ACCIDENTALLY IN LOVE

Book 13 in the Fircrest Series

Kam's Story

By Shannon Guymon

Dedicated to Travis – The love of my life

CONTENTS

CHAPTER 1

New Beginnings

GRACE JACKSON PUT her last box down on the floor and grinned at her new apartment. Sweet gig when your new boss lets you rent the apartment above his restaurant for next to nothing. She'd be able to pay off the last of her credit card debt within six months at this rate.

Then she'd do what she'd been dreaming of for the last few years, save up for two weeks in Bora Bora. She closed her eyes and sighed at the image of herself lying on a beach, next to her own private grass hut with a sweet, fruity drink in her hand. She scrunched her eyes and wondered if there was anyone lying next to her in her daydream. She sighed and opened her eyes, laughing at herself. Knowing her luck with men, *not likely.*

Her friends back in Seattle insisted she was just romantically delayed and that someday she would blossom into a temptress. Grace caught a glimpse of herself in the mirror on the hallway wall and paused for a moment. Yeah, that was never going to happen. She had shoulder length honey brown hair with generous blond highlights. She had large, blue eyes and a sprinkling of pale freckles across her nose and cheeks. She had an athletic, slim figure due to her long hours in the kitchen and her long walks with her dog. She was your basic girl next door with a touch of spice. She smiled a little, liking herself. If no one else did, then that was their loss.

Grace opened the windows of her little apartment to let the cool, spring breeze push out the stale air. She could tell the apartment had been empty for sometime now, which was a shame. It was an awesome apartment. Two bedrooms, one large bathroom with a shower *and* a bath and a surprisingly nice kitchen with granite countertops and new white cabinets. The family room wasn't huge but her comfy couch looked nice in front of the big screen TV where she loved to watch *Top Chef* and *Chopped* and all of her other cooking shows she devoured whenever she had the time.

She reached down and patted the head of her dog. "Hey, baby," she said with a grin, kneeling down to rub behind her Siber-poo's ears. She'd gotten the Siberian Husky, Poodle mix as a birthday present for herself last year. The name on her dog tag read, Rosemary, but she just called her Baby.

Baby licked her face and glanced around the apartment, as if to shrug and say, *it would do for now.*

"Wow, you're kind of a snob, huh?" she asked with a laugh and stood up. "Give me one more hour and then we'll go for a walk. My new boss wants to meet downstairs for dinner at seven, but until then we can explore. Sound good?"

Baby barked happily and wandered off to sniff every corner of her new territory. Grace dove into making her apartment a home. An hour later, she studied her new space and sighed in relief. *It felt good.* She had made the right decision to relocate to Fircrest. Seattle was fantastic, but she had needed a change and being in a new place was no big deal to her. She was good at making herself at home no matter where she was. She'd had a lot of practice as a kid. Being raised by the wild and crazy Jocelyn Jackson meant she'd had no choice. It was sink or swim with her mom. And thank heavens she'd learned how to swim fast.

"Come on, Baby," she said as she reached for the leash. "Time to let Fircrest know who's boss," she said with a smile and bent down to clip on the leash. Baby woofed softly in a very patronizing way and Grace laughed. It was good to have someone around to keep her humble.

CHAPTER 2

The Good and the Bad

ROB LOOKED UP from his laptop and held back a sigh of irritation. Taryn looked determined and he wasn't in the mood for a lecture from his little sister.

"Before you say anything, I have to finish this email and then I'm due to meet our new Sous chef for dinner. Wren's already downstairs. Can this wait?" he asked, sounding as impatient as he felt.

Taryn shut the door with her foot and shook her head decisively. "Nope."

Rob groaned loudly, not even trying to hide his irritation now. "*Fine*. Make it fast. You have two minutes."

Taryn frowned at him and sat down in a chair in front of his large, walnut desk. "I'm seriously ticked, Rob. You went over my head to hire this girl. *I'm* the one in charge of hiring for the restaurant and I had an incredibly talented Sous chef already picked out. I had to call Jason and rescind our offer. It makes us look bad. It made *me* look bad. *Who do you think you are?*" she asked, her voice rising even though it was still controlled. Not a good sign.

Rob looked at her steadily and leaned forward. "I'm the

owner of this restaurant is who I am. You're the manager. If you don't like the way I do things around here, then there are many other restaurants that would appreciate your skills."

Taryn's shocked expression had him sitting back and closing his eyes. Things had been tense the last few months between the siblings. Rob knew things weren't going well between her and Brogan and that his sister's marriage was struggling, but Taryn had the bad habit of bringing her bad mood to work and he was sick of it, along with everyone else who worked at The Iron Skillet. He hadn't invited her to be a part of the dinner with Grace because he was scared Taryn would make Grace want to quit before she even started.

"That's uncalled for," Taryn said stiffly, her eyes hurt.

Rob shook his head. "I've always hired the talent and you've always hired everyone else. You coming in here and asking who the heck I think I am? That's crossing the line. You haven't been happy here for a while now and it shows in your work and how you treat everyone, *including me.* You stomp around here like you're the queen from Alice in Wonderland, chopping off as many heads as you can and we're tired of it. You're on probation. I'll give you three months to figure out if you want to be here. If not, no hard feelings."

Taryn gasped and stood up, slamming the door seconds later with enough force to make him wince. Rob lay his head on his desk for a moment and tried the deep breathing exercises Wren had been telling him about for the past few months. Well, ever since Taryn had gone on the war path.

He stood up a moment later and grabbed his jacket off the back of his chair, slipping it on as he glanced at his phone. *He was late. One more black mark in Taryn's column*, he grumbled to himself as he walked down the hallway and into the main restaurant. He surveyed the crowded room and his heart eased a little. It was a good sight and always made him happy. He saw families eating and laughing and talking together and felt grati-fied that something he'd made could bring people together. He saw a few couples holding hands and staring into each other's eyes and grinned. This was why he did what he did. Taryn had just forgotten that work should be a joy, not a burden.

He hated hurting his sister, but he couldn't let her toxic attitude affect business. He knew from talk going around that Brogan had been pressuring Taryn to move to the East Coast but she'd been fighting it and now it was causing a strain on her marriage. He'd gotten a text from Brogan last week telling him that Taryn had told him to leave without her. Brogan was at his wits end and now thanks to Taryn, everyone else was on edge too. *Of course if she didn't have a job holding her back, maybe she'd be free to move with Brogan back East?*

He walked over to his usual table and was glad to see Grace and Wren were already there waiting for him. He grinned as he heard his wife's laughter and knew that was a good sign. Wren could be shy, so if someone could make Wren laugh and relax, he knew he was going to automatically like them. He paused before sitting down, taking the measure of his new Sous chef. He'd received glowing recommendations from her previous employer, and knew he was lucky to have her. Rob watched as Grace tilted her head back and laugh and his eyes widened in surprise. *She was darling.* He glanced back toward the kitchen and frowned, wondering for a moment.

Wren looked over and shook her head. "What are you doing just standing there, silly. Come meet your new Sous Chef. I already love her," Wren said, scooting over for him.

Rob pasted on a smile and sat down, reaching over and shaking Grace's extended hand. "It's a pleasure to finally meet you, Grace," he said and put his napkin over his lap. "We've been making do the last couple of weeks and Kam has threatened to kill me if I don't have someone for him by tomorrow. You're saving my life," he said with a wink.

Wren laughed and shook her head. "He's teasing you, Grace. Kam is one of my favorite people. You're going to *love* working here. When I was Head Chef and Kam was my Sous Chef, we'd have the best time. I was excited every morning to wake up and come to work because we had so much fun cooking together."

Rob snorted. "You woke up every morning, excited to come to work because you knew you were going to see *me*."

Grace laughed, and looked between him and Wren. "You two are so cute together. And I can't wait to start work. I've had a week off because of the move and I'm going crazy without a pan in my hand."

Rob sighed and began to relax. He liked Grace. She was down to earth, funny and he could tell by her eyes she had a good heart. She was perfect for The Iron Skillet.

"*This* is your new hire?"

Rob's smiled faded as he sat up straight and turned to see Taryn standing next to their table. He felt Wren's warning hand on his thigh and he took a moment before speaking.

"Taryn, I'd like to introduce you to Grace Jackson, our new Sous chef. We're very excited to have her here," he said in a warning voice. "Grace, this is Taryn Moore, my manager and my sister. You'll be reporting directly to Kam though, so you two won't have any interaction," he added quickly.

Taryn sniffed loudly, staring Grace down as if she were on the opposite side of a boxing ring.

"It's nice to meet you," Grace said when she realized Taryn wasn't going to say anything.

Taryn nodded her head regally. "Yeah, well, I hope you work out. We have high standards here at The Iron Skillet and if Rob hasn't mentioned it yet, we have a probationary three months to see if you work out. The last Sous Chef only lasted two months," she said and then walked away with what Rob would swear was a mean smile.

"She's killing me," he said under his breath to Wren.

Wren sighed and shook her head. "Grace, please forgive Taryn's behavior. She's been struggling lately. And the last Sous Chef quit because his wife got a job offer in San Francisco and they had to relocate. Please know that we're very happy you're here."

Grace shrugged her shoulders and glanced in the direction Taryn had disappeared. "People who are hurting, hurt others. It's not right but it's human and it's okay. I'll keep my head down."

Rob laughed with relief. "You're pretty tough if you're not scared off by Taryn. I like you, Grace."

Grace grinned and lifted her glass of water towards him in a toast. "To a long and happy career at The Iron Skillet."

Wren smiled at him as they clinked their glasses together. "It better be," Rob said with feeling.

CHAPTER 3

The Boss

GRACE WALKED INTO the kitchen the next morning with a determined smile on her face, ready to have a fantastic first day. She surveyed the already busy kitchen and noted the two prep cooks already chopping the vegetables for the day. She had been told that Candice was the other Sous chef but she only worked part time on the weekends. She watched as the older woman, probably somewhere in her fifties, began fabricating what looked liked a whole pig. She studied the people and the kitchen and nodded her head. They were professional, they worked well together, and the facility was clean and open.

She frowned, wondering what Wren had meant when she said working here was fun though. From the serious expressions on everyone's faces, fun wasn't part of anyone's vocabulary.

Now where was the head chef? Kam Matafeo was his name and from what Rob and Wren had said last night, he was a sweetheart.

"Hello, there. You must be, Grace."

Grace felt the timber of the low voice roll through her body like the bass turned up too loud on a car radio. She smiled brightly and turned around… and then had to look up. Way up. *He. Was. Massive.* Her mouth dropped open as she stared up at the mountain of a man. Why hadn't anyone warned her she was working for a giant?

"Holy cow. No one told me Shaquille O'Neill was the head chef. I'm Grace. It's an honor to finally meet you," she said brightly, noting his somber eyes lightened for a moment as if he was almost amused.

"The Shaq among Chefs. I like it," he said with a half smile. "Let me show you around the kitchen and introduce you. Then I want you to make me gnocchi. It's still our most requested side dish and we have a reputation for having the best. I'd like to see what you can do."

Grace grinned, excited at the chance to show off her skills. "You got it, Boss."

Kam's smile looked slightly less strained as he turned and walked away. She followed him and enjoyed meeting everyone. She noted that no one actually stopped what they were doing as they talked to her. They were all hard workers and well trained. Candice seemed the happiest to meet her. Manuel seemed like a nice guy, mid twenties and he had that dark look that so many women were drawn to. She noted the wedding ring on his left finger and smiled more easily. No awkward work place flirtations. *Good.* And James seemed like your typical college drop out, young and still looking for his way. He had a good natured, farm boy look to him. She hadn't sensed anyone was a diva in the bunch, so this could be a good situation.

"So glad you've come on board. Kam and I about died of exhaustion last weekend. We got a monster rush, Saturday at nine and weren't able to leave until one. We had Rob back here washing dishes. Anything you need, you just ask," Candice said with a warm smile.

"Will do." Grace said and clasped Candice's arm in

friendship before following Kam back to his office where he waited for her to sit down before shutting the door.

He took some papers off his desk and handed them to her before sitting down. "Here's the typical tax stuff. Just fill it out sometime today and get it back to me. I'll hand it off to Taryn. Rob told me she was pretty cold to you when you met her last night," he said with a slight rise of his jet black eyebrow.

Grace shrugged and leaned back in the hard chair, bringing her legs up to sit cross legged. "Not so much cold as just flat out mean. Rob said not to be scared of her and that she's just going through some stuff. No worries."

Kam nodded his head and smiled. "Easier said than done. She's made four waitresses and two waiters quit in the last month. If I had a dollar for every time I've seen someone cry this last week alone, I could buy myself a nice lunch."

Grace winced. "I've worked for some of the moodiest, nastiest chefs in the business. I don't scare easy but I have to admit, working in a toxic kitchen where I already have to watch my back isn't something I'm looking forward to."

Kam closed his eyes and sighed. "Taryn's drama will come to a head soon and then she'll come back down to earth. Until then, just stay out of her way. We all want you to be happy here so we'll look out for you."

Kam ran a hand through his long, wavy black hair and reached for a hair tie in his top drawer. She watched in fascination as he took the river of hair that flowed out of his head and began pulling it tightly back before securing it.

She blinked out of her stupor as she realized he was talking.

"I talked to Chef Andre' before we offered you the job and he was heartbroken you were leaving. He even told me to let him know when you got sick of us so he could tempt you to come back to Seattle."

Grace rolled her eyes and looked down at her hands before

replying. "Andre' loves drama. He's either passionately hating you or passionately loving you. There's no in-between with him and it changes weekly. Andre' is an incredible chef, but he's emotionally exhausting."

Kam laughed, the sound a little rusty and low. "Well, I already know I like you and I hate drama too. I think we'll make a good team."

Grace grinned. "I like you too, even though I'm jealous of your hair. Let me just get these forms out of the way and then I'll make you the best gnocchi you've ever tasted."

Kam stood up and handed her a pen. "The best gnocchi I've ever tasted still goes to Wren Downing. If you can beat hers, I'll be very impressed."

Grace cracked her knuckles. "Wren is going down," she said in a deep voice, making Kam make a huffing sound that might have been a laugh before he shut the door.

Grace glanced through the glass as the giant of a man walked back to the stove and shook her head in wonder. One of her best friends from college was Samoan so she was familiar with the open and friendly Polynesian culture. But Kam seemed different. He was so stoic and reserved. *Odd.*

She finished her forms quickly and then washed up. She made herself familiar with the walk-in and the pantry. She nodded her head in pleasure at the meticulous order of everything. It was time to make some magic. She slipped her phone and earphones out of her pocket and tapped her music app. She danced a little as she cooked and ignored everything and everyone as she created the world's best gnocchi.

*

Kam kept his eye on his new Sous chef as if she was a curious new animal at the zoo his son loved going to. He already liked her. *What wasn't to like?* She was easy going, tough, and she had kind eyes. Everyone he talked to said she was an amazing chef and from the smells coming from her station, he was going to have to lie to Wren about who cooked the best gnocchi. But there was something even more than that. He couldn't put his finger on it but it probably had something to do with the genuine warmth he saw in her eyes. He knew a lot of loving, kind women. He was surrounded by them. *So what was it about Grace Jackson that was so fascinating?*

He paused by the doorway and looked back at his new Sous chef as she danced to some music he couldn't hear. He could tell by the way she danced she didn't care what anyone else thought of her. Well, whatever it was, she was unique.

He smiled a little and then headed out of the kitchen and down the hallway to Rob's office. He tapped on the door lightly and walked in, sitting down in the chair opposite of Rob's desk as Rob finished up a phone call.

Rob smiled at him and held up one finger. Kam used the extra time to text his mom and ask how Natano was doing. He'd come down with a cold the day before and he was worried it might turn into something worse.

He's fine. He's working on some Legos right now. After lunch I'll try and get him to take a nap. But you know how stubborn he is.

Kam grinned. Oh yes he did. His boy Natano was a little ball of energy. He was also Kam's only joy.

Tell him Daddy loves him and I'll see him later.

Of course. Love you too, son.

"So, what do you think? Did I do good?"

Kam looked up from the picture his mom had just sent him of Natano building a tower and smiled easily.

"She's fantastic. I just assigned her to make me the best gnocchi in the world and she wasn't even fazed. It's like she was born making gnocchi and she's been training her whole life for this moment. She's got nerves of steel."

Rob clapped his hands. "Yes! I'm coming back with you. I've gotta taste this."

Kam laughed. "She's making enough for the lunch crowd so she's pretty confident."

Rob grinned. "Excellent. I love confidence. So you think you two will get along then? No personality conflicts?"

Kam shrugged. "Not yet. She seems like a nice girl. I asked her about Taryn and she honestly isn't worried about her. She's not happy about the instant antagonism but she can hold her own. I told her how many of the wait staff we've had to replace lately and she wasn't fazed. She's the perfect fit."

Rob scowled and looked out the window. "I swear, Kam, if we lose one more waitress, I'm firing her."

Kam winced. "She's had a rough time. Give her a break, Rob."

Rob shook his head in exasperation. "Yeah, her life is so hard. Her husband, who adores her, wants to move to the East Coast and she's too proud to move with him. Sorry, but I *don't* feel sorry for her. She needs to grow up and make some sacrifices for her family and stop ruining everyone else's life with her crappy attitude."

Kam looked down at his apron and paused before speaking. "It's more than the move, Rob. Let's leave it at that."

Rob frowned darkly at him. "You know something I don't? You better tell me, Kam. We're brothers and this is about our sister. We don't hide important stuff from each other."

Kam looked up at the ceiling knowing he was saying something he shouldn't. But he'd had a long lunch last week with Taryn and he knew more than most people. Definitely more than Rob.

"Brogan and Taryn's relationship is shaky right now."

Rob rolled his eyes. "Yeah, because Taryn won't move and support her husband."

Kam shook his head slowly back and forth. "*No*, it's more than that. Taryn found some emails from a business colleague of Brogan's that were flirty and inappropriate. She told Brogan if he moves, that it will be a trial separation. I don't think Brogan would ever cheat on Taryn, he loves her, but he didn't tell her about the emails either. Some of his messages back to the woman could be considered flirtatious as well. It's pretty much a mess."

Rob's face fell and he slumped back in his chair. "Freaking Brogan and his Ken doll looks," he muttered and massaged his temples.

Kam smiled a little at that and sat forward. "I've been try-ing to get them into my therapist. He's helped me and he works with couples too. I think they have an appointment soon."

Rob nodded his head, looking relieved. "Thanks, Kam. And thanks for telling me about what's really going on. I've been so angry at Taryn for the way she's been acting. I should have been a better brother and forced her to tell me what's really going on. This helps."

Kam sighed. "I figured."

Rob looked at Kam intensely for a moment and tapped his chin. A sure sign he was about to say something he probably shouldn't. "So if you haven't noticed... our new Sous Chef is kind of pretty."

Kam didn't blink an eye for five seconds. "I noticed."

Rob lifted an eyebrow. "*Well?*"

Kam frowned. "Well, what? Rob, we've had this talk before. You can't set me up with people, especially people who work here. It's inappropriate and awkward."

Rob rolled his eyes and stood up. "I can do whatever I

want, I'm the owner. Now all I'm saying is that if you like her, maybe you should think about asking her out."

Kam let the silence move into the awkward stage before standing up and putting his hands on his hips. "Rob, out of respect for you I'm going to say this more politely than I'd like to. *No.*"

Rob hurried around the desk and grabbed Kam's arms. "It's been three and a half years, Kam. It's time to live again. It's time to smile again. Please, bro. *Please.*"

Kam closed his eyes and shook his head. "I love my wife, Rob. She might not be here anymore, but that doesn't change the way I feel. I love my wife."

Rob's eyes turned suspiciously bright and Kam sighed.

"Kam, Bailey wouldn't want you to live the rest of your life in hibernation. She'd want you to be happy. She'd want Nate to have a mom. *Come on,* Kam. Just think about it."

Kam closed his eyes at Rob's words, wishing with all of his heart that Natano did have a mom. Wishing Bailey was still there with him so she could see her boy grow up. In his heart, he knew Bailey hadn't missed anything. She hadn't missed seeing her son walk for the first time or say his first sentence. She'd been there in spirit. He'd felt her presence on occasion and knew she was watching out for them. *But it still hurt.* He thought about what it would mean to marry some woman and bring her into his home and have her be a mother to his son. He shook his head quietly. He couldn't even imagine it.

"I don't want to talk about it, Rob. Come on. Let's go try Grace's gnocchi."

Rob hurried after him down the hallway, not saying anything else, thank heavens. Kam pushed through the heavy double doors and smiled to see everyone surrounding Grace with small saucers of gnocchi. He could tell by the smiles he was seeing that she did well.

"So does Wren have competition?" he asked Candice as he took the plate Grace offered him.

Candice laughed and glanced at Rob. "Don't tell Rob but his wife's gnocchi comes in a close second."

Kam and Rob shared shocked looks. "Give me a plate too," Rob ordered looking suspiciously at Candice.

Grace dished up a generous portion and handed him a fork. Kam and Rob took a bite at the same time, both of them closing their eyes and savoring the subtle flavors.

Kam opened his eyes first and smiled at Grace before turning to Rob.

"Sorry, Bro. Grace wins. The pesto and garlic sauce are divine and the gnocchi is so light and fluffy, I'm actually jealous."

Grace grinned as she accepted high fives from James and Candice.

Rob didn't answer as he was too busy stuffing another forkful into his mouth but his smile was promising. A minute later he finally spoke.

"Grace, I hate to brag, but I'm incredibly talented at picking out the best chefs. And I'll agree, this beats Wren's. But if you promise not to tell Wren yours is better, I'll make it worth your while."

Grace hooted and pumped her fist in the air just before her face turned white and her eyes went big. Rob stiffened and looked at Kam with fear in his eyes.

Kam turned slowly to see Wren standing right behind her husband. It was so easy *not* to see her when she was half the size of everyone else and a third the size of Kam. By the shocked look on her face she had heard everything her husband had said.

"Hi, Little Bird. You're just in time to try Grace's gnocchi. I want your opinion," Kam said softly and took the plate that Grace handed to him.

Wren scowled at him and Rob but obediently took a bite. She closed her eyes and chewed slowly, nodding her head as if listening to an inner dialogue in her mind. She opened her eyes and sighed before smiling brightly at Grace.

"Well, I guess no one can stay king of the hill forever. I bow to your gnocchi, Grace. You are the queen of potato dumplings."

Grace put a hand over her heart and laughed weakly. "Oh my word, you had me nervous there for a moment. I was worried for Rob's life."

Wren scowled at Rob briefly as he put his arm around his wife's shoulders. "I'll admit it's humbling to hear your husband praise someone else's food but I guess I better get used to it with you around."

Kam touched her shoulder and Wren looked up at him. "Little Bird, you will always be the queen of this kitchen. You know that."

Wren smiled sweetly at Kam and leaned up as far as she could to kiss Kam on the cheek. "Thanks, Kam. Love you."

Rob frowned at that. "How come you love *him*? He said it was better than yours too."

Wren put her chin in the air before dishing up more gnocchi. "Because he's not my husband. You're supposed to lie and tell me mine is the best no matter what."

Rob threw his hands in the air. "I was going to! I was going to bribe everyone else to lie too."

Wren and Kam laughed at Rob's exasperation.

"I'm sure some flowers will help me get over it," she said lightly and with a wave, disappeared out of the kitchen.

Rob watched his wife go with a smile on his face. "That woman. Man, do I love her."

Kam grinned. "You better. You answer to me if you don't."

Rob smiled and gave Kam a one armed hug. "I'd be scared except I know you love me just as much."

Kam grinned and fake punched Rob, making the man wince and flinch theatrically.

*

Grace watched the two men goof off with each other and realized something. These two men were much more than owner and Head Chef. They were family. She smiled quizzically trying to figure out their relationship as Candice wrote down her recipe.

"Candice? How are Rob and Kam related? I get this vibe that they're closer than friends."

Candice took a step closer and leaned her head in. "They're brothers in law. Kam married Rob's little sister, Bailey."

Grace nodded, hoping for more. Candice opened her mouth to say something but Rob and Kam looked at them both expectantly.

Grace widened her eyes at Candice who did the same back.

"Sorry, I missed your question," Grace said with a confident smile. It was always better to push forward than to cower in guilt for gossiping about your boss.

"I said, how did you get so good at making gnocchi?" Kam asked with a polite smile.

Grace shrugged modestly and stepped away from Candice. "My mother dated an Italian guy when I was fifteen and we had Thanksgiving at his parents' house. His grandmother was there and I spent the whole day in the kitchen with her. Best Thanksgiving of my life."

Kam tilted his head and studied her. "Interesting. You learned from your mom's boyfriend's grandmother how to make the best gnocchi we've ever tasted, and that was when you were fifteen. Is your mom still with this guy?" he asked curiously.

Grace laughed and shook her head. "Uh, *no*. That was one of her longer relationships though. They broke up right before

Christmas. Tony's grandmother had promised to show me how to make parrozzo. I was more heartbroken then my mom was when things fizzled."

Kam and Rob shared a look. "So did you ever learn how to make parrozzo?" Rob asked smoothly.

Grace flipped her hair. "Of course. I didn't learn until I was eighteen but it was worth the wait. You would die, it's so good, but I only make it at Christmastime."

Rob got a calculating look in his eyes. "I know it's only April, but if we could put parrozzo on the menu for tonight, I know *I'd* be extremely happy."

Grace narrowed her eyes at him. "How happy are we talking?"

Rob laughed and nudged Kam in the arm. "She's tough. I told you. So happy we'll forget about your three-month probation and just dive right into your bonus next paycheck."

Kam grinned at her and nodded his head. Grace twirled around in a burst of happy and did an elaborate bow in front of her two bosses. "Your wish is granted, kind sirs. Parrozzo is now on the menu. Wait, you've had it before, right?"

Rob sighed and closed his eyes. "One time. In Italy with Wren, on a second honeymoon. It would bring back good memories."

Grace sighed romantically. "Aw, well then I hope my parrozzo lives up to your memories tonight."

Rob fake scowled at her. "It better," he said and then patted her arm before whistling and walking out of the kitchen.

Kam folded his arms over his massive chest. "All right Gracie, you've got the boss wrapped around your finger. Now let's see what you can do."

Grace shook her finger at Kam. "Call me Gracie and that means we're friends. And correction, I have the *owner* wrapped around my finger. I'm still working on my boss though," she said with a wink before she whipped around and headed for the pantry.

*

Kam watched her go and only moved when someone cleared their throat behind him.

"She's a firecracker," Candice said, smiling as she put plastic wrap over the pesto sauce.

Kam nodded in agreement. "Firecrackers are usually too loud and too bright," he said, sounding worried.

Candice frowned and looked up at Kam. "This kitchen could use a little noise and lights. What's so wrong with dancing and music and yeah, maybe some pretty fireworks now and then?"

Kam frowned darkly. "To each their own," he said and walked towards his office.

Candice called after him. "I used to see you dance all the time."

Kam turned back, his hand on the door jamb. "That was a long time ago."

Candice frowned sadly. "Yeah, too long."

Kam shut the door to his office but ignored all the paperwork and food orders in front of him as he stared off into space. Grace was a gifted chef. Maybe she was friendly and could charm the socks off people. But could he handle someone laughing and dancing and teasing everyone in his kitchen?

He wasn't sure.

He massaged his heart and glared at his desk. It had been a long time since he'd danced and sang in the kitchen. He remembered all the fun times he used to have when he cooked with Wren and felt a moment of nostalgia.

But that was a lifetime ago. If Grace wanted to dance and have fun, then that was her business. *Him?* He preferred a calm, quiet, non-exciting work environment.

CHAPTER 4

The Belinda Girls

IN BETWEEN BAKING all of the parrozzo cakes, Grace took two fifteen minute breaks to check on Baby upstairs before she took her hour lunch break at three. She had so much to do she knew she'd be exhausted that night. She put the back down on her old blue, Dodge truck for Baby to jump up into and drove to the post office to set up a post office box so she could get her mail forwarded. She ran to the bank to set up her account and transfer her money from Seattle and by the time that was done, she had only twenty minutes before she had to be back at work. If she didn't relax for a few minutes, she was going to collapse. She glanced up and down the street and spotted a quaint looking bakery. *Perfect.*

Grace grabbed the leash and hooked it on Baby's collar. Baby jumped out of the truck and they walked across the street and down half a block. She wrapped the leash around the railing and ordered Baby to stay before pushing through the door. She stopped on a dime and closed her eyes as she smelled all the wonderful, delicious scents assaulting her senses. *Vanilla, chocolate, caramel and a hint of lemon.*

"Heaven," she finally said after a moment and opened her eyes to see two grinning women studying her.

"Sorry," she said, not feeling sorry at all. "But if a person doesn't stop and appreciate what you've done to the air, then there's something wrong."

The woman with long blond hair pulled back in a loose braid laughed and leaned her elbows on the counter. "Let me guess. New Sous Chef at the Iron Skillet? You smell the air like an expert."

Grace paused on her way to the display case and frowned. "How in the world could you know who I am?"

The attractive woman shrugged. "Wren's a good friend. She came in this afternoon a little put out that your gnocchi was better than hers. We had to comfort her with one of our caramel apples."

Grace laughed and joined the women at the counter. "That was very kind of you. Rob and Kam were trying to get everyone to make a vow of silence on behalf of my gnocchi but she appeared out of nowhere and the damage was done."

The beautiful brunette who was watching her with a smile laughed and she could see the resemblance between the women.

"That sounds like Rob and Kam. Don't worry about Wren though. She's actually very excited you're here and Kam will be grateful for the help."

Grace nodded as she scanned all of the yummy delicacies tempting her. "I'm excited to be here too. But you guys have to help me out. I only have fifteen minutes left to my break. What will give me all the energy I need to make it through the rest of the day?"

The women frowned and looked at each other before the blond spoke. "You're going to need a sandwich, some potato salad and two chocolate chip cookies. We'll make it to go so you can get back in time. You'll have to eat as you drive and then snack when you can."

Grace smiled and shook her head. "*You get it.* You get my life. Wow, thank you and that sounds perfect."

The brunette bagged up the food quickly, and handed it to her with a drink as well.

"How much do I owe you?" she asked, pulling her wallet out of her satchel.

Both of the women shook their heads simultaneously.

"Consider it our welcome to Fircrest gift. Just one condition. Come back tomorrow so we can get to know you. By the way, my name is Jane Matafeo and this is my sister, Layla Bender. We're the owners of Belinda's Bakery along with our other sister, Kit."

Grace was so touched she put her hand over her heart and paused, looking at the two women with glowing smiles and kind eyes.

"Okay, you've done it now. I'll be here tomorrow. You can count on it."

The women grinned and waved her off. She paused and turned back as she opened the door. "Jane? Any relation to Kam, my boss? I think his last name is Matafeo too."

Jane nodded her head and her smile dimmed slightly. "He's my brother-in-law. Or cousin in law. Mostly brother in law though."

Grace laughed. "Okay, now that's a story I have to hear. See you tomorrow." She hurried through the door, grabbing Baby's leash and slipping it over her wrist so she wouldn't drop anything.

She made it back to work and felt a hundred times better after eating half her sandwich, some of her potato salad and one of the cookies. She put the rest of her lunch in the walk-in next to Manuel's Big Gulp and knew she'd be snagging bites as often as she could.

"Holy cow, guys. I just found the best place. Belinda's

Bakery? Have you guys been there?" she called out generally to anyone who was listening. "The sweetest girls run the place. If I'm ever fired, I'm going there to work. The smell alone," she said.

Candice, Manuel and James all began talking at once, smiling and laughing and talking over each other as they each described their favorite dessert.

"I promise tomorrow when I go, I'll bring you all back a treat," she offered.

Candice laughed. "Grace, you are a breath of fresh air. And thank you. I've been craving cannoli lately."

Grace shrugged it off. "Of course. Life is too short to not share the goodies. What's Kam's favorite treat? I'll surprise him tomorrow too."

Everyone paused and looked in the direction of Kam's office. Manuel shook his head. "The man has no joy in food anymore. I wouldn't bother."

Candice frowned at Manuel. "Hush, Manuel. You don't know what he's been through. You'd lose your joy too."

Grace's eyebrows shot up. "What are you guys talking about?"

James made a slashing motion over his neck and everyone turned back to their work stations as Kam emerged from his office with his cell phone to his ear.

"Tate, I said *no*. Don't ask again. I'll come for dinner Sunday but that's it. Tell Jane I said hi," he said and then ended the call abruptly.

Grace walked over and began washing her hands as she processed everything. There was more to Kam Matafeo than she thought. She wasn't a fan of gossiping, especially about her boss, but she had to admit she was curious. What could make a man who cooks for a living lose his joy in food?

She had been wondering why Rob and Kam were worried

about her beating Wren's gnocchi. Why wasn't Kam's gnocchi mentioned? Shouldn't the Head Chef have the best food? And if not, then why in the world was he the Head Chef? Unless Rob had just hired his brother in law to give him a job. She'd seen nepotism in restaurants before. Usually restaurants that failed. If that was the case, then she was in fact going to be the acting head chef and Kam would just hold the title. *Yikes.*

Grace glanced over her shoulder at Kam as she dried her hands and frowned a little in worry. She saw a giant of a man with very sad eyes. Someone who looked tired. Not physically, but emotionally as if he was on his last rung and just holding on because he didn't know what else to do.

Grace felt a moment of compassion and nodded her head to herself. She'd do what she could to lift some of his load. Who knows? Someday she might need someone to help her out.

She walked over to Kam and smiled brightly at him. "Okay, Boss. Two questions. What's your favorite treat at Belinda's and what would you like me to do now?"

Kam frowned. "I haven't been eating a lot of sweets lately and I'd like you to be in charge of the scallop dish with the bacon braised chard and the spiced rubbed chicken thighs with ginger lime baby carrots for tonight. I noticed your porrozzo are done. Just make sure they get frosted."

Grace nodded her head with a frown of dissapointment. "Consider it done, Boss," she said softly and turned around and dove into her work.

The evening flew by and by seven she was in the swing of things as if she'd been working at The Iron Skillet for years and not hours. Just as she was hitting her groove and had turned up the music, a waiter popped back and asked her to come out to speak to the customers.

She frowned and glanced in Kam's direction. "Sorry, buddy. Head Chef gets credit."

The waiter who looked like all the other waiters did here, tall, thin and young, shook his head and glanced at Kam. "He never comes out. It's always the Sous Chef."

Grace blew out a breath in frustration before handing her pan over to Candice. She glanced around the kitchen but Kam must have taken a break. She held back the grumble that was stuck in her throat and instead nodded and followed the kid out of the kitchen.

He led her to a table close to the bar where two well dressed couples were sitting, talking and laughing and probably having a seriously decent time. *Good.* She'd smile, take the compliments and then run back before they got too behind.

"This is Chef Grace Jackson," the waiter said in introduction. "The owner told us that he stole her away from one of the best restaurants in Seattle."

Grace narrowed her eyes at the waiter and wondered if Rob had really told the wait staff that. It wasn't necessarily not true but it was definitely a very exaggerated version of what really went down.

The dark haired woman sitting furthest away looked her up and down and smiled warmly. "You look too young to be such an accomplished chef. We just wanted to tell you we've been eating here for years but tonight the food shined. There was a spark to the cuisine that we all loved and wanted you to know that we noticed."

Grace smiled in genuine delight at the compliment. Maybe coming out to talk to the guests wasn't such a bad thing after all?

"And, we'll be back next week. We were wondering if you were planning on making any changes to the menu?" the man sitting next to the blond woman asked.

Grace bit her lip wishing she knew the answer to that. Being the lowly Sous Chef meant she was not in charge. She could bring it up to Kam and see if he'd go for it, but he was so stern sometimes she was almost intimidated by him. Okay, she was flat out intimidated by him.

"Since today is my first day I honestly don't know, but I definitely have a few ideas that have been simmering. What suggestions would you have?" she asked, surprising the couples.

Everyone talked at once but they agreed they wanted more fresh, organic food. Grace talked to them for a few more minutes and then made her excuses before hurrying back. She pushed through the doors and came to an immediate standstill as she saw that the music had been turned off and everyone had tight, grim expressions on their faces.

"What in the world happened in the last five minutes?" she asked washing her hands again before diving back into the fray.

Candice grimaced and put a finger to her lips as if to tell her to be quiet. Grace frowned at her but looked to where Candice was pointing. Kam's office. She took a few steps forward to see into the tiny window and saw that Rob's sister Taryn was inside with Kam. Kam did not look happy. No one did.

"*Yeesh*," she muttered and wiped her hands before slipping back in front of the stove. Some people brought sunshine and some people brought rain wherever they went. Looked like Taryn brought thunderstorms.

She glanced at the orders coming up and was relieved to see they were still on schedule. Things were starting to slow down, which was typical of Thursday nights and she was grateful.

She whistled as she flipped some scallops but then felt an odd, cold shiver run down her neck as if she'd been walking through a cemetery at midnight. She glanced over her shoulder and jumped a little when she saw Taryn staring at her balefully with Kam beside her.

"Hi there," she said simply and then turned back around, not wanting to be the target of any misdirected anger.

"I hear your gnocchi is pretty good," Taryn said in a sugary sweet voice.

Kam's low voice saying Taryn's name was a warning. Okay, this girl needed a target for whatever emotion she was dealing with. *Fine*. Yell away. She turned around to face Taryn and smiled.

"Thanks, Taryn. I do okay. Can I make you something to eat?" she asked simply.

Taryn shook her head slowly. "Fraid not. I only eat food prepared by the Head Chef, not some subpar Sous Chef. You're basically just a prep cook."

Candice's snort was soft but unmistakable. Grace refused to let her smile waver. Never show them fear or weakness. That's how she always dealt with bullies. "Lucky for you Kam is right here. I'm sure he'll enjoy cooking for you. If you'll excuse me, I need to get back to *prepping* these orders," she said demurely and then turned around and flipped the scallops one more time before handing the pan off to Candice who began plating.

"Listen, Grace…" Taryn said in a scary voice.

Grace turned slowly around and speared Kam with her eyes. He'd told her he'd protect her from Taryn. Now seemed like a good time. She didn't have time for Taryn's bullying. She raised an eyebrow enquiringly at Kam and he nodded his head in acknowledgement.

"Taryn, let my people do the work we've hired them to do. If you want to get mad at someone, go yell at Brogan, not Grace. She doesn't deserve it. Now head on out," he said brusquely.

Taryn's head jerked back as if she'd been slapped.

"*Kam*, she's already trying to replace you! I overheard the diners tonight. They're raving about her cooking. You can't let this little know it all, push you out. I won't have it," Taryn sputtered, turning red in the face.

Kam shook his head slowly. "I threatened Rob I would quit

unless he hired her. None of this is your business, little sister. Just worry about the wait staff and leave my Sous Chef to me."

Taryn turned and glared at her, her dark brown eyes shooting fire. "I'm watching you," she hissed and then stormed off.

Grace frowned after the woman. "Wow, that was some real hate coming off that woman. Thanks for sticking up for me," she said stiffly to Kam as he watched her. It would have been nice if he'd stopped Taryn *before* she got going though.

Kam shrugged. "It's misplaced, but yeah, she hates you right now. Just ignore her, okay? There's nothing she can do to you. I won't allow it."

Grace paused, wanting to say more but instead nodded and went back to work. The music didn't get turned back on that night and when she finally made it upstairs, collapsing into bed as Baby licked her face, she wondered for the first time if she had made the right decision in coming to Fircrest.

But Grace's heart was never wrong and her heart had pushed her to come here. She'd give The Iron Skillet a three-month probation period and if she still had to deal with a vicious manager then she'd just look somewhere else. Life wasn't meant to be lived ducking in fear of crazy people. And if she had to cook in a kitchen with no music? Well, that would be just as bad.

She went to sleep that night and had a dream where she was thirteen. She was sitting by the window in their tiny apartment waiting for her mom to come home from her date. She listened to the screaming and yelling coming from the apartment next door and the sound of the police sirens racing down the busy road in front her apartment complex. And in the dream, she was wishing for something better. A place where she could be safe. A place where she could be happy. *A place where she could be loved.*

CHAPTER 5

Resurrection

GRACE WOKE UP the next day tired. It always took her a few hours to recover from bad dreams about her past and remember that life was okay now. She was happy and safe *and* loved. *At least loved by her friends.*

She tried to focus on everything she was grateful for. That was what her therapist had taught her to do on mornings like this. She was not that lonely, unloved little girl anymore. She'd conquered her past to become a woman she liked and respected. It was just a nightmare. That's all her past was and all it was ever going to be. She would never give it power to shape her future or cloud her vision ever again.

She took Baby out to do her business and then stood in the middle of her family room and looked around. She didn't need to be in the kitchen until one today since she'd be working late that night. Fridays and Saturdays were usually crazy. Good thing she liked crazy. But for now, she could relax, finish unpacking and take Baby for a walk.

She did just that and then took a long hot shower. She felt her old excitement for her new home return. Today was a new day and she was determined to win over her grim boss if it killed her. She didn't know why the man hardly ever smiled or laughed, but she was determined to make him smile at least once a day and laugh maybe once a week. She didn't want to push it.

She got dressed in her most comfortable ripped jeans and put on her favorite t- shirt. It said, O.U.R. and had the image of chains being broken on the front. It was her favorite cause to support and she loved wearing their merchandise. She pulled her hair up in a messy bun, put on some light makeup and she was ready. She had promised the Belinda Bakery girls to come for lunch again, and after the amazing food they'd so kindly given her yesterday, she was happy to oblige. That and she could use some friends outside of The Iron Skillet.

She took Baby with her and they made the two mile walk in no time at all. It was only eleven thirty, but she knew Friday night was going to stretch her, so an early lunch would be no big deal. She hooked Baby's leash to the railing outside and walked in, stopping and smelling again as the delightful scents of the bakery surrounded her in welcome.

"Are you going to do that every time you come in?"

She opened her eyes and laughed, as she noted the cute blond she'd met yesterday was grinning at her.

"You bet I will. How can anyone not?" she demanded and walked over to see all of the delightful creations in the cases.

"I guess we're so used to it we don't appreciate it anymore."

Grace frowned at her. "Just head over to the local dump for an hour and then come back here. Trust me, you'll notice a difference."

"No thanks. But I'm glad you came back today. Jane won't be in until two today. She'll be so ticked she missed you. But you'll get to meet Kit. She's going to cover for me while we have lunch and get to know each other."

Grace smiled at the complete welcome and open friendship

of this woman. It was rare and very appreciated. Most of her good friends had been slowly cultivated over years and years but here was this woman just feely offering her friendship as if friendship wasn't the most precious thing a person could give someone. *Amazing*.

"I'd love that," she said simply, not knowing how to express her gratitude yet.

A beautiful red-head with a toddler on her hip walked out with a pan of what looked like fruit tarts in her hand. The blond took the pan and expertly transferred them to an empty case while Kit kissed the little blond boy.

"You okay to take over?"

Kit nodded and then looked around, catching sight of her. "Of course, but first introduce me to the new Sous Chef. I've been dying of curiosity."

Grace grinned, amused that anyone could possible die of curiosity over her.

"I'm Grace and your little boy is gorgeous by the way."

Kit's eyes warmed and she smiled brightly at her. "He is, isn't he? I should be less prideful about my son, but I can't help it. He's the best little boy in the world."

Grace laughed as the blond rolled her eyes. "Ignore her. She's one of those obnoxious mommies who likes to brag about their kids constantly. If you give her an opening she's going to start showing you Danny's little crayon drawings."

Kit glared at her sister and Grace's eyes widened, wondering what would happen next. She'd never had a sister, but it looked kind of fun.

"And to think I was going to babysit for you tonight so you and Michael could go on a date. Forget it now."

The blond sister laughed and took off her apron. "I take it all back. Danny is an artistic genius."

Kit made a huffing sound and turned around, ignoring her sister now.

"So what will you have for lunch today?" she asked.

Grace shook her head, looking at the menu. "It all looks so good, but I'll try the pesto and turkey panini, the tomato basil soup and for dessert… hmm, surprise me."

"You got it. She walked around getting the food and Grace walked over and picked a table at the back of the bakery with a view of the street. Being the Pacific Northwest, the gray clouds were beginning to move in and she knew she'd be lucky to make it back home without getting wet at this rate. Sometimes she dreamed of moving somewhere sunny like California or Arizona, but this was her home. She could never leave.

"Here we are," said the blond sister.

Grace looked up and smiled at the array of delicious food in front of her. "And what do we have here?" she asked, staring at the cookie, feeling a little disappointed.

"Hey, no frowning allowed. If you don't like it, you can pick something else you like, but honestly, a simple oatmeal cookie after lunch is still the best thing in the world. Don't you know sometimes the showiest things are just all fluff and no substance? It's true to life and cooking. Didn't your grandma ever make you oatmeal cookies after school?" she asked.

Grace grinned, enjoying the conversation already. Life truths with food and friends. Could it get any better?

"Nope. No sweet grandma to speak of. But I'll trust you," she assured her and took a bite of her panini. "Oh, man, that is good," she said simply and shut her eyes in enjoyment.

"I have a feeling that you spend most of your life with your eyes closed, trying to pick out all the flavors of everything you eat or smell."

Grace blinked open her eyes and laughed loudly. "You happen to be right. What's your name, by the way? I have a super hard time remembering names and yesterday was so crazy and I met so many people that it all just leaked out last night."

The pretty blond flipped her long hair over her shoulder. "Layla. Layla Bender. Co-owner of Belinda's Bakery with my two sisters, Jane Matafeo and Kit Hunter."

Grace nodded, intrigued. "Three sisters running a bakery together. That's gotta be a dream come true."

Layla paused and then smiled sweetly. "Yeah, it really is. My family was what you would call dysfunctional and so when our grandmother left us her bakery in her will, it brought what was left of our family together. Now we're a family that is functioning and loving and we have a lot of fun together. All of our kids are growing up together and we have a network of friends and family now that works. What about you? Do you have family here in Fircrest? Or did you just come for an adventure?"

Grace paused and chewed her bite before answering. Layla was being open with her, so she should do the same. "Well, I don't actually have a family. My mom is living somewhere with someone doing something, but not sure on the particulars. And that's it. No dad to speak of either. He and my mom were never married and he was never part of the picture." she said, putting her hand over her heart as the pain flashed bright and then receded again. "So it's just me. I wouldn't say I was on an adventure so much as on a journey. Sometimes my heart tells me things and I've made it a rule to listen. My heart said it was time to move on and that Fircrest was the place to be. I have no idea why, but I can't wait to find out," she said, smiling out the window as she watched an older couple walk hand in hand down the sidewalk.

Layla made a humming sound in her throat as she took a sip of water. "Fascinating. I can't wait to find out either. So what do you think of The Iron Skillet so far?"

Grace shrugged as she stirred her soup and frowned a little.

"It's kind of a collage of different things right now. I could give you a fake answer but I'd rather not. It's good and bad. I'm in a kitchen where someone keeps turning off my music so I can't dance or sing. I have the restaurant manager glaring at me every chance she gets for no reason I can think of and my boss is stern, unhappy and not much fun. But other than that? It's okay," she said honestly and took another bite of her panini.

Layla frowned and put her sandwich down, as she leaned her chin on her hands.

"I'm not surprised by anything you just said, but knowing your heart brought you here, I hope you give it a good chance before you give up on Fircrest."

Grace smiled and nodded. "I'm tougher than I look, but I don't stick around in toxic environments either. We'll see if I can bring a little light to The Iron Skillet. If not, then there are other healthier, happier places to be."

Layla frowned and nodded. "True and smart. I agree, but I hope you do bring some of that light that you have. Out of all the places in Fircrest, The Iron Skillet's kitchen needs light more than any other place I know. Kam's had a lot of heartache and pain in the past few years. It would be so good for him to let some light in."

Grace's eyebrows rose as she looked back at Layla. "His eyes look so sad. I wondered if there was something wrong. Is it something you can tell me? If not, that's okay. I don't want to gossip, but if knowing what's going on can help me understand him, then I'd like to know."

Layla bit her lip and looked down at her hands for a moment before she looked up and nodded her head. "Okay then, I trust you with this information because I care about Kam. His wife, Bailey, died about three and half years ago in childbirth. It broke Kam's heart and this town's heart too. We've been hurting for Kam ever since. He's a single dad who's basically living for his son, Nate. But if you only knew him before Bailey died, you would have met the kindest, happiest, most incredible man in the world. Now he's just a shell of himself and that's the biggest tragedy of all."

Grace closed her eyes, feeling sad for her new boss and what he'd been through. "He needs a friend then? Is that what you're saying?"

Layla blinked a few times and shook her head slowly. "Oh, he has plenty of friends. The whole town loves Kam. And he has a huge family that surrounds him with support. *No*, I wouldn't say he needs a friend although I hope you and Kam can become friends. I would say, he needs someone to help him come back to life. I don't know if that's something you can do, but it would be interesting to see if you can."

Grace looked away and frowned. "*Bring a man back to life?* That's a lot to ask of someone. The best I can hope for is to bring music back to that kitchen."

Layla nodded her head in excitement. "But that's exactly what I'm talking about! Bring music back to The Iron Skillet. Dance in between orders. Bring some laughter and happiness back to that dark dungeon of a kitchen."

Grace shrugged, still a little taken aback. "All I can do is be me, Layla. I mean, my heart goes out to the man, but to be healed of *that* kind of pain, you have to *want* to be healed, you know? You have to actively seek out healing and light and he gave me the impression that he's very comfortable in the dark with the pain and that's where he wants to stay. If that's the case, then there's nothing I can do."

Layla sighed. "You're very perceptive and you're right. But it doesn't take that much light to break up darkness. One little match in a dark cave can do wonders. He's been cold and alone in the dark for too long. Maybe being around your light and goodness will make him remember what life used to be and what it could be again. It's worth a try, isn't it?"

Grace nodded her head, knowing that she'd been through some dark times too and she was so grateful she wasn't there anymore. Remembering her nightmare from the previous night, she nodded her head. If she could help someone, of course she would. She just felt weird having the responsibility squarely on her shoulders.

"I'll do whatever I can but in the end, it's his choice to be happy or not. No one can take on the responsibility for bringing a man back to life, no offense. But... I guess I can try."

Layla smiled brightly at her and motioned towards the cookie. "Of course you will. Now, try my cookie."

Grace sighed and picked up the unappealing cookie as she glanced at the cases of beautiful desserts she could be eating. She closed her eyes automatically and smelled the cookie before taking a generous bite. The smell of nutmeg and cinnamon made her smile. She chewed and paused and then chewed again before swallowing. She opened her eyes and grinned.

"I get it. Appearances are deceiving. This is incredible," she said, taking another bite. "The nutmeg is so warm and the chewy texture is incredible. I love it. But that doesn't mean I won't rest until I've tried everything you've made."

Layla laughed and sat back, looking very pleased with herself. "Excellent. Now, let's talk Taryn. You're helping the whole town out by helping Kam, so I'll help you with your mean Restaurant manager."

Grace frowned and picked up a crumb. "I'm not sure that's possible. Picture an angry tiger with an appetite for Sous Chefs and you've got Taryn. She took one look at me and automatically hated me. And I hate to brag, but I'm actually a really likable person. So this has come as a complete shock."

Layla laughed and crossed her legs. "Between you and me,

she's having some marriage problems. She doesn't feel she can trust her husband anymore and she's not happy about having to move cross country. She's taking it out on everyone around her. Trust me, I've heard from all of the waiters and waitresses who have passed through here on their way out of town."

Grace shook her head. "Sad, but how can you help me if I'm her new target?"

Layla pursed her mouth. "I can tell you her secret. Her one weakness is my flourless chocolate cake. You bring her one of my mini cakes in a cute box and I promise some of that fire will disappear."

Grace frowned as she finished her cookie. "And if you're wrong?"

Layla raised an eyebrow. "Are you putting my skills down?"

Grace grinned before laughing a little. "I wouldn't dare. But that reminds me, I promised all my new friends that I'd bring them a treat today from you guys. Candice wants cannoli but I have no idea about James, Manuel or Kam. Maybe Rob too just to be safe."

Layla popped up and walked over to the counter. "Kit, help me out. The kitchen staff at The Iron Skillet. Can you remember what they like?"

The pretty redhead walked over, the toddler nowhere in sight now as she looked at her curiously.

"Trying to bribe everyone?" Kit asked with a teasing look.

Grace laughed and shook her head. "Just trying to bring a little fun back to that kitchen. I get the feeling they've been making the same thing for so long that they don't even care anymore. I was thinking that if I jump started everyone's taste buds with some of these delightful pastries, they might be more excited about food."

Kit nodded. "Gotcha. But they're still going to love you for this. James and Manuel... it's been a while since they've been in but I'm thinking one of our mini-pineapple upside down cakes for Manuel and for James maybe one of our smore's cupcakes. Rob is a food snob, so I'd pick the roasted pear with the espresso mascarpone cream."

Layla nodded her head. "Kit knows her stuff. Good job."

Grace held up a finger. "What about Kam? He said he doesn't eat sweets anymore, but maybe something you guys have here might bring his appetite back."

Kit and Layla exchanged a sad smile before Layla spoke. "He used to love our Matafeo cupcakes. Jane created them for her hubby, Tate but all the Matafeo's are in love with them. I honestly don't know what could tempt him now. Kit?"

Kit walked back and forth, looking at all of the contents of their display case and shook her head in deep thought. Grace kept staring at the poppy seed cake with the passion fruit curd. That's what she'd get if she was Kam. Heck, that's what she'd get for herself.

"Add in a slice of that cake for me while you're thinking about it," she said, blushing as Layla glanced at her. "Hey, I know I just had a cookie, but you can't blame me. This place could tempt a saint."

Kit nodded. "It can tempt anyone except Kam Matafeo. But if I was a betting woman, I'd bet on our banana pudding parfait. It's simple. It's comfort food at it's best and it's non-confrontational, you know?"

Grace laughed. "Non-confrontational food. I know what you mean. I was looking at that roasted pear I'm getting for Rob and I was thinking, it would take a brave soul to think they're cool enough to eat that."

The sisters laughed and nodded. "That's the thing with Rob. He doesn't think he's cool enough to eat the best. He knows it," Kit said.

Grace grinned as the women boxed up all of her orders.

She took out her card to pay and then noticed a shelf of very innocent looking glazed donuts. "Give me one of those too," she said thoughtfully.

Kit frowned. "A glazed donut? Who in the world is that for?"

Grace shrugged. "I don't know yet, but I'm thinking someone needs one today. I'll let you know who it ends up with."

Layla sighed happily. "I actually really want to know now. Come in again soon, Grace. That light of yours is a lot of fun to be around."

Grace rolled her eyes. "That's what they all say. Have a good day, you gorgeous bakers. And come by The Iron Skillet one of these nights so I can cook for you."

Layla put her apron back on and nodded. "Why do you think Kit's babysitting for me tonight? Michael and I have reservations at seven. You'll have to come out to the table and meet my husband."

Grace smiled. "I'll make sure whoever waits on you lets me know. I'll make your dinner extra special," she promised.

Kit pouted. "Okay, I'm feeling very left out here. I didn't get to have lunch with you and now you're making her special food. Next week, it's my turn."

Grace opened the door as she held her large bakery box in one hand. "Listen, Red, there's plenty of me to go around. See you two later," she called out and hurried outside, glancing at her phone.

She barely had time to get back to work but that's what happens when you spend an hour talking with a new friend. Grace smiled as she took Baby upstairs to their apartment. She might have issues with work, but at least she'd made a couple friends so far.

She rubbed Baby's belly for a minute before heading downstairs with her treasures. She pushed through the big outside doors and walked into the bright light of the kitchen. She caught sight of the crew immediately and held her box up in triumph.

"Who deserves a treat?" she called out.

All three heads swiveled in her direction and Candice let out a squeal.

"If you have cannoli, I will love you forever," she said reverently.

Grace put the box on the counter and opened it slowly. The oohs and aahhs were loud and appreciated.

"Prepare to love me, Candice. Cannoli. For you, James. The cupcake. I think it's S'mores or something. And Manuel? Kit swears you love pineapple upside down cake."

Manuel shook his head in awe. "They remembered what I like? Amazing," he said and picked his dessert up. "Today is going to be a fantastic day," he said before taking a big bite.

Grace watched happily as everyone devoured their dessert and thanked her at least five more times.

"Who are you giving the rest to?" James asked, licking his lips greedily.

Grace shut the box and shook her finger in his face. "The boss and Rob. No touching, James."

James laughed and began whistling as he went back to work. Candice sighed happily and patted her tummy before disappearing into the pantry as Manuel slowly ate the rest of his.

"Rob will love that pear. But when Kam says no to that parfait, I'll gladly eat it," Manuel said casually.

Grace frowned, feeling determined. "Oh, he's eating it. Is he here?"

Manuel shook his head and washed his hands. "He's in with Rob, going over orders."

"Perfect. I'll kill two birds with one stone." She picked up her box and headed out of the kitchen and down the hallway. She knocked lightly on the door and walked in when she heard a voice calling out to come in.

She opened the door and walked in, noting the office was covered in baseball pictures and bats and jerseys. Dude was a little obsessed.

"Hi there!" she said brightly and plopped the box down on Rob's desk. "I brought some treats to work and wanted to share."

Rob looked surprised but pleased. "Wren's put me on a diet. I ate so much porrozzo last night I'm up a pound and I was supposed to lose ten by now for my New Year's resolution."

Grace laughed as she opened the box. "Well, this is a very light dessert that I think even Wren would approve of. It's roasted pear with espresso mascarpone. I have it on very good authority that you're a food snob."

She heard a snort to the side and glanced over to see Kam's mouth twitching. *Ha!* There was hope that the man actually had a sense of humor.

And for you, Boss, nothing quite so fancy. We're starting you off at the beginning again. Nothing scary. You get a banana pudding parfait."

Kam frowned at her but stood up to look in the box. "I told you I don't eat sweets anymore."

Rob frowned with his mouth full. "Bro, *why?* I still remember seeing you down five Matafeo cupcakes in ten minutes one time."

Kam shrugged, although he didn't sit down either. She could tell he was torn. Grace decided a little nudging wouldn't hurt. She walked over and picked up the spoon and dipped it in the parfait, holding it up to his lips.

"Fine, take one bite and if you hate it, I'll take it away. If you like it? Then what's the harm in enjoying a tiny little dessert?" she asked with a smile.

Kam rolled his eyes but took the spoon from her and ate the small bite. He didn't close his eyes to concentrate on the flavors like she usually did, but his eyes brightened and he actually smiled for real. It was small, but it was there! *Home run!*

"Yeah, it's not bad. Thanks, Grace. I think I will take it," he said graciously and picked up the parfait, sitting back down.

Rob grinned at her and nodded his head in her direction. "Thanks, Grace. A treat like this on a Friday afternoon is just what we needed."

She picked up the box with the one glazed donut and the flourless chocolate cake and her own special treat for later and headed for the door. "It was my pleasure. When I was at Belinda's Bakery looking at all the goodies, I felt selfish and decided to share the fun. Enjoy," she said in farewell. "Oh, and can you point me in the direction of Taryn's office? I got her a dessert too."

Rob and Kam's eyebrows shot up in unison as she waited patiently. Kam stood up and pushed the chair out of his way as he walked toward her.

"I'll show you where it is. I was just on my way over there, myself," he said, glancing back at Rob worriedly.

Rob's eyes were suddenly dark with worry too. "Uh, yeah. We'll finish up later, Kam."

She followed Kam out the door and down the hallway. Kam knocked lightly on the door and waited for a *'come in'* before opening the door and walking in. Grace noted that where Rob enjoyed all things baseball, Taryn enjoyed plastering her walls with pictures of her husband and son. The large portrait behind her desk showed a very different Taryn than the one before her. She looked tanned and happy with her husband's arms around her and their son standing with his hand in hers. Her husband was gorgeous. Blond chiseled beauty. And the way he was staring down at his wife, she could tell he was madly in love. *Aw*, the little boy was a spitting image of his dad. What a gorgeous family.

Today was no vacation at the beach though. Taryn had her hair pulled up in a tight ponytail and she was wearing an all black pantsuit. Her cheekbones were sticking out so much she wondered if she should have brought two mini cakes for her. Harder to see, were the dark circles under her eyes although she'd used a lot of cover up to hide them. She looked over-worked, miserable and tired and it was barely one in the after-noon. This might not go as well as Layla thought it would.

She glanced at Kam but he motioned with his head for her to take the lead.

"Hi, Taryn. I happened to be down at the bakery and Layla Bender mentioned how much you enjoy her flourless chocolate cake, so I brought you one," she said and put the box on the edge of the table. She gently lifted out the cake and set in in front of Taryn with a napkin and a fork. She smiled brightly and stepped back, wondering why Taryn still hadn't said anything.

Taryn blinked a few times and moved her lips as if to smile. "Thanks, Grace. I appreciate it," she said softly as a single tear slipped down her cheek.

Grace frowned and stepped forward, concerned. "*Taryn?* Is everything okay?" she asked hesitantly.

She didn't know Taryn at all but she'd heard twice now from other people that things weren't good at home. Things must be worse than not good though. Taryn looked like she was right in the middle of falling apart.

Kam touched her shoulder. "Grace, I know Taryn is very touched by this gesture. Why don't you head back to the kitchen? I need to discuss one of the wait staff with Taryn."

Grace nodded quickly and picked up her box and walked out. *Holy cow.* She shut the door and paused before walking away. One second later, she heard loud sobbing and the low sound of Kam comforting her.

She walked slowly back to the kitchen, feeling sad for the woman she didn't even know. No one should have that much pain. *Ugh. Men.* Pain and men went hand in hand in her opinion. She set her box on an empty counter and grabbed an apron, washing up and getting to work. It was none of her business what was going on in Taryn's life, but if Layla's chocolate cake could bring some comfort on a bad day, then that was a good thing.

Food to her was medicine and art combined. It could also be poison and addiction, but she chose to focus on the art and the healing power of food. Her joy in food and her passion for cooking had picked her up out of her dark and sad past and had given her a new purpose and identity all at the same time. She was so much more than she used to be and that was because of food.

And now, it was time to show Fircrest what she could do. It was date night and she wanted to bring the romance. If her food could sparkle and pop and make people feel good, then that was her contribution to all of the people in relationships tonight. And if someone was getting dumped tonight? Then hopefully her perfectly prepared steak or salmon would help numb the pain.

"Okay, people. I'm turning on my music and if anyone turns it off, *I will hurt you,*" she threatened, glaring at everyone in general.

Candice laughed and yelled across the kitchen, "Turn it up! I love to dance."

Grace gave her an air high five. "You got it!"

The men ignored her but she could see Manuel tapping

his foot to the music and James sang along to anything even slightly country. She decided not to stress out about her boss and his sad eyes, or Taryn and the agony in hers. Nope, today she was going to focus on the food and the fun she had making it.

By the time Kam walked back in, she and the rest of the kitchen staff were well on their way to being prepared for Friday night.

CHAPTER 6

Taryn

K AM WAITED UNTIL Grace had shut the door before he walked over and put his arms around his sister in law. "Taryn, honey, what happened?"

Taryn began sobbing loudly and so he just held on and waited. Finally, maybe ten minutes later, she was able to say something coherent.

"He wants a divorce," she whispered.

Kam nodded his head, not surprised by anything anymore. Saddened, but not surprised. "Why?" he asked simply.

Taryn clenched her eyes shut. "He says he can't live with a wife who doesn't trust him."

Kam nodded. "Did you go to the marriage counselor this morning?"

Taryn nodded her head, reaching for a tissue to blow her nose. "I, um, stormed out halfway through. Afterwards at home, I told him how useless counseling was and so he said forget it. He said he doesn't want to live like this anymore."

Kam sighed and ran a hand through his long hair. "Taryn, all I know is that you two love each other. If you don't want to lose your marriage, isn't it worth it to at least try? Why not hold your temper and hold onto your emotions and listen to what the counselor has to say?"

Taryn stared off into space as tears continued to run down her cheeks. "She said that I had things to work on too. She said that we both had to make changes. That's so insulting after everything I've been though. It was like having acid poured into an open wound."

Kam almost smiled. "It's hard hearing that we still have things to learn, huh? Listen, I'm going to grab Rob. I need to get to work, but I don't want to leave you alone like this."

Taryn shook her head quickly. "Rob's a jerk. He wants to fire me. No, Kam… please stay. Just for a little while."

Kam glanced down at the delicious looking cake and then back up at Taryn's thin, pale face and sat back down. "How about I eat my parfait while you eat your cake?"

Taryn snorted. "You haven't eaten anything sweet in years. Like you're going to eat that."

Kam frowned. It had been a long time since he'd indulged himself. "For every bite you take, I'll take one."

Taryn sighed but nodded. "Deal."

They sat quietly for the first few bites thinking their own thoughts.

"I probably shouldn't be so mean to Grace, huh?" she asked softly.

Kam looked up and noted the cake was half gone. "Probably not. She's pretty nice. She has kind eyes and she cooks like an angel."

Taryn nodded again. "I should probably even apologize. *Maybe*."

Kam hid his smile. "Is the cake that good?"

Taryn looked up with a watery smile. "It really is."

Kam laughed, the sound rusty and low. "Then that's okay then. There's no shame in apologizing, little sister. It just means your heart is open enough to see yourself clearly and that you're big enough to admit you're not perfect."

Taryn's face fell. "I'm so far from perfect, Kam, it's not even funny."

Kam nodded. "I know, Taryn. I'm not perfect either. None of us are. Brogan's not."

Taryn lifted her head slowly and stared starkly into his eyes. "Yeah, but I thought he was, Kam. That's what hurts the most."

Kam nodded. "That's what we do here. We love each other. We hurt each other. And hopefully at the end of the day, we forgive each other."

Taryn sighed and picked up her fork, taking another bite. "I'll make another appointment with the counselor."

Kam closed his eyes in gratitude. "You'll call today?"

Taryn nodded, still chewing.

Kam took another bite and then looked down in surprise. He'd eaten the whole thing. *And it had been wonderful.* He frowned noting that he felt good. The flavors had been a mixture of bold and subtle and the rich creaminess had surrounded him with what he could only be explained as a rush of endorphins. "*Wow,*" he said softly.

Taryn looked up at him surprise. "Wow, what?"

Kam motioned towards his empty parfait cup. "That. My dessert, Grace got me. It was so good."

Taryn looked at him curiously before her face lightened and she smiled. "Aw, good for you, Kam. You allowed yourself to enjoy something. I'm glad for you."

Kam frowned at her. "I enjoy a lot of things. I enjoy my son and Rugby."

Taryn lifted an eyebrow. "You enjoy rugby because it allows you to vent all of your aggression in a legal way. And yes, of course you love, Nate. But do you *enjoy* him?"

Kam frowned, surprised and hurt by her question. "Of course I do," he said simply and stood up, throwing away his trash in her small can by her desk. "Make that call, Taryn," he ordered and walked out of the office.

He looked back at Rob's office and frowned. He didn't want to face Rob and tell him his sister's marriage was even worse off then they thought. But he didn't want to walk back in the kitchen and admit how much he enjoyed Grace's dessert either. He didn't want her *seeing* him. He didn't want her enticing him with joyful food or anything joyful to be honest. He didn't want to see her dancing or singing or teasing Candice.

Or smiling at him.

He walked back towards Rob's office and decided not to ponder on the why of that. Some things were best left alone. Like him.

CHAPTER 7

Natano

GRACE WAS GOOD to her word and decided to keep it light. She worked, she danced, she sang a little and she cooked like she'd never cooked before. She was friendly to everyone and treated Kam just like she would Manuel or Candice. No matter what Layla had said that afternoon, the burden of bringing a man back to life was just too much. Being a candle in the dark, she could do, but only in her own way. It was almost as if Layla wanted her to be Kam's friend. But glancing at Kam and his perpetually grim face, she wasn't sure she was up for that. And Kam didn't look like he wanted a new friend. Besides, from what Layla had said, the whole town was his friend. Why in the world would he want more?

Grace blew out her breath and pushed all of the deep stuff away and focused on cooking the salmon in front of her to perfection. Layla and her cute hubby were here and the waitress had already come back to tell her how excited they were and that they'd want her to come out at some point.

She sang along to Andy Grammer's *Fresh Eyes*, swinging her hips as she cooked in time with the beat. She plated their meals herself and handed them off to the waitress and then put her hands on her hips.

"They better love it," she said to no one in particular.

Candice whistled. "I've never seen anyone cook as fast or as good as you, girl. You're a whirlwind."

Grace bowed her head at the compliment. "Thank you, Candice, my new best friend. What do we have next?"

Candice began to hand her the paper when she saw a little boy with tons of light brown curls run through the doors and right toward the stove where a large pot of water was boiling and a burner was on high.

"Oh no," she whispered and ran to intercept him. She caught the little boy in her arms, surprised at his strength as he struggled to get down.

"I want some fish and chips," he said in a high little boy voice.

"But sweetie, you can't just run towards the stove like that. It's hot and it could hurt you."

The little boy stopped struggling and stared at her. "*Who are you?*"

Grace grinned, entranced by his chubby cheeks and huge brown eyes. "I'm Grace. Who are you?"

The little boy frowned. "I'm Nate! I'm the best boy in the world," he said with such confidence she believed him.

She kept him on her hip as she walked over to a plate of grilled shrimp that had been sent back due to a mistake.

"We make fish and chips for lunch, but would you like some fried shrimp?"

Nate nodded his head and took the shrimp immediately, biting the top off expertly and chewing with his mouth closed. *Good boy.*

"I want more," he said promptly, smiling at her hopefully.

She glanced around the kitchen but everyone was working and Kam was no where in sight. This little boy had to be his.

Letting a little boy run wild in a busy kitchen was a recipe for disaster though. What was he thinking?

She grabbed a plate and scooped up some shrimp and grabbed her glazed donut too and took the little boy back to Kam's office and shut the door. She sat him on her lap while he ate and she asked him about his day. She soon learned that school, *preschool* she was assuming, had been fun because Max had shared the blocks with him. But he was mad at his grandma because he'd wanted to watch Doc McStuffins and she'd made him take a nap instead.

She grinned as the little boy talked and talked and ate the whole time. By the way he devoured the donut and shrimp she could tell he was hungry and it was past time for his dinner.

"So who are you here with? I don't see a lot of little boys running through my kitchen very often," she said once she could get a word in.

Nate looked at her like she was crazy. "I came to see my daddy. He's busy though so I decided to make dinner like he does."

Grace's eyes went big. He'd wanted to come back and cook like his dad did. *Scary.* "Well, why don't we go find daddy? Does that sound like a good idea?"

Nate licked his finger and nodded. "Okay."

She picked up the little boy and walked out of the office just as Kam burst through the door looking frantic.

"Natano!" he yelled and grabbed his son out of her arms. "I've been looking everywhere for you. Why did you disappear? I was talking to Grandpa and you were gone."

Natano patted his dad's cheek and touched his hair. "I wanted to make dinner in the kitchen like you do. But she wouldn't let me. Shrimp is yummy," he added.

Kam closed his eyes for a moment as a deep sigh of relief left his body. He opened his eyes and looked at her, shaking his head.

"Thank you and I apologize. This won't happen again," Kam said, holding Natano so tight the boy struggled to get down.

"Can I have another donut?" he asked, reaching his hand out to her.

Grace laughed and shook her head. "I don't think a dinner of fried shrimp and a donut is very healthy. I was actually just wondering what vegetables I should feed you."

Nate's eyes got big as he shook his head fiercely. "No, no. I don't like vegetables."

Kam snorted. "After what you just did, young man, you'll be eating vegetables for a month. Every meal."

Grace grinned at the father and son and thought they were the cutest thing she'd ever seen. A big, strong man holding a little boy with such tenderness and love.

"Well, Nate, it was nice meeting you but I've got to go say hi to some people who are dining with us."

Nate nodded gravely. "Next time I see you can I have another donut?"

Grace smiled and glanced at Kam. "That depends on if I get the chance to see you. I'm not sure little boys are allowed in the kitchen."

Kam frowned. "Only when dad is with you, right, Natano?"

Nate frowned back at Kam, "Then take me to the kitchen more. I never get to come back here," he pouted.

Kam laughed a little. "I'll bring you back next week for lunch if you're a good boy and promise to never run away again."

Nate nodded and Grace waved goodbye at the little boy who was looking at her so beseechingly she almost felt guilty for not having more donuts.

She moved quickly through the restaurant, finding Layla and Michael in a cozy booth, finishing up their meals as they talked and smiled.

"So how was the salmon?" she asked as they both looked up

in surprise. They'd been staring so deeply into each other's eyes, she could have stood there all day before they noticed her.

Layla grinned and motioned to her husband. "Grace, this is Michael. Michael, this is Grace, our new friend."

Michael reached out and shook her hand. "Grace, you're incredible. Dinner was outstanding tonight."

Grace smiled back and noted that Michael's masculine good looks were the perfect opposite to Layla's blond beauty. *Their kids must be models*, she thought.

"I'm so glad you enjoyed your dinner. What about you, Layla? What did you think?"

Layla pointed to her sea bass with papaya salsa. "I will literally do anything for this recipe. Seriously. *Anything.*"

Grace leaned her hip against the booth as she talked with the couple, enjoying their conversation.

"Well, I better head back to the kitchen before I get fired. You two have a beautiful evening," she said, noting how they held hands over the dinner table.

She walked back to the kitchen feeling a little churning in her stomach and frowned a little wondering at it. She wasn't jealous of Layla. She didn't even necessarily want to be with anyone right now either. But seeing the love they had for each other and the easy affection and kindness made her want something more. Maybe, if she was lucky someday, she could have a relationship like theirs. She'd certainly never had the experience of being around love like that. None of her mother's constantly revolving boyfriends had ever looked at her mom like that. Even her friends' boyfriends seemed too self-obsessed to care about anyone very deeply. *What would it be like to have a connection like that*, she wondered as she pushed through the doors.

She glanced at Kam who was talking to Nate and a large, Samoan man who had to be his father before heading back to her station. But a moment later, she felt a tap on her shoulder.

"Excuse me, but I just wanted to thank you for looking out for Natano when he got away from me. He's an adventurous little boy and likes to run wild. Just like his dad did at that age."

Grace smiled up at the man with short trimmed, white hair. "It was nothing. He's a darling boy."

Kam walked up to them, frowning again. *As usual,* she thought with a sigh.

"It's not nothing. Manuel told me he was running right toward the stove and he admitted he wanted to cook something. He could have burned himself and ended up in the hospital if you hadn't run across the kitchen and grabbed him. Thank you, Grace."

Grace patted Kam's arm before smiling at Nate, who was looking guilty and sad now. "Saving little boys is what I do when I'm not cooking. Me and my dog, Baby, walk around town looking for kids just like Nate to save. This was nothing," she assured the little boy.

Nate looked intrigued. "*You have a dog?* I want to meet your dog," he said eagerly.

Grace blinked, not sure what to say. "Well, next week when you come by the kitchen, I'll introduce you two. I live upstairs in the apartment. I run up on my breaks to say hi and take him outside. If it's okay with your dad, you can come help me," she said, looking worriedly at Kam.

Kam shrugged and nodded. "Sounds like fun to me. Natano loves dogs. I think you've just made a new best friend."

Grace and Nate looked at each other and grinned. "Good. Since I just moved here I was looking for a new best friend. You look like you're perfect for the job."

Nate bounced in his dad's arms. "I am! I'm the bestest friend in the world."

Grace laughed and looked at Nate's grandfather who was watching her intently with a smile on his face.

"Grace, I'd like to introduce myself to you. My name is Toa Matafeo. And to thank you for saving my grandson from disaster, I'd like to invite you to dinner this Sunday at our home. Please come," he said in such a way that it felt more like a command than an invitation.

"Uh, well,… um, that's very kind of you," she said, looking at Kam nervously.

Kam was looking at his dad in consternation but Nate looked ecstatic. "Bring your doggy, Grace!"

Toa nodded regally. "Yes, please bring your dog too. Kam will tell you the address. Lunch starts promptly at one," he said and slipped Nate out of Kam's arms and began walking away.

Nate waved at her over his grandfather's shoulder, leaving her in a very awkward silence with Kam.

Kam sighed and ran a hand over his hair as he stared at her. "I'm sorry about that. My parents are very old fashioned but they're kind, good people. I'd say don't come because I know you probably have a million other things you'd rather do, but they'd be offended. Sorry."

Grace shook her head. "I don't mind stopping by for an hour. And your little boy is so cute. I'll bring my dog and they can play catch for awhile. And if I get to try some authentic Samoan food, then it's all good," she said easily.

Kam looked relieved and smiled at her. "Good. That's good then. Okay, we're getting behind on orders. Let's get back to it," he said.

They both went to work and the time flew by, but she couldn't help noticing that Kam was singing softly to a couple songs. She smiled as she collapsed in bed late that night and wondered if bringing light to someone who'd been in the dark for so long was as simple as just being nice? If that's all she had to do, then this would be easy.

CHAPTER 8

Hope

TATE LOOKED AT Kam as they stood in the chilly, spring air and waited for the game to start. They'd been warming up for a good fifteen minutes, but the other team was late.

"Man, I hate when I have to wake up early just to have the game cancelled," Kam grumbled, rubbing his tired, blood shot eyes.

Tate nodded in complete agreement. "Late night?"

Kam shrugged. "Friday nights at The Iron Skillet. But it wasn't that bad last night. My new Sous Chef is incredible. She's fast and the patrons are raving about her food."

Tate's eyes widened slightly. "Jane told me about her. Grace, right?"

Kam smiled and put his hands on his hips. "Yeah, she saved Natano last night from hurting himself. *And* she brought desserts from the bakery for everyone. By the way, tell Jane that the banana parfait was delicious."

Tate blinked a few times, suddenly very interested in Kam's new Sous chef. "That's great, Kam. You've been needing someone reliable now for awhile. She sounds like she's perfect for the job."

Kam yawned loudly. "Yeah, she's amazing. Taryn could have scared her off too. She went after her, but Gracie didn't even blink an eye. She just brought in one of Layla's chocolate cakes and now Taryn loves her too. She's got this weird vibe about her, where everyone is drawn to her. It's the strangest thing."

Tate swallowed and closed his eyes, hoping that Kam might be one of those people. "Well, I'm curious now. Maybe Jane and I will stop by the restaurant so I can meet her and see how well she cooks," he said casually.

Kam nodded his head and began swinging his arms around in circles to warm up. "Yeah, do that. She's good at going out and saying hi to people too."

Tate snorted. "You mean she doesn't glare at people and tell them she needs to get back to work and that wasting her time talking is irritating?"

Kam paused and glared at Tate before punching him in the shoulder. "It got to be a pain in my rear, Tate. Everyone in the world wanting to talk to me when all I wanted to do was my job. It drove me nuts."

Tate laughed. "I know, I know. I'm just saying it'll be nice for Rob to have someone who knows how to schmooze the people."

Kam grumbled a little but didn't disagree.

"So are you bringing anything to dinner tomorrow?" Tate asked, yawning.

Kam shrugged. "Yeah, my Sous Chef. Dad invited her to dinner. Can you believe that?"

Tate's mouth fell open in shock. "What? *Our* dad?"

Kam turned and looked at him. "I was standing right there

and dad just invites her to dinner like he does that kind of thing all the time."

Tate shook his head, speechless. When he had asked Jane to marry him, he'd been disowned by his uncle and adoptive father. His mother and father were very traditional in their views and had wanted him and all of their children to marry Samoans. And when Kam had fallen in love with Bailey, although they hadn't disowned him, they hadn't been exactly happy about it either. And they'd probably just been relieved that Posey was willing to marry Pule, *but this?* Inviting Grace to dinner? Nah, it couldn't be their parents wanting Kam to date her?

He glanced at Kam and winced. *"You don't think... ?"* he asked.

Kam narrowed his eyes at him and shook his head. "Nah. Never."

Tate sighed, feeling a little let down. "What do you think of her. Is she cute?" he asked casually.

Kam opened his mouth to say something and then stopped. Tate waited, his heartbeat speeding up as hope began to fill his chest. He kept his face expressionless as he waited though.

"She's cute," he finally said and then wandered off to say hi to Pule who'd just shown up in time to be told the game had been cancelled. His loud complaining made everyone laugh.

Tate let out a breath as he stared at Kam's strong back. He took out his cell phone, turning around to stare at the misty, evergreen trees, surrounding the playing field.

He pressed Jane's contact and waited.

"Hey, gorgeous. Why aren't you playing? Did someone get hurt?" Jane asked worriedly.

Tate ran a hand over his short, cropped hair. "Nah, game was cancelled. The other team chickened out. Losers. But, baby, get this. Kam just told me he thinks his new Sous Chef is cute," he said, his voice choking up a little, shocking himself.

Jane was silent for a moment. "Oh, Tate... *do you think?*"

Tate swallowed hard, trying to control his emotion. "It's a shot. We're going to The Iron Skillet for dinner tonight. I've gotta meet this girl."

Jane laughed happily. "I've met her, Tate. She's more than cute. When she smiles, she's beautiful. She just doesn't know it. Oh my word. *Finally*, after all these years," she said with a shaky voice.

Tate closed his eyes. "Well, let's not get ahead of ourselves. We have a little hope. That's all it is. Just hope right now. He thinks she's cute. He hasn't said he loves her or anything."

"Hope is a wonderful thing. I'm calling Layla. It's her turn to babysit," she said and then said goodbye.

Tate slipped his phone in his pocket and wandered over to join the complaining. "Tai, do you still make those blueberry waffles with maple syrup?" he called out to his cousin.

Tai grinned and held his fist in the air. "Blueberry waffles! My place. Let's go, my brothers!"

They all shouted in happiness and headed toward the parking lot. He watched Kam pull Pule into a headlock and laugh and Tate stopped in his tracks. It had been years since he'd heard that sound. Not the stiff, polite, fake laugh that he'd heard too many times. No, this sounded like the old Kam.

Tate paused and rubbed a hand over his face, wiping away the stray tear that had appeared. Yeah, hope was more than wonderful. It was beautiful.

"Hey, Kam. Leave that kid alone. He's my ride," he yelled, and watched as Pule automatically glared at him.

They walked over and got in Pule's truck. Pule glanced at him, still ticked about the kid comment and then did a double take.

"Tate, what's the matter?" he asked, sounding concerned. "You look like you just saw a ghost."

Tate looked out the window. "I did. I saw the ghost of my old brother."

Pule nodded in understanding. "Kam about broke my neck, but it was worth it to hear him laugh like that again."

Tate gripped his phone in his hands. "Pule, there might be a girl Kam's interested in."

Pule frowned and rolled his eyes. "Dude, that's never going to happen. I know he seems like his old self today, but that doesn't mean anything."

Tate blew out a breath in exasperation. "Listen to what I'm saying. There is a girl. And dad invited her to dinner tomorrow. She's his new Sous Chef and from what everyone says, she's an angel. Kam thinks she's amazing. That's what he said."

Pule stared at him in shock. "Are you kidding me?" he whispered.

Tate shook his head. Pule pulled his truck over and leaned his head on his steering wheel as his shoulders began to shake. Tate unbuckled himself and scooted over, putting an arm around his cousin's shoulders.

"I didn't think this would ever happen," Pule said his voice thick with tears.

Tate wiped another tear away. "I know, bro. I know. But don't get your hopes up just yet. I'm going to check her out tonight at the restaurant. I want to see for myself."

Pule closed his eyes and lifted his head to heaven. "Thank you, God," he whispered reverently and then pulled back into traffic. "Well, I'm taking Posey to dinner tonight too, it turns out."

Tate laughed, wondering if the whole restaurant was going to be filled with his relatives and friends wanting to check out the new Sous Chef. That, and making sure she was good enough for Kam. They were all protective of Kam. He'd been through too much in the past few years and he didn't need any more pain in his life. If this girl was bad news, he didn't know what he'd do, but he'd do something.

"What if she's not good for him? What if she hates kids or we find out she's a racist or she doesn't like Kam's tattoos?"

Pule's eyes turned cold and mean as he looked back at him. "Then I'll take care of it. He's my brother and she'll have me to deal with if she hurts him."

Tate's eyes widened. For a second there, Pule looked scary. Pule's heart had broken a thousand times over for Kam through the years so it was understandable.

"You might want to give her a chance, Pule. Remember, if this is good for Kam, then we *want* to be nice to her."

Pule's face cleared immediately. "Do you think I don't know that? Geez, Tate. I'm not an idiot. I'll make up my mind tonight when I meet her."

Tate nodded as they pulled into the parking lot of Tai's diner. "We should tell Tai. He'll want to know."

Pule nodded. "Already done."

They walked into the diner and headed for the backroom where waffles were already being served. Tai must have called in the order on their way over. As they all began to eat, Tate watched Kam closely and counted six real smiles and a few booming laughs. He left an hour later, his heart so full, he could barely contain his joy.

Something had put a smile on Kam's face. Or more to the point, *someone* had put a smile on Kam's face. And he couldn't wait to meet that someone.

CHAPTER 9

Meet the Family

GRACE WAS EXHAUSTED and it was only seven on a Saturday night. This was not good. If she didn't get some energy and get some fast she was going to start cooking like a first year culinary student and that could not happen.

She glanced at Candice and blew a strand of hair out of her eyes. "Do you mind if we turn up the volume? If I don't get some inspiration I'm going to go slump in the corner and go to sleep."

Candice frowned at her worriedly. "Up late last night? Hot date?"

Grace laughed and stirred the gnocchi. "*I wish.* Nah, just some bad dreams."

"Then by all means, turn the volume up," Candice said, motioning to the Bose sound system in the corner.

Grace turned up the volume from her phone and began nodding her head to Macklemore's *Can't Hold Us.* She took a sip of water and squared her shoulders. She could do this. She *had* to do this.

Kam walked over and touched her shoulder. "What's wrong, Gracie? Not feeling well?" he asked, looking concerned.

"Everyone's got demons, right?" she answered with a half-smile. "Don't worry about me, Boss. I won't let you down."

Kam frowned. "I know a little bit about demons. Go take a fifteen-minute break in my office. Take a little nap or eat a snack. That's an order," he added when she opened her mouth to argue.

She smiled, touched that he was being so understanding. "Thanks. I really appreciate it," she said and took off her apron. She went into Kam's office, shut the door, and set her alarm for fifteen minutes. She walked over and sat in his huge, comfy chair and lay her head on her arms. As soon as she closed her eyes, she was asleep.

Fifteen minutes later when her alarm went off, she jerked awake and groaned. She stood up, smoothed her hair back and breathed in and out slowly. Her nap hadn't been nearly long enough but it had been long enough to get her through the rest of the night. She smiled and walked out of the office ready to work.

She spent the next hour trying to make up for lost time. She sang to the music and even got Manuel to dance with her for a few seconds so that was a victory. It was almost eight-thirty when a waiter came back and tapped her on the shoulder.

"It's time, Grace. We have three tables wanting to meet you. Kam said to leave you alone but they're insisting. *Loudly* insisting, I might add. Sorry."

Grace nodded and forced a smile. Tonight, she looked like she felt. Tired and drained. But if they insisted, then she had no choice.

"Thanks, Barry. I'll come right now," she said and whipped her apron off. She followed him out into the dining room and smiled brightly. She looked at all of the happy couples eating and laughing and wondered for a few seconds what that would be like. Having someone stare across the table at her with love in their eyes? She'd never had that. She felt a stirring of self pity and shook it off as Barry gestured to the people at the table.

Grace smiled at everyone in general and clasped her hands but did a double take at the woman sitting in the corner.

"*Jane?* My bakery buddy," she said, relaxing and smiling genuinely now.

Jane grinned and motioned to the man sitting next to her. "Grace, before I start embarrassing you with compliments, I want to introduce you to my husband, Tate."

Grace looked at the man sitting next to Jane and blinked in surprise. The man was gorgeous and was definitely related to Kam. "Well, what a handsome devil you are. He looks like he keeps you on your toes, Jane," she said, making Tate redden and laugh.

Jane hugged Tate and kissed his cheek. "He absolutely does keeps me on my toes. But I have to say, he's the best husband in the world. All the Matafeo men are pure gold."

Tate took a sip of water and shook his head. "Jane, you're supposed to be complimenting Grace, not me."

Grace laughed, enjoying torturing the poor soul.

"Oh, and this is Tai Matafeo, Tate's cousin and his wife, Cleo," Jane said, motioning to the couple sitting across from them.

Grace smiled and nodded at the couple, noting the strong resemblance between Tate and his cousin. "Wow, you Matafeo men won the genetic lottery. Cleo, how do you handle having such a beautiful husband? I think I'd be following him around all day glaring at all the women in a two block radius with a can of mace in one hand."

Tai tilted his head back and laughed so loudly all the

people in the vicinity turned around to watch. Cleo joined him and linked their hands.

"Well, I'll share a secret about the Matafeos. They adore their wives and are faithful through and through. Jane and I have never had one moment's worry. Have we Jane?"

Jane lifted an eyebrow and tilted her head towards her. "I don't know, Cleo. I think Grace is flirting with our men. What should we do? I can run out and buy some mace."

Cleo grinned and leaned over the table. "Nah, too easy. I say we complain to the Head Chef. He'll make her stay after and mop the floors."

Grace laughed, holding up her hands. "Okay, okay. I promise, no more flirting with your husbands, although they are too gorgeous to believe. But enough of them. Let's talk about me. How did you like your food?"

The table erupted in compliment after compliment and Grace realized that better than a nap or music, a good compliment could give you the energy of three Sous Chefs.

"Okay, guys. Okay. My head's going to explode and my boss is going to fire me if I don't get a move on. But thank you so much for coming in tonight."

Cleo took a sip of water. "Not so fast. First promise that you'll come to the next girl's night out. We insist," she said, looking at Jane.

Jane nodded. "I was just about to say that. You're coming and if I have to threaten Rob to give you a night off, I will."

Grace smiled, touched at the offer of friendship. "Consider me there. You all have the best night ever," she said and walked over to the next table.

Barry gestured to the guests. "This is Pule Matafeo and his wife, Posey. And this couple is Asher and Meredith Murphy."

Grace frowned and stared at Pule Matafeo. *Was the whole town nothing but Matafeos?*

"Uh, any relation to those guys?" she said gesturing over her shoulder to Tate and Tai. She looked back at the table and all four heads looked down as if they had been staring in her direction.

Pule smiled serenely and nodded. "Those two men are my cousins and Kam is my big brother."

Grace smiled and reached out her hand to shake. "It's a privilege to meet you. I have to say, I love working for your brother. He is so kind and thoughtful. I can't even imagine what it would be like to grow up with Kam as an older brother," she said.

Pule snorted and was about to say something when the woman sitting next to him elbowed him in the side. Pule smiled and nodded. "Kam was wonderful."

"He *is* wonderful," his wife said. "Hi, I'm Posey, Wren Downing's younger sister. She's told me about your gnocchi."

Grace grinned. "I love Wren! She's my favorite. Are you a chef too?"

Posey shook her head. "Oh, no. I can barely microwave food. I write children's books."

Grace shook her head. "That is so cool. Good for you."

"And I'm Kam's ex-girlfriend."

Grace swiveled her head to see an attractive blond with a razor sharp angled bob looking her up and down.

"Um, *okaay*. That's nice for you."

The man sitting next to her rolled his eyes and sighed loudly. "I'm Asher Murphy. And since you're new in town, we run the *Match and Mingle* web site for singles in the Fircrest and Tacoma area. The first month is free."

Grace frowned and looked down at her hands. "I probably should look into something like that but I have the worst luck with men. The last guy I dated, emptied out my savings account. I think I'll stick to what I'm good at. Cooking."

"Gotcha. You're a cat lady," Meredith said with a small, self-satisfied smile.

Grace turned and smiled directly at the woman, not breaking eye contact. She made it a rule to never back down from a bully and she wasn't going to start now, even if it was an ex of Kam's.

Meredith looked away first and blushed. "Sorry, that was rude," she finally said.

Grace didn't bother acknowledging the obvious and looked back to Pule and Posey. "So how was dinner tonight?" she asked, changing the subject.

Posey pointed to her almost empty plate. "I'm about to order another meal just so I can take home some leftovers. It was amazing, Grace. Truly, delicious."

Pule stopped glaring at Meredith to smile at her. "Let's just say we'll be coming back every week for dinner and twice for lunch if I have anything to say about it."

Asher put his fingers to his lips and make a kissing motion. "Perfection. Thank you for moving to Fircrest, Grace. We're all very happy you're here. *Right, Meredith?*"

Grace watched curiously as Meredith winced. If she wasn't mistaken, someone was getting kicked under the table.

"She might be a halfway decent cook but that doesn't mean that she's good enough for *K...*" she gasped suddenly and didn't finish her sentence. She glared across the table at Pule. "That hurt!"

Pule ignored Meredith and smiled up at her. "I think you *are* good enough for Calzones. I've been after Rob forever to add them to the lunch menu."

Grace smiled in confusion. "Good enough for calzones? Uh, sure. I'll see what I can do. You all have a wonderful evening. I have one more table to say hi to."

She walked away, motioning to Barry to show her the last

table. That was the weirdest encounter she'd had since moving to Fircrest. She was going to stay clear of Meredith. That woman was psycho.

"Grace, this is Anne Matafeo and her husband, Sefe. They've been very patiently waiting to meet you."

"Ah, another Matafeo," she said, feeling tired all of a sudden. The last encounter hadn't been very fun, but this older couple seemed nice enough.

"Yes, I'm Kam's uncle and Anne is Kam's mother-in-law. We just wanted to tell you how much we enjoyed your food tonight."

Grace smiled and bowed her head in acceptance. "Thank you so much. I wish I had more time to stay and chat, but I'm needed back in the kitchen. Please enjoy the rest of your evening and I'll tell Kam you stopped by."

Sefe nodded his head. His wife, Anne was staring at her unsmilingly as if she was measuring her and finding her wanting. Without another word, she walked quickly back to the kitchen. "*So weird*," she muttered and washed her hands before jumping back into the fray.

Kam walked over to her a little while later and touched her shoulder. She turned and smiled quickly at him before turning back to her clams.

"I'm not sure why all of my family showed up tonight. I, um… I hope everyone was nice to you."

Grace smiled and shrugged. "Oh, sure. I met Tate and your cousin Tai. Pule seems nice too. There was this one girl though that freaks me out a little. I'm thinking she's a touch psycho."

Kam grimaced and motioned with his hand. "Who was it?"

Grace shrugged. "Her name is Meredith. She accused me of being a crazy cat lady. Super weird. I've never met her before in my life and I'm getting all of these antagonistic vibes from her."

Kam sighed and looked up at the ceiling. "Yeah, well she is a psycho. Good call. Stay away from her. Anyone else?"

Grace frowned, not wanting to be a tattle tale. "I did meet your uncle and mother-in-law. Did I hear that right? Is your uncle really married to your mother-in-law?"

Kam bit his lip and put his hands on his hips. "It looks and sounds crazy, and I guess it is, but it works for them. Anne didn't say anything did she?" he asked lightly.

Grace shook her head, "No, just the opposite. She just stared at me the whole time as if I was a bug she wanted to squish. Next time they come in and ask to speak to the chef, you're going out. *Not me*," she said, shivering.

"I guess that's fair. I wouldn't like to be stared at that way either," he said and sighed. "Okay, enough of people wanting to talk to you. If anyone else comes back here asking for you, the answer is no."

They both heard someone clearing their throat and noticed, Clara, one of the new waitresses standing beside them looking as uncomfortable as she could.

"I hate to interrupt, but there are two tables asking to speak to you, Grace."

Kam glared at the waitress, making her step back. "Who is it?"

Clara cleared her throat nervously. "Garrett and Rayne Murphy and Becket and Ivy Lowell, um Sir."

Kam ran his hand over his hair and shook his head as she looked at him pleadingly.

"Oh and the other table is Tristan and Maya Jensen," she added quickly and then turned and ran out of the kitchen.

"I'm begging you, Kam. Please just let me cook. Any other day I'd be happy to talk to people all night long, but I just went through all of your relatives and I'm not having a great day as it is. Can you please just walk out and say hi? *Please?*" she begged.

Kam looked at her for a moment and nodded. "It's been years since I've gone out, but I'll do this for you. You've earned a break."

She watched him square his shoulders and head out, sighing in relief. Candice walked over and patted her shoulder.

"I overheard what you said about Meredith. She's a feisty one. She once sent back a dish three times because she wasn't happy with the way I prepared it. I once asked Rob to ban her from the restaurant."

Grace laughed. "I would sign that petition. She took one look at me and I swear, she hated me on the spot. I don't get it."

Manuel walked over and leaned in to whisper. "I heard from one of the old prep cooks a few years back that Meredith Murphy is Kam's ex-girlfriend from way back in the day."

Grace nodded. "And that's exactly how she introduced herself. As Kam's ex, right there in front of her husband. But I don't know why that means she has to hate *me*. I can't even imagine those two together. They're like polar opposites."

Candice nodded in agreement. "Kam's an angel and she's a devil, but I guess opposites attract and all that."

Grace pursed her lips. "From what I hear, they don't usually work out though. Probably why they're not together."

As everyone erupted with their opinion of Kam's previous relationship, she knew she had to put a stop to it or they'd get behind. "Okay guys, this was fun, but we better stop gossiping about the boss. Let's get back to work, my friends," she said and turned up the music to listen to *My House* by Flo Rida.

By the time Kam made it back to the kitchen, everyone was dancing and laughing and having a good time. Grace noted that Kam was smiling and knew that talking to old friends was probably good for him. Maybe she'd throw a fit every now and then for his own good.

*

Kam washed his hands after talking to his friends and turned to look at his crew. You wouldn't know by looking at them that they were doing the work of ten people but they worked in sync perfectly with each other all the while laughing and dancing and having a good time. He smiled as he watched Grace and Candice bump hips as they sang to Lady Ga Ga's *Just Dance*. A classic.

He went back to work and felt something he hadn't felt in a long time. *Good.* He felt good. He didn't want to push it, but he was almost having fun. The only thing not fun about the evening was the fact that his family had made it a point to come check out his new Sous Chef. He hadn't minded Tate and Tai. Tate had warned him he was planning on it and that he was just here to try out her cooking. *But Meredith?* Now that was a different story. She was acting exactly like a jealous ex girlfriend would. *And* right in front of her husband too. If he were Asher, he'd put a stop to that immediately.

He went to bed that night, tired but energized all at the same time. He couldn't put his finger on it, but something had changed. He frowned and turned over, fluffing his pillow as he tried to pinpoint what it was. But whatever it was, he kind of liked it.

CHAPTER 10

Munch and Mingle

GRACE SAT UP with a gasp and looked at the clock before sinking back into her covers with a groan. It was Sunday and her day off. She could relax. *Oh, wait.* No, she couldn't. She had a lunch to go to at Kam's parents' house. It shouldn't be too bad though. She could bring her dog and play with Nate and chat with Jane and Cleo. Kam would be there too of course. He wasn't one for lengthy conversations but it would be nice to know he was there. Kam had this protective, almost soothing vibe about him that she was starting to really like. At first, she'd thought he was super grim and un-fun but now she knew he was just dealing with a lot. She frowned up at her ceiling and wondered if they were actually friends yet. Probably not, but maybe they were in the process. Hanging out at his family party might be a good place to start.

She sat up and yawned, and knew there was no way she could go back to sleep now. Good time to think about what she could bring to the lunch. Kam's dad hadn't asked her to bring anything but she'd rather die than show up empty handed. She closed her eyes and mentally clicked through her recipes. She needed a side dish but one with some pop. She knew she'd go home feeling like a failure if she had to bring home leftovers.

Mmm, Hatch chili, corn pudding. It had some heat, a lot of cheese and was always a hit.

"Perfect," she said to Baby who was staring at her with his leash in his mouth. She laughed and rolled out of bed. "Give me five minutes."

Five hours later, she stared in the mirror as she fixed her hair. Usually, she had her hair up in a bun or pulled back in a ponytail, but she decided to put on some makeup and put a few beach waves in her hair. She glanced down at what she was wearing and wondered if she should change into her usual jeans and t-shirt. *Nah*, she never wore anything fun. She'd been holding onto this spring dress forever. It was cream and black striped and flowy and casual at the same time. But... if she wore her sexy red sandals? Grace frowned. That might be pushing it. But she never pushed it, so oh well, *she was wearing them*. All work and no play meant you never got to look pretty. And today, for some reason, she felt like looking pretty.

"How do I look, Baby?" she said, looking down at her Siber-poo. Baby woofed so she took that as a compliment. She walked over to her kitchen counter and picked up her casserole dish. "Time to socialize."

Twenty minutes later, she glanced at her google maps and back at the house. This had to be it. That and all of the cars parked out in front were a clue that something was going down. She got out of her truck and whistled for Baby to jump out of the bed. She picked up her casserole dish off the seat and shut the door with her hip. She heard the sound of Fleetwood Mac and relaxed. Anytime there was good food and good music, she knew she was in a good place.

She walked around to the back of the house. Even though it was April, it was a warm seventy-five and no one in the Pacific

Northwest was going to take that for granted. She whistled for Baby as she began sniffing something interesting under a bush. She walked through the wooden gate and around the corner, pausing to take in the scene before her.

She saw groupings of people all talking and laughing and glanced at her watch and frowned. They'd told her one but obviously the party had started earlier. That, or these people just enjoyed each other's company so much that they showed up early. She noted Jane and Tate were already here and so were Cleo and Tai, along with Posey and Pule, who she'd met last night.

"Doggy!"

She grinned as a curly haired bullet sped right for her. Baby barked in welcome as Nate stopped on a dime and began furiously petting her Siber-poo.

"Sweetie, just remember you have to be careful with dogs," she said, kneeling down carefully with her casserole dish in hand. "Baby is a nice doggy, but some doggies are nervous and will bite you if they feel scared."

Nate frowned up at her. "I don't scare doggies. I love doggies."

Grace grinned and put her hand on the little boys back as he showered her dog with love. "She likes you," she said.

Nate nodded knowingly. "Everybody likes me. Can I feed her?"

Grace frowned. "Well, she's supposed to eat special doggy food, but if you slip her a tiny piece of meat, I know she'll love it. Nothing else though, okay?"

Nate nodded his head gravely. "Okay, come with me, doggy."

Baby looked up at her as if to ask permission and she nodded. "Go with Nate, Baby. I'll catch up with you two in a second. I just need to say hi and put this with the other food."

Nate had already started walking away with Baby right behind him though.

"You're so good with kids. Do you have any?"

Grace jumped in surprise and turned to see Kam's father standing in the shadow of a tree.

She shook her head, smiling sadly. "I wish. No, I just love kids. Maybe someday I'll have a few myself. And thanks again for inviting me today. It looks like quite the party."

Toa looked over his shoulder at the large group of people and smiled. "Family and friends. What is life without them? Come join us, Grace. We've been waiting for you."

Grace frowned, wondering why they'd be waiting for her but agreed with him on the friends and family. She had plenty of friends, thank heavens. In the family department though, she was sadly lacking.

"I envy you, your large family. I'm pretty much on my own," she said, putting her casserole dish where he pointed on the large table covered with so much food she wondered how it was still standing.

Toa frowned at her and put his hand on her arm. "I can't imagine what it would be like to be so alone in the world."

Grace blushed and shook her head. "Oh no, I'm not really *alone*. I have my dog and my friends. I might not have family, but I think Heaven tries to make it up to me in other ways."

Toa nodded his head gravely. "Or, you could always have a family of your own. A husband and children of your own would be a good start."

Grace opened her mouth to say something but nothing came out and she shut it again. Toa smiled and took her arm, leading her over to a large group of people.

"Everyone, this is Kam's friend, Grace. She's his new Sous Chef at the restaurant."

Everyone stopped talking at once and turned to stare at

her. For the first time, Grace began to feel uncomfortable. "Uh, hi, everyone. It's nice to be here," she said lamely, feeling like a sixth grader being introduced to a new class by the teacher.

An older Samoan woman stepped forward and took both of her hands. "Thank you for coming to our home, Grace. My name is Pika. I'm Kam's mother. It's an honor to meet you."

Grace smiled warmly at the woman, touched by her formal hospitality. "Likewise. Kam is a wonderful boss. It's a pleasure to meet his family."

The people around Pika nodded their heads in approval and smiled at her. She felt a yanking on her dress and looked down to see Nate and Baby.

"Does she play catch?"

Grace laughed and picked up Nate easily, and put him on her hip. "She loves to. But first can you help me pick out something yummy to eat?"

Nate nodded his head and she smiled at the group of people before walking over to the table laden with at least fifty dishes.

"That's good," he said pointing to some pork dish. "But don't eat that," he said pointing to what looked like lumpy lettuce and peas. "It's so gross."

Grace grinned and put Nate down so she could fill her plate. "Okay, what next, Natano?" she asked, thinking she should be calling him by the name his dad called him instead of the shortened version.

Nate shook his head. "I don't want you to call me Natano."

Grace's eyebrow lifted. "But your dad calls you Natano. It's such a cool name. Why do you want me to call you Nate instead?"

Nate shrugged. "My friends call me Nate and you're my friend."

Grace smiled at the little boy, feeling her heart melt. "Aw, you're my friend too. Tell you what, you can call me Gracie. That's what *my* friends call me."

Nate grinned up at her and gave her hug around her waist. "Good, that means Baby will come see me all the time because we're all friends now."

Grace winced. "Well, Nate, I don't know how often I'll get to come see you, but anytime you want to see Baby, you just tell your dad. Deal?"

Nate nodded his head and hugged Baby too. "Deal."

Grace took her plate over to a shady tree and sat down with the little boy and her dog as she watched the people around her. She was more of an extrovert than an introvert, but she didn't mind taking a few moments to herself to get her bearings and to enjoy all of these new foods she hadn't tried before. Although she'd had a Samoan friend at culinary school, they'd mostly eaten fast food or what they made in class.

"These are delicious," she said picking up a little fried ball filled with what she would swear was Nutella.

"It's called panikeke. They're addicting."

She looked up to see Kam standing beside them.

"Daddy, we need a ball. Baby wants to play catch," Nate said, pouting slightly.

Kam pulled a tennis ball out of his cargo shorts and handed it to him. "Ask and ye shall receive."

Nate whooped and ran off with Baby right beside him. Kam took Nate's place beside her with his own plate of food.

"Overwhelmed or are you okay?" he asked, looking at her carefully.

Grace smiled and shook her head. "Totally, okay. I just wanted to take a minute to immerse myself in this food before I start talking to everyone. It's not often I'm invited to a Samoan get together."

Kam smiled and began eating some fish dish that she'd

almost picked and now wished she had. She noted that Kam's long hair was down instead of pulled back in his usual ponytail and he was wearing a short sleeved shirt, showing off some pretty impressive tribal tattoos. She tried to trace the tattoo with her eyes but then began to notice how the muscles in his arms rippled every time he moved. She blinked in surprise and quickly looked away.

Yikes, checking out her boss right in front of his entire family. *Real cool, Grace*, she scolded herself.

"I just met your mother. She's so sweet," she said, trying to think of something to say.

Kam looked over to where his parents were still talking to the large group of people and nodded. "She's already told me she likes you. My father thinks you're good with Natano, too."

Grace paused with her fork halfway to her mouth and laughed. "That's nice. Um, are they always this welcoming to your Sous Chefs?"

Kam snorted and shook his head. "Yeah, um *no*. Not at all. You're probably the first Sous Chef that they've met."

Grace waited for him to explain why but gave up with a small sigh. *Interesting.* "You'll have to try my corn pudding I brought. It's different than a typical corn pudding. It's got Hatch chilies and enough cheese to give you a heart attack."

Kam looked over at her and smiled. "I'll save room. You'll have to show me where it is though or it'll take me an hour to find it."

Grace smiled, excited for him to try something of hers not on The Iron Skillet menu. "I'll do one better. I'm going to grab you a small serving and be right back. Save my spot," she ordered and put her plate down and hurried over to the table of food. She frowned, noting that there were maybe only two servings left.

She scooped up a generous portion and practically ran

back to Kam. Kam laughed at her expression and took the small plate from her.

"You're really excited for me to try your dish, huh?"

Grace blushed but didn't deny it. "Well, you're my boss. It's my job to impress you."

Kam looked down at her red high heeled sandals and shook his head. "Seeing you run in those sandals impressed me. Trust me."

Grace blushed again and picked up her plate, not knowing what to say to that. *Was Kam flirting with her?* She looked at him out of the side of her eyes but he was already taking a bite of her dish and he was closing his eyes and concentrating. That was a good sign. She held her breath as he chewed and chewed and chewed. Finally, he opened his eyes and turned to look at her and a small smile began to tip his lips up.

"Best thing I've tasted all day," he said, his eyes smiling at her even though his lips were barely tilted up.

Grace let her breath out and looked up at the blue clouds feeling like the sun had come out. "Tell me why a compliment from you feels like ten from anyone else?" she said with a self-deprecating laugh.

Kam's eyes warmed up even more and he shook his head. "I guess that's a hint that I need to be more generous with my compliments. Gracie, you know I love your food. Everyone loves your food."

Grace shrugged and went back to eating. "Thanks, Boss. Maybe it's being the new girl but I absolutely need to impress you. You're an amazing chef and I want you to keep me around," she said with a wink.

Kam's eyebrows went up slightly as he watched her. "What if I told you that I already know I want to keep you around?"

Grace grinned and put her plate down, turning to give

Kam a hug. "Then that would make me the happiest Sous Chef in the world."

Kam looked frozen for a moment but when she picked up her plate again, he blinked a few times and let out a breath. "You know you're almost ready to be head chef somewhere. I'm surprised you haven't made that leap yet."

Grace shrugged and put her fork down, reaching for her lemonade. "It's part of my five year plan, but I have a couple friends who made that leap and they burned out fast. Two have quit and gone into other careers. They said the pressure was too much and they began to hate their jobs. I never want to hate cooking. It's been my passion and my life. I just want to enjoy what I do. I'll leap when I'm ready."

Kam nodded. "I know what you mean. There have been times I've been very close to burning out. Like last month for instance," he said dryly. "So tell me what would make you happy at work. I want you to be open with me. If there are changes that you'd like to make, tell me."

Grace licked her lips and turned to face Kam fully, putting her plate down and clasping her hands. "Okay, here goes. *If you're serious...*" she said, looking at him carefully.

Kam wiped his mouth with a napkin and put his plate down, turning towards her so she had his complete attention. "I wouldn't have said it, if I hadn't meant it, Gracie. Spill it."

Grace closed her eyes, feeling nervous all of a sudden, when she felt Kam's hand on her arm. She opened her eyes and nodded her head. "Okay, I would love to take lead on a few dishes. A few of my own dishes. I'd like to change up the menu. Not a lot. I know what you've got going is working, but we have a lot of regular customers who have mentioned wanting something new and different."

Kam nodded his head. "This is definitely something that you and I should talk to Rob about, but I'm open to new and different. Sometimes we all need a breath of fresh air. We haven't made any changes to the menu in awhile. It's probably time."

Grace felt her whole body smile as she gazed at Kam. "I could kiss you right now," she said, shaking her head in awe. It had been so easy! Kam was hands down the best boss in the world.

Kam stared at her for a moment before laughing awkwardly. "Ahh, um, that's probably not a good idea. I haven't kissed anyone in a few years. I wouldn't even know what to do."

Grace frowned at him before laughing. "I was teasing you, Boss. I don't want to get fired for sexual harassment."

Kam laughed and wiped his forehead with his napkin.

"*Sexual harassment?* It's a good thing we came over. Our conversation is boring compared to yours."

Grace and Kam looked up to see Jane and Tate and Pule and Posey standing in front of them. Pule and Tate were smiling at Kam while Jane and Posey were grinning at her and looking very curious.

Grace glanced at Kam with a wince. No way was she explaining how she'd just threatened to kiss her boss. She'd be kicked out of the party for sure.

"Oh, we were just talking about work protocol. I was warning Kam he'd better not come on to me. You know, the usual."

Kam began coughing as everyone laughed. Pule walked forward and began pounding his big brother on the back. "Is that true, Bro? Was she warning you about coming on to her?" he said, shaking his head in amusement. He obviously didn't believe it for a second.

Kam was still wheezing, his eyes watering. She couldn't tell if he was laughing or dying. Grace flipped her hair over her shoulder and lifted her chin.

"You guys know Kam. Such a flirt," she said breezily, making Kam cough even louder.

Tate laughed and put his hands on his hips. "Yeah, I know Kam. Such a lady's man."

Jane shook her head. "Well, he used to be. I remember the days when he could look at a girl and just make you sigh. You won't believe this Grace, but Kam really was a charmer."

Posey looked back and forth between everyone. "*Kam?*" she said doubtfully.

Kam wiped his eyes with a napkin as he tried to catch his breath. "Don't sound so shocked, Posey. Women used to fall at my feet everywhere I went. I was a Samoan Ryan Reynolds."

Everyone began laughing. Grace crossed her legs, enjoying teasing her grim boss. If she could make him blush or laugh, then she was doing pretty good.

"Posey, should we believe him? I don't know. Maybe we should make him prove it," she said, stirring the pot a little.

Everyone looked at her as if fascinated all of a sudden. Even Kam.

"Prove it?" Kam asked lightly, looking nervous almost.

Posey's eyes lit up and she clapped her hands. "Well, maybe you still have it, Kam. It would be sad to think you've lost your womanizing ways."

Kam snorted while Tate and Pule laughed. "Kam was never a womanizer. He couldn't help it that women fell at his feet," Tate said.

Pule nodded. "My brother was always very respectful of women. I remember hearing stories of him going out dancing and how all the girls would wait for a turn to dance with him."

Grace blinked in surprise and then stared at Kam. "*Seriously?* I can't even get him to dance with me in the kitchen," she said, turning to frown at Kam.

Kam shrugged and tried to look uncaring. "Maybe if you played better music."

Grace's mouth fell open. "Now, I'm offended. That's it. Tuesday morning, I better see some of these dance moves you're so famous for."

Jane put a hand on her arm. "Grace, I don't know if you're ready. If you see Kam dance, you'll probably fall in love with him and then you'll be too busy flirting to cook. We can't have that."

Kam began coughing again as Grace laughed. "Fall in love with my boss? Listen, his moves would have to be epic for that to happen. Last time I fell in love with someone for their dance moves, I was twenty and watching Maks on Dancing with the Stars. Sorry, Boss, but it takes a lot to impress me."

Pule was so busy laughing at Kam, Tate had to give Kam his napkin. "Okay, okay. I think we've tortured my poor brother enough today. If he swallows one more ice cube I might have to do C.P.R."

Grace nodded in agreement. Her quota was one blush or laugh a day. She didn't want to kill the man.

"Well, I'd love to tease my boss some more, but I've got a game of catch to get in on. It was nice seeing everyone again," she said as she caught sight of Nate and Baby.

*

They all turned and watched Grace walk away, heading for Nate and her dog on the other side of the yard.

Tate waited for Grace to be out of earshot before turning back to Kam who was trying very hard to look unaffected by the conversation.

"So, um... *Grace*. She's something, huh?" he said lightly as Jane slipped her arm through his.

Jane grinned up at him. "She's definitely something."

Pule took Grace's vacated seat and put his arm around his brother's shoulders. "Bro, I think she's in to you. What are you going to do about it?"

Kam sighed and shook his head. "She enjoys teasing me, but that doesn't mean she's *in* to me."

Jane and Posey shared a shocked look before Tate cleared his throat. Kam wasn't disappointed or mad that Grace was teasing him. He sounded like he was disappointed that she might not be in to him.

Jane folded her arms and stepped closer to Kam. "You know, Kam. You're such a charming, sweet guy. I bet it wouldn't take much to get her to be in to you. Dance with her like you used to with Wren. Joke around with her. Invite her to the beach with you and Nate."

Posey nodded and pushed her long, brown hair over her ears. "And Grace is awesome. Look at her. She's at a party and all she wants to do is play with Nate. She'd be the perfect girl-friend for you."

Kam stopped looking at Grace and his son and turned to glare up at Posey. "Posey, I don't need a girlfriend. I'm fine being on my own," he said gruffly and stood up to walk away.

Tate frowned and grabbed his brother's arm. "Bro, it's time," he said softly but firmly. "It's time to start living again."

Kam closed his eyes as if he were in pain. "But I don't know how to anymore," he said and shook off Tate's hand before walking away.

The group turned and watched Kam walk into the house.

Pule was the first to talk. "I don't care what he just said, he wants Grace to be into him. He wants her to flirt with him. I think he is ready."

Jane nodded. "I agree, Pule, but I think he's scared."

Tate frowned and shook his head. "My brother's not scared of anything, least of all a cute little Sous Chef."

Jane sighed and leaned her head against her husband's arm. "Honey, he's scared of being hurt again."

Posey put her hands on her hips as she turned and looked at Grace. "Well, I don't think she's all that terrifying. And the man blushed like four times and practically choked three. I think we have some serious potential here, folks. And hello, check her out. She's perfect for him. She's so cute and spunky and fun and she already loves his kid. Besides that, she teases him and makes him laugh. Who else can do that?"

Jane smiled. "No one. Seriously, no one has been able to do that. And I know every woman under the age of fifty and over the age of twenty who isn't married in Fircrest has tried. But how do we get him to feel it's okay to move on?"

Posey looked at Pule and her smile faded. "Maybe if Anne encouraged him to date Grace?"

Everyone's face fell.

Because that would never happen.

CHAPTER 11

A Chance to Show Off

GRACE WENT TO work on Tuesday with a smile on her face. And, okay, she always went to work with a smile on her face, but today felt different. No longer was she working with a grim, depressing boss and a restaurant manager who hated her. Now, she got to go to work with a boss who might actually be a friend.

And even Taryn was nicer. Saturday night as she was getting ready to go upstairs to her apartment, Taryn walked into the kitchen and apologized for being so cranky and told her not to take it personally. She'd then told her Rob had gotten tons of compliments on the food that night and that The Iron Skillet was lucky to have her.

Yeah, she was doing okay. She pushed through the doors and yelled out a hello to everyone and everyone yelled back, sounding happy to see her. It looked like everyone was in a good mood. Probably because Tuesdays were easy. Super slow and mostly fun. They usually had less than half of the patrons they usually had on the weekends so today would be a cake walk. She saw Kam sitting at his desk and poked her head inside.

"Hey, Boss. Just wanted you to know I'm here. Anything

you need?" she asked, noting his hair was pulled back in his usual ponytail. She kind of liked seeing it down like he'd had it at the party on Sunday. There was just something about seeing all of that wild hair free and fabulous.

Kam turned around, his eyes warming up as he sat back in his chair and looked at her. He bit his lip as his eyes narrowed at her and she felt her stomach flip over. *What was he thinking?* she wondered.

"Gracie, I've been talking to Rob about how talented I think you are. What would you say if I asked you to make us something for lunch all on your own? We want to see what you can do. If we like it… it's possible we could add it to the menu. Wow us. Make us cry with delight."

Grace's mouth fell open. "You're kidding me," she whispered.

Kam shook his head, his eyes smiling at her even though his lips weren't. She kind of liked that. She stopped staring at Kam's eyes and snapped back to reality.

Grace jumped up and down and screamed. Just a little, but it was a scream. "Thank you, Boss," she yelled and ran around his desk to give him a quick hug. Kam reached up and put his hand over her arms, keeping her in place.

"Now Gracie, remember, this is your chance. Don't screw it up," he said and let her go.

Grace ran out of the office, doing little ballet leaps. "I'm cooking!"

Candice laughed as Manuel and James walked over, frowning at her.

"She's lost it," Manuel said with a frown. "I knew she was too soft. Dang it, Candice. Now we have to find a new Sous Chef."

Grace stopped jumping up and down to frown at Manuel. "Uh, no I'm not soft and no there's not going to be any new

Sous Chef. I'm it, buddy. So get used to me. No, the boss just gave me a chance to cook something new today. If he likes it, we might be able to change up the menu a little," she said, squealing at the end.

Candice gave her a high five. "You've got this, Grace. I say blow their socks off."

James rolled his eyes. "As long as I don't have to do any extra work, I don't care."

Grace glared at James's back and stuck out her tongue. "Fine, you don't get to sample anything then."

James turned around with a suddenly sweet smile on his face. "I meant, I'll be happy to help you with anything you need, Grace."

Grace nodded her head. "Much better. Okay, let me grab a notebook. I need to figure out what I want to do. I can't believe this is happening," she whispered to herself, walking over to a counter where they kept old menus and pens. She grabbed a stool and sat down, taking out her phone and going through her notes app.

After a half an hour, she glanced at the clock. She had to make up her mind now if she was going to have time to prepare everything she wanted for lunch. She shut her eyes and tried to decide between going traditional or *doing what she really wanted to do…*

She was going for it. All the way. She ran to the walk-in and perused the shelf. "Yes!" she yelled and grabbed the lamb. "This is happening," she said as she grabbed all of the ingredients she needed.

Candice, Manuel, James, and Kam were taking care of all of the preparations for the lunch crowd while she zoned everything out and focused on creating the meal of her life. She turned the music up and began singing as she cooked. And every time Kam walked over to see what she was doing, she took him gently by the arms and escorted him right back to his stove. She could not do this with her boss staring over her shoulder.

Two hours later, she plated. She grinned as she stared at her creations. Even if they didn't like what she'd made, she'd never been so proud of herself. She took her phone out and took pictures so she could post them on Instagram and show her friends.

"What do we have here?"

Grace jumped a little and turned to see Kam staring at the three plates in front of her.

"If you'd be so kind to call in Rob and Taryn, I'd be happy to tell you in detail."

Kam bowed his head gravely and took out his phone, sending out a short text. She finished the final touches and stepped back. Candice handed her three forks and she held them in her hands as Taryn and Rob walked through the doors at the same time, looking curious.

"I have no idea what I'm smelling, but I know my stomach is excited to try something new," Rob said, rubbing his hands together.

Taryn's lips didn't exactly turn up enough to be described as a smile, but she didn't look angry either. That had to be a good sign.

"Rob, Taryn, Kam, allow me to describe your meal. The starter is fried goat cheese with pear, crispy prosciutto and balsamic reduction. Your next course is my crispy pan-fried shrimp with chorizo fideo cakes. If you're familiar with Spanish food you'll recognize the classic toasted pasta dish. You're going to love it. And your main course is a spice crusted lamb loin, Indian potatoes and Moilee-tomato sauce."

Rob held up a finger. "Lamb with Indian potatoes? Indian food is usually vegetarian. I'm surprised."

Grace nodded her head quickly. "You're right, Rob, however, I love to create fusions. Why not combine classic Indian flavors with meat? It's fantastic, I promise," she said handing out the forks.

Kam had remained silent while she spoke, watching her and studying the food. For some reason, she was most nervous about his reaction. She watched them closely as they took bites of each course and noted the smallest changes in expression.

Rob was the first to speak. "Grace, I have to admit, this is the best meal I've had in over a year. I'm stunned at your skill level. Truly amazing."

Taryn nodded and took another forkful of the Indian potatoes. "I agree with Rob. This is incredible, but, with that being said, I'm not sure it's suitable for The Iron Skillet and our clientele."

Grace's face fell as she turned to Kam. "Boss? What do you think?" she asked softly.

Kam had gone back to work his way through his starter. "Possibly the best meal of my life," he said simply and then looked up at Rob and Taryn. "You'd be crazy not to take advantage of this although Taryn's right. This is way beyond what we typically do. So why don't we have a special Fine Dining evening a month from now and charge a fortune for an evening of fine dining and maybe even some music and dancing. You could hire a band, go all out. Oh and get a few reviews while you're at it."

Rob's eyes began to glaze over as he stared at Kam. Taryn was frowning as she tapped her foot on the hard tile. Grace could tell they were thinking it over. Kam winked at her as she clasped her fingers tightly waiting for their answer.

Rob nodded his head before he spoke. "I love it, Kam. It's brilliant. What do you think, Taryn?"

Taryn frowned as she put her hands on her hips. "It has the

potential to get you a lot of press and a lot of new customers. I say it's a win-win situation. Do it quarterly and you'll have people making reservations a year in advance."

Rob's eyes widened as he rubbed his chin. "This is perfect. Okay, you two. Start planning it. You have a month."

Rob and Taryn both took their plates with them as they left the kitchen, obviously wanting to finish their food. Grace waited for the door to close before she turned to Kam and grinned.

"Is this really happening?" she whispered.

Kam shook his head. "You deserve this, Gracie. You're a talented and creative chef. This will be your ticket out of here though. Some chef from Seattle is going to find out about you and steal you from us," he said sounding sad.

Grace snorted. "I came here to get away from Seattle. This is where I want to be. I don't know why yet, but I know this is my place. No worries about me taking off, Boss."

Kam relaxed a little as he smiled down at her. "Then let's have some fun. Let's make everyone in Fircrest sit up and take notice. People are going to flip out when they find out what we're going to do."

Grace nodded, grabbing Kam's hands. "Add in a band and dancing and we're going to bring a little glamour to Fircrest."

Kam smiled, his eyes sparkling down at her. "I can't wait. But first, let me finish this meal. It would be a crime to let it go to waste."

Grace let go of Kam's hands and stepped back. "Mind if I join you?"

Kam shook his head and waited for her to plate some of everything before joining him in his office. They spent the next hour talking about menus and ambiance and even what music should be played.

When she stepped out of Kam's office, she knew two

things. She'd absolutely made the right decision in coming to Fircrest and Kam Matafeo might just be one of the best looking men she'd ever known. Why she hadn't realized that from the moment she'd first met him was a mystery, but for some reason, every day she knew him, he became more and more handsome. She jumped into the fray to help Candice with a dish going out but her mind kept going back to Kam.

She glanced at him a few times and shook her head in confusion. Had she been blind? Scared? Intimidated? *Nah, not her.* She watched as his back muscles rippled through his shirt and had to fan her face.

"You okay, Grace?" Candice asked, frowning. "You look red in the face."

Grace laughed and shook it off. "It's nothing," she said and got to work. *It had to be nothing.* Getting a crush on your boss was the dumbest thing you could do.

Grace looked over at Kam one last time. *But he was single...* why not? She remembered some of the drama from previous kitchens and winced. There were about a million reasons she shouldn't fall for her boss. And she was not dumb. If she wanted to make it as a chef someday, she had to keep her nose clean and her food on point. Mixing work with romance was a sure way to find herself cooking on a cruise ship leaving for Ensenada.

Yeah, she better sign up for that local dating website. *Fast.* Fixating on Kam would only mess things up for her *and* for him. Better to focus on someone else. *Anyone* else.

Grace stole one last look at Kam and sighed. But if she'd had a choice? Maybe she'd pick the kind, handsome head chef with the cute little boy and the sad smile.

Grace felt a wave of disappointment wash over her and frowned. This was like going to a restaurant and knowing you wanted the steak but getting the salad because you really shouldn't. It was unsatisfying and put you in a bad mood.

The rest of the day flew by as she focused on her future menu instead of her hot boss. When she went upstairs that night, she was more energized than she'd been when she woke up. And it all had to do with their Fine Dining night.

And *not* Kam Matafeo.

CHAPTER 12

Double Trouble

ANNE MATAFEO WALKED down the aisles of the grocery store, frowning at everything and not picking anything up. She needed to do her shopping but all she could think about was what Taryn had told her on the phone that morning. That Grace Jackson was incredible and that Kam thought so too. And she already knew that everyone in the Matafeo family thought Grace was fantastic.

Toa had even hinted that they wanted Kam to start dating her. *Ugh.* And when Pika had shown her a picture taken at the last family get together with Grace holding Nate on her hip and laughing at something he'd said, she'd wanted to throw up. The idea of some strange woman holding Bailey's son, as if Nate were her own, made her physically ill. *Her daughter had died giving life to that boy and you'd think they'd be careful about who had their hands on him,* she thought with a burst of anger.

If Grace thought she was going to waltz into town and snap up Kam and her grandson, she was sadly mistaken. Anne stopped and threw a box of jello in her cart with enough force to cause another shopper to look at her with a frown. Anne glared at the woman and walked on. *The nerve of that girl.* She didn't even know Bailey. If she had, she would know there was no way Kam would ever look at her twice.

Anne wiped away a tear as she thought of her beautiful daughter. She'd been gorgeous, true, but her heart had been so kind and good. And she'd loved Kam with all of her heart. How could he just turn his back on that? How could he forget what they'd shared? How could he even think of dating Grace when Bailey had died to give him their son?

Anne closed her eyes feeling the pain begin to overtake her and she had to concentrate on breathing in and out slowly.

"*Anne*? You okay?"

Anne blinked her eyes and turned her head to see Meredith Murphy standing beside her with a shopping cart. Meredith was dressed in a pale gray skirt, black high heels and a cream silk blouse. Her bright blond hair was almost blinding and she had to turn away for a moment.

"I'm fine, Meredith. Just thinking about what to have for dinner. How are you doing?" she asked, smoothing her hair and trying to smile.

Meredith shrugged and looked down at her feet. "I'm actually glad I ran into you. I don't know... everyone keeps talking about how Kam should be dating his new Sous Chef, Grace, but it just bugs me. Are you okay with this happening?" she asked, her tight mouth turning down into a frown.

Anne's mouth fell open and she stepped closer to Meredith. "*No!* No, I'm not okay with it happening. How could I be?"

Meredith sighed and clasped her arm. "Forget shopping. Let's go over to the bakery and talk. I swear, you're the only sane person in this town."

Anne nodded her head sharply and took her one jello box out of her cart and put it on the shelf next to the spaghetti sauce. "Let's go. My treat."

Meredith's face lit up and they both left their carts in the middle of the aisle. "Now you're talking."

The women met up at the bakery five minutes later and took the nearest table next to the bakery cases. Meredith ordered a hot chocolate and a croissant while Anne chose a Diet Coke and Mocha bread pudding.

Meredith took a sip of her hot chocolate and one small bite before leaning over the table. "We have to do something about this, Anne. If we don't, someone like Tate or Pule or who knows, even his parents are going to set Kam up with Grace and then watch them get married. I won't stand for it, Anne."

Anne nodded her head, feeling her heartbeat speed up at the thought. But she paused, blinking in confusion. "Wait, I know why *I* don't want Kam marrying some flaky cook from his restaurant, but why do you care?" she asked bluntly.

Meredith paused and licked her lips, sitting up straight and lifting her chin. "Anne, there was a time I cared for Kam. And the fact is, I still care about his happiness. I know this girl isn't good enough for him. *I know it.* I was at the restaurant last week and just watching the way she talks and the way she looks... Anne, he can do way better. I don't even think she's that cute," she said with a sniff.

Anne shrugged. "I agree. If I hear one more person tell me how pretty Grace is, my head is going to explode. It's like they've completely forgotten how beautiful Bailey was. How could they forget my daughter?" she demanded, her eyes closing in pain. "It's offensive. And Kam is just vulnerable. The poor man doesn't even realize what she's doing. I get it, Kam is lonely. But to even think for a moment that he could replace my daughter with some stranger just kills me. It really does," she said, swallowing hard.

Meredith frowned and shook her head. "This whole town needs to wake up. It's like they've all lost their minds. They think, okay, it's been three and a half years, it's time for Kam to move on so they're all going to pressure him into this relationship just because they think it will make him happy. I know what would make Kam happy. A woman who is smart and beautiful and who can make him laugh. *That woman? She's a mess!*"

Anne sighed and took a sip of her Coke. "I've heard the talk. I know they all think it's a done deal. And every time I hear them say something like, *when is Kam going to ask her out,* it's a dagger in my heart. They have no empathy for me. Or Kam for that matter. Why don't they just leave the man alone? He's perfectly happy raising Nate on his own. There's no need for him to move on. We all help him with Nate. He has so much family, the man is *never* lonely. Everyone just needs to mind their own business," she said with a firm nod of her head.

Meredith smiled and took another bite. "Agreed, Anne. So what can we do to get people to stop with this ridiculous idea that Kam and Grace would make a good couple?"

Anne tapped her chin. "Well, it's simple. We have to get rid of her. Everyone knows I'm a nice person, but this isn't a situation where we can just hope for the best. Kam might very well just marry this girl because he's pressured into it."

Meredith's eyes lit up. "We'll run her out of town. *I love it.*"

Anne sighed happily and took a bite of her bread pudding. "I'm so glad I ran into you today, Meredith. I feel much, much better now."

"*Do you two need anything?*"

Meredith and Anne looked up to see Kit standing beside the table with a polite smile on her face.

Meredith nodded and pointed to some crumbs on the table. "Well, I didn't want to say anything, but this table is dirty. Could you wipe it down and then get Anne a refill on her Coke? She's almost out."

Kit smiled and wiped Meredith's croissant crumbs off the table. "I'll be right back with that refill."

*

Kit's smile disappeared as soon as she turned around. "Little twit," she muttered as she refilled Anne's cup. She walked back to the table just in time to hear the words, *we could make something up?*

Kit cleared her throat and the women stopped talking immediately. "Here you go, Anne. I was meaning to tell you next time I saw you what a gorgeous little grandson you have. Nate was in here last week with his other grandma picking out a cookie and he was so polite."

Anne's face lit up and she smiled up at Kit. "He's the best little boy in the world. If I could just get Kam to cut his hair. All those curls are so wild, I just want to take a comb to that boy every time I see him."

Kit nodded and leaned her weight on her hip. "Well, dads are funny. If you ask me, Nate needs a mommy," she said with a wink and walked off.

The sound of furious whispers made her smile a little as she took out her phone and sent out a group text to Jane, Layla, Cleo, Wren, and Posey.

> *Emergency! Anne and Meredith are here at the bakery and they're hatching a plot to run Grace out of town. Neither one of them wants Kam to date her. I just heard them trying to decide on what lie to tell about her. Be here at noon. We need to nip this in the bud.*

Kit waved goodbye to Anne and Meredith as they left fifteen minutes later. Kit had tried to do some dusting by the cases closest to the two women so she could hear more of their plan, but every time she got close, they began to whisper. Kit walked over to the door and looked out the window just in time to see Anne give Meredith a tight hug. Meredith looked way too self-satisfied in her opinion. Kit glared at the blond as she sauntered towards her flashy new, white BMW.

"Not on my watch," Kit said out loud and grinned as she saw Jane pull up at the same time as Layla. The two sisters raced up the steps and Kit held the door open for them.

Jane put her umbrella down and took off her rain coat as Layla smoothed her damp blond hair back.

"I leave for one hour and this happens?" Jane asked with a frown.

Kit shrugged and walked back to the counter. "Can I help it if all the juicy stuff happens on my shift?"

Layla sighed and walked around the counter to grab a water bottle. "I knew this was too easy. Of course Anne and Meredith have to try to ruin everything."

Kit's eyes narrowed. "I can see why Anne would. She's still mourning her daughter and doesn't want to see her replaced. It's sad and selfish considering how lonely Kam is and how much Nate needs a mommy, but still, human and understandable. *But Meredith?* She was worse than Anne. She kept saying how Grace wasn't good enough for Kam and how she wasn't even cute."

Layla rolled her eyes. "She's jealous. She's catty and acting like a thirteen-year-old."

Jane's eyes narrowed and she tapped her foot in frustration. "If she really cared about Kam, she'd understand how much pain the man has been in and see how Grace could help him heal. Doesn't she have a heart?"

Kit snorted. "That's always been up for debate."

Layla held up her hand. "Let's not fall her to her level. But that doesn't mean we look away and let her ruin this for Kam, either. We have to stop them."

Kit nodded her head, smiling in relief. "I knew you guys could fix this."

Layla and Jane looked at each other and winced simultaneously.

"You know Anne. She's a force of nature and Meredith can be a dirty fighter. It'll take a village." Layla said worriedly.

Jane looked down at her phone. "Everyone should be here any minute. Hopefully one of us will be able to figure out how to protect Grace from two of the craziest women in Fircrest."

Kit nodded. "I'll set up some snacks and we'll shut down the bakery for an hour. This is too important for distractions."

The women pushed the tables together and put out drinks and sandwiches and cookies. Every single woman showed up looking grim and determined. Kit filled them in on everything she'd overheard and the women broke out in anger and outrage immediately.

Layla stood up and held her hands up until everyone quieted down. "Okay, before we go further, we need to ask ourselves, is it worth it? All of us going up against Anne and Meredith isn't going to be easy. So do we know for sure that Kam actually does like Grace. Should we even get involved?" she asked calmly.

Posey nodded her head and everyone looked at her. "I was at the party last Sunday and I saw them together. Grace was playing with Nate and her dog and I was watching Kam watch them. When Grace leaned over hugged Nate and showed him how to throw the ball, Kam's whole face lit up. *He smiled.* Not his fake smile either, it was his real smile. I'm telling you his eyes were glued to her. And from what Pule has told me, this is the first time Kam's had this kind of reaction to a woman, well, *since…*"

Wren held up her hand and Posey let her sentence fade. "Rob and I have been praying every night that Kam will fall for Grace. He's been smiling and laughing since she's come to work. It makes Rob cry just thinking about it."

Kit leaned forward. "It doesn't bug Rob that Kam might move on? That he would somehow forget about Bailey?"

Wren shook her head quickly. "He loves Kam like a brother. He was there with Kam when Bailey died. He loves Bailey but he hates seeing Kam just walk around like a shadow of himself. We've seen little glimmers of the old Kam lately and I swear if Anne and Meredith mess this up I'm going to run them over with my car," she swore sounding serious enough to make everyone stare at her in shock.

Jane laughed nervously and pushed a plate of cookies towards Wren. "Okay, it's safe to say that this is a serious possibility for Kam. Are we ready to do whatever it takes then to make this happen?"

Cleo cleared her throat. "It sounds like this is going to cause some serious drama in our quiet, little town. Wren, you're going to be on the opposite side of your mother-in-law. And we all run into Meredith at yoga and zumba. Having her as an enemy will make life harder for everyone."

All of the women looked at each other for a moment before Wren spoke up. "I know I'm not Kam's real sister, but we love each other like brother and sister. And I cared for Bailey too. I truly believe she'd want Kam to move on and be happy. She'd want Nate to have a mom who loved him. Let's not just do this for Kam, but let's do this for his son *and* for Bailey."

Jane nodded. "I agree, Wren. This whole town can't move on because Kam can't move on. The sun needs to come out again. All in agreement, raise your hand," she said, her brown eyes looking serious and determined.

Layla smiled and looked at all of the women surrounding her raising their hands. "Excellent. Now, what do we do about it?"

Everyone remained silent before Kit spoke up. "Meredith mentioned making up stories about Grace. Lying to get her to leave town. That's pretty low in my book."

Posey glared at the table. "I know what it's like to be lied about and to have a whole town think the worst of you. I almost did leave town. It could work."

Cleo sighed. "I say we just tell Kam the truth. *Hey, buddy, your mother in law and ex are freaking out at the possibility of you dating someone and so they're going to trash her reputation so much that she leaves town.*"

Wren shook her head. "I don't think he's ready to even acknowledge his feelings for Grace though. If we confront him with what's going on, he'll run back to his dark cave and pretend he was never thinking about Grace that way. He needs time. This relationship needs time to grow and that can't happen if Anne and Meredith get in the way, but it can't happen either if we all surround him and tell him that his romance is in jeopardy."

Layla sighed and ran her hands through her long hair. "This is a mess. For now, let's just go home and tell our husbands. Jane, Tate needs to know but stress the fact that we can't tell Kam or else he'll go into hiding. Posey, same thing with Pule. They're closest to Kam. Just make sure if anything happens, they're there to throw some water on the fire."

Wren stood up and picked up her purse. "Sorry guys, I've gotta get Jackie to preschool but I'll talk to Rob and let him know what his mom is up to. Maybe he can talk some sense into her."

Everyone waved goodbye to Wren. As the door closed, Kit pursed her lips and crossed her legs as she sat back in her chair. "Do you think Rob has a chance of talking some sense into Anne?"

Posey bit her lip and shook her head. "All I know is that Anne is still mourning her daughter and that if Kam moves on, that means we've all forgotten Bailey. I think she needs therapy."

"Agreed," Layla said, "but in the meantime, we have to neutralize her. Now, how to neutralize Meredith?"

Cleo narrowed her eyes. "I wonder what her husband thinks of his wife acting like a jealous girlfriend who still isn't over her ex?"

All of the women looked at each other with wide eyes.

"But that could cause some marriage problems for Asher and Meredith," Posey said worriedly.

Kit sniffed. "Granted, but Meredith doesn't even hesitate to ruin Kam's chance at happiness. Maybe this will be a good wake up call for her. Maybe she needs to spend more time worrying about her own love life instead of Kam's."

Jane massaged her temples. "She's my friend, guys. I can't ruin one relationship to save another."

Layla shook her head with a frown. "I don't think there's any harm in pointing out what's happening to Asher. Who would he listen to?"

Cleo answered. "That's easy. His brother Garrett or Becket. He trusts them. I could tell Rayne and Ivy what's going down. Let me talk to them and see what they think."

Layla stood up and walked over to the door, turning the CLOSED sign to OPEN. "Okay, Ladies, the battle begins. Let's all do our part to protect Kam and Grace and keep Anne and Meredith from causing too much damage."

All of the women stood up, hugging each other and promising to stay in touch.

Kit stood with her sisters as they waved goodbye to everyone. "If this works out and Kam ends up marrying Grace and Nate gets a mommy, we deserve a trip to Hawaii."

Jane laughed and shut the door. "I know, we'll all go to Hawaii with Grace and Kam for their honeymoon. He'll love it."

Layla snorted as they moved the tables and chairs back. "We'll have the knowledge that we brought some happiness to a broken-hearted man. I think that's thanks enough. But speaking of Hawaii, I'll talk to Michael tonight. A family trip somewhere warm and sunny sounds like heaven right now," she said, staring out the window at the rainy, gray day.

Kit put her hand on her sister's shoulder. "I'll tell Hunter to start booking hotel rooms."

Layla turned around hugged her sister. "I really hope you're not kidding. And thanks for being on watch today. If you hadn't been listening in, we wouldn't know what Kam and Grace are up against. Now they have a chance."

Kit stopped in her tracks and put a chair down. "Hey, we talked about telling Kam and decided against it. But we never talked about telling Grace. Does anyone even know if *she* likes *him*? What if she doesn't?"

The three sisters stared at each other with identical frowns.

Layla gave a tired laugh and sat down. "I guess we all just assumed she would automatically fall for Kam. From what I can tell, she's friendly and kind of flirty with everyone. He might be misreading this. But oh my word, what if he gives his heart to her and she doesn't want it? I don't think this town can handle another Matafeo heartbreak."

Kit shook her head. "No need to stress if this isn't an issue. The guy is gorgeous, sweet as honey and he's had every unmarried woman in a twenty-mile radius after him. I'm betting she likes him. But we need to find out for sure."

Kit and Layla turned and stared at Jane. Jane sighed and sat down next to Layla.

"Fine. I'll do it. But how? I can't just walk into The Iron Skillet and say, *hey, have you fallen for your boss yet?*"

Kit winced and Layla rubbed her sister's back.

"People love to open up to you, Jane. Complete strangers walk in here every day and pour their hearts out to you. You're like a bartender except you peddle sugar instead of alcohol. She won't be able to help it," Layla said soothingly.

Jane stood up and grabbed her purse. "Well, the sooner we find out the better. Wish me luck."

Layla and Kit watched Jane walk out the door and looked at each other with twin grins.

"I love pawning off hard chores on the youngest sister. It makes me feel so powerful," Kit said, grabbing a rag to wipe down the tables.

Layla laughed and walked behind the counter, grabbing an apron and wrapping it around her waist. "I'm relieved Jane is doing it. I don't think I could handle standing there and hearing that she didn't like Kam. I'd be trying to convince Grace that she did or something insane like that."

Kit paused and tilted her head. "That's not a bad idea, actually. Even if she doesn't like Kam, we could do our own manipulating. She might just see him as her boss *now*, but we could um, design a few spontaneously romantic situations that would push them together."

Layla stared at Kit with an arrested look on her face. "Kit, you know you're kind of brilliant, right?"

Kit blinked in surprise with a wide grin on her face. "I thought I was going to get a lecture on ethics."

Layla swished her hand in the air. "No way. Some people don't know a good thing when they see it and need a little prodding. Maybe our little Grace is slightly blind when it comes to gorgeous, single Samoan men."

Kit laughed and put her hands on her hips. "What would this town do without us?"

Layla grinned back at her sister. "The poor dears don't know how good they have it."

CHAPTER 13

Going for It

G RACE GLANCED UP at the huge clock on the wall and sighed. Wednesdays were typically just as slow, if not slower than Tuesdays, but she had some errands to run and needed her full lunch hour.

"Okay if I take off, Boss?" she asked, already taking her apron off.

Kam looked up from his calamari and nodded. "Of course. Enjoy your break, Gracie."

Grace smiled and touched his arm as she walked past him. "You're an angel. Let me know if you need anything and I can bring it back for you."

Kam smiled and tilted his head. "I've been craving another one of those banana parfaits you got me last week. If you stop by the bakery would you grab me one? Pick out something for yourself too, my treat."

Grace laughed and took the bill he handed to her. "You got it. That's the best deal I've gotten in months."

Kam narrowed his eyes at her and shook his head. "That is a shame if it's true. I can't believe there aren't hundreds of men lining up to spoil you."

Grace stopped in her tracks and laughed. "*I wish*. I can't even imagine what that would be like. Forget hundreds. I'd take just one," she said with a wink and pushed out the door.

She hurried to do some grocery shopping, picking up Baby's favorite dog food and some toiletries. She then took Baby to the park down the road and threw a Frisbee to her for fifteen minutes before heading to the bakery. She was not going to miss out on seeing that look of pleasure on Kam's face. She had to admit that knowing the banana parfait she'd bought him had brought him a little happiness filled her with joy.

She left Baby in the back of her truck and ran up the steps to the bakery. She was craving another pesto sandwich and wanted to pick out something for herself more decadent than an oatmeal cookie to get her through the rest of her day.

She pushed through the door to see Kit, Layla and Jane all standing behind the counter, looking grim and worried.

"Hey there, bakery sisters. Why the sad faces?" she asked, walking over to the counter.

Jane lurched forward with her mouth open in surprise, her big brown eyes lighting up to a bright amber.

"I was just at the restaurant looking for you! You are a hard woman to hunt down."

Grace smiled, touched that Jane had been trying to find her. "We must have just missed each other. Well, I'm here now. What can I do for you?" she asked, feeling curious.

Layla and Kit joined Jane at the counter, looking at her with serious eyes. Grace frowned. "*Wait*, am I in trouble?"

Kit laughed and Layla shook her head. "Not at all. Um, Jane... why *did* you want to see Grace?" Kit asked, turning to look at Jane with a raised eyebrow.

Jane turned and glared at Kit before turning back to her. "I was just wanting to catch up with you is all. I hope you're here to have lunch. I'd love to join you."

Grace smiled and nodded but then narrowed her eyes. "You went all the way to my restaurant to find me to ask me to have lunch with you?"

Jane cleared her throat but nodded firmly. "I sure did. Pesto again? Or do you want to try our BLT? We just added it to the menu."

Grace relaxed and looked at the menu up on the wall. "I've been dreaming of another pesto sandwich. I'll try the BLT another time. And if I could have one of those Matafeo cupcakes too. It looks way too naughty, but I'm in a naughty mood," she said with a smile at Layla.

Layla laughed and reached for the cupcake. "Anything else?"

"Um, a water bottle for my lunch, oh and add a banana parfait to my order. Kam asked me to bring him one. I swear, that man was on a 40 year fast or something and one bite of the parfait brought his little soul back to life. If I could, I'd bring him twenty banana parfaits."

The girls all smiled brightly at that. "Well, three years fast anyways. But yes, Kam is slowly waking up," Layla said, her eyes gleaming brightly.

Jane came around the counter and ushered her to a table at the back. Kit brought over their sandwiches and water bottles and then left them alone.

Grace took a big bite and groaned. "So good," she said and Jane preened in delight.

"It's such a compliment to have a talented chef enjoy a simple sandwich I made."

Grace laughed and picked up a potato chip off her plate. "It's the simple pleasures in life that mean the most, I've found."

Jane nodded her head. "I completely agree. Just like friendship. What's life without good friends?"

Grace smiled, warmed by Jane's kindness. "Absolutely. Life without friends is no life at all. I have to admit I've been missing all my friends back in Seattle. My friends are basically my family and I've been a little homesick without them."

Jane crossed her legs and took a sip of water. "Well, unless you haven't realized it yet, you have some new friends. Me, for instance and Kit and Layla too. Wren loves you, so you're kind of set. And all the Matafeo's think you're amazing as well. I think you have more friends than you think."

Grace smiled and crossed her legs too. "You're right. That's a nice feeling. I have to admit, I wasn't sure about Fircrest when I first got here. But it was a good move."

Jane smiled brightly. "And how's Kam as a boss? Is he good to you?"

Grace's eyes widened and she leaned forward. "At first I thought he was so grim and kind of depressing, but he's actually the sweetest man I've ever met. Really, he has the kindest heart. He's protective and old fashioned while at the same time, he has these impressive tribal tattoos and wild hair. *He's…*" she paused, blushing and looked out the window, not finishing her sentence.

Jane smiled and grabbed her hand. "He's *what*, Grace?" she asked softly.

Grace glanced around as if to see if anyone was listening in. "This is so bad."

Jane winked. "Then you're in good company. Spill it."

Grace laughed, not believing it for a second. "Well, I was going to say, he's so *hot*. But that's the thing. I absolutely should *not* be thinking that my boss is hot. I've witnessed disaster after disaster in the few kitchens I've worked in, where the Head Chef dates a Sous Chef or the owner gets involved and then it's nothing but a nasty, messy disaster. And I do not want to mess this up. I mean, I'm happy here. I'd hate to have to move again."

Jane licked her lips and sat up. "Sure, *sometimes* work place romance doesn't work out, but sometimes it does. It doesn't mean it shouldn't ever happen if the circumstances are right."

Grace shrugged and looked out the window with a frown. "Ah, he doesn't think about me that way so it's a non-issue. He's super sweet and kind but he's never flirted with me or anything. I was actually thinking about signing up for that local dating website that witchy girl and her husband run."

Jane laughed at that and took a bite of her sandwich. "Yeah, Meredith can be witchy. But Grace, are you really the type of woman to meet some stranger at a Starbucks? Why not try things out with Kam first and then if that doesn't work out, just remain friends and branch out to the online thing?"

Grace put her sandwich down and stared at Jane. "What exactly are you saying? Are you saying you think I *should* go for Kam?"

Jane smiled so big Grace wondered if she was seeing all of her teeth. Jane nodded, clasping her hands on the table as she sat forward.

"Tate was telling me that his family thinks you're amazing. They love the way you're so good with Nate. And Kam already thinks you're wonderful. I mean, what if true love was sitting right under your nose this whole time and you just didn't realize it?"

Grace frowned and studied her sandwich for a moment as she thought about it. "Ugh, *no way*. Last time I went after a guy, I made a fool of myself. I mean, if I thought for a moment that he might like me that way too... then, *maybe* I'd put myself out there. But with him being my boss, yeah, *no*. Too much of a gamble."

Jane frowned and stared at the table for a moment. "So you just need a sign then, is that it? You need to see some kind of evidence that Kam is attracted to you?"

Grace sighed and ran her hand through her hair. "Look,

I'm not the most beautiful girl in the world. And he's kind of… well, too much for the mere mortal to handle."

Jane laughed at that. "That's all the Matafeo men. But you're crazy if you don't think you're beautiful. I have news for you, Grace Jackson. When you smile or laugh, you make the whole room stop and stare. When you smile, everyone smiles. When you laugh, everyone wants to be closer to know what the joke is. You're exactly what this town needs, and you know what? You're exactly what Kam needs."

Grace licked her lips and crossed her arms over her chest. This conversation was getting kind of deep. "What do you mean, *Kam needs me*?"

Jane's smile disappeared and her eyes grew sad. "It's no secret, Kam is a single dad. His wife, Bailey, died in childbirth. Nate's never even known his mom. And Kam, well, he was devastated. He hasn't dated at all. And believe me, women have tried. But we all think he's ready to live again."

Grace sighed. "That's what Layla told me. She said I could bring him back to life. I thought she was just talking about getting him to smile and try new fun foods again. But you're talking about bringing his heart back to life. That's a completely different story."

Jane nodded slowly, looking deep into her eyes. "We all love Kam. We just want him and Nate to be happy. And you know what? It's the biggest compliment we could pay you, to entrust Kam to you. We *all* think you're wonderful."

Grace cleared her throat, feeling boxed in. "*We*, huh? So this is the town's consensus then?"

Jane blushed and looked away. "Okay, I'll admit a few of us have discussed the possibility of you and Kam getting together. And it's crossed your mind too. So why not give it a try?"

Grace pushed her hair over her ears and looked away. "So here's the deal and it's kind of embarrassing too, so this stays here. I'm not that great with men. It's the same scenario every time. I pick the coolest guy I can find and then he magically turns into a loser. The last guy emptied out my bank account. The guy before that cheated on me with one of my friends. *Ex* friend now. The guy before that was a narcissist and insisted I get plastic surgery to uh, *augment* certain parts of my body. And I could go on and on starting with my first kiss at seventeen. I'm just not good at this kind of thing."

Jane smiled with compassion. "Well, guess what. Your luck has just changed, because Kam is none of those things. He's one of the best men I know. He's a man of integrity and honor. He'd never cheat on you and he has treated every woman he's dated with consideration and respect. Trust me, if you don't date Kam, you're missing out on the experience of a lifetime. Don't you want to know what it's like being treated like a queen? Who wouldn't want to know what that feels like?"

Grace smiled at that and took another bite of her sandwich. "You know you sound a lot like a used car salesman, right?"

Jane laughed nervously and sat back. "*Sorry*. I don't mean to pressure you into anything. *I just*… I just want Kam to be happy and I meet you and you're so fun and full of light and you have kind eyes and a cool dog and Nate loves you and I can't help connecting the dots. But none of this matters if you don't like him. And if you don't? Well, that's okay too because we'll all still love you."

Grace shook her head. "Oh, I *like* Kam. I'm trying as hard as I can *not* to like Kam."

Jane frowned at her. "Well, knock it off. I give you permission to like him. Now go for it."

Grace frowned back at her. "You're so bossy and maybe I will."

Jane blinked in surprise and then let out a loud whoop. "Oh, man, you just made my day."

Layla and Kit walked over with bright eyes and big smiles. "So what's going on over here?" Layla asked.

Grace blushed and motioned to Jane. "Your sister here, has been threatening my life if I don't fall in love with Kam. She's basically the love mafia."

Kit and Layla's mouths fell open simultaneously as Jane tilted her head back and laughed loudly. Grace laughed too, and watched as Kit and Layla continued to stare in shock at their sister.

"She's kidding! Grace, tell them you're teasing," Jane begged.

Grace snorted. "It wasn't much of an exaggeration, but to let the cat out of the bag, I'm considering going for Kam. He's fantastically gorgeous and he has a good heart and the cutest little boy in the world. I'd kind of be crazy not to go for it, right?"

Layla and Kit nodded their heads frantically. "Totally crazy," Kit assured her.

"It's all about that light, Grace. Remember what I said," Layla said.

Grace grinned and stood up, picking up her water bottle and her box containing the parfait and the cupcake.

"You three are like the love witches of Fircrest, you know that, right?"

Kit covered her mouth with her hand. "Oh my word, I love that. I'm making t-shirts."

Grace frowned. "As long as I'm not turned into a Voodoo doll when this turns into a disaster and I leave town in a tornado of embarrassment."

Layla laughed. "We'll lock up all of our Voodoo dolls. You're safe, we promise."

Jane sighed happily and stood up, walking forward and giving Grace a big hug. "Honestly, you got this, Grace. Just remember that you're just as amazing as Kam is. I truly believe you guys could make each other deliriously happy."

Grace looked up at the ceiling with a pained expression. "Does that mean I have to try to flirt now?"

Layla laughed. "You're the biggest flirt Fircrest has ever seen, and that's saying a lot."

Jane agreed. "As if that's a problem for you. Last week, you had Tate and Tai both blushing so hard, me and Cleo had to take pictures with our phones."

Grace sighed. "It's easy when it doesn't matter. It's when it *does* matter that I can't flirt. Ugh, you guys. *Ugh.*"

Kit walked her to the door and opened it for her. "You poor thing. Romancing the hottest guy in Fircrest. Yeah, we're feeling so sorry for you."

Grace stuck her tongue out at the sisters. "You really don't know my pain."

Jane smiled kindly at her. "I do, Grace, trust me. Just don't stress out about it. Let it happen naturally. All I'm saying is, don't hold yourself back. That's it. Stop convincing yourself you don't like him, and see what happens. Easy."

Grace nodded and took a deep breath, letting it out slowly. "Well, when you put it that way, it doesn't sound so bad. Okay, I can do this."

Layla pumped her fist in the air. "You can do this!"

Grace walked down the steps to the sound of the bakery sisters clapping for her. It was one of the weirdest yet most heartwarming moments of her life. She waved at the girls from her truck and laughed all the way back to the restaurant.

"Baby, you will not believe what I just went through," she said to her dog and then filled her in on the way back to work.

By the time she got back to the kitchen she was calm

enough to smile breezily at everyone and not stutter like an eighth grader in front of Kam. That and watching him eat his parfait made her think that yeah, maybe it was time to try out a little workplace romance. Like immediately.

*

Kam closed his eyes to enjoy the banana parfait Grace had brought him and let out a moan of pleasure. When he opened his eyes to thank Grace for the dessert, she was staring at him with narrowed eyes and her cheeks were redder than normal. He blinked in surprise and stared back at her, wondering if he was reading the signs right. Because if he was, Grace was looking at him as if *he* was a banana parfait and she was starving.

"Um, thanks, Gracie. I appreciate it," he said, licking some cream off his lips.

Grace's eyes widened as she stared at his lips for a second and then fanned her face.

"They should put warning signs up around here. *Do not watch Kam Matafeo eat a banana parfait. Fire extinguisher will be needed.*"

Kam's mouth fell open at the blatant flirtation and then he tilted his head back and laughed.

Grace grinned and fanned her face theatrically. "I might just buy you a parfait every day at this rate."

Kam cleared his throat, feeling slightly self-conscious but yet very flattered. "I um, wouldn't mind that at all."

Grace winked at him and turned and walked away.

Kam watched her go and began fanning his own face. "That is a dangerous woman," he said out loud before taking another bite.

He finished his dessert and then went back to work alongside his pretty little Sous Chef. Today, he was the one who turned up the music.

CHAPTER 14

Meredith

MEREDITH SAT ACROSS from Rayne and Ivy at The Iron Skillet and frowned at the sisters. Rayne's husband Garrett was her husband's brother and since Becket and Garrett were practically brothers anyways, that made her and Ivy unofficial sisters-in-law as well. But right now, they were seriously getting on her nerves.

"You're saying, you think Kam *should* go out with Grace? Are you kidding me?" she said, her mouth feeling tight as a sudden headache began to pound.

Rayne frowned at her and glanced at Ivy quickly before leaning forward across the table, her long, dark brown hair, falling over her shoulder. "Well, of course I do. From what I can tell, Grace is sweet and wonderful. She'd be perfect for Kam. He could use a little sweet and wonderful in his life."

Ivy nodded her head quickly. "Totally agree, Rayne. Becket and I ordered the chocolate soufflé for dessert for lunch yesterday and we forced our waiter to pull her out of the kitchen and come talk to us. She came right out and was so gracious. I was thinking of inviting her to our book club."

Rayne smiled at her sister. "She'd be fantastic. Let's do it."

Meredith stared at the ceiling for a moment and breathed in and out before answering. This was not going the way she'd pictured it in her mind.

"Here's the deal. She's *not* that great. Kam deserves way, *way* better than Grace Jackson. Really, *who is she?* She's just a runty little Sous chef. I mean, this isn't some average guy looking for a date. Kam's a single dad and he's our friend. Don't we want the best for him?" she asked, her voice rising slightly.

Rayne blinked a couple times and then her mouth hardened. "You dated Kam, isn't that right, Meredith?" she asked in a calm, smooth voice that had Meredith sitting up straight for some reason.

Meredith cleared her throat and nodded once. "Oh, a long time ago. We dated a little."

Ivy tapped her fingers on the table. "It kind of sounds like you're a little possessive of Kam, no offense," she said, in the same narrowed eyed gaze as her sister.

Meredith pushed her bright blond hair over her ears and glared at the sisters. "That's actually very offensive and no, of course I'm not. What a thing to say. All *I'm* saying is, there's no reason to push this woman on Kam if he's not ready. What's the harm in being cautious until we know more about her? She might be a serial killer for all we know," she said with a brittle laugh.

Rayne blinked at that and glanced at Ivy again. Meredith was beginning to think the two sisters could communicate telepathically.

Ivy shook her head. "Wren says she's a beautiful, fun person. And I heard the other day that Taryn was being kind of rude to her, but Grace won her over with kindness. I'm sorry that you feel so strongly about it, but from where I'm sitting, I think she would be good for Kam."

Rayne took a sip of water and smiled at Ivy. "I agree.

This would be good for Kam *and* for his little boy. I think, Meredith, since you have such strong feelings about this, *and* since it's none of your business, that maybe you should keep your thoughts and feelings to yourself. I would hate for this to get back to Kam."

Meredith's mouth fell open at the direct way Rayne was talking to her. Her cheeks turned red and she looked down at her lap to control her breathing.

"Well, that's rude," she said, looking up and staring Rayne in the eye.

Rayne raised a dark eyebrow and met her gaze head on. "Really? How's that?"

Meredith stood up and threw her napkin on the plate. This hadn't gone the way she'd imagined it would when she and Anne had planned it out. Everyone was supposed to believe her and turn against Grace, not imply that she was possessive of Kam. Which wasn't true at all. *The nerve.*

"I have a genuine concern for a friend and you're implying that I don't have his best interests at heart. I consider that rude," she said, slipping her purse over her shoulder and picking up her sunglasses.

Ivy frowned at her. "His best interests? You'd rather he stay alone and sad? That actually sounds like the exact opposite of his best interests. Meredith, you need to do a little soul searching."

Meredith rolled her eyes and swore she'd never have lunch with Rayne and Ivy again. Total brats.

"I guess we'll have to agree to disagree, then won't we?" she said tightly.

Rayne shook her head. "I *don't* agree. It sounds like you want to make sure they don't get together. As a friend of Kam, that worries me."

Meredith tapped her foot on the floor and crossed her arms over her chest.

"Try and stop me," she said and turned and walked away.

"Of all the nerve," she huffed under her breath and stomped away. She walked around the corner and then paused, leaning against the wall and putting her hand over her chest as she took a minute to control her heart beat.

She straightened herself and stared down the hallway at the kitchen. It wouldn't hurt to say hi to Kam. She walked down the hallway and pushed through the door just as Grace walked past her.

The runty little Sous Chef smiled at first and then narrowed her eyes, her smile fading. "I think you're lost," Grace said to her.

Meredith ignored her and smiled at Kam who was talking to one of the other cooks by his office.

"Hi, Kam!" she called out and walked over to her ex.

Kam turned towards her and smiled. "Hi, Mer. What brings you back to the kitchen? Was your lunch okay?"

Meredith forgot what she'd ordered since she hadn't stayed to eat it. "Um, yeah, it was fantastic. As always. I just wanted to drop in and say hi. I've been worried about you lately," she said, putting her hand on his arm.

Kam frowned and motioned to his office. She walked in and sat down, waiting for him to shut the door. He sat down across from her and looked at her, waiting. He was so beautiful. How could one man be so blessed in the looks department? Of course, Asher was gorgeous too in his own way, but Kam was, well, *Kam*. No one could compare.

"Well?"

Meredith jumped in surprise. She'd been so busy staring at him, she'd forgotten to come up with something to say.

"Oh, well, what I was saying, was that I was worried about you," she mumbled, looking down at her knees.

Kam sighed. "Worried about what?"

Meredith looked up and glanced out his window at Grace who was doing some kind of weird chicken dance with Candice. *What a nerd.*

"Well, I heard a rumor that a few people are trying to pressure you into dating your new Sous Chef, Grace. And I know how upsetting that would be for you," she said in a low voice as she frowned at him.

Kam's eyes widened. "*Pressured?* Yeah, no one is pressuring me to do anything."

Meredith sat back and frowned even more. "Well, if they haven't yet, I'm sure they will, so just be prepared. I can talk to Rob for you if you want me to. There are so many talented Sous Chefs around. It's not like The Iron Chef even needs Grace Jackson. Haven't you noticed she's kind of irritating? And she's really not that cute," she added as an after thought.

Kam's eye widened as he shook his head. "You're saying that you want to talk to Rob about getting Grace fired?"

Meredith laughed and waved her hand in the air. "Oh, of course not. *Unless she's bothering you.* But I wonder what Bailey would think of you dating someone like Grace. I knew Bailey, and I know for a fact she'd be horrified," she said, nodding her head firmly.

Kam frowned at that and looked away. "I wasn't aware that you and Bailey were that close."

Meredith cleared her throat and it was her turn to look away. "Well, we weren't best friends, but I know she wouldn't like you dating someone like Grace. I heard the other day, um… that she's kind of icky. Tons of men. So many ex-boyfriends she can't even keep count. Really trashy," she said, feeling a little guilty at the blatant lie.

Kam's eyebrows shot up and he glanced out the window at his Sous Chef. "Well, it sounds like you've been listening to gossip, Mer and I don't waste time with that junk. You shouldn't either. Listen, it was good to say hi, but I need to get back to work. You take care and tell your husband I said, hi," he said standing up.

Meredith stood up slowly and fixed her purse on her shoulder as she stared sadly at Kam. "Do you ever wonder what it would have been like if you and I had ended up together?" she said softly.

Kam frowned at her, his eyes hard. "No, Meredith. I'm sorry. I don't."

Meredith took the hit to her heart and turned around, walking out of the office and out of the kitchen without another word. The poor man was so good, of course he wouldn't want to speculate. She was married to Asher and if he had said anything it would have been inappropriate, *but she knew*. She knew he had to wonder. The poor man was so lonely, how could he not?

Meredith drove away in her car and smiled to herself. She'd look out for Kam, even if no one else would.

*

Kam watched Meredith walk out and shook his head. She was acting crazier than usual. *And who was gossiping about Grace?* he wondered, looking around his kitchen. He looked at Manuel and shook his head. Candice? *Nah.* James? He and Grace barely spoke. It didn't make sense. And Grace dating around and being *trashy*? He watched her sway to the music as she prepared a beet and goat cheese salad. He couldn't see it. There was literally nothing icky or trashy about her. More like the opposite. Every good thing he could think of was wrapped up in one cute as heck woman with a smile that could light up his cold heart.

"Hey, Grace," he said, walking up beside her. "How's it going?"

Grace smiled up at him and motioned to her salad. "Fantastic per usual. And you, Boss? You doing okay? I saw you talking to dragon lady. I'm glad to see you're still alive."

Kam laughed at that and leaned his hip against the counter. "Still breathing. She uh, seems worried that people might be pressuring me into dating you," he said and watched her expression closely.

Grace stopped what she was doing as her cheeks turned bright red. "*Seriously?* She came in here to warn you about dating me?"

Kam shrugged. "Well, to warn me that people might pressure me into dating you. She seemed worried that you would just add me to a long list of lovers."

Grace snorted at that, shaking her head before laughing. "Oh wow. You're kidding me. *You're not kidding me, are you?*"

Kam smiled and shook his head, relaxing even more as he watched the play of emotions on her face. Embarrassment, amusement and then more embarrassment.

"Well, that's pretty interesting. Does that make me seem more exciting and exotic?" she asked, smiling up at him suddenly.

Kam laughed, enjoying himself. "Not really. No worries, I don't listen to gossip about my friends. I just thought you should know. I'll let you get back to work," he said as he turned and walked away.

"But what would you do if someone *did* try and pressure you into dating me?" she called after him.

Kam turned back to see her grinning at him. He smiled back. "I'd probably thank them," he said and lifted an eyebrow at her before walking out of the kitchen. He had a meeting with Rob to go over the budget and he was already five minutes late because of Meredith.

He knocked on Rob's door and walked in, sitting down in the comfortable chair across from his boss and putting his hands behind his head as he waited for Rob to get off the phone.

"Mom, I think you're being silly. *Relax.* If Kam did date Grace, would it really be that tragic?" Rob said, rolling his eyes and pointing to the phone as Kam's smile faded.

Something was going on here. It sounded like Meredith and Anne were on the war path about Grace. He sighed and tilted his head back, suddenly tired.

"Yeah, well, I don't care. I say Bailey would love to see Kam happy again. Don't you want Nate to have a mom?… Yeah, well a grandma just doesn't cut it, Mom.… No, I don't. No, Mom, I don't. Listen, Kam's here, I gotta go… no, I won't tell him to not date Grace, sheesh, Mom, calm down. Go play bingo or do yoga or something," he said and hung up the phone.

Rob sighed loudly and picked up a baseball off his desk and threw it up in the air. Something he did when he was stressed out. Anne had obviously done a number on him.

"My mom's a little nuts. Sorry, Kam. I guess she's heard that your family loves Grace and automatically thinks that means that you two will end up together and then all hell will break loose which will usher in the end of the world."

Kam didn't say anything. He didn't know what to say.

Rob looked at him sadly for a moment before shaking his head. "For the record, bro? I think it would be wonderful. Wren thinks so too. We all do. You've been alone too long, my friend. It's time to live again. If you date Grace? Cool. Go for it. No guilt. If you don't? No problem. This is *your* life and no one should have a say in it. Especially my mom."

Kam swallowed and nodded. He forgot sometimes what a

decent guy Rob was. "Thanks, Man. I appreciate it. Thanks for calming Anne down too. She's not the only one either. Meredith was just in my office trying to convince me not to date Grace. She even asked me if I thought about the two of us being together? Can you believe that?" he asked with a laugh.

Rob blinked slowly and shook his head. "Um, no. I don't. That's weird, dude. Sounds like Asher needs to sign up for couple's counseling if you ask me. Stay away from Meredith. And stay away from my mom too for that matter. That's an order."

Kam laughed. "Will do, Rob. So um, what do *you* think about Grace?" he asked casually.

Rob smiled, his eyes warming. "I think she's wonderful, Kam. She's kind. She's smart and she's not afraid of bullies. She's a talented chef and she loves dogs and kids. What more could you want?"

Kam shrugged. "I was just curious what you thought. Doesn't mean I'm going to ask her out or anything," he said gruffly.

Rob threw the ball in the air again. "Nah, you do you, Kam. If you want to go on a date, *go*. If not, there's always a game playing at my place. This is your life. You don't need anyone telling you what to do or *when* to do it."

Kam smiled and relaxed again. He had good friends. No pressure. "Onto the budget for the month. Let's talk crab legs."

Rob frowned. "Do we have to?"

Kam nodded. "Yes we do."

Kam spent a half an hour going over prices with Rob before heading back to the kitchen. When he returned, Grace was already gone for the day. He forgot she had asked for Wednesday night off. He frowned, feeling let down for some reason. He looked around the kitchen and wondered where the light had gone. It seemed so dark now without her.

He went back to work, wondering what Grace was doing.

CHAPTER 15

Enemy #1

IT WAS A week after Kam had hinted at liking the idea of the two of them together and then... *nothing*. Grace frowned at Kam's back. He was either extremely slow and cautious when it came to dating, which granted, the man hadn't dated in a very long time, *or* he had decided he wasn't interested in her.

Ouch

She'd flirted with him casually throughout the week, and he'd smile and look flattered and then... *nothing*. She sighed as she mixed her gnocchi dough and stared across the kitchen at the small window letting in some rare Pacific Northwest sunlight. She should be at the park with her dog, throwing a Frisbee instead of in this kitchen, making gnocchi for all of the gnocchi obsessed residents of Fircrest.

Grace closed her eyes and thought of three things she was very grateful for, her dog, her friends and her health, and then she smiled. She knew just the physical act of smiling could do wonders for her mood so she forced herself to stretch her lips. It was that or quit her job, grab her dog and head to Hawaii where she could be a homeless bum and learn to surf.

"What's putting that smile on your face?"

Grace jerked out of her reverie and looked up to see Kam smiling down at her. She shrugged and continued to mix her batter.

"Just daydreaming of running away to Hawaii, the land of sun and surfboards."

Kam frowned at that and crossed his massive arms over his chest as he rested his hip against the counter. "Running away, huh? Anything in particular you're running away from?"

Grace blew a strand of hair out of her eyes and shook her head. If she said, *him and his non-existent ability to ask her out*, he'd faint with shock. She'd keep it simple.

"Not really. It could just be the fact that we finally have a sunny day and we're all stuck inside. Or it could be this Adele song. Have you noticed that she's a little obsessed with her ex? I swear, every song is about trying to get him to reconnect even though he's moved on. I'm thinking about writing Adele and inviting her to Fircrest. We could have dinner, hang out by the water and have a heart to heart about letting go of the past. What do you think?"

Kam laughed. "Adele is a voice among voices but you're right. Girl needs to move on. I'm hoping her third album will be a little more emotionally healthy."

Grace grinned and went back to her dough as Kam took a phone call. She'd noticed Kam's questioning look at her before he'd walked away. She'd decided yesterday to tone down the flirting. This couldn't be all one sided. No way was she going to make a play for her boss if he wasn't reciprocating her feelings. She'd lay off and see what happened. Probably nothing, but it wouldn't hurt to play it safe. But the looks he kept giving her made her think *maybe* he missed her flirting.

Grace smiled at that. But if he wanted her to flirt, then he'd have to do a little flirting himself. It was only fair.

She finished making her gnocchi and then began the first orders for lunch. After a busy lunch rush, she threw off her apron and grabbed her purse. "I'm running to the hair salon. If you need me, text," she called out.

Kam popped his head out of his office and lifted an eyebrow. "Any chance you'll be stopping by the bakery?"

Grace laughed and shook her head. "I'll be lucky to make it back before my break is over. But speaking of the bakery, if *you* happened to stop by Belinda's, I know I'd *love* another Matafeo cupcake. They're addicting."

Kam gave her a pouty face, but then winked at her before disappearing back into his office. She smiled and walked out into the sun.

She hurried over to the Fircrest Cut N' Curl and pulled open the door. She frowned at the 1980's feel of the place but Jane had assured her that everyone went to the Cut N' Curl. She ran a hand through her hair as she stared at the three little ladies sitting in old fashioned chairs getting tight little perms.

Would Jane set her up? If this turned out bad, she was never speaking to Jane ever again. *Ever.*

"Hi, there. Are you Grace?"

Grace turned around with a smile to see a tall Black woman with long braids smiling politely at her.

"I am. Are you, Sonja? Jane told me I had to see you."

The attractive woman smiled and motioned to the chair closest to them. "Jane is one of my favorite customers. And that has nothing to do with the fact that she tips me in cupcakes. Have a seat and tell me what you have in mind."

Grace sat down and set her purse on the counter. "My hair has been dull and boring. I'm always working in a hot kitchen and my blond highlights are fading. I need some pop. I need healthy hair. I need a miracle."

Sonja ran her fingers through her hair and made a hmm

sound. "Your hair is a little damaged. Have you been doing coconut oil treatments? Any deep conditioning?"

Grace winced and shook her head feeling like a naughty little girl. "Yeah, no. I've been so busy with the move and my new job, I've ignored my hair. And my skin. And my wardrobe. And everything."

Sonja laughed and made a tsking sound. "So why do you want a change now? Hot date coming up?"

Grace grinned and shrugged. "A girl can hope. There's this gorgeous Samoan chef I wouldn't mind going out with. I keep getting mixed signals from him though."

Sonja smiled serenely. "Well, let's wake him up. How about I just retouch your roots and then do a gloss treatment for the rest of your hair? You'll look and feel like a million bucks after I'm done. Your hair will be soft and shiny. You'll love it."

Grace grinned and lifted her hair for the drape. "That sounds wonderful. Thanks Sonja."

Sonja walked off to mix the gloss so she picked up a magazine.

"*A hot Samoan Chef?* You're not talking about Kam Matafeo, are you?"

Grace whipped her head to the side to see an older woman with dark hair sitting next to her. She was getting a trim and the girl working on her had wide eyes and looked nervous. The woman looked kind of familiar.

No way. Kam's mother-in-law. Of course she'd get caught talking about wanting to date Kam. Yikes.

"I am, yes," she said simply and then began flipping through her magazine. Better to act confident instead of the intimidated and nervous woman she was now. This woman could throw a fit right here and now if she wanted to. She was the mother of Kam's deceased wife and she probably wasn't happy about the fact that some strange woman wanted to go out with her daughter's husband. *Ugh.* Drama.

"I don't think that's a good idea," the woman said with a snap in her voice.

Grace closed her magazine and turned her head to look at the woman. She was sitting up super straight and her eyes were bright and narrowed. She looked ticked. This was not good.

"Why's that?" she asked calmly.

The woman bristled and turned to glare at her. "I know who you are. You work for my son, Rob. Now listen to me, *you leave Kam alone.* He's not ready to date anyone, least of all a little nobody like you."

Sonja walked up just then and looked between the two women. "Problem?"

Grace licked her lips and shook her head. "Not at all. This woman just called me a nobody and ordered me not to date her son-in-law. This feels like some bizarre reality show."

Sonja frowned at the woman. "Anne, we've talked about this. No more antagonizing other customers while you're here."

Anne rolled her eyes and crossed her arms. "I'm almost finished with my trim and then I'll leave. But I will say this. With one call, I could have you fired. *One. Call.* So you better watch yourself. If I hear that you've been bothering Kam or even flirting with him, you're out. Capiche?"

Grace snorted, almost amused by the woman's cockiness. "Holy cow, forget the bad reality show, this is a gangster movie. And just to make things clear, I *do* plan on flirting with Kam as much as possible. If you want to get me fired, go for it. But we have a Fine Dining experience for The Iron Skillet coming up and you might want to wait until that's over. It's going to be huge for the restaurant."

Anne sniffed and looked away. "I did hear about that from Taryn. She's very excited about it. But that won't stop me from getting you fired if you take one step near Kam. I won't have it, I tell you. I won't. Kam doesn't need you in his life."

Sonja began to speak but Grace held up her hand, turning her whole body to face Anne. "Look, I get it, seeing Kam move on after losing your daughter, sucks. But life has to go on. Life can't stop forever. Why not let Kam find love again. Wouldn't that be the best thing for him and his son?" she asked softly.

Anne held up her hand and stood up, ripping her drape off. She took a few bills out of her purse and threw them on the counter. Grace noted that only half of her hair had been trimmed and now she had an odd crooked look to her shoulder length brown hair.

"I will not stay here another second and listen to this. You don't know anything about it. You didn't know Bailey. You didn't know how much they loved each other. He *still* loves her and he always will. Why would you want to be with a man where you know you'll always be second place?" she asked with a mean look in her eye before stomping out.

Grace's stiff smile slowly faded as she watched Anne walk past the window.

"Wow, she kind of has a point, doesn't she?" Grace said softly to herself.

Sonja squeezed her shoulders. "Honey, you just ignore all that spitefulness. You live your life and do what your heart tells you to. Now, let's get started," she said and began applying the chemicals to her hair.

Grace zoned out, only coming out of her fog when Sonja handed her a mirror and twirled her chair around to show her the back of her hair.

"Well, what do you think?"

Grace blinked and sat up straight, staring at her now shiny, silky hair.

"Oh, Sonja. I love it. I truly love it. It's just what I needed.

I feel like a new woman," she said, standing up and pulling her drape off. "You come by The Iron Skillet any time and I'll make you something delicious."

Sonja grinned. "Absolutely. You can count on it."

Grace hugged Sonja, handed her a check and then hurried outside. She would be five minutes late, but it was worth it. She flipped her hair and smiled happily before jumping up in her truck. She drove quickly back to work and then frowned as she parked.

She walked slowly to the back of the restaurant and sighed before pulling the door open. Anne might be mean and spiteful, but she had a point. Did she really want to come in second place in Kam's heart? And could she live her life knowing that he would always be missing his first wife? She clenched her eyes shut and tried to push the thoughts away. It was a non-issue anyways. Kam couldn't even bring himself to ask her out.

She opened the door and walked in, washing her hands and picking up her apron.

"Gracie? Come in here for a second."

Grace looked over her shoulder at Kam standing in the doorway of his office and swallowed hard. She squared her shoulders as she walked into Kam's office.

"Shut the door, please."

Grace bit her lip but did as she was told before sitting down and staring at the man in front of her. *Why did he have to be so good looking? Why torture innocent women?*

"You know what? I think you should cut your hair," she said, without thinking.

Kam's eyes widened as he automatically pulled his hand over his ponytail. "What? *Why?*" he demanded, frowning at her.

"Because it tortures women, that's why," she snapped, crossing her arms over her chest. "And maybe wear long sleeves, too. Those tattoos are just as bad."

Kam blinked a few times and then grinned at her. "Wait. You're saying I'm torturing you?"

Grace nodded her head, frowning at him. "It's cruel to be honest."

Kam laughed and pushed a small box closer to her. "Well, maybe this will make up for it."

Grace felt her stomach growl as she reached for the box, hoping against hope that it was what she thought it was. She hadn't had time for lunch and this could very well put her in a better mood.

"Oh please, please be something yummy," she murmured, opening the lid to see the biggest, most decadent cupcake ever made by human hands. "Oh my word. It's too beautiful to eat."

Kam shook his head. "Not even. Take a bite."

Grace lifted the large cupcake out of the box and stared at it for a moment before taking a large bite. She closed her eyes, shaking her head at the explosion of flavors in her mouth.

"It's too much," she whispered, licking her lips. "This has to be what heaven is like."

Kam laughed and put his hands behind his head, leaning back in his chair. "Your hair is pretty."

Grace smiled and leaned back in her chair, now much much happier than when she'd entered his office. "Really? Thanks, Boss."

Kam smiled back at her, just looking at her. Grace blushed, now feeling weird, eating in front of him as he just sat there watching her.

"And what did you pick from the bakery today? Did you stick to the parfait, or did you venture out and try something new?"

Kam motioned to an empty box on his desk. "Kit convinced me to try her newest creation. It was a looped churro dipped in chocolate and nuts. It was amazing," he said, sighing happily.

Grace laughed and licked some icing off the side of her cupcake. "And to think I had to force that first banana parfait on you. I love it. Next time I'm there, I'll pick up a couple for both of us."

Kam cleared his throat and looked down at his large hands. "Um, yeah, that would be great. Maybe we should just uh, go together sometime?"

Grace raised an eyebrow at Kam over her cupcake as he looked at her with a strange expressionless look on his face. She tilted her head as she studied him. Two things. The man had just sort of asked her out. And he was super nervous about it. She grinned at him and pointed her finger at him.

"Boss, you just asked me out."

Kam cleared his throat again and began fidgeting with a pencil. "Nah, not really. It was more like, if you're going and I'm going and we happen to be going at the same time and we both want a churro, maybe we should just go together. That's all."

Grace laughed and shook her finger at him. "No way. You just asked me out."

Kam's face reddened as he looked up at the ceiling and sighed pitifully. "Why do women make life so hard?" he asked the ceiling.

Grace sat back and sighed happily. "Oh you've done it now. We're going on a date. We. Are. Going. On. A. Date."

Kam groaned and rubbed his face before staring at her in exasperation. "Well, can you blame me? You come in here, singing and dancing and tempting me with desserts and making me laugh. *And Gracie, you flirt.* You flirt with me like crazy. What's a man to do?" he demanded.

Grace grinned and took a bite of her cupcake as she wallowed in her happy glow. "Oh I get it. I forced you to ask me out. Is that it? You poor little thing."

Kam sighed and shook his head, looking even more befuddled. "Of course not. No, I've been wanting to ask you out for two weeks now. I've just been,... I've just been a little hesitant is all."

Grace smiled at him. "*Two* weeks? You know, I was about to give up on you. I was thinking if you didn't ask me out, I was going to take Baby and run away to Hawaii."

Kam grinned, looking very satisfied for some reason. "Oh, that's why you wanted to run away, huh? Good to know."

Grace raised an eyebrow at that. "Oh, so you *do* enjoy torturing poor, innocent women. Well, then I deserve this date. For making me wait, for the hair and the tattoos, I think I deserve something more exciting than Belinda's Bakery though."

Kam tilted his head. "Oh yeah? What did you have in mind?"

Grace sat forward, grinning. "*Dancing.* I want to go dancing with you."

Kam narrowed his eyes at her. "We'd have to leave a little early Saturday night, but there's a club I know that stays open until two. If you're not too tired, we could leave here at ten."

Grace stood up and popped the last of her cupcake in her mouth. "It's a date then," she said and saluted him before walking out into the kitchen.

It was only later that night when she was laying in bed, trying to fall asleep that Anne's words about always coming in second place in Kam's heart began to play on repeat through her mind. She sighed and turned on her stomach, watching the shadows play against her wall.

Could she do it? Could she allow herself to fall for a man who would only give her half his heart? She frowned at that, feeling the automatic punch to her gut.

The answer to that was, *she didn't know.*

CHAPTER 16

2ⁿᵈ Place

THE NEXT DAY, Grace drove to Belinda's for her lunch break, promising to bring everyone back a goody. But it wasn't the cupcakes or the churros she was after today. No, she wanted to talk to Jane, Kit and Layla.

She ran up the steps to the old home, turned bakery and ripped the door open. She saw the three sisters standing together behind the counter and raised her arms in a Rocky stance.

"I did it!" she yelled, a little louder than she should for a public place.

The three women stared at her for a moment before they began jumping up and down, screaming as loud as she did. She laughed and bent over, resting on her thighs as the women ran around the counter to hug her.

"We knew you could do it," Layla said, hugging her tightly.

Kit patted her on the back. "You, Grace Jackson, are a woman to be reckoned with. Good job."

Jane shook her head and patted her cheeks like a grandmother would do. "Good girl. You get a treat for that. Anything you want. Kit will even make you something custom if you want."

Kit snorted. "Yeah, right. She marries the guy, then yes. Custom all the way. Heck, I'll make a wedding cake for you. But just a date? Girl, you get a churro and you'll be grateful."

Grace laughed and walked over to the counter, pulling a crumpled list out of her jeans pocket. "Here's my list from everyone back at the kitchen. I'm their new errand girl since they know I come here practically every day. But I could use a sandwich and a little conversation. Because although I do have a date this Saturday night, Anne threatened to have me fired yesterday if I even so much as flirt with him. I think I'm in trouble."

The three sisters stared at each other in horror before Jane began making the sandwich and Layla and Kit got everything else. Grace walked over to the table and pulled over another chair so everyone could sit down.

Within two minutes, they were all sitting down, looking grim. Grace was just glad to be eating her sandwich though and decided to let the sisters stress over Anne.

"*Mmm*, this is good," she said, pointing to the BLT. "I love your pesto, but this is a close second place."

Jane smiled and pushed the bag of kettle chips over to her. "I added extra bacon for you."

Grace smiled at Jane and took a sip of water. "Thanks, Jane. So what do we do? I was getting my hair done, by the way, *love Sonja*, and there's Anne listening to me jabber on like an idiot about trying to get my hot Samoan boss to ask me out and she flips out. Seriously, I'm talking foaming at the mouth. She got up and left *halfway* through her haircut. One side of her hair is longer than the other. I am not lying."

Layla groaned and leaned her head in her hands. "And she actually said the words, *I'm going to have Rob fire you?*"

Grace nodded. "She said it like, three times. Anne doesn't play."

Kit snorted. "No, she doesn't and she never has. I could tell you stories about Anne that would singe your eyeballs. Okay, just one. A long time ago, she was so mad at me that she had nasty reviews printed in the paper and online about our bakery. We lost a lot of revenue because of her temper."

Grace blinked in surprise. "And no one has burned her at the stake?"

Jane shook her head. "She married Sefe Matafeo a few years ago and really mellowed out. But Kam is a sore spot."

Grace sighed. "Well, maybe you girls could help me out then. What should I do?"

Kit, Layla and Jane all looked at each other with pained expressions.

Jane patted her hand. "We don't know, but we'll think about it. You're not nervous about going out with Kam? You're not going to back out are you?"

Grace shook her head, frowning. "Nah, I don't scare that easily. But she did say something that I'm having a hard time working out in my head."

Layla sighed. "*Oh, no.*"

Grace winced. "Oh, yeah. She said, *why would I even want to be with a man where I knew I'd always come in second place in his heart?*"

There was dead silence for a minute before Kit leaned back in her chair and cracked her knuckles.

"Well, that was a cruel thing to say."

Grace raised an eyebrow. "But not necessarily untrue, either. You guys knew Bailey. Were they really in love?"

Layla smiled kindly at her. "Yes, Grace, they were. Kam was head over heels in love with her and Bailey was, well, she was beautiful like a model. She'd had some struggles in high school, so she was kind of like this aloof princess in the tower. I think Kam loved the idea of being her knight in shining armor. The man who would keep all the bad guys away."

Jane stole one of her potato chips and nodded. "But she truly loved him too. She wasn't very fond of men, but Kam helped her to relax and trust again. Sorry, Grace. It was kind of beautiful. I think that's why it's been so hard for Kam to move on. Because he did love her so much."

Layla took a sip out of her water bottle. "But, and this is a big but, why should that be a problem? The fact that Kam knows how to love and how to treat a woman is a good thing. That means he'll treat you with respect and kindness and love too."

Grace held up a finger. "That I believe. It's the always coming in second place part I might have a problem with. I mean, isn't that the fairytale? You meet the man of your dreams and *tada,* you're soul mates and you live happily ever after. I don't know if I'm the type of woman who could be happy loving a man who's heart already belongs to someone else."

Layla reached out and grabbed Grace's hand in hers. "But what if Kam's heart is so big and so beautiful that he's able to have *two* soul mates. What if he can love Bailey and love you too?"

Grace felt depressed all of a sudden. "I can see it now, we'll have pictures of Bailey all through the house. I'd constantly be seeing this amazing, practically perfect, gorgeous woman looking at me live *her* life with *her* husband and *her* son."

Grace surprised herself, by flicking a tear away. "*What would that be like?*" she asked in a whisper. "Looking down from heaven at the life you should have lived? The man you loved and the child you died bringing to life, loving a new woman? Oh my heck, that hurts my heart."

Jane shook her head. "Well, here's what I think. I think you are an amazing woman with a huge capacity to love too. Not just to love Kam, but to love Nate too. And not only that, but to love Bailey and have compassion for the fact that she *isn't* here loving Kam and raising her son. I know you can love her like a friend and allow for the fact that she'll always have a place in Kam's heart and Nate's heart. I know you have the capacity to honor that and respect that and not be intimidated by it *or be diminished by it.*"

Grace sat back and stared at Jane, who's cheeks were red and her eyes bright.

"*Wow,*" Layla said and hugged Jane.

Kit shook her head. "Yeah, wow. Jane, anytime I need a pep talk, you're the one I'm going to. Heck, I feel like loving Kam and Nate now and I'm happily married with two kids."

Grace gave a watery laugh and leaned her head in her hands. *Could she do it?* Did she have the strength and the capacity to love so unselfishly?

She raised her head and sighed, trying to smile. "Well, we'll see. We have our first date Saturday night. This could develop into a fun friendship or we could date for a few months and things fizzle *or* we might fall in love. At this point, I don't know. I'm really just looking down the road and asking what if. But I'll be okay, one way or another."

Layla nodded her head. "I believe that. But will Kam be okay? What if he falls in love with you and wants to be with you, but you don't think you can handle the second place thing? What then?"

Kit frowned and stared at her. "Yeah, forget the down the road business. You better make up your mind *now.* I don't want Kam hurt any more than he's been hurt. If you're not in all the way right this second, then just break it off before it even begins. *Please,* for his friend's and family's sake, make up your mind now. This man should not have to have his heart broken again."

Jane smiled as she stared at her. "Ah, don't worry about Grace. Look at her eyes. She's already in."

Grace frowned at the sisters as they all stared at her. As if on cue, all three sister's faces relaxed and they smiled.

"Oh, she's totally in," Layla said with a relieved grin.

Kit smiled and shook her head. "Sorry. I should have looked closer before I got all intense on you."

Grace took a sip of water and shook her head. "You girls are witches and that's all there is to it. If you weren't my friends, I'm telling you, I'd be scared."

The sisters stood up as one as the bell above the door dinged and a group of young moms walked in.

"That reminds me, the Love Witches t-shirts should be arriving any day," Kit said breezily as she walked away.

Layla grinned at her. "We own it."

Jane watched Layla and Kit for a second before turning back to her and putting a hand on her shoulder. "You're going to be just fine, and what's even better, Kam and Nate are in good hands. We trust you, Grace."

Grace sat by herself and finished her lunch while she stared outside at the white clouds passing by and thought about everything the sisters had said to her. Maybe she was underestimating herself?

She heard the bell ring again and looked up to see Taryn walk in. She slumped down in her chair and popped a potato chip in her mouth. Maybe Taryn would be so busy she wouldn't notice her?

Taryn ordered a flourless chocolate cake and looked around, immediately spotting her. Grace smiled and waved, hoping that Taryn would take her cake and leave. *But no, she was heading over.* Grace sighed. She'd made peace with Taryn, but that didn't mean that she wanted to sit and talk with her either. And besides that, Taryn was Anne's daughter *and* Bailey's sister. She might be getting ready to be threatened away from Kam. *Again.*

She glanced at the sisters for help, but they'd all disappeared into the back room. She was on her own.

"Mind if I join you?"

Grace motioned to the chair. "Please. How are you, Taryn?"

Taryn gave her a tight, unhappy smile and shrugged. "Fantastic. And you?"

Grace smiled and motioned to her now empty plate. "Full and happy. You should try one of their sandwiches. *Divine*."

Taryn shrugged. "I haven't been very hungry lately. The only thing I want is this dumb flourless chocolate cake. Everything else tastes like cardboard."

Grace frowned and sat up, leaning forward. A woman or man who had given up on the joys of food was dealing with a lot of pain. Kam had taught her that.

"Are you okay?" she asked softly.

Taryn pursed her lips and stared out the window. "How to answer that? Do I tell the truth or do I say what I always say and tell you I'm fine?"

Grace bit her lip. "Give it to me."

Taryn sighed, her face falling. "Life is horrible. Life is pain and heartache and then there's just more pain. And I'm so tired," she whispered. "I'm just so tired."

Grace reached over and took Taryn's hand. "Only a man could cause that much pain."

Taryn snorted. "Only the most beautiful man in the state of Washington. I guess it's no secret that I'm having marriage problems. Brogan wants to move across country for a work opportunity and I don't want to. Come to find out that part of this work opportunity is the chance to work with a woman called Tiffany Sanders. She's a former Miss South Carolina," she said with a bitter twist to her mouth.

Grace frowned. "Uh, I hate to break it to you, but you're

just as gorgeous as any model or Miss any state. *So what?* Brogan has you."

Taryn looked up with tears in her eyes. "Yeah, well I found some super flirty text messages and emails between them. That's what."

Grace felt her stomach drop. "Oh wow, I'm so sorry. Nothing, uh... *physical* though?"

Taryn shook her head. "No and I believe him. It's called an emotional affair. That's what our marriage counselor called it. Brogan says he's sorry and it won't happen again, but this woman, *Tiffany*, wont stop texting him and messaging him and Linked-in'ing him and on and on. She says she's in love and she's willing to fight for him."

Grace felt nauseated for Taryn. "Let's go beat her up. You book the flight and I'll get online and order the brass knuckles."

Taryn stared at her for a second and then burst out laughing. *"Really?* Because I will so take you up on that."

Grace nodded her head. "I'm there. The nerve of her. But what does Brogan say about this?"

Taryn sighed and closed her eyes. "Everything he's supposed to say. He's so sorry. It started out innocently, just work stuff and before he realized what was going on, things had gone too far. He's blocked her on everything and says that he'll never talk to her again."

Grace nodded, feeling slightly better. "But then why does he still want to move across country? Wouldn't that put him right in her lap, so to speak?"

Taryn groaned. "He still wants to move. She works in a different department than he would but it's still the same company. It is an amazing opportunity for him, but I can't imagine living my life constantly wondering, you know? Are they going to lunch together today? Are they passing each other in the hall today? I'd be miserable. *I can't.* I told him if he takes the job, we're over. And,… he's thinking about it."

Grace's mouth fell open. "You're kidding me," she whispered.

Taryn shook her head jerkily. "Sadly, no."

Grace shuddered. "What an idiot. I'll go help you pack up his stuff and throw it on the front lawn."

Taryn smiled at that. "In front of my son? I don't want to traumatize our child. But the old me would have been all over that. The new me is trying to be mature and think about what would be best for everyone."

Grace frowned. "That sounds horrible."

Taryn laughed, sounding sad rather than amused. "It is."

Grace watched as Taryn stood up and picked up her bakery box. "Sorry to dump on you. It felt good to talk to someone who wasn't my brother or my mother though."

Grace smiled. "Anytime. Seriously, you and me? We're friends,"

Taryn's eyes lit up. "I could use a friend right now. Thanks," she said and walked out.

Grace threw away her trash and waved goodbye to the sisters who were helping another customer. She picked up her box of goodies for everyone back at the kitchen and headed out to her truck.

She stared up at the sky and wondered how she could be on the brink of what could be a fantastic, romantic relationship, while Taryn was on the brink of what could be an emotional disaster. She closed her eyes for a moment and sent up a short prayer for Taryn.

CHAPTER 17

Warnings

WHEN GRACE FINISHED passing out all of the donuts and cupcakes she grabbed Kam's arm and whispered in his ear, "Can I talk to you in your office?"

Kam grinned and nodded, putting his hand on the small of her back as they walked across the kitchen. She waited for him to shut the door and sat in the chair across from his desk.

"Thanks for the cronut," he said, popping the last bite in his mouth.

Grace waved her hand in the air and leaned forward. "Anything for you, Boss."

Kam frowned and shook his head. "*Kam.* I want you to call me, Kam. That's who I am to you. I don't want you to see me as just your boss."

Grace smiled and nodded her head. "Okay, *Kam.* I want to do something for a woman I'm worried about, but I need your help."

Kam nodded and leaned forward. "Of course. Anything. What can I do to help?"

Grace paused and smiled at Kam. There was no hesitation.

Someone needed help and he offered his assistance immediately. *Maybe she could love this guy.*

"It's Taryn Moore. I ran into her at the bakery and she's dying inside. Someone needs to knock some sense into her husband and I think you're the man for the job. You know him. You know Taryn. And if I'm not mistaken, you probably already know the situation too. She really wants to save her marriage, but she can't if they move across country and she has to deal with the fact that her husband is working with a woman who would love to break them up."

Kam closed his eyes and sat back as he pinched the bridge of his nose. "Gracie, getting in the middle of marital problems is the best way to get yourself beat up and lose a friend at the same time."

Grace snorted and shook her head. "Like anyone can beat you up. And what's the harm in having a heart to heart talk with a friend to help him out? Kam, *she loves him*," she said in a pleading voice. "And, this is killing her."

Kam sighed. "I know she does. And he loves her. But this is complicated and I think they need to work it out on their own."

Grace glared at Kam for a moment, irritated she wasn't getting her way. "She gave him an ultimatum. If he takes the job, their marriage is over. She says he's thinking about it."

Kam's eyes widened at that and he shook his head. "Crap."

Grace nodded. "Exactly my feelings. *Please?* I'll cover the dinner shift. I'll do everything. Just please, call Brogan and take him out for pizza and golf or something manly."

Kam gave her a half-smile and crossed his arms over his chest. "You're a little fixer, aren't you?"

Grace blinked in surprise. "I haven't ever thought about it, but I guess so. If someone's in pain, how can I stand by and just watch without doing something to help?"

Kam nodded slowly and smiled at her. "Okay, you've convinced me. I'll call Brogan right now."

Grace sighed and clasped her hands together. "You are the best, Kam," she said and stood up, walking around his desk and putting her arms around his shoulders, hugging him tightly.

Kam reached up with his hands, putting them on her arms as if to keep her in place. They stood like that for a long time before she pulled away. She stood up and looked at the door just in time to see Rob standing there, looking through the window, with his mouth hanging open.

She jumped away from Kam as he stood up and walked around the desk to open the door.

"Hey, Rob. Care to join us?" Kam said dryly.

Rob nodded his head, looking red in the face. "Uh, yeah, sure," he said and shut the door behind him. Rob motioned to the chair. "Grace, you might want to sit down for this."

Grace felt her face redden as she sat down. She glanced at Kam worriedly but he was smiling serenely at Rob as if he was caught hugging women in his office every day.

"Um, I'm glad you're uh, both here," he said, clearing his throat. "There's something I need to talk to you about."

Kam nodded. "Sure, Rob. We're on track for the Fine Dining experience coming up. The menu is set and I've ordered everything. Taryn told me that we're already over-booked."

Rob nodded and rubbed the back of his neck. "Yeah, this is more on a personal level. I just had lunch with my mother and she spent the good part of an hour trying to convince me to fire Grace."

Grace's face turned white and she felt her hands begin to shake as she stared at Rob's grim face.

"Aw, that's too bad," Kam said calmly, "Because if Grace goes, then I go too."

Rob rolled his eyes and leaned up against the wall. "Like

I'm going to fire anyone. Geez, Kam, as if I'm that stupid. No, I just wanted you two to be aware of the fact that my mom is on the war path. I don't know what's fired her up, but she's got a bee in her bonnet about Grace and wants her gone. She'll probably go to Taryn next since I shot her idea down. She's worried that you're going to date Grace and fall in love, etc. etc."

Kam turned and looked at her and smiled encouragingly. "Anne has always been overly emotional. She'll calm down in a few weeks."

Rob rolled his eyes. "Yeah, right. Because she's so good at calming down. Well, I just thought I'd warn you and give you my blessing, or whatever you want to call it. From what I can see, you two are well on your way to dating bliss," Rob said with a genuine smile on his face.

Grace bit her lip and looked up at Kam who was laughing softly.

"Rob, you crack me up. It was just a hug. You're acting like you caught Grace and I making out."

Rob rubbed his hands over his face. "Oh mercy. I'm betting I will at this rate. I need a vacation. Between you and Taryn, I deserve a week in Italy, far away from all of this drama."

"You'd miss it," Kam said and stood up, hugging Rob so tightly the man made a squeaking noise.

"You're breaking my ribs again," Rob shouted before Kam loosened his grip.

Kam laughed. "You're a good man, Rob. Give your mom a hug and kiss for me and don't worry about anything. Gracie is a good woman with a good heart. And you're welcome to let anyone know that we *are* dating and we're going to be dating for a long time and that's okay. Everything is okay," he said in a soothing voice.

Rob smiled and hugged Kam again. "Love you, Bro. I'm

happy for you. See you, Grace," he said and walked out of the office.

Kam walked over and pulled Grace up from her chair, hugging her next. Where Rob's first hug had been deathly tight, the hug she was getting was gentle and warm and an experience that she didn't want to end. He let her go a few moments later and smiled down into her face.

"Now, if you'll excuse me, I need to call a friend and invite him out to dinner."

Grace grinned and went up on tiptoe, kissing him on the cheek. "You are the best."

Kam grinned and pointed to the door. "Out before you start making out with me."

Grace laughed and walked out of the office feeling a hundred pounds lighter now that she knew Kam was willing to help Taryn and Brogan patch things up. She waved happily at Kam as he left a half an hour later to go home and shower before taking Brogan out.

It was hard taking over the running of the entire kitchen by herself, but she was happy to do it and worked extra hard. Thank heavens there were no complaints that night. She would hate to let Kam down. By the time she went to bed that night, she was tired but hopeful. Hopeful for Taryn and Brogan and hopeful for herself too.

CHAPTER 18

Brogan

KAM SAT ACROSS from Brogan at Tai's diner and watched his friend inhale his Cuban sandwich.

"Dude, when's the last time you ate? You look like you've lost at least fifteen pounds."

Brogan wiped his mouth on a napkin and took a sip of water. "Taryn hasn't been cooking much since we started marriage counseling. She uh, wants me to know what being a single dad is going to feel like, I guess," he said with a bitter twist of his mouth.

Kam frowned and took a bite of his Philly steak and cheese. "She might have a point, Brogan. At the rate you're going, you're going to be living off of fast food and canned chili."

Brogan frowned and stared at his hands before looking up.

"She told me if I take the job our marriage is over, Kam. How's a man to put up with an ultimatum like that?"

Kam shrugged and stared Brogan in the eye. "The girl you were involved with is with the company you want to work for. How could she live with that, Brogan? Have you thought of that?"

Brogan made a huffing sound and looked away. "I told her

it was over. I told her that it was nothing, just harmless flirting and chit chat. She needs to trust me when I tell her it won't happen again. It wasn't like I was unfaithful to her, Kam. Geez, she blew this whole thing up into something so huge and stupid, it infuriates me," Brogan said tightly, looking angry.

Kam shook his head, not understanding his friend at all.

"Let's see if you can put yourself in Taryn's shoes for a second. What if it was her and she'd gotten a job offer in New York, working at the same office with a man that you knew she'd been having an emotional affair with? How would that make *you* feel?"

Brogan glared at him and shook his head. "It's not the same thing at all and you're completely taking her side."

Kam raised an eyebrow. "There are no sides, Brogan. And I think we're all aware that emotional affairs are just as damaging as physical affairs, if not more so."

Brogan glared at his hands and then his face collapsed as he closed his eyes.

"I don't know what to do," he whispered. "I feel like the worst person in the world. I can't believe I've hurt Taryn so much. And now she looks at me like I'm a different person. I don't even know if she loves me anymore. I've ruined everything and now, all I want to do is leave. Leave here, leave the pain, leave the guilt and just start over."

Kam frowned. "Start over? *With this other woman?*"

Brogan groaned. "*No...* I don't know."

Kam grimaced wondering if knocking Brogan in the head would help clear his thinking. "As your friend, I'm going to be honest with you. You're ruining your life. Grow up and start acting like the man Taryn thought she was marrying. I don't know what's happened to you, but you've changed. The Brogan I used to know would never be acting like this or treating the woman he loves like she doesn't even matter."

Brogan ran his hands through his hair, making it stick up and for some reason, made him look even more like a lost model from New York.

"I don't disagree with anything you've just said. Just tell me what to do to make this nightmare go away."

Kam sighed and reached over the table and patted his friend on the shoulder. "That's step one. Admit you're being a jerk. Step two, go home and tell your wife you love her and tell her that you're *not taking that job*."

Brogan frowned and shook his head. "I can't do that. Taryn will never let me live this down. If I don't take this job, she'll look at me as weak."

Kam shrugged. "No, you've already proven that, Bro. This would be you proving you're strong. A strong man knows how and when to apologize. A strong man doesn't let pride get in the way of marriage and family."

Brogan groaned again. "It's like I've drawn my line in the sand and she and I won't cross it. We can't get to each other."

Kam felt like pulling his hair out. "Dude, she can't get to you because you've basically told her that you're picking another woman over her."

Brogan blinked a few times and shook his head. "Why is life so messed up? Life used to be so easy. Taryn and I were so in love and then one day I wake up and I look at my life and… *I'm bored*. There's nothing exciting or fun to look forward to. Taryn is so busy with work and our son that there's nothing left for me. I have no one."

Kam frowned at that, feeling a sliver of compassion. "Have you brought this up in counseling, Brogan?"

Brogan shook his head, sneering cynically. "A strong man like me actually talk about his feelings? You're kidding, right?"

Kam snorted. "You've got some weird ideas about what the definition of a strong man is. Bro, go home and love your wife.

Love your wife and *talk* to her. Tell her what you just told me. If you're willing to make changes for her, then I'm sure she'll be willing to make changes for you. It goes both ways."

Brogan nodded and tried to smile. "That's the dream anyways, right? But what if you're always the one to give in? What if you're the only one who's *ever* made changes? Taryn's such a force of nature that I *always* give in to her. And I'm just sick of it. If just once, she'd compromise for me, or put me first, or heck, even notice I was there, I don't know. I guess I'd be... *happy*."

Kam smiled. "Now we're getting somewhere. Talk to Taryn tonight but make another appointment with the marriage counselor tomorrow. There's hope."

Brogan made a hoarse sound that might have been a laugh. "That's the best thing I've heard all day. *Hope*. I thought I was out of that."

Kam smiled and talked to his friend for another hour before driving him home. He watched as Brogan walked through his door and shut it and put his hands in his pocket. Good marriages didn't always stay good. It took a lot of work, a lot of compromise, a lot of forgiving and a whole heck of a lot of not getting caught up in inappropriate relationships on social media.

Kam turned the key in his ignition and pulled out into the street. Thanks to Gracie he had the rest of his evening free and he knew just who he wanted to spend it with. He was heading home to his son.

*

Tai watched his cousin talk to Brogan Moore and shook his head at the changes he could see in Kam. He was talking, smiling and doing what looked like the best he could to knock some sense into a drowning man. He'd watched the past three years as Kam walked through life like a shadow of himself. The man he was seeing tonight? He was engaged. He was alive. He was Kam Matafeo, back from the shadows.

Cleo walked over to him and slipped her arms around his waist.

"Baby, he looks so good. He looks worried about Brogan, but beyond that, he looks happy. Do you know when he walked in, he smiled at me and gave me a hug," Tai said, his voice cracking.

Cleo nodded and rubbed Tai's back soothingly. "He's coming back to life. Now if we can just keep Meredith from ruining it," she said under her breath.

Tai frowned and turned to face his wife. "*What was that?*"

Cleo smiled brightly and waved her hand in the air. "It's nothing. Forget I said anything."

Tai took his wife gently by the arm and pulled her into the back room. "What is Meredith up to?" he demanded.

Cleo shrugged, looking helpless before sighing and sticking her hands in her back pockets. "Kit overheard Meredith and Anne plotting to ruin Grace's chances with Kam. They've even talked about making up lies about her to get her to leave town. They both don't think she's good enough for him. I don't think either one of them want to see Kam move on. Meredith's been acting, um, kind of possessive of Kam to be honest. I haven't said anything to you about it because we're worried that it will get back to Asher and cause her some marriage problems."

Tai frowned and turned his head to look at his cousin one more time. He watched as Kam stood up and gave Brogan a hug and patted his cheek as he spoke to him.

"Nah, my cousin is back. No one is shoving him back in the lonely dark again. I'll take care of this," Tai said and took off his apron.

Cleo's face whitened. "Wait, Tai. What are you going to do?"

Tai grabbed his car keys and his wallet and shook his head. "It's time Meredith paid attention to her own personal life and stayed out of Kam's."

Cleo covered her mouth with her hand as she watched Tai leave. "Crud," she whispered.

Tai drove over to Asher's house and knocked on the door. *Enough was enough.* Plotting to ruin his cousin's happiness? Yeah, not if he had anything to do with it.

Meredith opened the door and smiled at him. "Hey, Tai. Are you here to see Asher?"

Tai nodded brusquely. "Yeah, I'd like to talk to him if he's here."

Meredith smiled and looked over her shoulder. "Honey? Tai's here to see you. Come on in."

Tai shook his head. "No thanks. I'll wait out here."

Meredith frowned at him, tilting her head as she studied him. "You look upset. Is everything okay?"

Tai nodded. "It will be when I talk to Asher."

Meredith frowned at him and stepped aside as Asher came to the door.

"Hey, Man," Asher said, walking out on the porch and giving him knuckles. "Come on in. We haven't hung out in forever."

Tai nodded. "Actually, I was wondering if I could talk to you privately. Can you go for a walk with me?"

Asher looked back at Meredith. "I'll be back in a little while, Mer."

Tai walked down the steps, waiting for Asher to join him. He waited for Meredith to close the door but he could feel her gaze on him from the window.

"So what's up?" Asher asked, not wasting any time.

Tai sighed. Now that he was here with Asher, he wasn't sure how to say what needed to be said.

"Well, you've probably heard that Kam is interested in Grace Jackson, his new Sous Chef."

Asher grinned and nodded his head. "I heard. Garrett and Becket came over the other day and told me how happy Kam is. Like they had to convince me or something. They had a rugby game last Saturday and Kam didn't break even one bone. They said he actually smiled and joked around with everyone. Meredith doesn't seem to think it's a good idea, but everyone else seems to think it's awesome."

Tai nodded. "And what do you think?"

Asher shrugged. "If she can bring a smile back to his face, who am I to say anything about it? Nah, I think it's great. She's an amazing cook, too. I had her blackened salmon the other day for lunch and just about cried it was so good."

Tai smiled briefly. "Agreed. She's amazing. So here's the problem. A lot of people have noticed that Meredith isn't happy about Kam moving on with Grace. She was even over-heard talking to Anne about ways to break them up. Kit heard them plotting to make up lies about Grace so she'll leave town. None of us want to see that happen. Not now when Kam is happy again."

Asher stopped in his tracks and stared at him, frowning. "Wait, *what?* What are you saying, Tai? Are you saying that you think Meredith wants to break up Kam and Grace? That's crazy! Why would she even care? I mean, I know they used to date and everything, but that's insane."

Tai frowned, hating to hurt his friend. He put a hand on Asher's arm. "It is a little crazy. But it also scares me. I've seen my cousin smile for the first time in over three years. And buddy, I'll do anything to see that smile stay. Even if it means, talking to you about your wife's possessive feelings towards an ex-boyfriend," he said softly.

Asher's eyes widened as if he'd been punched in the gut.

"Don't say that," he said in a hard voice.

Tai sighed and let his hand drop. "Do you think I want to? Do you think I want to come over here and have this conversation with you? Dude, *please*, just talk to Meredith and let her know that we all know what she's doing and what she's been trying to do. Please tell her that we all want her to stop. Everyone who loves Kam *wants her to stop*. Kam's happiness and his healing are on the line and we don't want her to ruin it."

Asher's face turned hard as he stared at his feet. "You really think she feels possessive about Kam?" he asked in a quiet voice.

Tai licked his lips and stared up at the night sky. "Yeah, it looks that way. That doesn't mean she doesn't love you, Asher. It just means that there might be some lingering connection there that needs to be snipped. And as her husband, I hope you get the scissors out."

Asher nodded his head slowly. "Will do," he said and turned around, walking slowly back to his house without another word.

Tai watched his friend walk away and hurt for him. He walked back to his car and watched the shadows in the family room window walk back and forth. He couldn't hear any screaming. He didn't *want* Asher to scream at Meredith. He just wanted him to stop her before she did something irreversible.

When the lights turned off he got in his car and drove back to the diner. Hopefully Kam and Grace were safe from Meredith now. If not, he'd talk directly to Meredith and Anne too if needed. Family was everything to him and Kam's happiness was just as important to him as his own.

*

Meredith sat on the couch and stared at Asher in shock. "How *dare* you accuse me of having feelings for Kam?" she whispered, whisking angry tears off her cheeks.

Asher stared at her with his arms folded across his chest. "And here I was thinking it was time to start a family with you and this whole time you've been plotting with Anne to break up Kam and Grace. For what purpose, Meredith? So he could come back to *you*? Tell me, I'm curious."

Meredith looked away, feeling a wave of shame wash over her. *Why had she been trying to keep Kam and Grace apart?* It had all made so much sense when she was talking to Anne. But right now, with Asher staring at her with accusations in his eyes, she wasn't sure. She just knew in her heart, she didn't want Kam together with Grace. *She didn't want Kam together with anyone.* She could at least admit that. She licked her lips and looked at her lap. She had no excuses and it looked like Asher knew it.

"Look, this all sounds horrible and the spin Tai put on it puts me in a very bad light. He's making it seem as if I want to have an affair with Kam or something," she said with a brittle laugh, looking anywhere but at her husband. "I mean, it's beyond ridiculous. Besides, why *can't* I look out for Kam? Maybe I just want him to be with someone fantastic. Someone who's beautiful and smart and who would fit in with his life here in Fircrest. From everything I've seen, Grace isn't that person," she said with an automatic sneer as the image of Grace popped up in her head. Her cute, spunky personality and that big smile that lit up her face. *Gag.*

"You've seen her, Asher. She's just not that cute. I mean, look at me. I make sure my hair and make-up are perfect if I'm going to be seen in public. She puts her hair up in a rubber band. Rayne and Ivy think she has a great smile, but *really*? Seriously, get some braces. Major snaggle tooth on the left side. She's just not what I would picture for Kam. I mean, of course

I set the standard pretty high, *but Grace?* Seriously, if not me, then someone needs to do an intervention with Kam."

Asher closed his eyes as if he were in pain. "Holy crap, Tai's right," he said softly to himself. "You're still not over Kam. My wife isn't over her ex-boyfriend. And here I am planning to put an addition on our house so we can have a nursery. What an epic joke on me," he said and sat down in a chair on the opposite side of the room as if he were exhausted.

Meredith gasped and stood up, rushing to his side, kneeling down in front of him and taking his hands in hers.

"*Asher!* It's not like that at all. I *am* over Kam. I promise. I was just worried is all. It's nothing. I swear I won't say another word about Grace. I won't even talk to Anne about her anymore. It's over. Please, please, don't think these horrible things about me," she begged.

Asher refused to look at her and stood up. "I'm going to bed. Tomorrow I have a lot of meetings and then I'll be having dinner at my brother's house. I probably won't see you until late. Don't wait up for me."

Meredith stood up, tears steaming down her face as she stared at him in shock. "Stop, Asher. Don't act like this. This is nothing. I *want* the nursery. I *want* to start a family with you. Please don't listen to Tai."

Asher stared at her sadly. "I'm *not* listening to Tai. I'm listening to *you*. And just for the record, Grace Jackson is beautiful. Not in a fake, manufactured way, but in a good, sweet and kind, from the inside way. Everyone sees it but you. Goodnight, Meredith."

Meredith collapsed on the chair and sobbed into her hands. This was not what she'd planned. Not even close.

CHAPTER 19

Book Club

ALL OF THE women sat at the large, round table The Iron Skillet used for company meetings occasionally and which Rob let them use for their monthly book club. Everyone was there, Layla, Kit and Jane, Rayne, Ivy and Cleo, along with Posey, Wren, Taryn and Maya.

"I feel bad not having Grace here," Jane said, pouting as she took a big bite of her crab cake.

Wren nodded as she took a sip of her lemonade. "Let's move it to Monday and she could totally do it. We'd just have to switch it to Tai's Diner or the Mexican place."

Posey cleared her throat. "Um, did we forget to invite Meredith? She usually comes to book club."

All of the women stared across the table at each other with identical unhappy frowns.

Taryn raised her hand. "I was the one who sent out the group text. I forgot to include her. *On purpose.*"

Layla winced and clasped her hands in front of her on the table. "Well, it would be a little awkward to have a conversation on how to protect Grace and Kam from Meredith if she's sitting right there listening in."

Cleo cleared her throat and leaned forward as everyone turned to look at her. "Well, remember I was going to tell Tai what was going on so he could help out? Well, after thinking about it, I decided against it because I was worried about Meredith's marriage. Well, I let it slip last night. Tai was just standing there, looking at Kam and Brogan having dinner and he was so happy that Kam was back, you know. So I let it slip. Tai was gone in less than five minutes. He talked to Asher about what Meredith's been up to."

The sound of gasps filled the room and Cleo winced staring at all the shocked faces. "He says Asher was very calm about it and that he followed him home and waited outside in case there was any yelling. He said he could tell they'd talked a little but then the lights went out and they must have gone to bed. It's possible Asher didn't even say anything to her."

Maya shook her head. "I think he must have. Meredith was in my hot yoga class this morning and I could swear she was crying the whole time. I asked her if she was okay and she just said she was extra sweaty."

Everyone turned and looked at Jane. Jane rolled her eyes and pulled out her phone. "Fine, I'll text her."

Everyone waited silently, sipping on water and munching on their crab cakes as Jane waited for a response. A few minutes later she held up her phone.

"She says, I'm fine. Just not feeling that great is all. Oh and don't count on me for book club this month. I'm busy right now with work. TTYL"

Jane frowned at her phone and put it down. "Meredith loves book club. She must know that we're all upset with her for what she's been up to."

Kit shrugged. "*Good.* I hope she does feel shame and remorse for what she's done. Nothing wrong with that. I mean, why all the sad faces? Seriously, we should be toasting Tai and the guts it took to stick up for his cousin."

Taryn sighed. "As someone who has struggled with their marriage lately, I don't wish it on anyone."

Layla nodded. "I think we can have enough compassion for the fact that Meredith made a mistake that's making her miserable right now."

Wren pushed a long strand of strawberry blond hair out of her eyes. "I'm with Kit. Meredith needs to grow up. Meredith also needs to figure out her past so she can focus completely on her husband and maybe this needed to happen for her to get closure. And last but not least, Meredith can be a brat. If she knows that the whole town knows about her and Anne, then that's okay. Actions have consequences. She's in her late twenties and she thinks it's okay to act like she's still in Junior high."

Jane winced. "So harsh, Wren."

Posey frowned at Jane. "No she's not. Wren's right. Pain's a good teacher. This experience might be the catalyst that Meredith needed to become a better person and wife."

Layla raised her hand. "Okay, Meredith will now be dealing with her consequences. Moving on. We still have Anne on the warpath though."

Taryn sighed loudly, "Rob told me yesterday that he and my mom had lunch and for over an hour she tried to convince him to fire Grace. Of course he didn't but she's going to be a harder nut to crack. She's *not* hung up on Kam. She's angry that Kam's moving on from my sister."

The group of women all stared at each other with hopeless eyes.

Kit reached for a second crab cake. "Well, what can she really do? She obviously can't get Grace fired. Any gossip that she tries to spread about her has to go through us and we won't be spreading it. I don't think we have anything to worry about."

All the women looked at Kit doubtfully. Rayne raised her hand and everyone turned and stared at her.

"Garrett's working on the landscaping on her house. I could have him feel her out and see if she's still dangerous."

Ivy nodded. "I'm helping them plant some flowers tomorrow. She always brings out drinks to everyone. I know she'll talk to me. I'll text everyone and let you know what she says."

Jane shook her head. "Why do I have a bad feeling about this?"

Layla rolled her eyes. "Because we're talking about Anne Matafeo, that's why."

Taryn glared at Layla. "Hey, that's my mom. She might be crazy, but she's still my mom."

Layla grimaced. "Sorry."

Wren cleared her throat loudly. "Okay, enough of Meredith and Anne. Does anyone know if the romance is heating up between Grace and Kam or are they still in the friend zone? I would hate to see all of our worrying go to waste."

Jane grinned and drummed her hands on the table. "Ladies, I'm pleased to inform you that they are going dancing tomorrow night after work."

Everyone began clapping and shouting. A few waiters and waitresses peeked their heads into the conference room, so they quieted down.

Wren laughed in relief. "This is fantastic news. I know Kam's an amazing dancer. They're going to have so much fun. I can just see the sparks flying now."

Taryn frowned a little and took a sip of water. "But sparks die. The question is, how to turn those sparks into a bonfire? I love my sister, Bailey, but watching Kam be so lonely and miserable is nothing she'd want for him. And it breaks my heart that Nate doesn't have a mommy to look out for him. They need Grace. But romance? It's not what's it's cracked up to be," she said, twisting her wedding ring around her finger.

All of the women turned and looked with compassion at Taryn. Ivy who was sitting next to her, put an around her shoulders and gave her a hug.

"This group is made up of women of action. You say the word and we'll break Brogan's knee caps. Or at least, I'll have Becket do it."

Taryn laughed and shook her head. "No, he actually came home last night from having dinner with Kam and he was different. He wasn't so angry and mean. He was actually kind of nice and sweet. We have another appointment with our marriage counselor next Tuesday."

Layla smiled at that. "That's fantastic news. It sounds like he's had a change of heart. And you said he had dinner with Kam last night? *Wow*."

"Wow, what?" Taryn said.

Layla shook her head. "Nothing, it's just that we've all seen Kam in a fog for the past three years. If he's putting himself out there and reaching out to a friend to help him, then that's a sign right there. Our boy is back."

The women all smiled happily and gave each other high fives.

"You know, even if Grace and Kam don't end up together, she's still brought him back to life. Maybe these two will just be good friends?" Rayne suggested.

Jane frowned and shook her head. "Nah, way too much chemistry. She thinks he's hot."

Kit grinned. "She thinks me, Layla and Jane are witches. *Love* witches."

Posey frowned. "That's so unfair. Why don't we all get to be love witches?"

Kit glared at Posey. "But I already ordered the t-shirts. Just three of them. Bright pink with bedazzled black lettering and a witch's hat. I designed them myself."

All of the women glared at Kit. "You better order more or you Belinda witch girls aren't invited to the next book club meeting," Cleo threatened.

Jane stood up and raised her hands to get everyone to quite down. "No burning the witches at the stake here. I'll order more t-shirts but seriously, where are we going to wear them?"

Ivy laughed. "Easy. To Grace's bridal shower of course."

The women grinned and congratulated themselves and didn't once bring up the book they were supposed to have read that month.

CHAPTER 20

Disowned

PULE STARED AT Kam dumbfounded. "What do you mean, you're going dancing?"

Kam glared at his little brother and remembered all the reasons his mom would be sad if he hurt him.

"I didn't realize I wasn't allowed to go dancing," he said dryly and went back to his computer. If he didn't get the order for next week's seafood in, no one would be enjoying scallops or salmon or crab cakes.

"So who are you going dancing *with*?" Pule persisted, putting his feet up on Kam's desk, automatically making Kam's blood pressure go up a few more degrees.

"Someone. Are we done here? I need to get back to work," Kam said, motioning for the door.

Pule grinned and shook his head, obviously enjoying himself. "Uh, uh. So let me guess. Grace Jackson, you're cute little Sous Chef, who I hear from Tate, likes to bring you treats all the time."

Kam closed his eyes for a moment and counted to five. "Yeah, I'm taking Grace. There's no need to make a big deal about this. Geez, you act like I've never gone on a date before."

Pule's eyes dimmed a little and his feet came down as he leaned over his brother's desk. "No, I think it's great. And to answer your question, I'd go to Cloud Nine. It's a newer club so you probably wouldn't know about it. I'll text you the address."

Kam nodded his head in thanks. "See you later, Pule. Be good."

Pule stood up and shook his head. "You know, I'm not nine anymore. You don't have to tell me to be good."

Kam's eyes softened as he stared up at the large man who all in all was a good guy who'd had his back these past few years. "I know, Pule. It's just habit. That's how I tell you I love you, man."

Pule walked around and hugged his brother. "Love you too, Bro. Now don't have too much fun Saturday night," he said and yanked softly on Kam's ponytail before walking out.

Kam smiled and looked back at his computer screen before jumping up and hurrying out of his office just in time to see Pule cornering Grace by the stove.

"Yeah, I remember you from the party at my mom and dad's house. So tell me more about yourself. Any prior arrest records? Any unfinished relationships back in Seattle."

"Pule!" Kam barked, making Pule jump and look around guiltily.

Grace's eyes were wide as she looked around his brother to stare at him.

"I'm guessing it's protocol to do background checks before dating you, huh?" she asked with a twinkle in her eye.

Kam relaxed a little but didn't stop glaring at Pule. Scaring off his girl. *His brother was going to die.*

"You have ten seconds to disappear and then it's going to hurt. I promise you," he said softly.

James and Manuel whistled loudly and Pule grinned unrepentantly.

"Just looking out for my brother," he said and then left out the back door before he could reach nine.

Kam walked over to Grace and put a hand on her shoulder. "Sorry about that. My little brother can be a pain. Just part of the Matafeo legacy. It's tradition that every generation has their own version of Pule. My dad had Sefe, my uncle. He's a trial but we love him."

Grace laughed and continued to stir her bouillabaisse. "I'm jealous you have a brother that likes to tease you. I don't even know what that's like. But it sounds like he's just being protective of you. And to clear the air. No arrest records ever, although when I was ten I did shoplift a few candy bars. That's it, I swear."

Kam frowned. "Did you return the candy bars?"

Grace's mouth opened before she looked up at the ceiling and winced. "Yeah, *no*. I ate them. You're judging me now, I can see it in your eyes."

Kam laughed and shook his head, enjoying teasing her. "Not at all. Just don't tell my brother Tate that story. He might still want to lock you up. Pule would help him."

Grace bit her lip and looked back at her pot. "You have a such a big family and they all care about you, I can tell. Are they going to be okay with you asking me out?"

Kam shrugged and leaned his hip on the stove next to her. "They're welcome to care about me, but I make up my mind who I date. They've all been trying for the past year and a half to set me up with all the single girls in Fircrest. I think they'll all be thrilled when they find out we're dating."

Grace's eyebrows went up a little at that. Dating? She wasn't sure going dancing on Saturday night meant they were dating but she wouldn't argue with him. *Yet.* She'd wait to see if he was a good kisser first.

"Well, I'm excited for tomorrow night. I bought a new

dress and shoes," she said smiling happily to herself. "I haven't had the chance to really dress up in a long time, so I'm going to make the most of this date," she said with a wink.

Kam laughed and touched her shoulder. "I can't wait," he said and walked back to his office.

*

After finishing up his orders, he helped Grace and Candice with the dinner rush. By nine o'clock, he was getting tired though and looking at the clock.

"Hey, Kam. Table twelve wants to see you."

Kam frowned, turning around to see a new waiter they'd just hired looking at him nervously.

"I don't go out," he said unemotionally and went back to his sauté pan, where he was putting a nice color on his scallops.

"They're insisting. And they said if you refused to come out that they'd complain to the owner."

Kam's eyebrows went up at that. "They're threatening me?" he asked and felt Grace walk up next to him.

"I'll go out," she said quickly, taking off her apron.

The waiter shook his head and pointed to Kam. "They said they didn't want to talk to the Sous Chef. They want Kam."

Kam growled but took off his apron, stomping out of the kitchen and into the dining area. Some days he hated being a chef. He rounded the corner and spotted the table and stopped.

Just one person.

Anne Matafeo. *Bailey's mother.*

He walked slowly to the table, waving to everyone who was calling out his name. He crossed his arms over his chest as he stared at his mother-in-law and shook his head.

"Anne, we talked on the phone just yesterday afternoon. What is it you want?" he asked bluntly, not wanting to hurt

Anne, but getting mighty tired of Anne's insistence on sticking her nose into his business.

"Have a seat," she said, pointing to the chair in front of her.

Kam glanced at his watch. "Two minutes, Anne. That's it."

Anne frowned at him and pushed her plate away. She'd ordered the lasagna as usual with a side salad and bread sticks.

"I'm not happy with the way our conversation went yesterday and you don't seem to be answering my texts anymore. So this is what I have to resort to."

Kam shrugged and sat down. "I have nothing left to say on the subject, Anne. I'm sorry that you're upset that I'm dating Grace, but I'm sure that when you think about it, you'll see that it's a good thing for me and my son."

Anne glared at Kam and banged her palm on the table. "Well, it's not good for *me*. What would Bailey think? Huh? What would she think of you taking up with some Sous Chef?"

Kam almost smiled. *Taking up?* "Anne, Bailey had a very loving and giving heart. I know she wants me and Nate to be happy. The only person in this town who doesn't, seems to be you."

Anne blinked at that and glared some more. "It has nothing to do with happiness and everything to do with decency. How can you honor my daughter's memory if you're in love with another woman? I thought you promised to love Bailey forever?"

Kam closed his eyes at the automatic slam of pain to his heart. "I did promise that and I still do. I'll always love Bailey, Anne. Nothing could ever change that," he said softly. "And I honor Bailey every day by doing the best I can to raise our son to be happy and healthy."

Anne sniffed and took a drink of water. "Well, I don't approve of this and I never will. If you keep moving forward with this relationship, I'll never speak to you again. You'll be dead to me."

Kam frowned and shook his head, in awe at the lengths Anne would go to get her way. "So that means that you'll be shutting Nate out of your life then as well, right?"

Anne's mouth dropped open and her eyes went wide. But she slowly nodded her head. "Nate needs his grandmother. He needs me and if you do this, then yes, *you're* the one responsible for pushing me out of his life."

Kam shook his head slowly. "I'm not pushing you, Anne. You're the one making the ultimatums and leaving our lives."

"Uh, what's going on here, Mom?"

Kam looked up to see Rob and Taryn standing next to the table. He motioned to their mother and stood up, pushing the chair back in.

"I've just been informed by your mother that she will never speak to me or Nate again if I date Grace," he said dryly, looking at Anne and noting the red splotches on her cheeks.

Taryn gasped and Rob groaned.

"Kam, I'm so sorry. Mom's not been in her right mind lately. She doesn't mean it," Rob rushed to say.

Taryn clenched her hands into fists. "Mom, I swear if you don't knock it off, Rob and I will stop talking to *you* and see how you feel."

Anne pounded her fist on the table. "I will not be spoken to like this," she said shrilly.

Rob shook his head, looking embarrassed and upset. "But you think it's totally fine to talk to Kam this way? This has to stop," he said.

Kam looked at Taryn, Rob, and Anne one last time before walking back to the kitchen without another word. He loved the Downings with all of his heart, but *man oh man* were they a lot of work.

He went back to work by Grace's side and began to relax as she serenaded him to Rob Thomas's song, *Hold on Forever*. He could feel all of his stress and anxiety over Anne melt away as he began humming along to the song. Every time Grace hit the high note, she'd pause and close her eyes and he'd have to watch her food to make sure it didn't burn.

He loved it.

Driving home that night, he smiled to himself thinking that in less than twenty-four hours he and Grace would be on their first official date. He went to sleep that night with a smile on his face.

CHAPTER 21

Jocelyn

GRACE WOKE UP the next day feeling excited for the evening. It had been at least five months since she'd been on a date. Being a chef meant dating was never easy. Not many guys wanted to wait around until ten thirty or eleven to begin their date with someone who was exhausted.

She walked to her closet and pulled out her apricot wrap dress that went to her knees and was very flattering if she did say so herself. She picked up her new shoes she'd found at the Rose boutique yesterday and sighed in pleasure. She didn't often spoil herself but when she did, she sure enjoyed it. She took the dress and held it up to herself in the full length mirror and twirled a little.

Her glossy hair swished around her shoulders and the color in her face let her know what she already knew. She was very excited for this date. Most of the time when she was asked out, she never really enjoyed it. She was either stressed out, wondering if the guy really liked her, or she was insecure and wondering the whole time if she looked okay, or she was dreading the party they were going to. But tonight was different. Tonight, she was going out with someone she truly liked and respected and someone she had fun with and could relax with and be herself.

That and *he was so good looking*. She put a hand on her stomach to keep it from jumping around. She couldn't remember the last time she'd felt butterflies for anyone. Grace frowned at her reflection. *Well, it was about time.* She was going to soak up all the butterflies she could.

She didn't have to be to work until one today. She could go see an early movie or clean her house. *Or* she could take Baby down to Point Defiance and hang out by the water. She'd been so busy with moving in and getting settled she hadn't really taken any time to enjoy the Puget Sound. Her life in Seattle had been too busy to spend very much time enjoying the water. But that's why she'd moved here, to slow down and to find her place.

She lay her dress down on the bed and turned to Baby. "Want to take a picnic to the beach?"

Baby jumped up and barked. That was a yes. She threw on some shorts even though it was only seventy-two degrees and grabbed Baby's beloved Frisbee. "Just need to stop by Belinda's for my pesto sandwich and we'll be on our way."

The drive down to the bakery only took a few minutes. She told Baby to stay in the back of her truck and ran up the steps to the bakery, flinging open the door and taking in the delicious smells.

"Man, I love this place," she said aloud.

"Man, you're annoying."

Grace opened her eyes to see Meredith staring at her unhappily.

"Ignore her. She has marriage problems because she's still hung up on her ex," Kit said, sounding snappy from behind the counter.

Meredith turned back to Kit and stuck her tongue out. "You're a brat, Kit Hunter and you've always been a brat. Stay out of my business and stop gossiping about me."

Kit shrugged. "When you plot to destroy someone's happiness, *for instance*, Grace's here, then I think it's okay for friends to step in and stop the crazy."

Meredith began breathing fast and her knuckles were turning white on the bakery box she was holding. "You are such a witch. You don't know anything about it. If you and all of the other brats had stayed out of it, life would be just fine. Now it's a hot mess because of all of you busy bodies."

Kit opened her mouth to say something but stopped when Jane came out of the back room holding a pan of éclairs.

"Hi, Meredith," Jane called out, not realizing that crap was going down.

Grace shuffled away from Meredith in case she decided to attack.

"Jane, you're just in time. Meredith was calling me to repentance for being a gossiping busybody and not allowing her to lie and destroy Kam and Grace's happiness."

Jane put the tray down on the counter and stared at Grace first and then Meredith and then Kit as the horror on her face grew. "*Okaaaay*. Grace? Will you turn the sign to CLOSED. I don't want any customers coming in on all of this drama."

Grace did as she was told and flipped the sign to CLOSED as Meredith glanced at her with cold fury.

"*She's* the one you want Kam to be with?" she said, pointing to her as if she was a homeless person with a police record.

Grace frowned and put her hands on her hips. "Look, Barbie Doll, you don't know me. You don't get to judge me. If Kam and I want to go out on a date, then that's between him and me. You know it's true. You are acting like a weird, possessive ex-girlfriend." she said with a shake of her head.

Jane blinked in surprise as Kit smiled at her and gave her a thumb's up. Meredith on the other hand opened the box of cupcakes she was holding and picked up a large chocolate one.

"I can't stand you," Meredith said with a bright smile. "You blow into town and everyone's *oohing* and *ahhing* over the cute little Sous Chef and there goes Kam, acting like an idiot over you. So yeah, I think I *will* judge you. I don't like you and I think your cooking stinks," she said and licked some icing off the edge of her cupcake.

Grace's eyes narrowed. *Such a low blow.* "That's not what your husband said yesterday when he asked me to come to his table. He said he loved my cooking and thought I was wonderful. How's your marriage doing, by the way?" she asked with an identical bright smile to match Meredith's.

Meredith put her cupcake down, her smile now gone as she glared at Grace and then turned back to glare at Jane and Kit.

"Not so great thanks to all the women in town who like to ruin marriages," she said looking like what she was, a miserable woman looking for someone beside herself to blame.

Kit sighed and leaned her elbows on the counter. "Ironic, considering you didn't hesitate to plot with Anne to ruin Kam's chances with Grace."

Meredith rolled her eyes. "It's completely different. Anne and I actually care about Kam and want the best for him and Nate. All you guys want to do is gossip and hurt people and stick your noses into places you don't belong."

Jane frowned and walked around the counter coming to stand in front of her friend. "Mer, if you truly believe that then you don't really know me or any of the other women in this town. We didn't want to hurt you, that's why Cleo waited so long to tell Tai what you were up to. It was Tai who made the decision to tell Asher. Kam's family wants him to be happy. We all do. Why can't you see that?"

Meredith wiped a few tears off her cheeks. "I can see just fine, thank you. But now that I do, Asher isn't talking to me and I haven't even seen him for three days. He's gone before I wake up in the morning and he comes home at night after I've gone to sleep. So I hope you're all happy. I'm probably going to be served divorce papers soon."

Kit rolled her eyes. "Stop being so overdramatic. Get over Kam and then go apologize to your husband. He's hurt and betrayed. Do something about it."

Meredith groaned. "Easier said than done, you brat. But now that you've fixed Kam's life, you can all figure out how to fix mine."

Jane nodded her head and grasped Meredith's shoulder. "We will. None of us want to hurt you or see you unhappy, Mer. Whatever we can do to help, we will."

Meredith sighed and nodded. "I'll hold you to that. Now, if you'll excuse me, I have to go eat all of these cupcakes."

She turned to walk past Grace and stopped, her hand on the door. "Look, I'm sorry for saying those things just now. You're probably okay and I um, I guess you're kind of cute in your own unique way. You should really think of braces though. But if you make Kam happy, then... whatever," she said stiffly.

Grace smiled and nodded her head, accepting the apology. "For what it's worth, I hope that everything works out with you and Asher. He's a great guy *and* super cute."

Meredith glared at her. "Keep your hands off my husband. You've already taken my ex-boyfriend. Geez," she said and stomped out the door.

Grace's mouth fell open in shock as the door shut. "Can you believe her? *Keep your hands off my husband?*"

Jane shook her head and pulled her over to the counter. "Just ignore her, she likes to get the last word in."

Kit sighed. "She's exhausting. But the good news is that

she's been neutralized, *thank you Tai Matafeo*. So your date tonight should be fantastic and perfect. I hear dancing is on the agenda."

Grace grinned and stared at all of the wonderful creations in the cases. "It is. The only dancing I do is in the kitchen, so I hope I don't embarrass myself tonight with Kam. From what I can tell, he's a good dancer."

Jane nodded. "He's one of the best. You're are going to be in date heaven. Now, what can we get you?"

Grace ordered a lunch to go and chatted with Kit for a few minutes while Jane rang her up. The bell rang over the door and Kit's face froze.

Grace turned around slowly to see Anne Matafeo and Sefe walking in, talking with their heads together.

Kit leaned over and grabbed her arm. "Go out through the back door in the kitchen. *Hurry*, I'll distract them," she hissed.

Jane shoved her bag at her and Grace hurried around the counter and through the doors into the kitchen. She didn't even stop to talk to Layla as she made a dash for the door.

Grace felt her heart beating fast as she drove down to Point Defiance. Running into Meredith was one thing. Running into Anne Matafeo the day of her date with Kam was just too much to deal with.

She turned up the radio and tried to relax as she sang to James Arthur's *Say You Won't Let Go*. She found a parking spot and whistled for Baby as she jumped out of her truck. She found a sunny section of sand close to the water and laid out her old, beach blanket. She threw the Frisbee to Baby for a half an hour and then walked her up and down the beach before taking out her paperback book and getting comfortable as Baby barked at all the seagulls and chased leaves over the sand.

"*Whatchya reading there?*"

Grace looked up, shading her eyes from the sun to see Pule

Matafeo and Posey standing beside her. She sat up and smiled, showing them the cover of her book. "Romance. I'm a happily ever after kind of girl."

Posey sighed and took the book from her. "This is one of my favorites. Oh my word, you have to read the sequel. It gets even better."

Grace laughed and took the book back. "I didn't even know there was a sequel. And I will. How are you two lovebirds doing this fine day?"

Pule kissed Posey's hand. "It's always a perfect day when you're with the one you love."

Posey sighed and stepped closer to Pule as if she wanted to kiss him but was holding back. "I can't argue with that. Speaking of love. I hear you have a date."

Grace laughed and sat cross legged. "I think everyone in town knows I have a date tonight."

Pule smiled happily at her. "Welcome to Fircrest. But to be honest, we probably wouldn't all be so nosy but you're dating my brother and we're all revved up about it."

Grace swallowed. *Yikes, no pressure.* Just the whole town excited about her going on a date. Baby walked up and woofed at the strangers. Pule and Posey knelt down and made friends with Baby, and Grace automatically liked them even more.

"I don't know, Pule. I bet we'd be just as nosey even if she was dating Manuel or James," Posey said laughing as Baby licked her face.

Grace groaned and Pule shook his head. "Why would she date those guys when she could date a Matafeo? Kam's the greatest man in Fircrest and possibly Tacoma. Present company excluded. Seriously, Grace, you're a lucky girl."

Posey sighed and stood up, brushing the sand off her knees. "Okay, you don't have to sell the poor girl on your big brother. She already said yes to the date. We'll let you get back to your book. But good luck tonight," she said and waved as she pulled Pule away.

Grace waved them off and sat back on her elbows as she enjoyed the breeze off the water and the sight of the waves hitting the sand. She closed her eyes and let all of the breath out of her lungs and then she felt it. *Relaxation.* There was just something special and healing about being near the water.

Life before adulthood hadn't been very relaxing or peaceful, so she treasured the moments of peace as much as she could. She heard the chirp of her phone and rolled on her stomach to grab it.

Hey, heard you moved down to Fircrest. Me and Billy will be by to see you tomorrow. That's probably your day off, right? We'll need a place to stay for a few days. A few weeks at the most. See you soon! Mom

Grace sat up, all relaxation and peace now completely gone as she stared in horror at her phone. She'd done a pretty good job of building boundaries between herself and her mother but every now and then Jocelyn Jackson would sneak in, rip things to shreds and then take off, not to be heard of for a year or two or three.

"This can not be happening to me," she whispered. "And who the heck is *Billy?*"

Grace closed her eyes and groaned before looking at her phone again.

Hey, Mom. Good to hear from you. I'm looking forward to seeing you since it's been so long, but I can't offer you a place to stay. I'd be happy to help you find a hotel though.

She looked at her text critically and then pushed send before she changed her mind. Two seconds later, she got reply.

Haha, funny. See you tomorrow. Can't wait to take a shower and eat some of your amazing food.

Grace frowned at her phone, remembering all of the emotional trauma she'd experienced as a child and teen from her mother's whirlwind lifestyle and constantly changing men. She began breathing fast as the stress crept into her neck and shoulders.

"Unreal," she whispered, as Baby nudged her arm with her nose, whimpering as she sensed her turmoil.

She practiced her deep breathing exercises her old therapist had taught her as she spoke empowering mantras to protect herself from this kind of situation.

"I am strong. I am good. I am light. I am beautiful. Nothing and no one can harm me. I am safe. I am okay," she said over and over again.

Five minutes later, she could do it.

No. This is not okay, Mom. You and Billy can NOT stay with me. I'd be happy to meet you somewhere to catch up, but anything else is out of the question. No discussion.

She re-read her text and sighed, hating that this was what her relationship with her mother had come to, but knowing that for her own emotional well-being, this is the way it had to be.

She stared at her phone and jumped when it chirped, signaling a new text.

One little poop emoji.

Which could mean anything. It could mean that her mother was respecting her wishes or it could mean, *haha, poop is on you because me and my biker boy, Billy are going to be there to trash your house and smoke things that shouldn't legally be smoked and then get you fired and thrown out of your new apartment.*

Grace flung herself back on her blanket as Baby lay her head on her chest. She stared at the blue sky above her until her alarm beeped. She had just enough time to get back home and get ready for work. She blinked in surprise and remembered she got to see Kam soon and that she was lucky enough to be going on a hot date later. All she had to do was control her mom and life would be perfect.

CHAPTER 22

The Date

KAM WATCHED GRACE work efficiently and quickly as she plated meal after beautiful meal. But she wasn't dancing. She wasn't smiling. And she wasn't having fun. She looked lost in her thoughts. *Thoughts that weren't about him.* Or their date later that night. Nope, definitely sad thoughts.

He frowned and looked at the clock. They were having a nice lull. Maybe he should force her to take a ten-minute break?

"Grace, come keep me company in my office while I take a break," he said, taking off his apron and grabbing a cold water bottle for both of them.

Grace blinked in surprise as if she was coming out of a daze. She smiled in thanks and took her apron off too.

He opened the door to his office for her and waited while she sat down. He took a long draw from his water bottle and then sat back, smiling at her.

"What's going on, Gracie? You look sad and you never look sad," he said softly.

Grace bit her lip and looked over his shoulder as if she was thinking of what to say. She shook her head and reached for her phone, opening it and looking at something that made her eyes go dark.

"I guess I am a little sad. I got a text from my mom today while I was down by the water. She wants to stop by with her newest boyfriend for a few days or a few weeks which probably means a few months. And I *can't*. I can't do it. Not this time. I'm happy. I'm doing great. I have a job and I have a date with my super hot boss and I'm happy. *I can't*... I can't allow all of the toxic bad crazy back in my life. I told her I'd be happy to see her for lunch, but that she couldn't stay with me."

Kam's eyes widened at the information. "Doesn't sound like a very stable parent."

Grace snorted and shook her head, rubbing her temples. "Stable is not in Jocelyn Jackson's vocabulary. If she's not living by the seat of her pants and creating some kind of havoc, then she's not really living."

Kam frowned and looked down at his hands. "How can I help?"

Grace shook her head and took a sip of water. "I don't think anyone can help me," she said quietly. "I moved out the day I turned eighteen and that was the best day of my life. I've been in therapy for years trying to unravel all of the bad and keep the good. And I'm in a good place. I'm strong, I'm happy and I'm stable. But keeping my mother at bay, sometimes that's an impossible task and then I'm left to clean up the mess she leaves behind."

Kam sighed. "You can always say no and keep saying no."

Grace finally looked him in eyes and shook her head slowly. "You haven't met Jocelyn. No one can tell her anything. Least of all no. But I did today. She responded with, *ha ha* and a poop emoji."

Kam rubbed his chin. "She doesn't know where you live or where you work though, right?"

Grace shook her head. "I'm not that dumb."

Kam nodded. "Meet her for lunch at my parent's home. We're having a family dinner tomorrow and you were invited anyways. By the way, my parents will be offended if you don't come. She can meet you there so she won't know where you live or work. And if anything gets out of hand, then you have me and my whole family to back you up."

Grace looked at him, blinking her eyes quickly as her lips trembled. "*Back-up?* I've never had that before," she said softly.

Kam smiled at her and stood up, opening his arms to her. "Well, you do now. More back up then you'll ever need. No one messes with the Matafeos."

Grace stood up and walked into his arms, feeling safe for the first time since she'd gotten her mom's text. "One problem. I'm not a Matafeo," she said quietly.

Kam laughed softly to himself. He'd forgotten for a moment she wasn't.

"Well, you've been adopted into the Matafeo clan. You're one of us now and that means we look out for you. Text your mom and give her my parents' address and tell her dinner's at one. We'll be proactive with the situation so she's not the one calling the shots."

Grace sighed happily, still leaning her head against Kam's strong chest. "Okay. And thanks, Kam. You might not have saved my life, but you just saved my sanity. I owe you."

Kam frowned and pulled back. "You don't owe me anything, Gracie. You mean a lot to me. I'd do anything I could to help you," he said, looking deep into her eyes.

Grace stared up into his big brown eyes and knew if she went up on her tiptoes and he leaned down just a teeny little bit, she could kiss him. Kam leaned his head just a little bit closer to hers and she moved up, her lips just a breath away

... and then the door opened with a bang.

"Oh, uh,… *crap*. Sorry to interrupt what looks like could have been an amazing kiss, but we've got an emergency."

Grace and Kam sprung apart to see Rob standing in the doorway looking tense.

"What is it?" Kam demanded looking worried.

"Meredith and Asher are in a screaming match right now in the middle of the restaurant. I don't want to call the cops on them since they're friends but no one can calm them down and people are complaining and some people are even leaving. Since it's about *you*, I was wondering if maybe you could fix this?" Rob said glancing at her apologetically.

Kam glanced at her with a wince and nodded before following Rob out of his office. Grace walked out of the office and ran to Candice's side.

"Can you cover for us for a few more minutes? I want to see what's going on," Grace whispered hurriedly.

Candice nodded. "There's so much drama going on, there are no orders. That and people are leaving. Go snoop and then let me know," she said, swishing her hand at her to hurry.

Grace ran after Kam. By the time she made it down the hall and around the corner, Kam was already standing between Asher and Meredith.

"Asher, you shouldn't be treating Meredith this way," Kam said in a low, mean voice that she'd never heard him use before.

"Don't tell me how to treat my own wife, Matafeo. Besides, this is all about you anyways. I'm actually glad you're here. Finally, we'll have an answer. Please for the love of heaven, please once and for all, tell Meredith that you don't love her and that you two are over. Because trust me, she doesn't get it. She still thinks you two are a thing even though she's wearing my ring. She's got some strange romantic idea in her head that you two are still in love with each other and you're both just wasting time until you can be together again," he said bitterly, looking at Meredith with something close to hate in his eyes.

Grace covered her mouth with her hand and looked at Meredith who was standing with her shoulders slumped, looking defeated and embarrassed.

"I told you that's not how it is," Meredith said softly, with her eyes down and her hands clasped together.

"Asher, this is not the place to have this conversation. What are you trying to do? Publicly humiliate your wife?" Kam asked, sounding furious.

Asher put his hands on his hips and lifted his chin in the air. "Why not? She publicly humiliated me by trying to break you and your girlfriend up. I heard all about it from your cousin, Tai. He told me to control my wife so you could be happy. The whole town knows what Meredith and Anne have been up to. It's no secret. Everyone knows my wife is still hung up on you," he barked, still glaring at Meredith.

Rob stepped forward. "Listen, Asher. I told you that if you didn't stop, I'd call the police. I've already called Garrett. Don't make this any worse. Meredith is miserable. Isn't that what you wanted? Now just go," Rob said in a firm voice.

Asher shook his head. "No, I'm not going anywhere. I'm sick to death of this. This ends now. I want to know if Meredith is going to choose me or choose Kam. I'm sick of being second place in my wife's heart."

A tall man with blond hair and the face and build of a model walked over and put his hand on Asher's arm.

"Asher, take it from someone who's really messed up and knows a little of what you guys are going through. Public shaming isn't going to do your marriage any good. Come sit down with me at my table. I'm waiting for Taryn. We'll help you out. I know a great marriage counselor who can help you guys get back on track. Please," the man said in a kind voice that had Grace biting her lip in hope.

Asher snorted and shook the man's hand off his arm. "Like I'd take any marriage advice from you, Brogan. No thanks."

Kam's shoulders tensed and Rob and him exchanged a look before Meredith cleared her throat.

"If calling me out in public will make you happy, Asher, then fine. Keep going. I love you. I keep telling you I love you, but the way you're treating me is ridiculous. I've never cheated on you."

Asher raised an eyebrow. "Really? It feels like it to me. Looking at me for the past few years and wishing someone else was there instead? Isn't that the same thing?"

Meredith wiped the tears away from her eyes and shook her head. "That's not true. Please believe me."

A large man with dark brown hair and silvery blue eyes walked into the room and made a beeline for Asher. Asher looked up and noticed the man and his face fell as if all the bluster and rage had just faded.

"Asher, what are you doing?" the man asked softly as he put his hands on Asher's shoulders, looking down into his eyes.

Whatever he saw on Asher's face had him shaking his head and pulling him into his arms for what was the sweetest thing she'd ever seen. A grown man, comforting another grown man as if he were his son. *Or brother.* She remembered him now. This was Garrett Murphy.

Asher put his arms around Garrett and hugged him back. Garrett leaned down and spoke softly in Asher's ear and a moment later, Asher nodded his head.

Garrett looked up, his arm still around his brother's shoulders as he looked around at Rob, Kam and Brogan.

"My brother's coming home with me. We apologize for disturbing your dinner," he said with an apologetic smile.

Meredith took a step forward, her hand reaching out toward Asher, but Garrett turned his fierce eyes on her and she took two steps backwards.

"Good night," Garrett said to everyone in general and then led his brother out of the restaurant, leaving a deafening silence in his wake.

Everyone's eyes then turned to Meredith who was busily wiping tears from her eyes.

"Please accept my apologies for ruining everyone's evening," she said in a husky voice and then turned and walked over to her table, picking up her purse and taking out her keys.

"Meredith, you're in no state to drive. I'll take you home," Rob said and took the keys from her. "Brogan, will you follow me?"

Brogan nodded immediately and the trio left without another word. Grace watched as the people began to whisper furiously around the restaurant, building slowly to a low roar.

She felt a touch on her arm and looked up to see Kam frowning at her.

"Let's get back to work," he said, sounding sad.

She nodded and followed him down the hall and back into the brightly lit kitchen. She looked at Candice who raised her eyebrows. Grace mouthed the word, *later*, before walking over to the stove.

Kam walked with her. "Well, that was crazy."

Grace nodded her head in agreement. "Do you think he's right?" she asked softly so no one could overhear. "Is Meredith not over you?"

Kam's eyes darkened and he shook his head and then shrugged. "If she wasn't before, she is now. I think seeing how much she hurt Asher finally killed any remaining feelings she had for me. I don't agree with how Asher handled it, but the man's heart is broken. It's hard to judge him."

Grace looked up at him with narrowed eyes. "I don't know. You looked pretty ticked out there. I was worried you were going to pick him up and throw him out into the street."

Kam smiled briefly. "That's the old, Kam. The new me realizes that talking is better than violence."

Grace smiled and shook her head. "I can't even imagine you being violent. You're the gentlest man I've ever met."

Kam laughed at that, his eyes lightening. "Remind me to invite you to my next rugby game."

Grace nodded, feeling intrigued. "I'll be there."

Everyone went back to work, but so many people had left that it was as slow as a Wednesday night. By the time Kam and Grace left for their date, the kitchen was already cleaned up.

Grace whipped off her apron and pointed to the ceiling. "Let me just freshen up and change. Give me ten minutes, tops."

Kam nodded as he folded his apron. "No hurry. We'll have to stop by my house so I can change too."

A half an hour later, they walked into the dimly lit night club and Grace grinned. "This is perfect," she said in Kam's ear. "I haven't been dancing since I moved here. Come on," she said and pulled him out onto the dance floor.

Kam laughed. "Don't you want to get a table and a drink first?"

Grace shook her head as she began dancing, grabbing his hands so he couldn't get away. "No, let's work up a thirst first."

*

Kam grinned and began to relax as they danced, laughed and flirted. He hadn't had this much fun *since,...* Kam felt the metal door of pain slam down on his heart as thoughts of Bailey and dancing with his wife slipped in.

Grace stared at him, frowning slightly. "*Hey there*, I think

I could use that drink now," she said and pulled him off the dance floor.

They got a table and he ordered a Coke for her and a water bottle for himself.

They talked for a while as they watched the other dancers. Kam took a long pull from his water and then choked as he saw his little brother, Pule dancing in the corner with his wife, Posey.

"You've gotta be kidding me," he said, shaking his head, knowing this was no coincidence. His brother was spying on him.

Grace touched his arm. "You either have a really bad headache or you're mad about something."

Kam forced his expression to relax as he pointed to Pule. "My little brother is spying on us. I'm going to kill him."

Grace leaned forward and gasped a little as she caught sight of Pule and Posey. "Spying on you? *Why?*"

Kam sighed and closed his eyes for a moment. "Because my family is nosey and annoying."

Grace laughed and grabbed his arm, pointing toward the bar. "Kam, I hate to tell you this, but I swear I just saw Tai and Cleo by the bar."

Kam growled as he strained his neck to see a glimpse of his cousin. "Seriously? I go on a date and my whole family has to show up? This is embarrassing. I am so sorry, Gracie."

Grace covered her mouth with her hand as she began to laugh. Kam stared at her and let his head fall back. "Great. Who now?"

Grace pointed past his shoulder at the front door. Kam turned around to see Jane and Tate walk in.

"That's it," he said, standing up and throwing a few bills on the table. "Let's go back to my place. We can talk and watch The Office on Netflix."

Grace jumped up and took one last sip of her Coke. "Sounds like heaven. Let's go."

They snuck out the back before anyone would notice they were gone and drove fifteen minutes to Kam's house. Grace stared at the modern house and nodded her head.

"It suits you," she said with a smile and walked in.

Kam followed her in and locked the door. "It's a good house and it's by the water. Natano and I have been happy here."

Grace raised an eyebrow at that but wandered around, picking up pictures of his son. Nate was a happy little boy, but Kam had been grim and emotionless when she'd first met him. Happy wouldn't have been the word she'd use to describe him. She walked back to his family room and looked out the huge floor to ceiling windows at the moon shining down on the Puget Sound.

*

"This is incredible," she said softly.

Kam walked over and stood by her side, studying her profile as she stared at the water. What was it about her that pulled at him? She wasn't as pretty as Bailey, but there was something *more* there. He couldn't stop looking at her. He would notice something new and wonderful about her face or eyes or lips every time he looked at her. And when Grace smiled at him, there was such a goodness in her soul that it reached out and grabbed his heart and made him feel... made him feel whole again.

He put a hand on her shoulder and turned her to look at him.

"Gracie, I'm going to kiss you now," he said softly.

Grace's eyes warmed at that as her mouth tilted up in a smile. "Good. I was just wondering when you were going to stop being so shy," she said and went up on her tiptoes, putting her hands on his shoulders.

Kam smiled at her confidence and leaned down, gently touching his lips to hers. Grace allowed him to kiss her softly for a moment before she sighed and wrapped her arms around his neck, pulling his head closer.

"You're so sweet," she said smiling into his eyes before she began to kiss him in a way that only Grace would. With confidence, a lot of spark and a whole lot of energy.

Kam pulled away, laughing as he kept his arms firmly around her.

"Kissing you is a lot of fun. I had a feeling it would be."

Grace laughed softly and kissed him lightly on the cheek. "If it's not fun, you're not doing it right."

Kam blinked at that and pulled her over to the couch. "I think you're right. But I promise that I didn't just bring you home to make out with you. Cuddling on the couch and watching The Office is still part of the plan."

"Darn it," Grace said, fake glaring at him and making him laugh again.

After two episodes, Kam got them a large bowl of ice cream to share and they watched one more. They laughed and talked and kissed some more and by the time Kam took her home, he knew something.

He never wanted to watch TV without Grace in his arms ever again.

CHAPTER 23

Family Reunion

GRACE WOKE UP Sunday morning feeling slightly on edge. True, she'd had the best date of her life with a guy she might or might not have some serious feelings for but that didn't change the fact that she had to see her mom in four hours.

She took Baby for a walk and then jumped in the shower. She'd make her go to dessert to take to Kam's mom and dad's house. She was a chef, not a baker, but her salted caramel, chocolate chip cheesecake was easy and she'd never met anyone who didn't love it.

She made her cheesecake while she let her hair air dry so she could have some natural waves today. For some reason, she wanted to look extra pretty for Kam. It probably had nothing to do with the fact that he'd kissed her senseless last night. *But then again...*

She sang along to Fifth Harmony as she put her cheesecake in the oven and then walked over to the window. Even though the news had called for a rainy, gray day, the sun was shining and it was a warm seventy-five.

She tried not to think about her mom and Billy wanting to

move in with her and instead focused on the fact that she would have Kam and all of his family surrounding her and supporting her today. Hopefully her mother would take defeat gracefully and be a good sport. She crossed her fingers that Jocelyn wouldn't throw a screaming fit. She still remembered her mom throwing a tantrum at the store when one of her credit cards was declined.

She leaned her head against the glass as she thought of all of the things she had in common with her mom. She hoped anger and a fluid sense of morality wasn't one of them. Her mom always seemed to pick the wrong guy too. She always went for the bad boys. They had to have a motorcycle, at least a dozen scars and most recently, prison records.

She was aware that she'd had issues with self-esteem in the past, but she'd grown up a lot lately and hopefully that showed in her interest in Kam Matafeo. The man was a rock, he was stable, he was kind and good and he was a father. He was compassionate when it came to his ex-girlfriends and he was respectful of women period.

Yeah, it was safe to say that she wasn't interested in deadbeats and bad boys. Why choose drama when she could choose cuddling on the couch and giggling over Michael Scott? Well, that and kissing. She *loved* kissing Kam.

Grace smiled dreamily and closed her eyes, wondering for a moment what it would be like to really be Kam's girlfriend. To have someone she could depend on, someone who would love her and someone she could love in return?

She sighed and shook herself. They were just feeling things out right now. They'd only been on *one* date even though the whole town had practically thrown them together with the exception of Anne and Meredith. But that was fine with her. If the town of Fircrest wanted her to be with Kam Matafeo, then by all means, she would go along with it.

She sighed one more time over her last kiss with Kam and then did her laundry. When it was time to go to Kam's parents' house, she glanced at her phone. No texts from her mother. *Weird.* Usually her mom would send her text messages, taunting her and teasing her if she thought it would upset her. Jocelyn Jackson got a kick out of torturing her for some reason. But not today.

She drove twenty minutes to the Matafeo's and only got lost once. She whistled for Baby and they walked around the house to the backyard, just like last time.

And just like last time, a little bullet of a boy ran right for her.

"*Gracie!* You came!"

Grace handed her cheesecake to Kam, who had appeared at her side so she could pick up Nate and hug him.

"Of course I came. I knew I was going to see you," she said, kissing his cheek.

Nate laughed and touched her hair. "Can I throw a ball to Baby again?"

Grace let Nate down and patted Baby's back. "Baby would be so sad if you didn't."

She smiled as Nate and Baby ran off to play and looked up at Kam. "They love each other."

Kam smiled down into her eyes. "Kids love dogs and dogs love kids. They go together."

Grace nodded her head. "Absolutely. I would have killed for a dog when I was a kid. You should get Nate one."

Kam's eyes narrowed at her. "Or we could just borrow yours. You like to share, Gracie?"

Grace laughed and leaned up on her toes to kiss him on the cheek. "I adore sharing as a matter of fact."

Kam's arm snaked around her waist as he pulled her close. "I was hoping you'd say that. Let's put this down by the other desserts and we'll get you a plate of food. Your mom and her boyfriend are talking to Tate right now."

Grace's face froze as she turned and scanned the yard. Yep, there was her mom, wearing a pair of holey jeans and a faded black, Harley Davidson T-shirt. Billy had to be at least ten years her senior and had a beard that came to the middle of his chest. He looked like a typical Jocelyn boyfriend. *Scary*.

"I guess we better go say hi," she said unenthusiastically.

Kam squeezed her side again. "Hey, stop worrying. We're all here for you. Nothing bad will happen. I promise."

Grace tried to smile and was grateful for the support of Kam's arm. She loved her mom, but the drama and the emotional drainage was hard to deal with.

"Hi, Mom," she said softly as they approached.

Jocelyn turned around and smiled brightly. *Too brightly*. Her eyes looked glazed and her hands were shaky. Her long, wavy brown hair now had some silver streaks in it and her makeup was a little smeared.

"Hi, Grace. Long time no see," she said and walked forward to give her hug.

Grace hugged her back, taking in the scent of marijuana. "It's good to see you too,"

Jocelyn pulled back and gestured to her boyfriend. "Billy, Grace. Grace, this is Billy, the love of my life."

Grace sighed at hearing that. She'd heard her mom introduce so many men as the love of her life that the term actually made her shiver. She behaved herself and smiled. "Hi, Billy."

Billy stared at her with dead looking eyes. "Hey," he muttered, looking just as unhappy as she felt about meeting him.

Tate cleared his throat. "I was just telling Billy here that I recognized him. He's got a couple warrants out. I'm off duty and he's a friend of yours, so I mentioned that if they take off, I probably won't follow them."

Grace's face turned red in embarrassment and her stomach dropped as Jocelyn flipped her long wavy hair over her shoulder. "It's so ridiculous. Billy is totally innocent, Grace. It's just a weapons charge with a breaking and entering. Seriously no big deal. His ex lady threw a fit when he started dating me and lied about him. As soon as we can get a lawyer this will all be cleared up."

Grace grimaced, feeling shocked, but not surprised. "Sure."

Kam put his arm around her shoulders and looked Billy up and down. "Sorry your visit is being cut short. When you have things taken care of with the law, you're welcome back."

Billy rubbed his beard and then spit in the grass next to his feet. "Let's go Joss."

Jocelyn pouted. "I think I'll stay with Grace for a few weeks. You deal with the warrants and we can meet up later."

Grace felt her heart sink but didn't say anything. If her mother wanted to get away from this guy then she couldn't turn her away. This guy had a bad, creepy feel to him. On the other hand, *Jocelyn in her home?* There would be no peace, but she'd survive. She always did.

Billy stared at Jocelyn for a minute, unblinkingly. "Have it your way but I'm not coming back for you."

Jocelyn glared at Billy as she put her hands in her back pockets. "You promised we'd spend a few months by the ocean. I told you I don't stay with guys who break their promises to me."

Billy shrugged. "So let's head down to California. I got a buddy down by San Bernardino who's offered me a trucking job. We can have some fun."

Jocelyn's face brightened up. "I'd love a little sun right about now."

Billy walked over to the food table. "Let's grab a plate of food and get going before this guy goes for his cuffs," he said, his voice gravelly.

Jocelyn looked back at her and smiled, her eyes filled with excitement. "Well, this didn't work out the way I wanted it to. I was hoping to crash at your place for awhile but if your boyfriend's brother is going to throw Billy in jail, then we'd better head out."

Kam nodded and Grace swallowed, feeling slightly nauseous. "Okay, well keep in touch, Mom. And be safe."

Jocelyn laughed and walked over to stand by Billy. "That sounds so boring. Why be safe when you can have fun?" she said with a wink.

Grace walked her mom and Billy out to their old beat up, red Mustang and held their plates as they buckled up.

"You don't happen to have a few bucks I can borrow, do you?" Jocelyn asked, looking hopeful. "Things have been tight and all since I lost my waitressing job."

Grace dug the check out of her pocket, she'd made out for a hundred dollars that morning, knowing her mom would be asking. She always did. "Be happy," she said and stepped back as the door shut with a bang.

She watched her mom and Billy drive away in a cloud of exhaust smoke and felt guilty by the huge wave of relief she felt.

"He's got a rap sheet a mile long, Grace. He's not a nice guy and that's an understatement."

Grace looked up to see Tate standing next to her. She nodded, feeling sick at heart and empty. "That's how she likes them. Mean and bad. And it doesn't matter how many times she gets burned. She keeps touching that stove," she said quietly, wishing with all of her heart that it wasn't true.

Tate put a hand on her shoulder. "Believe it or not, I actually know how you feel. Sorry, Grace."

She walked with Tate back to the party and joined Kam, who was now sitting with Nate and Baby and trying to get Nate to put the ball down long enough to eat a hot dog.

"No hot dog, Daddy," Nate said with a frown and threw the ball as far as his little arms could, which was actually pretty far.

Baby and Nate ran off laughing and Grace's heart eased a little. "What is it about hearing a little boy's giggle that heals a heart?"

Kam smiled and patted the seat next to him. "He's definitely healed my heart. Natano's so full of happiness and light. He saved my life after I lost Bailey. If it weren't for him, I don't know how I could have kept living."

All thoughts of her mom and Billy left as she sat down and put an arm around Kam's shoulder. "I hope you feel safe enough with me that you can talk to me about anything. I *want* you to talk to me about Bailey," she said softly.

Kam nodded, his eyes softening. "I appreciate that. It's been hard to talk to anyone about her except my therapist. Everyone else had to grieve too, you know."

Grace nodded. "I know. I can feel it when I talk to people."

Kam raised an eyebrow and looked at her.

Grace blushed and looked away. "The bakery sisters have been after me for a while to go out with you and Jane and I have talked about how hard it's been for you to get over Bailey."

Kam sighed and looked away. "I don't know if I've gotten over my wife, but I do feel like my heart is ready to love again. Does that make sense?"

Grace nodded and pushed a long strand of curly hair off his cheek. "It does. I can't ever know what you went through, but I can hug you when it hurts."

Kam turned back and looked at her, his lips lifting in a sweet smile.

"And that's why I'm dating you. *Right there.* Because you make my heart feel light and free. I feel so good when I'm with you."

Grace grinned. "Wait. *We're dating?* Is this official?"

Kam smiled and shrugged. "Why, is there someone else you'd rather be dating?"

Grace laughed and stole a cherry tomato off his plate, popping it in her mouth. "Like there's anyone who can compare with you. *Heck no*, there's no one else I'd rather date. Especially after that kiss last night. I think you're stuck with me."

Kam laughed and leaned over, kissing her lightly on the lips. "You haven't seen anything yet."

Grace blushed as she shook her head. "You know your whole family is watching us, right?"

Kam looked around and sure enough, his whole family was staring at them, smiling so big, all she saw was a sea of white teeth. He leaned over and kissed her again for good measure. Grace heard a loud whoop from the other side of the yard and pushed Kam away, laughing in embarrassment.

"You're causing a scene. I don't want Tate to arrest me."

Kam cleared his throat. "Hey, that's no joke. Tate really did arrest Posey one time. You'll have to ask yourself if it's worth it to date me."

Grace's mouth fell open. "You're kidding me."

Kam shook his head slowly. "Ask Tate."

Grace's eyes widened and she licked her lips. "*Yikes*. Remind me not to mess with the Matafeos."

Kam grinned. "All you have to do is be a good girlfriend, kiss me every day and go dancing every now and then and you're safe."

Grace sighed. "That's easy. I can do that in my sleep."

"*You kissed my dad on the lips. Ick!*"

Grace jumped and looked down to see Nate and Baby at her side. She cleared her throat in embarrassment as Kam picked Nate up and put him on his lap.

"Is that okay?" Kam asked, looking down into his son's beautiful big, brown eyes.

Nate frowned. "You never kiss anyone. Why are you kissing Gracie?"

Kam looked over Nate's head at her and smiled. "Because I like Grace. I like her a lot. You know how you like Baby?"

Nate grinned and leaned down to pet Baby. "I love Baby. Do you love Gracie?"

Kam reddened as she grinned at him, waiting for his response. "Yeah, Kam. *Do you love me?*" she teased.

Kam shook his head, grinning. "Yeah, maybe I do," he said looking her in the eyes as he said it.

Grace's eyes widened and she felt her heart catch as Kam's hand reached out for hers.

Nate turned and looked up at her. "Does that mean I get to keep Baby? Because if Daddy can keep you, then I get to keep Baby," he said louder and jumped off his dad's lap. He leaned over and hugged Baby and ran across the yard to his grandmother.

"Grandma! I get to keep Baby!" he yelled over and over.

She laughed as Nate ran around to everyone there, announcing that he got to keep Baby.

She looked at Kam and squeezed his hand. "Well, you've done it now," she said softly.

Kam leaned over and kissed her on the cheek. "I hope so."

Pule and Tai walked over with their wives and joined them, pulling up chairs so they could talk easier.

"So we thought you guys were going dancing last night," Pule said with a frown. "Did you guys cancel your date?"

Kam frowned at his little brother and shook his head. "Why would you think I needed my brothers and cousin for back up?"

Tai and Pule exchanged quick glances and smiled easily at Kam. "Ah, it wasn't like that. We just wanted to be there in case you forgot how to dance with a woman or you know, talk or breathe," Tai said with a grin.

Kam narrowed his eyes at his cousin. "*Funny.* How'd I do, Gracie? Did I do okay?"

Grace put her arm around Kam's shoulder and gave him a hug. "I have no complaints, gentlemen. Your brother is a charmer."

Jane nudged Cleo's shoulder with hers. "Oh my word, Cleo. She looks like she's been kissed. I thought there were rules about that. Aren't you supposed to wait until the third date?"

Cleo nodded, her blue eyes glowing mischievously. "I think Kam forgot about that rule, Jane. Yep, Grace looks like her date went a little *too well.*"

Pule and Tai grinned at Kam as he shared a pained look with Grace.

"So is he a good kisser or has he forgotten how?" Pule asked in a serious voice that had Kam's arm muscles bunching.

Grace laughed and shook her hair back. "Well, I can safely say that Kam is absolutely the best kisser I've ever known."

Tai frowned. "You must not know very many men then. This guy couldn't be that great."

Kam sighed. "That's it. I'm going to kill you both now."

Grace put her arm around Kam's shoulder, keeping him in his chair as everyone laughed.

"Okay, enough teasing. But I will say, that yes, Kam is a divine kisser and I can't wait to go out with him again and again and again. He's gorgeous, he's sweet and he's got the cutest little boy in the world. It's safe to say, I have a huge crush on this guy."

Kam laughed and relaxed. "You heard it from the lady. She's practically in love with me. Now leave us alone."

Jane and Cleo's mouths were hanging open as Pule and Tai stared at them with what looked like joy in their eyes.

"I gotta go find Tate," Pule said, his voice sounding weird and low.

Tai just kept shaking his head back and forth, blinking fast.

"Okay, um, I'm going to grab seconds before Sefe gets here and eats everything," he said and turned and walked away quickly.

Jane and Cleo leaned over and hugged Grace. "This is so cool. I've gotta text Kit and Layla and let them know that everything is going according to plan," Jane said taking out her phone and walking away.

Which left Cleo standing there, smiling sunnily at them.

"You know when life gets messy and hard and painful and then suddenly all the knots come loose and the colors you thought were so messy actually turn out kind of beautiful and this crazy picture you thought was ruined and torn to bits actually begins to start looking like a masterpiece?"

Grace stared at her in confusion as Kam nodded his head. "Um, yeah, I guess so."

Cleo nodded her head and sighed. "That's what you guys are. This messy, beautiful piece of life. I love it," she said and walked away.

Grace bit her lip and looked up at Kam. "Do I have to take a yoga class from her to translate that?"

Kam laughed. "She's just trying to say that life is crazy and hard but sometimes it's amazing and beautiful too. *We're* what's beautiful. You and me."

Grace felt her heart melt as she stared at the man next to her. "We're beautiful *together*."

Kam laughed. "We better stick together then."

Grace breathed in and let it out slowly feeling the joy of that sentence fill her heart. "That sounds good to me. I say we shake on it."

Kam shook her hand firmly. "You know a handshake is an old-fashioned contract, right?"

Grace raised an eyebrow. "That sounds pretty serious. What happens if you break this contract?"

Kam's eyebrows rose as he smiled down at her. "I'd be the

dumbest man in the world if I let that happen. And, Gracie, I'm not dumb."

Grace leaned into his side, just to feel his warmth and strength and let herself relax into the happiness. They finished their lunch and then walked over to talk to Kam's mom and dad, Toa and Pika. Grace appreciated the fact that they didn't ask too many questions about her mom or Billy.

Tate walked up a few minutes later and hugged Kam. He didn't say anything, just hugged him. Long and hard. Kam didn't seem embarrassed at all either. He just hugged him back, holding his brother.

Grace watched in fascination, wondering what was going on. She didn't have any siblings and wondered if this was the norm. When Tate stepped back, he looked in Kam's eyes and smiled. "This is good," he finally said.

Kam looked back at her for a moment before answering. "It's more than good."

Tate nodded his head once and walked away.

Grace wasn't sure if it was a Samoan thing or what, but she'd never seen two men communicate that way.

Kam kept his arm around her shoulders after that but when Sefe and Anne showed up and hour later, he suggested they take Nate and Baby back to his house and watch a movie.

She agreed and they ended up spending the whole day together. He kissed her good night after he walked her to her car and stood in his driveway as he watched her leave.

She stared at him in her rearview mirror and wondered why her heart felt like bursting. That and for once, she didn't want to leave. She wanted to stay with Kam and his son in the house by the water.

She wanted Kam.

CHAPTER 24

Love Witches

ALL OF THE women stared at each other unhappily as they quietly ate scones and drank vanilla bean steamers.

"Sorry, but I feel bad for her," Jane said, sitting up straight and looking around the table at her friends. "I mean, think about it. She's lost her husband and her friends. What does she have left?"

Kit snorted. "I'll tell you what she doesn't have. *Kam.* She lost everything because she stood in the way of his happiness. Ask yourself why. *Why, Jane?*"

Layla sighed and put a hand on Jane's arm. "Give her a break, Kit. She cares about her friend. And even though you don't like her, for the most part, we're Meredith's friends too. Come on, you don't want to see Meredith alone do you?"

Kit rolled her eyes. "I guess not, but honestly, if she doesn't grow up after this, I'm done with her."

Cleo took a bite of scone and chewed for a moment as she closed her eyes. "It's only good karma if we help her. If she can fix things with Asher, I know she'll never take him for granted again. I bet you a million dollars their relationship will be ten times better after this."

Rayne cleared her throat and put her steamer down. "Well, I've had a front row seat to their relationship and it's fair to say that Asher has been running after her the whole time. She wears the pants in that relationship and always makes him feel like he's not good enough for her. I think after this, it will be much more even."

Ivy raised her hand in the air. "All in favor of helping out a poor, lost soul, raise your hand."

Maya, Rayne, Layla, Jane, Cleo, Posey and Wren all raised their hands. Everyone turned and stared at Kit who sat with her arms folded.

"Sorry, I can't be fake. Not about her. I wish you all well, but she deserves this. She needs to sit and stew in her pot of misery for a while before you all charge in and save the day."

Layla stared at her sister and shook her head. "No compassion at all? What if it were you? What if you and Hunter were on the verge of breaking up?"

Kit narrowed her eyes and sat forward. "It wouldn't be because the whole town knew I was hung up on an old boyfriend."

Wren, who was sitting on the other side of Kit rubbed her back soothingly. "What about, *judge not, lest ye be judged?* That kind of thing? Let's just help her out and leave the punishment to someone else."

Kit's face remained stony and she looked away.

Posey, who was sitting across from her, frowned at Kit. "I think you're being kind of mean, Kit. Why wish unhappiness on anyone?"

Kit blinked in surprise at being called out. "Look, it's great everyone wants to help Meredith but it's always the same story. Meredith is a selfish brat and everyone steps in to make it all better for her. When is she going to learn? Let her deal with this like an adult. I mean, what are you going to do? Huh? Go up to Asher and tell him to love his wife again? Tell him he can trust her again? You don't even know if he can. All I'm saying is, stay out of it. I think we need to sit this one out," she said and stood up, taking her scone and steamer with her to the kitchen.

Jane watched her sister with sad eyes and shook her head. "Just give her time. But she does have a point. When it comes to marriage problems, this is between them. There's nothing we can do to reconnect their hearts."

Wren shrugged. "Taryn and Brogan have reconnected theirs. At least I think so," she added with a happy smile.

Everyone turned with hopeful smiles to stare at Wren.

"I was wondering why she didn't show up today. I texted her," Ivy said.

Wren took a sip, still smiling. "Rob told me that Brogan asked to borrow the boat. He took Taryn out on the water yesterday for a few hours. Kam told me he made them a picnic basket and Rob said when Brogan returned the boat, he was smiling from ear to ear."

Everyone grinned and began talking at once. Layla whistled to get their attention.

"We might not be able to fix marriages, but we can certainly help things along. It just takes two willing hearts and the perfect set up. I know The Iron Skillet is doing this fancy fine dining thing next week. We bought tickets. Does anyone know if Asher and Meredith did?"

Jane nodded her head. "We bought them together. But there's no way Asher will show up now."

Ivy and Rayne looked at each other and nodded their heads. "We can get him there. Garrett and Becket will be going. We just need to get Meredith to show up," Rayne said.

Posey leaned her elbows on the table and looked excited.

"We can play their favorite love songs. It'll be perfect. Romantic music, good food and dancing. This has to help."

Wren frowned and looked at Ivy and Rayne. "One problem. I heard from Rob that Garrett is just as mad at Meredith as Asher is. He's a protective older brother looking out for a boy he practically raised. Will he get in the way?"

Rayne sighed and glanced at Ivy. "He's furious. I'll try and calm him down. Ivy, you work on Becket."

Ivy nodded her head. "Will do."

Jane ran her hands through her long brown hair and looked around the table at all of her friends.

"It comes down to forgiveness. Who knew that perfect marriages aren't so perfect and that everyone would need so much forgiveness?"

Layla took another bite of scone as she nodded her head in agreement. "All of the best marriages I know are built on kindness and a lot of forgiveness. It doesn't matter how big and beautiful your wedding reception is, or how beautiful you are or how flat your stomach is or how much money you have in the bank. It's two people working hard, all the time, to make it work."

Posey scrunched up her face. "I have a friend from back home who just got divorced. She wanted a Pinterest life she said. She found the cutest boy she could, planned the perfect wedding and life and then when it was all over, she was stuck with this guy she didn't know very well, didn't like very much and didn't have anything in common with."

Maya, who had been quiet the whole time tapped her nails on the table. "We compare everything these days because of social media. Everyone thinks we live in an Instagram life, but we don't. I shut down all my accounts and I'm ten times happier."

Everyone looked at her in shock.

Wren shook her head. "I'd die."

Cleo laughed and agreed. "There's no way, Maya. But I'm glad to know you didn't unfriend me. I was wondering."

Everyone laughed and finished their scones and drinks.

"Okay everyone, divide and conquer. We've got one week to get Meredith and Asher ready to reconnect those broken hearts of theirs. Jane and Cleo, you know Meredith the best. You two work on her and make sure she's okay. Everyone else, do your part, whatever that is," Layla said and stood up.

Everyone nodded their heads in agreement.

Wren cleared her throat. "We haven't even talked about Grace and Kam though."

Layla laughed and sat back down. "Any news?"

Jane smiled happily and looked across the table at Cleo. "They were at Tate's parents' house yesterday and Kam had his arm around her shoulders the whole time. I counted at least seven kisses."

Cleo grinned and let out a loud whoop. "Ladies, I don't want to jinx this, but it's happening. I saw Kam. Tai saw Kam. That man is in love."

Jane clasped her hands together and sighed. "Tate was in tears too he was so happy. He went up and hugged Kam so hard I thought he was going to pop a rib. He couldn't stop talking about how happy Grace made Kam. And Nate loves her. He ran around telling everyone that Grace's dog was now his. It's the cutest thing."

Cleo frowned and bit her lip. "Yeah, but her mom and that guy were super icky. He gave me the willies."

Jane frowned and nodded as everyone stared at her expectantly.

"So Grace's mom shows up unexpectedly with the scariest guy I've seen since I watched The Walking Dead last week. Tate recognized him immediately and says he's got a long rap sheet and he's not a nice guy. If Grace's mom is hanging out with him, she's in for trouble."

Maya frowned, looking worried as she rubbed her arms. "What about Grace? She's not in danger, is she?"

Jane shook her head quickly. "It sounded like they were on their way out of town."

Ivy sighed. "I hate trouble. Maybe you witchy sisters can put a charm on the town to protect our little lovebirds."

Jane and Layla looked at each other and grinned. "Speaking of which," Layla said and stood up, walking around the counter and grabbing a large box. "This arrived yesterday. I almost forgot."

All of the women watched as Layla pulled out pale pink t-shirts with the words, *Love Witches* in bold black letters with a witch's broom in the middle.

The women all jumped up to grab one.

Layla handed them out. "If I don't get to wear this shirt to a bridal shower, I'm going to be ticked."

Maya held hers up to her shoulders and smiled. "I should have specified maternity sized."

Everyone began screaming and Kit came out to see what was going on. After everyone hugged and congratulated Maya, Kit took her shirt and smiled.

"I've decided to help Meredith. Ten minutes of washing dishes can do wonders for your soul."

Everyone hugged Kit too as Jane turned the sign to OPEN. She and her sisters watched as everyone left, holding on tightly to their new shirts.

"If we can make this happen, we really do deserve that trip to Hawaii," Layla said, looking at Kit.

Kit shrugged and checked the size on her shirt. "No wedding, no Hawaii."

Jane and Layla grumbled and began cleaning up the crumbs from their book club meeting.

"Funny how we meet all the time for Book Club but we haven't read a book in two months. I'm starting to think all we do is meddle in people's lives," Kit said.

Layla grinned. "Someday we'll read a book again. Real life just happens to be more interesting right now."

Jane laughed and grabbed an apron. "Who knows, maybe Posey will write a book about all of this someday."

Layla paused and stared out the window at the cloudy day and smiled at the thought. A book about Fircrest might be a good idea.

CHAPTER 25

Betrayal

I T WAS GRACE'S day off and she had all morning to herself. Kam was running errands with Nate until he had to go pre-school at one. That's when she and Kam had plans to meet up for a hike and a picnic. She took a luxurious bubble bath and then took Baby to the park. She thought about running by the bakery but decided to pass since she'd be having lunch soon.

Maybe she should go shopping? Next week was their Fine Dining experience and for the last hour, Candice, James and Manuel were going to take over for her and Kam so they could dance and mingle with everyone. Which meant she needed a dress.

She glanced at her phone and knew she didn't have enough time to run down to Tacoma and be back in time. But she loved the Rose boutique where she'd gotten her dress that she'd worn to the Matafeo's lunch.

She helped Baby into the back of the truck and drove over, parking in front. She hopped out and told Baby to stay as she walked in the quaint old store front. She paused as her eyes adjusted and looked around. There were tons of boho clothes, the kind she liked, and a wall of dresses from casual to elegant. She saw a multi-colored midi dress with short sleeves and walked over to touch the material.

"Gorgeous," she whispered.

"That's vintage, by the way. Pure silk."

Grace turned around to see a girl in her twenties with bright pink hair and a nose ring.

"It's fantastic. How much?"

The girl walked over and flipped the tag around. "It's a hundred and sixty-seven but we're having a Spring Sale. I'll give you fifty percent off."

Grace squealed and hugged the dress. "Where's the changing room. If this fits, I'm going to pee my pants."

The girl winced. "Yeah, please don't."

Grace laughed and hurried to the changing room. It was so dark and dim that it was hard to really see what she looked like. But if the mirror wasn't lying to her, which had happened so many other times in the past, then she was going to rock this dress.

She practically floated to the checkout counter and handed the dress to the clerk. "It's perfect."

The girl nodded. "I've been eyeing this dress for a month, but it'll look fabulous with your eyes."

Grace preened. "You are an amazing sales clerk."

"Thanks, it's a gift. That'll be $87.93, please."

Grace pushed her debit card across the counter and waited as she checked her text messages.

"Uh, this isn't going through. Your card was declined," the girl said with a frown.

Grace frowned, knowing she had plenty in her account. Even though her ex had emptied her out of everything, she'd been frugal for the last little year and had been saving every penny she could. She had at least five thousand in the bank.

"That can't be right. Try it again," she said, feeling a cold wash of anxiety rip through her.

The girl frowned at the machine and shook her head a moment later. "I can hold the dress for you for two days. Sorry."

Grace sighed and shook her head, "This cannot be happening to me," she said to herself and took her card back feeling mortified and confused. "I'll be back."

The girl nodded, looking at her with what could be either compassion or pity. It was hard to tell sometimes.

She walked out to her truck feeling all the happy excitement that she'd been relishing, slipping through her fingers. She jumped in the truck and drove down to the bank. She felt like throwing a fit. If she lay on the floor, kicking and screaming, would that make this nightmare disappear?

She walked up to an open teller and pushed her card across the counter. "My card was just declined five minutes ago. I'd like to know why" she said as politely as she could.

The guy standing in front of her looked like he was barely twenty. His tie was too tight and he looked like he'd rather be anywhere but where he was.

"Let me just check your account," he said with a derisive upturn of his lips.

Grace stared at him, unblinkingly as he entered her account number and stared at a screen for what seemed like a very long time. She began to sweat as her stress levels began to rise.

"Looks like you came in this morning and emptied your account out," he said looking at her as if she was insane.

Grace felt her stomach drop as she leaned over the counter. "One small problem. *I didn't.*"

The guy stared at her for a second, his eyes going wide. "Let me go get my manager."

Grace closed her eyes, feeling sick. How could this be

happening to her? *Again?* The feelings of betrayal and stress came slamming down on her bringing with it an instant headache.

An older man with glasses and a tan suit walked up to her and asked her to join him in his office. She felt like crying, but followed him into a small, dark room.

After she explained that whoever emptied her account wasn't her, he turned his monitor around so they could look at it together. "Your account was emptied at 9:05 this morning. Do you recognize any of these people?"

Grace stared at the people walking into the bank and frowned, concentrating on the small, sort of blurry images of people. "It's so hard to see," she muttered and then froze as the image of a woman with long, wavy brown hair walked in, wearing faded jeans and a white t-shirt.

Grace stared at the image of her mom and felt a part of her soul die. "I know her," she whispered, pointing to her mom. "That's my mother."

The bank manager nodded his head, looking sympathetic and picked up the phone. She listened as he called the police and waited, feeling numb.

When someone touched her shoulder she looked up to see Tate Matafeo dressed in his uniform looking down at her. He knelt beside her and took her hand in his.

"I'm sorry, Grace. We'll put out a warrant, but they're probably to Oregon by now."

Grace nodded her head. "She took everything I had. My card was just declined. What am I going to do?"

The bank manager, *Stan,* as she now knew him as, pushed a document toward her. "Fill this out. This is a classic case of identity theft. We can have your money refunded. They used a personal check and changed the amount which means they committed fraud and our clerk didn't catch it. But I have to warn you, the bank will prosecute to the fullest extent of the law. I'm sorry the thief was your mother, but we need to recoup our losses."

Grace stared at the wall in front of her and sighed. Putting her mom in jail. This is what her life had come to.

"Grace, I can loan you some money until the bank comes through for you. It should only be a few days," Tate said.

Grace swallowed hard and nodded her thanks. "I appreciate it, Tate. But I'll be okay," she said, wishing her voice didn't sound so wimpy and small.

"What was it you were trying to buy when your card was declined? I'll take you there now and you can get it. On me."

Grace closed her eyes and shook her head. "I wanted to buy a dress for the Fine Dining dance next week. I wanted to look pretty for Kam."

Tate's face stiffened and his eyes went dark. "Let's go get that dress."

Grace stood up and shook her head, feeling so embarrassed she could die. What must Tate think of her and her family?

"Tate, I truly appreciate the offer, but... *I can't.* This is killing me as it is and if you're nice to me right now I'm going to start crying," she said smiling too brightly.

Tate stared at her for a moment and then nodded his head. "Fine. But if you need *anything* and I find out you didn't come to me or Jane I'll be offended."

Grace nodded her head quickly as her eyes began to fill. She turned so Tate couldn't see her eyes and shook Stan's hand before being led out to her truck.

"I'd appreciate it if this stayed between you and I," she said, looking at her feet. "I'd hate for Kam to know. I'd hate for anyone to know that my mom just took all my money."

Tate stared at her for a moment and shook his head. "Listen, Kam would want me to help you. I won't tell him if you'll just let me help you," he finally said, putting his hands on his hips.

That did it.

Grace let her head fall forward as the tears she'd been fighting started to fall. She covered her face with her hands, trying to stop the sobs, but she couldn't. She felt Tate's arms come around her as she began to shake and couldn't do anything to stop it.

A long time later, she lifted her head, feeling even more mortified, but too empty to do anything about it.

"I just want to go home," she whispered, digging in her pocket for her keys.

Tate frowned, keeping his hand on her shoulder. "Can you drive?"

Grace nodded, sniffing hard. "It's just a block down the road, Tate."

Tate nodded and walked with her to her truck. He opened the door for her and waited while she buckled her seatbelt.

"Everything will be fine, Grace. Don't take this to heart so much. Your money will be returned and no one will ever need to know."

Grace closed her eyes and wished her lips would stop trembling. The feeling of overwhelming betrayal was threatening to drown her. But she knew Tate wouldn't let her go unless she reassured him.

"I'll be okay. I guess it was just a shock. Sorry, I'm a little emotional right now but thank you for everything," she said and put her hand on the door.

Tate frowned at her, obviously not buying it. "Okay, but I'm going to check on you later."

Grace nodded and flicked a few more tears away. "Thanks, Tate. I can see why Kam loves you so much."

Tate's eyes softened and he nodded. "Drive safe."

Grace didn't answer and shut the door. She knew Tate would watch her drive away so she put all her energy into driving as safely as she could. She made it home and ran up the back entrance to her apartment with Baby. She collapsed on the couch and pulled her knees up into a fetal position as the tears came harder.

She felt her phone vibrate in her pocket and jerked up, scrambling for her phone. She glanced at the time and groaned as she read the text.

See you in five minutes. Can't wait. I've been looking forward to seeing you all day.

Grace ran to the bathroom and stared at her wrecked makeup and blood shot eyes. There was no way. She texted as fast as her fingers could move,

Kam, I'm so sorry, but I don't feel well right now. Can I take a rain check? Maybe we can meet up later tonight?

She stared at her phone, holding her breath as she waited for his response. She knew he'd been getting the food ready for their picnic and she felt horrible canceling, but if he saw her now, he'd insist on knowing what was wrong. And she didn't have the strength right now. How could she tell the man she was falling in love with that her own mother had just stolen all of her money? She'd be humiliated and he'd probably be shocked and horrified.

Still no text back.

She walked over to her fridge and opened the door, looking at the empty contents. She'd been so busy lately she hadn't really done much shopping. *Dumb. Dumb. Dumb.* Now she had no food and no money. She bit her lip and glanced at her wallet. She did have an emergency credit card. If she was really desperate, she could pull it out and worry about the interest rate later.

She sat back on the couch and crossed her legs, appreciating Baby for coming over and laying her head on her knee.

"You'd never betray me, would you, Baby?" she asked softly and smiled a little at Baby's answering woof.

She heard the ping of her phone and looked down, biting her lip in dread. *What if he insisted on coming over? What if he got mad at her and broke up with her?*

She breathed in and out slowly and then calmed herself. The reason she liked Kam in the first place was that he was a gentleman. He was kind and he was not a jerk. She could read the message.

She touched her message icon.

I'm so sorry, Gracie. I'm going to bring the picnic over and put it on your doorstep. I would love to see you tonight as soon as you're feeling better. If not, I can wait. Call me if you need anything.

Grace re-read the message three times and then shut her eyes in relief and awe. Kam Matafeo was a man among men. The world needed more men like him.

She texted him back a smiley face emoji and told him she would absolutely text him later.

She threw her phone on the carpet and rested her head on the arm of the couch. Today was turning out to be horrible, but hopefully tonight would be better. She was sad to miss out on a romantic picnic with Kam, but there was no way she could fake being happy and present when she was a mess inside.

Fifteen minutes later, she heard the unmistakable sound of a large man walking up her metal steps. She froze like a rabbit, wondering if Kam would knock on the door or give her the space she needed.

The sound of footfalls going back down the steps had her

falling more in love with Kam then she was before. Sensitivity. He had it and thank heaven for it.

She waited five minutes and then opened the door slowly to see a large brown grocery bag. She picked it up, surprised that it was so heavy and shut the door with her foot. She felt her stomach rumble as she opened the bag to see four plastic containers of food.

She opened one to find a caprese salad. Another contained chocolate cake. *Mmm.* Another contained what looked like seasoned pork roast. And the last one contained what had to be BBQ potato chips.

It was official.

She was in love.

The man knew her perfectly. She smiled, feeling her heart fill with light as she sat down and began eating. Afterwards, she felt much, much better. She decided to take a nap and grabbed a throw off the back of her couch and cuddled up, turning her phone to silent.

She just needed a little time to recuperate from the vicious blow her mother had dealt her. She picked up her phone one last time and looked up her mother's contact info. She scrolled down and swiped the block option. She stared sadly at the phone before facing it down on the carpet.

Now she could rest.

CHAPTER 26

The Thief

SHE CREPT THROUGH the back door, using the key she'd taken last week. No one would know. Rob was such a trusting soul, he didn't even have security cameras. Crazy man. She walked through the kitchen and down the hall to Rob's office. She'd heard him talking to Wren one night about how he kept all the keys in his bottom drawer. She walked behind the desk and leaned over, pulling the drawer open. Yep. Keys. Five of them. She took them all out and walked over to wall safe. She tried three keys and on the fourth try, she felt it slide and click.

"Bingo," she breathed out softly as she pulled the safe door open.

Rob had taken Wren and the kids up to Seattle for the day and so he hadn't been in to take all the money from Saturday night to the bank. She frowned at the vault and reached in for the bags of money. He must not have been to the bank all week.

"Idiot," she breathed out, shaking her head. "But all the better for me."

She pulled the bags out and slipped them into her over-size purse. No one would suspect anything if they saw her. She could count it all later. She emptied the entire safe and then shut and relocked it. She put the key back in the bottom drawer and turned off the light, shutting the door and walking back to the kitchen.

Easy. Stealing all of The Iron Skillet's money had been the easiest thing she'd ever done. It might be time to consider a new career. She stopped with her hand on the knob and looked back. *Crud!* She'd forgotten the most important thing. She set her heavy purse down and ran back to Rob's office. She took one of Grace Jackson's hair clips and put it down on the carpet right under the safe.

"Perfect," she breathed out.

She laughed as she turned and ran back to the kitchen. She picked up her purse and walked out into the sunlight, locking up after herself. She got in her car and drove away smiling at the thought of Grace Jackson in handcuffs.

Kam wouldn't think Grace was so special once everyone found out what a thief she was.

CHAPTER 27

Kam and Comfort

K AM STARED AT Grace across his kitchen table and frowned. Something was not right. The light in Grace's eyes was dim today. It was as if someone had thrown a bucket of water on her inner fire. She'd told him she hadn't been feeling well, and maybe that was it... *no*. It couldn't be. Something was wrong. And she wasn't telling him.

"Uno!" Natano shouted, making him and Grace laugh.

"Natano, why do you always beat me?" he asked with a growl.

Natano giggled and put his fists in the air as if he was Rocky. "Because, I'm the best," he said gleefully.

Grace ruffled Natano's hair and smiled at him. "You deserve a treat for that. I made some chocolate chip cookies. Would you like one before you go to bed?"

Natano nodded his head. Smart kid. Who in their right mind would turn down a homemade chocolate chip cookie?

Grace walked over to the counter and brought over a plate of cookies, setting them in front of him and his son. He and Natano both took two. She didn't take any.

"Not hungry?" he asked, raising an eyebrow.

Grace winced and shook her head. "Not today. But that's no reason that you two shouldn't enjoy yourselves," she said with a smile that didn't reach her eyes.

Kam frowned, not liking this. If something was wrong, then Grace should tell him. He'd have to wait until Natano went to bed though.

"Well, buddy. It's time to brush your teeth and head to bed," he said as soon as Natano put the last bite of cookie in his mouth.

Natano frowned, his eyebrows slamming down. A sure sign there would be a fight. He stared at his son and shook his head and Natano grimaced and nodded. He'd promised Natano a special treat if he was on his best behavior for Grace. Good boy.

Fifteen minutes later, he was standing on his back deck with Grace, looking out over the water as the sun began to set.

"Thanks for coming over tonight. I know you aren't feeling well, but it's good for my heart to see you and know that you're okay," he said, putting his hand on her shoulder and pulling her closer to his side.

Grace's head fell to her chest and she sighed softly. "I feel so bad for cancelling on you today, Kam. Especially since you went to so much trouble, making the lunch and everything. I promise it won't happen again," she said grimly.

Kam frowned. Something was definitely up. "Is there something you'd like to talk to me about?" he asked, not knowing how to let her know that he was there for her.

Grace shook her head immediately, making her blond streaked hair swing out. "Uh, no. Everything's fine. Listen, I should probably get going."

Kam's head shook this time. "Oh, no. You're not going anywhere. I can tell you're upset about something. Let's go inside and cuddle on the couch and watch The Office. You need some endorphins and you need to relax. That means me, my couch, and Michael Scott."

Grace looked up at him, meeting his eyes for the first time that day and smiled. "Why are you so good to me?" she asked, wonderingly. "Most guys would act hurt and selfish and make it about them. But you… you honestly care about *me*," she said, sounding surprised.

Kam pushed her hair away from her face and leaned down, looking into her light blue eyes. "Because I want to be good to you, Gracie. Something inside of me just wants to reach out and grab on. I hate not seeing a smile on your face. And if there is something or *someone* who's taken your smile away, it's my job to get it back. So please let me."

Grace's shoulders relaxed a little and she nodded. "Cuddling with you and watching The Office sounds like exactly what I need right now."

They spent the next couple of hours talking and laughing and by the time she went home, she felt almost normal. There was something about being kissed by Kam that breathed life back into her.

CHAPTER 28

The Guilty Party

ROB STARED AT the empty safe with his mouth hanging open in shock. "Oh, no," he whispered, feeling ill as he put his hand to the very back of the safe feeling nothing. He swallowed hard and then ran down the hallway to his sister's office.

"Taryn, did you come in yesterday and make the deposit?" he asked, sounding as desperate as he felt.

Taryn put her phone down, shaking her head with a frown. "No, you always do the deposits unless you're out of town. What's wrong?"

Rob ran his hands over his face and as a wave of nausea rolled through his body. "It's gone. It's all gone. I was supposed to come in yesterday and do it but I took the family to Seattle instead. It was the money from the last couple of weeks, Taryn. I've been so busy lately I just figured I'd make the deposit today and now it's all gone."

Taryn stood up and rushed past him and down the hall. He followed her back to his office and watched as she searched the completely empty wall safe. She turned and looked at him with wide eyes.

"We've been robbed."

Rob nodded his head, hating the sound of that. He felt so helpless. And that made him furious. He put his hands on his hips and paced his office as Taryn continued to stare at the empty safe in shock.

"Who could have done this to me?" he growled.

Taryn turned and grabbed his arm. "It had to be someone who had access to your key."

Rob's face went white as he closed his eyes. Someone he knew and trusted had done this to him. He ground his teeth as rage poured into his veins. "When I find out who did this, I swear I'm going to kill them."

"Rob, how much? How much do you think they took?" Taryn asked quietly.

Rob clenched his hands into fists. "At least eight grand. Maybe more."

Taryn covered her mouth with her hand. "No," she whispered. "We need that money for rent and payroll. What are we going to do?"

Rob walked over to his window and took out his phone. "We're going to find out who robbed me and get our money back."

He dialed 911 and within ten minutes, Tate and Pule Matafeo were standing in his office. He told them everything as they wrote down notes.

"Had to be an inside job. There's no sign of a busted window or locks," Pule said somberly after a thorough look at the exterior of the building.

Rob nodded his head. "It has to be."

Tate sighed. "It's been a bad week for people in Fircrest. You're not the only one who's been betrayed by someone they trust."

Rob could feel his blood pressure rising as he thought of

the person who would steal from him. "I swear I want a public flogging for this."

Pule snorted and walked over to the safe. "You and everyone else who's been taken advantage of. Due process, buddy."

Tate sighed and put his hand on his arm. "Please tell me you put in the security cameras I told you about last year."

Rob's face flushed red as he shook his head. "I didn't think anyone would do this to me. I mean, we live in Fircrest, not Seattle. We know everyone who lives here. *Practically.*"

Tate frowned at him. "Well, we'll start doing interviews and hopefully we'll be able to flush out the culprit. We'll get a team in here to do fingerprints as well so if they're in the system, we'll know."

Taryn flipped her hair over her shoulder. "Well, it had to be someone who was hurting for money, right?"

Tate shrugged. "Depends on their motive for doing it. Any enemies, Rob?"

Rob blinked in surprise. "*Enemies?* No way. Everyone loves me."

Taryn snorted at that and Pule grinned. "I can think of a few guys from that last team we played. Remember that one guy who threatened to break your knees?"

Rob laughed and then frowned. "Yeah, I guess I might have a few enemies. Holy crap. I can't believe this."

"Wait, what's this?" Pule said, leaning down and picking up a hair clip.

Rob walked over and looked at it and then turned to Taryn. "Is this yours?"

Taryn walked over and took the hairclip and frowned, glancing at Tate. "No, but I know who it belongs to."

Rob huffed out a breath in exasperation. "*Who, Taryn?* Who?"

Taryn looked away and sighed. "Grace Jackson. She wears these hair clips."

Tate's eyes widened as he took the hair clip back from Taryn. "Has Grace been in your office lately, Rob?"

Rob shook his head slowly, his eyes grim and mean looking. "Not lately. I always go to the kitchen if I need to talk to her. She hasn't been in my office for about two weeks."

Tate sighed and Pule frowned. "I don't believe it. Grace wouldn't do something like this," Pule stated.

Rob snorted. "Based on what? The fact that she's dating your brother? Come on."

Tate cleared his throat. "Innocent until proven guilty, Rob. I know you're angry and you want someone punished right now, but just because there's a clip here that belongs to your Sous Chef, doesn't mean she's the one who took the money. Maybe your cleaning crew picked it up and it fell out of someone's pocket as they vacuumed. I'll interview them too. Get me their names and numbers."

Rob rolled his eyes but gave him the number of their cleaning crew.

"We all like Grace," Taryn said, sounding sad. "I mean, I didn't want to like her, but she's so dang likable, how can anyone not? I was going to invite her to get our nails done this week for the dance."

Pule cleared his throat loudly. "Your mom has no problem hating her."

Taryn waved her hand in the air, ignoring him. "My point is, she's got us all beat when it comes to personality, wit and charm, but that doesn't necessarily make her a good person."

Rob sighed. "I really thought she was though. Remember when you were being such a witch to her and she brought you a treat?"

Taryn blushed and folded her arms over her chest. "In my

defense, I was going through a hard time and really, anyone who was female and pretty was on my hate list."

Tate patted Taryn's arm. "Understandable. But again, let me stress that this is circumstantial evidence. You have no proof that Grace took the money."

Rob shook his head. "Well, like you said, we need to find out if she recently had some financial troubles. Maybe she needed the money?"

Tate's face froze and he looked away. Pule frowned, staring at him.

"Hey, *didn't you mention...*" Pule began but was interrupted by Tate.

"We'll start interviewing everyone now and get out of your hair. You're going to need our police report to give to your insurance company. I'll have that to you by the end of the day. We'll figure this out, Rob. I promise."

Rob nodded, looking even angrier. "We better, or I'm going to burn this town down until I find out who did it."

*

Tate and Pule walked out of Rob's office and headed straight for the kitchen. Pule grabbed his arm and pulled him to a stop.

"Tate, I saw that police report. You didn't say anything but I know Grace's mom emptied out her bank account. Do you think Grace stole the money?"

Tate looked up and down the hallway and shook his head. "I don't. And don't you dare breathe a word about Grace's money situation to anyone. That's between me and her and her mother. She didn't want anyone to know. Especially Kam. She's humiliated and hurting right now."

Pule shook his head, looking obstinate. "How well do we really know this girl? Sure, Kam likes her. She's pretty and fun and makes him smile. But that doesn't mean she didn't steal the money, Tate. We need to keep an open mind."

Tate frowned at him. "Pule, do you really think so little of your brother to think that he'd fall in love with a thief?"

Pule glared at his cousin. "Dude, do your job and be a cop. This has nothing to do with Kam. We've all been fooled before," he said and walked into the kitchen, letting the door swing.

Tate sighed feeling tired all of a sudden. He pushed through the door and went right for Kam.

"Hey, Man, let's talk," he said, pointing to his office.

Kam was talking to his prep cooks but nodded, looking concerned. "Sure thing."

He and Pule followed Kam to his office and shut the door. Tate glanced through the window and noticed Grace was over in the corner prepping what looked like a whole pig. Gross.

"She's a hard worker," he said softly, nodding his head toward his brother's Sous Chef.

Kam stood next to him and Tate looked up in time to see a sweet expression come into Kam's eyes. "She's the best,"

Tate turned and looked at Pule grimly. Pule rolled his eyes and shook his head.

"Kam, we're here in an official capacity. The Iron Skillet was robbed sometime between Saturday night and this morning. Rob estimates that about eight thousand dollars was taken from his safe. There's no sign of a forced entry, so we're left to conclude that this was an inside job."

Kam blinked in shock, not saying anything for a minute. "*Robbed?* Someone came in and stole from us?" he demanded, sounding almost as ticked as Rob.

Pule nodded his head, looking disgusted. "Someone we all know, too."

Kam's eyes turned dark as he looked at his hand. "James

has been complaining about money troubles lately. He had his car impounded last week. I hope it wasn't him."

Tate cleared his throat. "We'll interview everyone, Kam. I just wanted to make you aware of the situation before we start pulling out your cooks."

Kam nodded, folding his massive arms over his chest. "Whoever it is, they better get a head start on me because when I find out who did it, they're going to pay."

Pule's eyes widened and he glanced at Tate.

"Kam, I'm telling you this as your brother and someone who loves you. They found one of Grace's hair barrettes by the safe. Has she been acting different lately?" Tate said quietly.

Kam's head whipped back as if he'd been struck. "*What?* How do you know it's Grace's"

Tate put a hand on his brother's arm to calm him down. "Taryn recognized it as one of Grace's. Don't worry about it. It does make her look a little suspicious, but it's not proof of anything at this point. But just be aware that Rob is close to losing it. He might come in here yelling. You never know with the Downing's."

Kam closed his eyes and breathed in and out slowly before shaking his head. "He better not even look at her the wrong way. If anyone accuses Grace of anything, they'll have me to deal with. And I won't be nice," he said in a deadly voice.

Pule swallowed and looked down as Tate smiled at him. *Smart kid. Keep your mouth shut.*

"I agree, Kam. Grace is fantastic and I don't believe for a second she did this. But we do need to find out who did and do it fast. So help us out. Have you seen anything unusual around The Iron Skillet lately? Anyone acting different?"

Kam sat down and shook his head. "I'm going to have to think about this, but right off the top of my head, no. Even

James has been acting normal. He's been grumbling about his car but he's not trying to hide his money problems either."

Pule cleared his throat. "Yeah, because someone trying to hide their money problems would automatically look guilty, huh?" he asked, looking pointedly at Tate.

Tate glared at Pule before looking back at Kam. "Okay, we're going to get started with Grace just because we have to go through everyone. Don't be upset by it though," he said calmly.

Kam glared at him. "I don't want her interviewed. Just take my word for it. She didn't do it."

Tate shook his head. "Protocol, Kam. No reason to get upset. The sooner we get through everyone, the sooner we'll be out of your hair. We'll use your office so you can be sure we're not hurting your girlfriend," he added with a smile.

Kam frowned at him suspiciously but nodded his head. "Fine, I'll go get her, but if you make her cry, I'll make *you* cry."

Tate sighed. "Kam, seriously?"

Kam walked out of the office, letting the door slam loudly. Tate turned and walked over to Pule, putting a finger in his chest.

"Listen, you little punk. She's not trying to hide her financial problems from people. She just didn't want Kam to know because she doesn't want him to think badly of her because her mom cleaned her out. She was out trying to buy a dress to look pretty for him for the dance this Saturday. You keep pushing this and I promise, Kam will be breaking one of *your* bones. Not mine."

Pule pushed him away. "Fine, I won't say another word. But if it turns out she is the one who did this, I want a huge apology and a promotion."

Tate snorted and sat down in Kam's chair. "And if I'm right, I get to demote you and give you a pay cut."

Pule began arguing but the door opened and Grace walked

in. Tate smiled at her kindly and pointed to the chair. "Pule, while I talk to Grace, I'd like you to go interview the wait staff."

Pule grumbled something under his breath but walked out. Grace looked at him worriedly but sat down.

"Tate, is this about my mother?" she said in a weak voice. "Did you find her?"

Tate shook his head. "Don't worry. Billy and your mom won't be able to hide much longer. We'll find them. No, this is about The Iron Skillet. Over the weekend, The Iron Skillet was robbed. About eight thousand dollars has gone missing from Rob's safe. We're here to interview everyone to see if we can figure out who would do it."

Grace's mouth fell open and she turned pale. "Oh, no," she whispered. "Poor, Rob. I know exactly how he feels. He must be sick to his soul," she said sounding pained.

Tate nodded. "He is, along with a good case of rage."

Grace sighed and leaned her head in her hand. "I can't believe someone would do that to Rob. He's the nicest guy in the world. I'm just so shocked."

Tate nodded his head. "He's a great guy, but volatile too. So we better figure it out soon. Oh, one thing before you send Candice back. They found one of your hair clips on the floor by the safe. I don't suspect you at all, but I thought you should know."

Grace froze in the process of rising to stare at him as her mouth opened. She slowly lowered back to the chair as if she'd lost all strength.

"*My* hair clip?" she asked in a whisper.

Tate nodded slowly. "We're not sure how it got there."

Grace's eyes were wide with horror and he knew she got it. It looked bad for her.

"It's just circumstantial evidence, Grace. There's a dozen

ways that clip could have ended up there. I just wish Rob had listened and put in a camera system like I told him to."

Grace closed her eyes as if she were in pain. "Wait, are you saying that Rob thinks it's me?"

Tate cleared his throat and looked at his hands. "I'm not saying that at all, but Rob might."

Grace stood up, looking shaky and miserable. "Okay then," she said quietly and walked out without another word.

Tate stood up and watched as she walked over to Candice. While Candice walked across the kitchen toward him, he watched as Kam hurried to Grace's side and put his arm around her shoulders. Tate studied the way Kam stared down into Grace's eyes, his face full of concern and what very much looked like love.

Tate's mouth thinned to a grim line. Grace either had very bad luck or someone was setting her up. Tate's breath caught as he thought about who might want to see Grace gone and behind bars.

He closed his eyes and shook his head. Hunter had been going on and on about a group vacation to Hawaii. If he could get through this robbery, he was going to take his brother-in-law up on the offer. He was going to need a week of sun and surf if he had to throw Meredith into jail.

CHAPTER 29

Coming Clean

GRACE TOOK AN early lunch break and sped all the way to Belinda's Bakery. If she didn't get a pesto sandwich and a cookie soon she was just going to melt into a puddle of misery.

She told Baby to stay, promising her a walk in the park and then ran up the steps to the front door. She opened to the happy sound of bells ringing and walked right to the counter where Jane was standing, talking to Kit and Layla. All three turned and looked at her with wide eyes.

"Oh, my word, Grace. Are you okay?" Kit asked, looking at her with a frown.

Grace paused, looking down at her feet. She'd just barely found out about the robbery. *How in the world did they know?*

"I'm hanging in there," she said quietly, not sure exactly what they were talking about.

"We've had four people come in today, talking about the robbery and about your hair clip," Jane said, looking worried. "Were you in Rob's office?"

Grace felt like throwing up and leaned on the counter for

strength. People were already suspecting her. Grace shook her head.

"No, we're not sure how it got there," she said, her voice sounding reedy and weak.

Layla frowned at her. "You don't look so well. Come sit down. We'll bring over a sandwich and a cookie."

Grace stumbled to the back table and leaned her head in her hands. After she got her breathing under control she took out her emergency credit card to pay for the lunch. If this wasn't an emergency, she didn't know what was.

She handed her card to Layla when she brought the food over and picked up the sandwich. She had been craving a sandwich just minutes before but now as she put the food to her mouth, the thought of eating made her ill. She lowered the sandwich and took a drink of water instead.

All three sisters were staring at her expectantly as if they were waiting for something.

"I didn't do it," she said simply and the girls looked relieved to hear her say it.

"Of course you didn't," Kit scoffed, pulling a chair up next to hers. "But how crazy is it that *your* hair clip was found in Rob's office."

Grace shrugged, holding her water bottle in her hands. "Yeah, crazy."

Layla shook her head. "They'll figure out who did it. Tate's like a blood hound. He won't rest until he figures out who stole the money."

Jane nodded. "The man is unstoppable."

Grace tried to smile. "Good to know."

She felt her phone vibrate in her pocket and looked down to see who was calling her. She frowned when she didn't recognize the number but answered it anyways.

"Hello?"

"Hello, Ms. Jackson. This is Stan from the bank. I just wanted to let you know that we had an anonymous bank transfer of eight thousand, seven hundred and forty-two dollars put into your account this morning. It looks like maybe your mother had a change of heart. I just notified the police department so they're aware."

Grace's heart sunk as she struggled to form words. "Are you sure?" she whispered.

Stan laughed. "We're the bank, Ms. Jackson. We're always sure. Have a good day now."

Grace stared in shock at her phone as she lowered it to the table. She heard someone clear their throat but couldn't for the life of her look up.

She was done.

She couldn't handle anymore.

Grace stood up and picked up her water bottle, leaving her sandwich and cookie on the table.

"Thanks for lunch," she said woodenly and walked out of the bakery to the sound of Layla, Kit and Jane calling her name.

She drove around town as the bank manager's word ricocheted in her mind like a bullet. The same amount of money that was stolen was put into *her* bank account. Stan had already called the police and informed them. On top of that, her hair clip was found by the safe.

Everyone in town would assume by the end of the day that she had stolen from The Iron Skillet.

And just when she thought life couldn't get any worse. Now she was going to go to jail for twenty years. Grace laughed hysterically and looked down at her gas tank. She was on empty. Of course she was.

Well, if she was going to make a run for it, she'd need to fill up, she thought to herself, as a plan to run away to Alaska with Baby filled her mind. Sure, she hated snow and being cold but if it meant she'd stay out of jail, it might be an option.

She pulled into the first gas station and took out her magic emergency credit card. No way was she using her debit card and touching one penny of Rob's stolen money. The very thought of it made her ill.

She began pumping gas, staring off into the gray clouds as she wondered again how her life could be in such shambles when just a couple days ago she'd been so happy. Happier than she'd ever been to be honest.

Thoughts of Kam entered her mind and she felt like collapsing and giving up. She had come to Fircrest for a new start and a new adventure. She'd had no idea she'd fall for her boss or that he'd fall for her. Or that she'd make so many new friends. Or that the sight of Nate giggling and running into her arms would fill her heart so full she wanted to burst.

She wiped a few tears away and leaned against her truck.

"I hear you're thief of the year."

Grace slowly turned around to see Meredith Murphy standing by her car, looking perfect as usual. She wiped another tear off her cheek and stared silently at the woman smiling at her triumphantly.

"I knew there was something up with you and now everyone else will know it too. I got a call from Anne, early this morning, telling me everything. How they found your hair clip and how the money was put into your account. You didn't even try to hide it, did you?" she asked with a laugh.

Grace licked her lips and stood up tall. No way was she going to let this little bully kick her while she was down.

"And how's Asher doing?" she asked simply, and watched as Meredith's face crumpled and she turned her face away.

"I'll be so glad when you leave town with your tail between your legs. I swear you brought nothing but bad luck with you when you walked into town," Meredith finally said, as she swiped her credit card with a flourish.

Grace glared at Meredith and pulled the automatic receipt out and shoved it in her pocket.

"Meredith, your bad luck was of your own making. I had nothing to do with it," she said quietly.

Meredith sneered at her. "Anne is right. You're not good enough for Kam and you're not good enough for Fircrest. Why don't you just leave?" she asked with a syrupy smile.

Grace blinked quickly and looked away. That was exactly what she'd been planning on. Leave everything and sneak out of town, never to be heard from again. But the triumphant look on Meredith's face had her second guessing herself. Leave town with her tail between her legs?

Yeah, that wasn't going to happen.

"No such luck, honey. You're stuck with me," she said with a big smile and blew Meredith a kiss.

Meredith scowled at her as if she'd been expecting a different reaction. "When Kam realizes you're guilty, he'll dump you. He hates people who are dishonest."

Grace raised an eyebrow. "Oh, darn. Then you can have him. *Right?*"

Meredith tilted her chin in the air. "Like I care."

Grace laughed at that and opened the door to her truck. "Keep telling yourself that. Oh, and tell Asher I said hi," she added for good measure before jumping in her truck. She revved her engine a few times, making sure Meredith was covered in exhaust before driving out of the gas station.

She looked in her rearview mirror and smiled as Meredith gave her a rude hand gesture.

"Back at ya, Sweetheart," she murmured.

She drove past the interstate onramp and the road to Alaska and instead drove down to the beach. She let Baby out and took her water bottle down to the edge of the water. She glanced at her phone and groaned when she saw she only had twenty minutes left to her lunch break.

As if she could go back to work now. The police were probably staking the place out, waiting for her with handcuffs. On the other hand, Alaska was out for the simple reason that she couldn't give Meredith the satisfaction. It had been a bad idea anyways. No, she'd have to stay and fight this one out. Running away from your problems was something she'd learned at the knee of her mother. But she wasn't her mother. She was Grace Jackson, and she was a woman of integrity and honor. And this town was going to realize that soon enough.

In the meantime, someone wanted badly to trash her reputation.

She took a long pull from her water bottle, and frowned as her stomach rumbled. She'd left her entire lunch back at the bakery. Ugh.

She reached for her phone, knowing she needed to text Kam. He deserved to know what was going on. She swiped his contact and began texting.

Kam, can you meet me down by the water? Point Defiance. Second beach exit. We need to talk.

She re-read the text and hit send. Fifteen minutes later, Kam was sitting next to her. She felt her heart beating twice as fast as normal as she watched the large, silent man look at her. He wasn't going to say anything. *Okay.* She had plenty to say, he could just listen.

"On Monday morning, I went to buy a dress for Saturday night," she said, looking away from Kam's piercing eyes and out across the water instead. Much easier than seeing his love for her die a fast death.

"My debit card was declined. I ran over to the bank to find

out what the problem was, and it turns out my mom had taken the check for a hundred dollars I'd given her on Sunday and turned it into a check for *five thousand* dollars. She took everything I had. Tate showed up and took down a report and put out a warrant for my mom's arrest. And I was crushed," she added, letting the sand fall between her fingers.

"I didn't want you to know," she said quietly. "I was falling for you and I was starting to think that you were falling for me and it was pretty much the best feeling in the world. And if you knew how horrible my mother was, then you might think I might be horrible too," she said with a mirthless laugh.

"I begged Tate not to tell you. He wanted to go buy the dress for me but I wouldn't let him. He's a really nice guy, by the way. And then today, I find out that someone stole over eight thousand dollars from Rob with my hair clip, conveniently left right in front of the safe. And then, just a half an hour ago, I get a call at the Bakery from my bank manager telling me that someone anonymously deposited money into my account. Stan thinks it was my mom, having a guilty conscience. But the amount was a little over eight thousand dollars."

She closed her eyes and breathed in and out, letting the pain wash through her. "Kam, I don't expect you to believe me, but I didn't do it. I know this sounds paranoid, but I think someone is setting me up," she said, finally looking at him.

Kam's eyes were shadowed as he reached over and pulled her towards him. Grace pulled back for a second, confused, but when his arms wrapped around her, holding her gently against his chest, she began to shake.

And then she began to cry. *Again.* She'd been doing that a lot lately.

She wrapped her arms around his waist and held on as if her life depended on it.

"*Shh*," he said, kissing her forehead as if she were a child.

"Of course you didn't take the money. Anyone who thinks you did is an idiot," he said in a grim voice.

Grace hid her face against his chest and breathed in the comfort and safety that she felt in his arms.

"Everyone will think I did, though," she mumbled into his chest.

Kam shook his head. "Anyone who wants to think you did, will have me to deal with."

Grace looked up and wiped her eyes as she looked at Kam. "I ran into Meredith at the gas station. She told me she'd heard from Anne early this morning that I stole the money. She even knew about my hair clip being in Rob's office. She's probably told at least twenty people by now."

Kam's eyes narrowed. "Did she?"

Grace nodded her head and then went back to the support of his chest. It felt much better, hiding in the strength of Kam's arms. Maybe she could just stay here forever?

"I'm taking you home. Rob shut down the restaurant today since everyone's being interviewed by the police. I want you to relax and not think about this okay? I've got to run some errands but tonight I'll take you back to my house and make you dinner."

Grace snorted. "Kam, I'll be in jail by then. Come on. But I think this would be a good time to ask you if you believe in prison romance?"

Kam laughed. "Tate tries to put you in jail and he'll need to bring back up. No one is touching you, Grace. *No one.* And when I find out who set this up, they're going to regret it."

Grace frowned at the violence she heard in his voice and sighed. "I've never had anyone stick up for me before. I kind of like it."

Kam kissed her forehead. "Get used to it. Grace, you know I care about you, right?"

Grace sniffed and looked up at him, knowing she must look like a makeup smeared hag. "*Why?*" she asked in confusion. "Why in the world would you care about me?"

Kam laughed and took her face in his two hands so gently she wanted to weep. "Because you're the sun in my day. You make my heart beat and you make me want to dance and sing again. Grace, I love you. I can't keep myself from kissing you and holding you and wanting to be with you every second of the day. I need you. I'm a mess without you."

Grace stared at Kam, humbled by his simple words. No games. No half-truths. Just a man expressing his feelings for her. *Wow.*

"If you only knew how much I love you too," she said and began crying again.

Kam laughed softly and held her close as she sobbed into his chest.

"And it's all ruined. I was so happy and everything was so perfect and then life just crumbled on me. And the thought of moving to Alaska and never seeing you or Nate again made me want to die," she said, wiping her eyes on his shirt.

Kam sighed and closed his eyes as he held her hard.

"I would have just followed you. Natano and I would hunt bear and live off of salmon. We could have made it work."

Grace laughed and shook her head, feeling so relaxed now, she could barely move.

"We'd live in an igloo and wear fur year long. I like it. Let's leave now."

Kam grinned and tilted her head up, touching his lips to hers lightly. "Nah, I want to clean up this mess. Besides, my family would miss me too much. And you too. Everyone loves you, Grace. This is your home now."

Grace's eyes clouded over. "*Someone* doesn't love me very much. Whoever transferred all that money into my account hates my guts."

Kam growled low in his throat. "Speaking of that. Let's get you home. There are some things I need to take care of."

Grace nodded and tried to stand up. Kam stood up and picked her up easily in his arms and walked with her to his car.

"*But my truck...*"

Kam whistled for Baby and helped her into the car. "You're in no condition to drive. I'll get Pule to pick up your truck later. Besides, this way you can't run away to Alaska without me."

Grace laughed softly and buckled up. "Like I could ever leave you."

Kam drove her home and waited for her to get inside before he left. She went straight to her bed and fell on it, covering herself with her blanket.

Maybe she'd take a nap and by the time she woke up, life would somehow be better and she wouldn't be headed for jail. She wanted with all of her heart to believe Kam, that somehow he could save her from her fate. But really, what could one man do when someone was determined to destroy her?

CHAPTER 30

Celebrating

ANNE MATAFEO WAS in a good mood. Life was starting to look up. And when she was happy, *she shopped*. Of course, when she was sad, she shopped too, so there wasn't that much difference. But today there was a purpose. She needed a dress for the Fine Dining experience at The Iron Skillet this Saturday. She wanted to dance the night away with her Honey and eat amazing food too.

That, and celebrate the fact that she'd singlehandedly gotten rid of Grace Jackson. She laughed at the memory of Rob calling her, upset that all of his money was gone. As soon as everyone finds out that all the money just happens to be in Grace's bank account, she was going to leave town faster than you could say *prison*.

Anne leaned out the window and waved at Cleo Matafeo. "Hi, Cleo!" she yelled, as Cleo waved back.

It was like the sun had finally come out. She should have realized sooner that all she had to do was take matters into her own hands. That's the only way things got done anyways.

She pulled up in front of the Rose boutique, a store Wren always talked about, and hopped out. She pushed through the door and frowned at the dim lighting. Of course that might be a blessing. She perused the racks of clothes and didn't see anything she liked. She went up to ask the clerk a question and saw the perfect dress. A long, flowing dress in red with gorgeous, bright flowers – It would be perfect for Saturday night. A little long on her, but she could have someone hem it before Saturday.

"That's the dress I want," she said, pointing to the dress hanging behind the clerk on a separate rack.

The clerk glanced behind her and shook her head. "Sorry, I'm holding it for a customer. If she doesn't come back by tomorrow you're welcome to have it."

Anne frowned, hating the fact that she could see the dress she wanted but she couldn't have it. "Look, I'll pay you extra for it. I really want it and I have the money right now. I'll pay cash."

The clerk frowned at her and shook her head. "No, she was a nice girl and she was in love with this dress. Come back tomorrow though if you're still interested."

Anne glared at the girl and lifted her head in the air, wondering why anyone would dye their hair pink. *Tacky.* "Afraid I won't be back. You just lost my business."

The girl shrugged and went back to her laptop. "We'll try and survive," she said dryly.

Anne made a huffing sound and pulled the door open with enough force to send the bells ringing like crazy.

"The nerve of her," she muttered.

She decided to drive down to Belinda's Bakery and grab a few cupcakes for Sefe. The man was obsessed with them and he deserved a treat for putting up with her for the past couple of months. She hadn't been in the best of moods. She arrived a few minutes later and entered the bakery to the sound of people talking and laughing.

Anne waited patiently until she was the last one there and pointed to the Matafeo cupcakes. "I'd like six of your biggest cupcakes," she said smiling brightly at Kit.

Kit nodded her head and began boxing up the cupcakes while Jane walked over to say hi. *Nice girl.*

"Hi there, Anne. You look so happy. Good news?" she asked.

Anne shrugged, knowing she couldn't say anything. "Well, I'll just say that life turns out the way it should sometimes. And I'm not ashamed to say that makes me happy."

Kit narrowed her eyes at her and glanced at Jane.

"You're glad that life turns out sometimes? That sounds kind of cryptic. That's not like you, Anne. You're such a straight shooter," Kit chided.

Anne preened and then couldn't stand it. She had to say something.

"Well, I'm sure you've heard by now, but Grace Jackson stole all of Rob's money out of his safe. *All of it.* I even heard she had the gall to deposit it in her own account. I told everyone that girl was trash. And here, everyone was determined to push her on our Kam. As if she was good enough to be my grandson's mother. The very idea is offensive," she said, frowning that it came so close to happening.

Jane's mouth was open and Kit looked shell shocked. Layla who had been wiping down a table walked over and put her hand on her arm.

"Anne, how do you know all of this?"

Anne flipped her hair and shrugged. "Rob called me and told me about the missing money."

Layla nodded. "But did he actually say that *Grace* was the one who took it?"

Anne shook her head. "No, the poor man is so naïve. But I know it was her."

Kit frowned. "But then how did you know the money was deposited into her account?"

Anne rolled her eyes, feeling irritated. "Why so many questions? *I just know, okay?* Now how much do I owe you? I'm in a hurry to get home. I'm celebrating tonight."

Layla cleared her throat. "Wait. You're going to celebrate someone's misery? Anne, that's unkind, even for you."

Anne put her hands on her hips and glared Layla down. "Look here, Layla Bender. I told that woman she should stay away from Kam. If she's going to ignore me, then she's going to have to pay the consequences."

Kit shook her head slowly. "And those consequences are being meted out by you," she said slowly as if to make sure.

Anne shrugged and smiled brightly. "No one messes with me *or* my family. You should know that, Kit," she said sweetly.

Kit rang Anne up without saying another word and Anne walked out with her cupcakes, having gotten the final word in for once with the bakery girls.

And it felt amazing.

She drove home with her good mood returning immediately. She should invite Kam and Nate over for dinner Sunday. It had been too long since she'd seen her grandson. And now that Kam had finally learned his lesson, it was time to make amends. Kam would now be able to see how unsuitable Grace was, and he'd apologize nicely and things could go back to the way they should be. Her, Sefe, Kam and Nate and everyone else. Her family.

Hers.

Not Grace Jackson's.

CHAPTER 31

Fired

KAM TEXTED TATE and told him to meet him at the restaurant and was grateful when Tate showed up within twenty minutes. They sat in his office and looked at each other for a moment.

"What are you thinking?" Tate finally asked, sitting back and resting his ankle on his thigh.

Kam shook his head. "Tate, I'm telling you Grace was set up. Someone did this to her."

Tate didn't say anything for a moment. "What makes you say that?"

Kam leaned forward. "Her hair clip *right* in front of the safe? Are you kidding me? That's so obvious, it's ridiculous. A child would do that. And I just talked to Grace. She said she was at the gas station filling up and Meredith was there. Grace said that Meredith was going off about Anne calling her this morning to gloat about her stealing money. Tate, she said, *this morning*. No one even knew until ten when Rob called you guys. I asked Rob. He didn't call his mom until eleven. Something is fishy, Tate."

Tate sighed and rubbed his face with his hands. He was

already exhausted from talking to all of the employees at the restaurant along with trying to get security footage from the dry cleaners across the street.

"Kam, I'm not an idiot. I know Grace didn't do it. Here's my problem though. The bank notified me that someone, an *anonymous* someone, deposited the exact amount that was stolen from Rob, into Grace's account. Right there, I know it wasn't her. Nobody is that dumb and I know a lot of dumb criminals. So relax, I'm way ahead of you. And I have two suspects. Pule is talking to Meredith right now down at the station and I'm getting ready to go talk to your mother-in-law."

Kam sighed in relief and closed his eyes, lifting his clasped hands up to heaven. "You're the best Tate. You can be my best man at my wedding."

Tate grinned at that, his face relaxing with happiness. "Dude, you serious?"

Kam grinned back. "Would I joke about something like this? Of course I'm serious. I love her. I love her so much it hurts."

Tate sat back and shook his head. "Kam, you know I care about you so I have to ask. Are you *sure* it's love? *Hold on, hold on.* Don't get mad. Let me finish," he said as Kam stood up and crossed his arms over his chest. A sure sign that he was ticked.

"I just have to ask because this all happened so fast and she's the first girl you've dated since... since you lost Bailey. Maybe you just feel comfortable with her? Or maybe you're just good friends? *Maybe you're just lonely?*"

Kam looked at his brother and shook his head slowly. "I've been in love, Tate, so I know what love is and I know what it isn't. What I feel for Grace is love."

Tate frowned and looked down at his hands. "Is it the lasting kind though? Is this the kind of passion that has the power to last? Or is this the kind of love that's sweet and nice and fades because you're really just friends who care about each other? I don't want to see you end up divorced in a few years. None of us do."

Kam blinked a few times and sat down. "How do I explain this?" he muttered. "I loved Bailey with all of my heart, you know that. But this is different. With Bailey, I was just so in awe of her beauty and how incredible she was. I felt like every day was precious because I was blessed to have this delicate princess in my life. And it felt like that. Like I was living a fairytale. But Grace is different. She's down to earth and she makes me laugh. I relax around her because she's always teasing me or making me sing or dance. I feel more like me with her than when I'm alone. She makes me happy, Tate. And she also makes me want to kiss her. *A lot*," he added, turning red.

Tate grinned and stood up. "Well, that answers that then. You're in love, brother. Congratulations and yes I'll be your best man. Now I gotta go save your girl."

Kam smiled in relief and walked him out. "My life is in your hands. No pressure. But if you do feel like you need to arrest Grace, I'm taking her and disappearing."

Tate glared at Kam. "Stop being ridiculous. I told you that wasn't going to happen."

Kam tilted his head and looked at him like he was on the opposite side of a Rugby match. "It better not. Because you'll have to bring an army if you do."

Tate rolled his eyes. "You're killing me, Kam. Seriously killing me. Go kiss your girlfriend and let me handle things."

"What choice do I have?" Kam grumbled.

Tate glared at him. "None."

Kam smiled as Tate drove away and was grateful for his family. He relaxed a little as he walked back into the kitchen. He needed to lock up and make sure everything was ready for tomorrow before checking on Grace.

When he walked out of the pantry, he was surprised to see Rob standing in the middle of the kitchen looking miserable.

"Rob, you okay?" he asked, walking over and grabbing Rob's shoulder.

Rob shook his head. "Kam, how could I be? Someone stole from me and it makes me sick to my soul. I don't want this to come between us, but I think Grace did it. There's no one else it could be."

Kam sighed and motioned for Rob to come to his office.

"Rob, it wasn't Grace," he said firmly as if talking to a child.

Rob sat down and stared at him with blood shot, worried eyes. "Of course she did. You just can't see it because you're interested in her."

Kam shook his head. "I'm more than interested in her and I can see just fine. Ask yourself something first before you make any more accusations. Who stands to benefit if Grace takes the fall for this?"

Rob frowned and shook his head. "I know there are a couple people in town who have made it clear they don't like Grace, but neither one has the audacity to steal from me," he said firmly.

Kam stared at Rob, not wanting to fight with his friend and his boss but needing to defend the woman he loved, too.

"Rob, listen to me. Grace didn't do this. And if you look at all the facts, they point to your mom being the one. *The hairclip*, Rob. Just lying there in front of the safe to implicate Grace. That has your mom written all over it."

Rob stared at him quietly for a moment and then stood up, turning toward the door. "Because we're friends and I care about you, I'm going to forget that you just said that. Because if I didn't, I'd have to fire you right now."

Kam frowned, following Rob out of his office. "Then you

better go ahead and fire me then, because Grace is innocent and your mom has been known to act crazy when it comes to her family. Understandably so, but Anne has a track record for doing the unthinkable sometimes."

Rob turned back, his eyes glowing with anger now. "Have it your way. You're fired. Clear out your things. I'll send your last paycheck in the mail."

Kam stared at Rob, shocked that he'd take it that far but he nodded his head slowly. "See you around, Rob."

Rob didn't answer and stomped out of the kitchen, leaving Kam standing by himself, stunned at how quickly that had happened.

Kam shook his head sadly. Rob was going to hate finding out his mom had something to do with it. He whistled as he locked up and left the kitchen, shutting the door firmly.

He had a feeling it wasn't his last day at The Iron Skillet. How was Rob going to refund all those dinner tickets for the Fine Dining experience if he didn't have a Head Chef or a Sous Chef who happened to be the mastermind behind the Fine Dining experience in the first place? Kam grinned at Rob's dilemma and walked up the back steps to Grace's apartment. It was nice to have a day off every now and then.

CHAPTER 32

The Interrogation

PULE WATCHED AS Asher stormed into the police station and made a bee-line right for him.

"I am not paid enough for this," Pule muttered and shut his laptop as Asher stopped beside him, breathing heavy and looking like he wanted to get in a fight with someone.

"What's this about my wife being arrested for framing Grace Jackson? Something about money being stolen from Rob's restaurant? *Are you kidding me?*" he exploded, making all the heads in the room turn in their direction.

Pule controlled his automatic anger at being yelled at and motioned for his friend to have a seat. He counted to five as he searched for his empathy instead of his baton.

"Meredith was questioned, Asher, *not arrested*. I don't know where you're getting your information, but they have it wrong. As a matter of fact, you just missed her. If you hurry, you can catch her," he said, hoping that Asher would run after his wife.

Asher looked at him coolly and shook his head. "No, *you're* the one I want to talk to. Who do you think you are, bothering my wife and treating her like some common criminal?" he demanded, pulling his suit coat away from his body.

Pule rolled his eyes and counted to five. *Again.* "I just asked her a few questions, Asher. No big deal. Now, I'm busy, so if you'll excuse me."

Asher's face went hard. "Pule, *answer me.* Why was Meredith being questioned?"

Pule leaned forward, almost out of patience. "Because it's no secret Meredith was furious that Kam was dating Grace. Everyone and their dog knows your wife hates Grace. Grace was set up to take the fall for a robbery and there are only two suspects. Your wife and one other woman."

Asher groaned and leaned back in his chair as if he were exhausted. "Pule, why is this happening to me? Why can't my wife just love me like Posey loves you? What would you do if the whole town knew that your wife might have set up another woman because she was jealous over an ex?"

Pule grimaced and shook his head. "It wouldn't feel good, Man. I agree. But if it makes you feel any better, I don't think it was Meredith. At least she didn't cross that line."

Asher snorted. "What's your definition of the line? Because with me, she crossed it a long time ago."

Pule nodded, in total agreement. "Have you talked to Meredith about counseling? I know you guys love each other. It's possible you can work this out if you're both willing."

Asher looked away as he fidgeted with his tie. "That's the problem. Do I *want* to work on a marriage where my wife doesn't see me as her number one? I'll always be her number two or whatever number I am in her heart."

Pule shook his head, feeling sick for his friend and the pain he was going through. "But what if this was a big wake-up call for her? What if counseling could make your marriage even stronger now? What if you *are* her number one and she's just been immature and blind?"

Asher smiled cynically at Pule and stood up. "That's a lot of what ifs. Sorry to bother you, Pule. I'll see you around."

Pule stood up and watched Asher walk out of the police station, a miserable man who didn't know what to do. But Pule knew one thing. Asher loved Meredith. If he didn't, he wouldn't be in so much pain.

He reached for his keys but then stopped as Tate walked in, followed by Sefe and Anne. They both looked royally ticked and Tate looked exhausted. He'd better stick around. He nodded at Tate and followed them back to the interrogation room.

He sat down next to Tate as Sefe and Anne took their seats on the opposite side of the scarred, wooden table. Tate reached for the recorder and turned it on.

"You have the right to a lawyer," he began but was interrupted by Sefe.

"Let's just get this over with," Sefe said, sounding impatient. "I have spring training tonight and I don't want to miss it. I can't believe you'd think for one moment that my sweet Anne would do such a thing, Tate," he scolded. "When I tell your father about being dragged down to the police station, he's not going to be happy with you."

Tate wasn't surprised at his anger and confusion. Sefe was a good man but if it didn't involve football then he just wasn't that interested. It was very possible that Sefe had spaced the fact that Anne hated Grace and set her up. "I'll keep that in mind, Sefe."

Tate turned to Anne who was attempting to look stoic but was having a hard time pulling it off because she kept smiling happily.

"Anne, thanks for coming down. Do you know why we want to talk to you?"

Anne nodded, her lip curling up slightly. "Of course. *Everyone* knows. You can't go anywhere and not hear about how

Grace Jackson stole all of my son's money. She's a low class, thief. Toa and Pika told me how sketchy her mom and her boyfriend are. And you know what they say, the apple doesn't fall far from the tree. Good riddance, I tell you. Tate, I wouldn't be surprised if she hasn't already left town. I think you should send a policeman over to check on her."

Tate frowned at Anne. "Well, if that were true about apples, then I'd be the worst apple around."

Anne looked away, not saying anything.

Tate continued, feeling Pule's hand on his back as if to comfort him. "And don't worry about Grace's whereabouts. She's with Kam, right now and she's perfectly fine. And just to be clear on the matter, Grace *isn't* the one who stole the money," he stated and then watched as two bright red circles appeared on Anne's face.

"*What did you say?*" she gasped, staring at him in surprise.

Tate almost smiled. "*I said*, Grace didn't do it. Or do you mean the part where I said, Kam was with Grace? It's pretty sweet actually. Sometimes trials bring people together, you know? I think the thought of Grace being framed pushed Kam over the edge. You know how protective he is. Kam just asked me to be his best man when he marries Grace," he said, smiling happily.

Anne slammed her hand down on the table so hard, Pule jumped in his chair.

"No he isn't," she hissed furiously. "Over my dead body will Kam marry that sleazy woman. Over my daughter's dead body!" she shouted.

Tate frowned and glanced at Pule. Pule met his eyes and nodded his head. They were together on this. Anne on the brink of losing it was a strong indication that she was the one they wanted.

"Anne, please calm down. You seem very upset." Tate said in a soothing voice.

Sefe stared at his wife in confusion. "Anne, what's wrong? You're acting like a crazy woman."

Anne ran her hands through her hair, making it stick up wildly. "*Are you kidding me?* After everything I've done, he's going to marry her now?"

Tate nodded and tried to look as pleased as he could. "My whole family is thrilled. And Kam is happier than I've *ever* seen him," he said, wincing at the pain he knew those words would cause Anne and wishing he didn't have to. But if he was going to get Anne to admit that she'd been the one to steal the money, he'd have to push her to her breaking point. And her breaking point was Bailey.

Anne's face turned white and she stared at him with rage in her eyes. "Kam's happier than he's ever been?" she whispered.

Tate nodded and turned to Pule. "Wouldn't you say so, Officer Matafeo?"

Pule laughed and nodded his head. "I heard him just the other day, Tate. He said he's never been happier than he is now with Grace. No offense, Anne. I know he loved Bailey, but Grace is something special, you know? I've never seen him so in love."

Anne's hands began to shake and Sefe put a hand on her shoulders, looking at her worriedly. "Honey, you need to calm down."

Anne stood up, visibly shaking and pointed a finger at Tate.

"I will not stand for this," she whispered. "I refuse. Bailey deserves better than this. *She died,*" Anne whispered, beginning to cry. "She's not here. She's not here take care of her family, so *I* have to. It's the only thing I can do now to help her. I *had* to protect Kam and Nate. It's what she would have wanted."

Tate nodded, feeling compassion for Anne. "And how did you do that, Anne? How did you protect Kam?" he asked softly.

Anne ignored the tears streaming down her cheeks as she stared past Tate's head at the empty wall. "I made sure Kam would never want Grace. *But he does.* How can he want Grace after she stole all that money?" she asked, shaking her head in confusion and sounding sad.

Pule leaned forward. "Because he loves her, Anne. He knows her and he knows she could never have done something so horrible."

Anne's mouth worked for a moment as she shook her head back and forth erratically. "He can't love her. He loves Bailey. *He. Loves. Bailey,*" she said over and over as she collapsed into Sefe's arms.

Tate watched as Sefe soothed his wife and felt horrible for pushing Anne so hard. But he had to finish it.

"Anne, you're the one who stole the money from Rob, aren't you?" he asked softly as she continued to sob in her husband's arms.

Sefe's head whipped up at that, looking shocked but Tate ignored him.

"I get it, Anne. I mean, if I were in your place, I don't know if I wouldn't have done the same thing. Everyone knows how much I love Jane. I know if something ever happened to her, I'd *never* marry again," he said, not knowing if that was true or not, but needing to get Anne's reaction.

Anne cried harder, nodding her head. "*Exactly,*" she practically shouted. "He loved Bailey with all of his heart. How can he move on? *And with Grace Jackson?* She doesn't look anything like Bailey. She doesn't act like her. She's practically the opposite of Bailey. How could Grace take my daughter's place? It's a joke," she insisted.

Sefe took his wife's face in his large hands and made her

look at him. "Honey, Grace isn't taking Bailey's place. No one could do that. But Grace has her own place in Kam's heart and you need to respect that. And if you've done something to hurt Grace, then you need to make it right. Tell Tate the truth, Anne. Did you take the money from Rob to make Grace look bad?" he asked softly.

Tate looked at his uncle in surprise, impressed that he was the one to push Anne for the truth and very much appreciating it.

Anne looked up at her husband with wet eyes and lowered her head a few inches. "I did," she whispered. "I just wanted her to leave and never come back. I'm sorry, Sefe. Please don't hate me."

Sefe made a huffing sound and hugged his wife hard. "I could never hate you, Sweetheart. You're the love of my life. Now let's fix this mess, okay?"

Anne leaned her head on Sefe's shoulder as if she was emotionally drained. Tate felt Pule's hand on his back and appreciated the support.

This wasn't going to be easy. Anne had committed a felony and framed an innocent woman. This wasn't just a mess. This was a disaster for their community.

"If you'll excuse us for a second, I need a minute with Officer Matafeo," Pule said, standing up and opening the door.

Tate frowned, but followed Pule out into the hall. "*Now*, Pule? I just got a confession out of her. What could be so important?" Tate demanded.

Pule took him by the arms and looked him in the eyes. "Don't do it. Don't charge her."

Tate stared at his cousin in awe. "You're kidding me, right? She just committed a felony with the intent to commit *another* felony. There's no way I *can't* charge her."

Pule shook his head. "Rob won't press charges. We'll get the money out of Grace's account and all of this will go away."

Tate groaned and rubbed his neck. "One small problem. *Grace*. Why in the world wouldn't she press charges? And if she doesn't, the D.A. will. Anne framed her in cold blood. Anne would have been totally fine if Grace had spent the next twenty years in jail."

Pule stared at him for a moment and shrugged. "I don't know, but I do know that if we can work this out between everyone without involving the courts, this family might have a chance to heal. Can you imagine Anne in prison?" he said with a shiver.

Tate snorted. "She'd be running the joint within weeks."

"First let's call the bank and take care of the money and then let's talk to Kam and Grace," Pule said.

Tate nodded. "I get what you're saying, but what about consequences? Anne's just going to walk away without any punishment for what she did? The woman stole a lot of money and framed Grace for it. I'm telling you now, she wouldn't have felt any guilt about Grace going to jail or leaving town in humiliation. That doesn't sit well with me. It would be unethical to just sweep this under the rug. And I can't. I took an oath and so did you."

Pule nodded in agreement. "Tate, she lost her daughter. She lives with that pain every day. I know it's no excuse and it's definitely not rational, but can't we have some pity on her?"

Tate threw up his hands. "I know, I know. But there has to be justice too."

Pule sighed, rubbing his chin. "We need time to figure this out. Why don't we put her in a jail cell overnight? That will wake her up. Cuff her and read her her rights. Tomorrow we'll see about releasing her."

Tate smiled a little, liking the idea. "We could have Rob

and Taryn come to the jail to visit her. Not being able to be with her family might be the wakeup call that she needs."

He slapped Pule on the shoulder. "You're a good cop and a good man," he said, grinning.

Pule smiled, "Thanks. About that raise?"

Tate snorted. "Dude, you're getting demoted and a pay cut, but you're still a good cop."

Pule groaned and followed him back into the room.

Tate went through the process of reading Anne her rights and putting cuffs on her as Sefe watched helplessly.

Anne stood there without any expression until he handed her off to Officer Whitfield, a female officer who would take over. She looked back at him with panic in her eyes.

"I didn't mean it, Tate. Please don't put me in jail," she whispered, her voice trembling.

Tate forced himself to show no emotion. "Just think how Grace would have felt today, being locked up for a crime she didn't commit," he said evenly. He watched as Anne's eyes hardened and he sighed as Anne turned and walked away.

Anne might need more than one day in jail.

CHAPTER 33

The Dregs of Society

ROB SAT NEXT to Taryn and stared at his mother on the other side of the safety glass. Ever since the phone call from Pule, he'd been in a state of shock.

Taryn picked up the phone and motioned for Anne to do the same. "Hi, Mom."

Anne tried to smile but grimaced instead. "Hi, honey. Thanks for coming down to see me. I can't believe they're making me wear this hideous orange jumpsuit. I don't understand why they won't just let me wear jeans and a t-shirt or something normal."

Rob grabbed the phone from his sister. "*What were you thinking?*" he yelled through the phone, feeling his anger win out over the overwhelming embarrassment of the situation.

Anne shrugged helplessly. "I guess I wasn't thinking. I just wanted Grace gone. I mean, how could I stand by and watch Kam ruin his life with that woman? I owed it to Bailey," she said, righteous anger lifting her chin in the air.

Taryn snorted beside him and Rob closed his eyes and tried not to have a heart-attack. "You *owed* it to Bailey to hurt Kam? Is that it?" he asked softly.

Anne frowned and shook her head. "Of course not. I would never hurt Kam. He's just confused. He doesn't know what he wants. When this all dies down and Grace leaves, it'll go back to the way it was. The way it's supposed to be," she said earnestly.

Taryn was leaning in to hear their mom, but grabbed the phone from him as soon as their mom's words left her mouth. "You mean when Kam was miserable and lonely? He has a chance to be happy, Mom. Why would you ruin that for him? I'm telling you right now, Bailey would want Kam to be happy and to live a full life with love and companionship and, and... *fun.* And you thought you'd just take that away from him because you know what's best? Mom, I'm so ashamed of you," Taryn said, tears thick in her voice.

Anne blinked a few times and looked away as if she was confused. Rob firmly took the phone away from his sister and waited until his mother looked at him again.

"Taryn is right, Mom. Kam deserves to live again and smile again and be happy again and Grace gives him that. They have a chance to be a family. Think about someone besides yourself for once. Nate needs a mom and it turns out, Kam wants a wife."

Anne bared her teeth and glared at him. "Nate has me," she spit out.

Rob shook his head. "And you see him, *what?* A few times a week for a few hours at the most. What about bedtime stories and someone to comb his hair in the morning and tell him they love him as he goes to school? Grace loves Nate and he loves her. You need to think about what you did, Mom. You took it upon yourself to decide for Kam what was best for him and his son. That's not love. That's control."

Anne shook her head. "You don't understand, Rob,

because you're not a mother. It's my job to look out for this family. *My job.*"

Rob nodded. "But it's not your job to *ruin* this family, or to steal from me or to frame an innocent woman. You did all of that. And now the whole town knows what you did. Kam knows. Do you think Kam will ever want you around Nate now that he knows what you tried to do to the woman he loves?"

Anne whisked away a tear from her cheek. "He doesn't love her," she insisted. "He's just confused."

Rob glanced at Taryn who was still staring at their mother in shock. "No, Mom. You're the one who's confused and now you're the one in jail. And sadly, you're the one who is going to spend twenty years in prison for felony theft."

Anne's face froze as she looked back at him. Reality finally starting to sink in. "Do you think Sefe will divorce you? I mean, at his age, he doesn't have time to wait for you to get out of jail," Rob asked, looking at Taryn.

Anne gasped and covered her mouth with her hand. Taryn took the phone from him and waited for Anne to look at her.

"Mom, I love you but maybe this needed to happen. You go through life doing what you want, saying what you want and not caring who you hurt. Well, you've hurt a lot of people now. And I'm going to speak for my sister since she can't speak for herself. *Leave Kam alone.* Don't you ever meddle in his life again. He doesn't deserve this."

Anne tried to lift her chin but instead put the phone down and stood up, walking away with her shoulders shaking.

Rob took the phone and hung it up before looking at Taryn. "I hope that got through to her."

Taryn sighed, looking tired. "We can only pray. *Holy crap,* Rob. Our mom is in jail," she said and then stared at him as she covered a laugh with her hand.

Rob stared at her for a moment and then leaned back,

laughing too. "It's better to laugh than cry, huh? I guess we shouldn't be surprised though. Come on. I'm going to take you out for ice cream. We deserve a treat after having to visit our mom in jail."

Taryn stood and smiled, linking her arm with his. "I want a double scoop for this."

Rob opened the door for her. "You got it."

Ten minutes later they were sitting at Tai's diner, eating ice cream in an old fashioned red vinyl booth.

"So putting mom's disastrous life aside for a moment, how are *you* doing?" he asked looking at his sister. She no longer had that haggard, drained and empty look.

Taryn gave him a half-smile and shrugged. "We're doing okay. Not great. Not perfect. But okay. Which is a thousand times better than it was, so that makes it feel almost like heaven," she said wonderingly.

Rob smiled and nodded his head, taking a bite of his mocha almond fudge. "That's pretty good then. So is Brogan going to take that job?"

Taryn shook her head with a real smile this time. "No. We've been going to counselling for awhile now and during the last session, he told me he turned it down. He said he never wanted me to worry about him again. We're going to stay put and work on our relationship."

Rob sighed in relief, grateful that his sister's marriage was doing so much better. "That's fantastic, Taryn. Why don't you and Brogan come over for dinner Sunday? It's been awhile and it would be good to see you all together again."

Taryn smiled, her eyes lighting up. "That sounds wonderful. Thanks, Rob."

Rob smiled and then noticed Tai at the counter, talking to Pule and Tate.

"Oh, crud. The Matafeo's are over at the counter. Should we duck and run?"

Taryn sighed and looked over her shoulder. "Those Matafeo's are law abiding people. The salt of the earth. And here we are, the dregs of society now."

Rob wanted to argue with his sister, but shut his mouth. There was really nothing he could say to that.

"Hey, Rob. How's it going, Man?"

Rob looked up to see Tai standing beside him. Tate and Pule right by his side.

Rob couldn't even smile. He felt like dirt. "Yeah, I've been better. Your cousin there just locked up my mom."

Tate shrugged. "Well, when someone steals a lot of money and then frames an innocent person, that's kind of what happens."

Taryn blew out a breath and scooted over. "It feels weird having all of you guys standing there looking down on us lowly Downing's. Have a seat."

He scooted over and Tai sat next to him while Pule pulled up a chair and sat at the end of the booth with Tate sitting next to Taryn.

Tate looked at him and shook his head. "It's a mess, Rob. There's no way around it. How did talking to your mom go? Was there any remorse?"

Rob cleared his throat, feeling even more embarrassed if that was possible. "Uh, *no*. Not only is there no remorse, but she thinks she's justified in doing what she did. I'm going to get her a lawyer tomorrow and get her out on bail. But sitting in jail tonight is probably good for her."

Taryn nodded, frowning at her half eaten ice cream cone. "It's so weird what people do when they can rationalize their behavior. Our own mother stole all of the money out of our safe. It's kind of hard to digest."

Tate put his arm around Taryn's shoulders and gave her a hug. "It'll be okay. I bet tomorrow morning your mom might have a little more remorse than she does right now."

Rob sighed feeling tired all of a sudden. "And if she doesn't?"

Pule shrugged. "Rob, you should know that you don't have to press charges. We've already talked to Sefe and we're all in agreement that Anne really does need to learn her lesson though."

Rob stared at Pule and then Tate. "*That's right*. I wasn't even thinking. I don't have to press charges. I mean she is my mother," he said in relief, feeling the weight of the world fall off his shoulders.

Tate cleared his throat. "But she needs to understand that what she did was wrong. I don't know if Kam will ever speak to her again after this."

Rob shook his head and looked away. "Heck, I don't even know if he'll speak to *me*. I fired him yesterday."

Pule, Tate and Tai all stared at Rob while Taryn made a choking sound. "My family is crazy," she announced loudly to the diner. "It's official. The Downing family is completely insane. *Rob, how could you?*" she demanded, looking furious.

Tate frowned at him. "Yeah, why would you do that?"

Rob looked at his hands and couldn't meet their eyes. "Because I was convinced that Grace took the money and he was convinced that she didn't. He told me that he thought my mom took the money to frame Grace and I was so offended by that, that I um, fired him on the spot," he said, feeling sick to his stomach and ashamed at being so blind.

Pule blew out a breath. "Dude, that was such a mistake. Who's going to cook now? *Manuel?* Because I know from Kam, that he's not that great. He's okay at prep but don't expect him to sauté anything."

Rob groaned and took another bite of his ice cream in misery. "Kam and Grace will probably move to Seattle and open up their own restaurant and I'll go out of business and end up selling sports equipment and doing bad commercials."

Taryn laughed. "That would actually be hilarious. Mr. Cool Baseball man's fall from grace, because of Grace. Well, because of our mom, but that's semantics."

Pule laughed. "Good one, Taryn."

Taryn sighed, her smile fading fast. "I guess I better start looking for a new job. The Iron Skillet is well on it's way to being turned in the next Chuck-A-Rama. You hiring, Tai?"

Tai nodded immediately. "For you, Taryn, I won't even make you fill out an application. You can start bussing tables tonight."

They all laughed, but Rob wasn't happy. His mom had some thinking and soul searching to do.

But then again, *so did he.*

CHAPTER 34

The Picnic

KAM PICKED UP Grace later that day and they drove to Hunter and Kit's house. "My buddy loves kayaking and he said we could borrow his equipment. We'll kayak over to an island he was telling me about and have that picnic you still owe me."

Grace smiled and pulled her hair up into a ball cap. "I've never been kayaking, I'm excited."

Kam smiled and pulled up in front of a gorgeous house that looked like a work of art.

"No way. Kit lives *here*?" she asked, looking in awe.

Kam laughed. "She does indeed. I'll introduce you to Hunter sometime. He's brilliant, funny and super down to earth. You'd never know in a million years that he designs video games and is pretty much a genius. Kit adores him."

Grace shook her head as she followed Kam around the house to the dock. "I can see why."

Kam shook his head. "Oh, she didn't fall for him because of his money. They're crazy for each other. Watch when you see them together. They're constantly kissing."

Grace smiled, happy that her friend was in love with her

husband. "That's so sweet," she said and walked over to Kam and went up on her tiptoes and kissed his cheek. "There. Now you know what that's like too."

Kam grinned and put his backpack down. "Well, she kisses him on the lips, not the cheek. It's a little more passionate than a peck on the cheek."

Grace laughed and put her backpack down too in order to wrap her arms around his neck. "Is it like this?" she asked softly and went up on her tiptoes again, tilting her head to the side and pulling his face down to hers. She caressed his lips with hers slowly and then deepened the kiss.

She knew she was attracted to Kam, but the chemistry she was feeling lately, was off the charts and nothing she'd ever experienced before. Just being around him drove her crazy. She always had to stop herself from touching his arm or playing with his hair. Well, today she wasn't going to hold back.

Kam took control of the kiss and bent her over his arm as he took the kiss to a new level. She pushed her hands into his hair and held on. When he finally pulled away, they stared at each other, both a little surprised.

"*Seriously?* You're going to kiss me like that and then expect me to kayak? None of my muscles will work," she said, looking at his lips and hoping he'd kiss her again.

Kam grinned and pulled her close again, but only kissing her on the temple this time. "I'll do most of the work while you recuperate."

Grace laughed and hugged him back. "Did you know my favorite place to be is in your arms?" she said quietly, feeling his heart beat against her ear.

Kam sighed, his whole body wrapped around her. "Did you know that my favorite place for you to be is in my arms too?"

Grace lifted her face to his, smiling ear to ear. "This is too easy. I don't get it. I'm crazy for you, you're *obviously* crazy about me. We love being together. Where's the drama? Where are the fights and the tantrums? This is just... fun," she said in confusion.

Kam shook his head and pushed some hair over her ear. "Because you're in a relationship with *me*. And I will treat you with respect and love and kindness. Why would I want to hurt you by making you question my feelings for you or by treating you badly? What kind of man would I be?"

Grace shrugged, feeling a sense of wonder. "No man at all. By the way, I'm all for this, whatever *this* is that we have going on. I'm getting addicted to it."

Kam laughed and pulled her toward the end of the dock where Hunter already had the kayaks tied up.

"You're not sure what *this* is? I hate to break it to you, but you're falling in love with me. I know we talked about love the other night, but I think you might be confused. *This* is different. You're *in* love with me. You need to get used to that."

Grace laughed and shook her head, blown away by the conversation they were having. "You know, I've never had a guy explain my feelings to me before. Especially when it comes to love. Most guys run screaming from the room if you even start to say the word."

Kam rolled his eyes. "Sounds like you knew a lot of idiots. You're gorgeous, fun and full of kindness and sweetness and love and every good thing I can think of. Of course I'm in love with you."

Grace stopped and stared at him as he hooked her life jacket into place. "Wait, this sounds serious. Are you really standing here, on this dock, telling me that you love me and that I love you?"

Kam paused for a moment, a smile lingering on his beautiful lips and nodded. "Yeah, it looks like it."

Grace smiled, taking it in for a moment and then surprised

both of them when she began to cry. She leaned her head against his chest and let her tears wet his shirt while she tried to get herself under control.

"Sorry, happy tears. Don't be scared," she said quickly, wiping her eyes.

Kam wiped a tear away with his thumb and kissed the other tears away with his lips. "Those are the best kind. Now, let's get going. I'm starving and I know the perfect place to lay a blanket down and kiss you."

Grace's eyes widened and she grinned. "Let's hurry then."

Kam tilted his head back and laughed. "Another reason I love you. Get your booty in the kayak, woman."

They spent the next hour kayaking until Kam led them to a small island with a small rocky beach. He pulled the kayak out of the water and helped her out. He carried the backpacks up a small hill where there was some wild grass and laid their blanket down. She sat down cross legged and began unloading everything Kam had brought.

"You know, I cook too. It's possible I can stretch my skill set and make a picnic. I feel like you're spoiling me."

Kam sat down next to her and handed her a water bottle. "Next time you can pack the lunch. But isn't it okay if I spoil you?"

Grace shrugged. "I don't know, I've never been spoiled before. But I have to say, it feels pretty good."

They ate the fried chicken, homemade potato salad, and rolls as they talked and laughed.

"So, did Rob call you this morning?" Grace asked, looking at him from under her hat.

Kam leaned back on his elbows and stared at the clouds before answering. "He did. He begged me to come into work today, but I said no."

Grace sighed. She'd gotten separate phone calls from Jane,

Cleo and Posey last night telling her all about Anne getting arrested for stealing the money. And although she was relieved that she wasn't in jail herself, it was still sad.

"*That's it?*" she asked, frowning at him.

Kam sighed. "No. He was pretty upset. He saw his mom in jail and feels horrible for not believing me and trusting you. I do feel bad for Rob, but he did fire me and it's nice to have some time off to spend with my girl."

Grace grinned. "So are you going to go back to work tomorrow?"

Kam shrugged. "Probably. He needs to think about controlling that temper of his and hopefully having Candice, Manuel, and James take over today will help him figure that out."

Grace looked down at her plate and frowned. "He never called me to ask me to come back to work."

Kam shook his head. "No, I told Rob he wasn't allowed to call you and that he needs to apologize to you in person before you go back to work."

Grace grimaced. "I guess he's eating a lot of humble pie today."

Kam laughed. "Not as much as you think. Wren texted me this morning and she's filling in for tonight but she's given Rob an earful and so has Taryn. And no, Wren doesn't want to work tomorrow so I say we go in and give Rob a break."

Grace grinned, glad that everything could go back to the way it was. "Sounds good to me. Did he offer you a raise or anything?"

Kam laughed. "He offered me the use of his boat for a whole year if I'd come back to work. Baby, we're going to teach you to waterski."

Grace gasped. "*No way!* I can't wait."

Kam took a sip of water and leaned on his side to look at

her. "It gets better. Rob's making you *co*-Head Chef. You just got a raise too."

Grace threw her napkin at him. "And when were you going to tell me all of this?" she demanded.

Kam threw the napkin back at her. "Right now."

Grace gave up and leaned over, kissing him hard on the lips. "It's a good thing you're so cute, you know that."

Kam grinned. "I'm aware. Now finish up your lunch. We have some kissing to get to."

Grace held up her hand. "Before we get to kissing. Have you heard anything about Anne? Are they going to press charges? Is she going to go to prison?"

Kam frowned, his eyes sad now. "No, I talked to Rob and Tate about it. Rob's not going to press charges but they're going to leave her in jail until they feel like she has some kind of remorse for what she tried to do to you."

Grace gulped, feeling a shiver go down her back. "You know, it was a close thing there. I could have easily ended up in jail or been halfway to Alaska by now."

Kam nodded, his mouth thinning. "Which is why I'm glad that Anne is in jail right now. Tate went in todayand talked to her and she still feels justified in what she did. There was a lot of tears but that was mostly over the color of her jumpsuit and the fact that she missed an episode of The Bachelor."

Grace bit her lip and looked away. "I heard from Jane and Cleo the kinds of things she was saying about me. That I'm not good enough for you. That she doesn't want me around her grandson. It's weird to know that someone can hate me so much and not even know me."

Kam reached over and touched her leg. "Honey, she's not thinking clearly. She's still mourning her daughter and she can't move on."

Grace tried to smile. "I know, but it makes me feel so strange and... vulnerable."

Kam sighed. "I would too. But she'll have to make peace with the fact that we're going to be together. If she doesn't, she's going to be a very miserable, lonely person."

Grace took a bite of potato salad and stared at the seagulls flying over the water. "Do *you* think I'm good enough for you?" she asked quietly.

Kam laughed. "I think I just expressed my feelings for you very clearly back at the dock. Of course you're good enough for me. You walked into the kitchen that first day and my heart started beating again. You forced banana parfaits on me and I began to breathe again. You made me dance and sing with you in the kitchen and you brought happiness back to my life. Grace, I love you. End of story. No more talk about who's good enough for who. You just are."

Grace smiled at Kam and knew she'd always remember this moment. "I guess I feel a little insecure sometimes because of my mom and the things she does and who she does them with. *Sorry.*"

Kam shook his head and pulled her over to sit in his lap. "You're nothing like your mom. You're amazing and good and honorable. No one looks at you and sees your mom."

Grace leaned her head back against his shoulder. "Well, Anne does. That might be why she hates me so much."

Kam kissed her cheek. "She would have hated anyone I fell for. Don't take it personally."

Grace turned and looked at him. "Is that the same reason Meredith hates me too?"

Kam groaned. "That's a different situation. She's figuring things out though. I don't think you have to worry about her anymore."

Grace wrapped her arms around Kam's waist and

squeezed. "Good. Anymore jealous girlfriends or mother-in-laws I need to know about before this relationship goes any further?"

Kam laughed. "That's it. I promise."

Grace turned in his arms and linked her hands behind his neck. "Now about that kissing."

Kam smiled and twisted her body around so she was laying on the blanket. "Your wish is my command," he said and began kissing her senseless.

Grace had to admit after he dropped her off that night, that she'd put up with twenty jealous girlfriends and ten mother-in-laws if she got to keep Kam.

CHAPTER 35

Second Chances

MEREDITH STARED ACROSS the blanket at her husband and was grateful for the breeze off the Sound that cooled her hot face. She had chosen to meet him down at the beach at Point Defiance instead of at The Iron Skillet, their favorite restaurant. She couldn't forget the last time they'd been their together and her public humiliation. At least here, if he began yelling, it wouldn't cause a scene.

"Thanks for coming," she said, wishing her voice sounded stronger... *that she was stronger.*

Asher ignored her as he stared at the waves. He wasn't dressed for the beach. He was wearing dress pants and a nice shirt. She studied his profile and wondered again how one man could be so good looking. She sighed and looked away.

"So I just want to know where we stand. You haven't been home in over a week. I never see you. I never hear from you. I can't keep living my life in limbo, waiting for you to notice me," she finally said, tired of waiting for him to say something.

Asher shrugged. "I'm surprised you even noticed I was gone. I mean, Kam's the love of your life. Aren't you constantly obsessed with him and who he's dating and fun things like that? Why waste your time worrying about a husband when your life is so full with your ex-boyfriend?"

Meredith closed her eyes, accepting the punch to her heart and nodded her head. "I guess that's fair. An *I'm sorry* won't cut it, huh?" she asked dully.

Asher shook his head and glanced at her, his eyes filled with pain. "Doesn't look like it. Let me ask you a question, Meredith. If it was me, and I was fixated on an ex-girlfriend and couldn't or *wouldn't* get over her, to the point where I made a public spectacle of myself and humiliated *you* in public, what would you do?" he asked evenly.

Meredith paused, blinking quickly. She hadn't really thought of it like that before. She took a few minutes to process that, feeling a fresh new wave of shame wash over her.

"To be completely honest, I'd already be gone and you'd have a nice set of divorce papers in front you," she said quietly, whisking a few tears off her cheek.

Asher's shoulders relaxed a little. "Then this won't come as a surprise. Meredith, I'd like a…"

Meredith turned and held up a hand. "Stop right there. Don't even say it."

Asher frowned at her. "*Why not*? You just admitted that you'd kick me out if I'd done to you what you've done to me."

Meredith put a hand on her chest, trying to calm her racing heart. "But there's one thing you're forgetting. *I love you* and I need you to forgive me," she said earnestly, grabbing on to his hand.

Asher slowly but firmly pulled his hand away. "That's asking way too much of me right now. Garrett set up an appointment with a divorce lawyer for me tomorrow. I think we should both go."

Meredith clenched her fists in her lap and shook her head.

"What a nice big brother, helping you get rid of your wife," she said, bitterly, wondering if Garrett had ever liked her.

Asher shrugged. "He is a good big brother. He's very loyal, unlike you. Which is why we need to be there tomorrow."

Meredith breathed in and out slowly, fighting the urge to jump up and run away. But she knew if she did, her marriage was over. She had to fight for Asher.

"I love you, Asher. I'm so sorry I hurt you. Please let me make this right."

Asher groaned softly and shook his head. "*Why?* So we can go back to the way things were? I don't like the way things were. It's been pointed out to me by a few people that you don't treat me very well. I've been told by a few people that I bend over backwards to spoil you and treat you like a queen and I get nothing in return. I'm starting to wonder what it would be like to be in a marriage where it's equal. Where two people love each other completely and put each other first and are kind and faithful and appreciate one another. I've never had that."

Meredith tried to swallow and couldn't as she let her head fall. "I've made a lot of mistakes with you. I can admit that. I've been narcissistic and selfish and immature, but I've always loved you and I've always been faithful to you."

Asher's head swung in her direction, his eyes blazing at her. "We have very different definitions of what being faithful means."

Meredith winced. "I've changed my definition to fit yours. *I have.* I guess I had this weird hang up when it came to Kam dating other girls after Bailey. I'm not in love with Kam or anything, I just have a soft spot for him because I did used to care for him. I was a brat and I was mean and I acted badly and I'm sorry."

Asher raised an eyebrow. "I'm surprised you're not in jail

with Anne Matafeo. You guys were the only ones in the hate Grace club."

Meredith grimaced. "I might be a brat, but I'm not crazy."

Asher just looked at her as she reddened. Meredith rolled her eyes, fighting the urge to snap back at him.

So the whole world lumped her into the same category with Anne. Jane had called her and told her what had happened and she'd been so sick about it she'd stayed in bed, staring at her ceiling. She'd done a lot of soul searching and knew that she and Anne had been horrible. If she'd been a better person, she could have talked some sense into Anne and calmed her down *but no*, she'd egged her on and she bore some of the blame for Anne being where she was.

"*I'm not crazy*," she said again. "But I'd be crazy if I let you go," she said softly.

Asher looked away from her and glanced at his watch as if he wanted to leave. As if he couldn't stand to be with her another minute.

"I know we can work through this, Asher," she said, feeling desperate. "You're the only man I love. You're the only man I want to father my children. I can't imagine my life without you."

Asher snorted. "Oh, I can think of one other guy you can imagine yourself with. Let's not lie to each other."

Meredith glared at him. "Look, I'm not proud of the way I acted. I'm completely humiliated. Did you know I go shopping now at midnight so I don't have to run into anyone I know? I work from home and I don't ever go out anymore. I'm a pariah in town now that everyone thinks that I hate Grace. But I'm not lying. I love you, Asher. And if Grace didn't exist and Kam did want me back, *which he doesn't*, you have to know that I would never choose him over you. I *don't* love him. I love *you*. What I want to know, is if you still love me?"

Asher sighed and looked at his large hands. He stared at his wedding ring and pulled it off, watching as the sun gleamed on the single diamond in the middle. Meredith felt her heart speed up, praying he wasn't going to chuck it into the water. He twisted it in his fingers and then slowly slipped it back on his finger. Meredith let out a ragged sigh of relief and felt like crying again.

"I can't seem to stop. Garrett says the feelings will fade with time, but I don't know."

Meredith ground her teeth thinking of all the things she'd like to say to Garrett at that moment, but pushed it away as hope filled her heart. "Then we have a chance. Asher, I love you with all of my heart. And if you still love me, then let's work on our marriage. Lets not throw it away. *Please.*"

Asher looked at her sadly and shook his head. "I can't be in a marriage where I only have a part of your heart. I love you but that's torture and that's misery for me. I feel like the only solution is to walk away."

Meredith scrambled to her knees and grabbed Asher's hands in hers, staring down into his face. "But you do. I swear you do. You have all of my heart, every piece and corner is yours."

Asher closed his eyes, refusing to look at her. "How in the world can I ever believe that, knowing what I know?"

Meredith bent her head and kissed his knuckles. "Because I've cleaned out all the other rubbish. All of the immature infatuations I had left over are gone. Please believe that these last two weeks I've grown up a lot. I'm not that selfish, stupid girl I was. Coming close to losing you has been the hardest thing I've ever experienced and I will do whatever it takes to win you back. *Anything.*"

Asher's lips twitched at that and he shook his head. "Fine. I'll postpone my appointment with the lawyer tomorrow.

Garrett's going to kill me but I'll give you a chance to win me back."

Meredith's eyes widened and she felt lightheaded with relief. She threw her arms around Asher's neck and held on as she began to shake.

"*I love you, I love you, I love you,*" she whispered over and over as he gently pulled her arms from around his neck.

She watched as he stood up, whisking the sand off his pants. "I guess I'll see you around then," he said and walked off without another word.

Meredith watched him go with a frown on her face. Before, any affection she'd given Asher, he'd grabbed onto greedily. But he definitely had his walls up now. Well, he'd given her a chance to win him back. Now all she had to do was figure out what that meant and how to do it.

She collapsed back on her blanket and stared up at the clouds for over an hour, trying to come up with a plan. But all she could think of was telling him she loved him and she'd already done that. She needed to do something huge. A grand gesture. She rolled over on her stomach and watched a family play Frisbee and wondered if that would be her and Asher someday, with their two kids and a dog.

She stood up and picked up her blanket, smiling grimly. *It would be her and Asher someday.* She was determined to get her man back.

CHAPTER 36

Cutting the Strings

KAM WALKED INTO the jail visitor's room of the police station and nodded to Pule. "Where do I sit?"

Pule pointed to one of the tables in front of the bullet proof glass. "We'll bring her out. Just pick up the phone to talk to her."

Kam nodded and sat down, looking around and taking in all the details. It was a sad, depressing place and one he never wanted to spend time in.

He waited for over ten minutes before a female officer brought Anne through the doors. He was glad to see she wasn't in handcuffs but the orange jumpsuit had to be demoralizing.

He watched her sit down and pick up the phone before he reached for his.

"Hi, Anne," he said and watched her. She looked the same except for the clothes. Her hair was done and her makeup was on and she was smiling serenely as if it was a normal every day occurrence for him to come visit her in jail.

"Thanks for coming to see me, Kam. Rob said you weren't going to want to see me after what I did, but I knew that couldn't be true. Our bond is deeper than any feelings you could have for that woman," she said with a satisfied smile.

Kam blinked slowly and prayed for patience. "I came to see you out of respect for Bailey but you need to know that Rob is right. I don't see the point in having a relationship with you any longer. It's obviously not safe. You're not someone I can trust around my family or the people I care about."

Anne's head whipped back as if she'd been slapped. "*What? Why would you say such a thing to me?*" she demanded.

Kam raised an eyebrow. "You stole money and blamed my girlfriend for it. According to Rob, Tate *and* Pule, you don't have any remorse for what you did."

Anne frowned and looked down at the desk. "Well, of course I feel bad," she finally said.

Kam grimaced. "Yeah, you feel bad you were caught. If it was Grace sitting where you are now, you'd be completely fine with it and throwing a party."

Anne pursed her lips and looked at her nails. "Well, if you had just listened to me and realized that Grace is not the woman for you, then none of this would have happened. If you think about it, this is all your fault," she said with a small, self-righteous smile on her lips.

Kam closed his eyes and wondered how Rob, Taryn and Bailey had turned out even half-way normal. Anne was flat out crazy. He thought about hanging up and walking out but remembered his uncle Sefe and how upset he was by the fact that his wife was still in jail. They'd sat him down and browbeat him into not posting bail for his wife but he wasn't happy about it.

"And that right there, is why you won't be allowed near my son ever again," he said sadly, wishing things could be different.

Anne's eyebrows snapped together as she glared at him. "You would keep me from my grandson? *How dare you,*" she sputtered. "I'll sue you! Grandparents have rights you know."

Kam shrugged. "You're unbalanced and talking like a crazy person. You rationalize your behavior and have no qualms about ruining other people's lives because you think you know better than everyone else. You don't even know Grace. You took one look at her and made a snap decision. And now your reputation is ruined. You've humiliated your children and your husband is heartbroken at home, alone. Was it worth it?"

Anne continued to glare at him but her eyes softened at the mention of her husband's name. "Tate says I'll be able to go home soon. Something to do with getting the right lawyer," she said with a wave of her hand.

Kam ignored that. "*Was it worth it, Anne?*" he asked again.

Anne shrugged and looked away. "It didn't turn out the way I had planned. I didn't really *want* Grace to go to jail or anything. I just wanted her to leave town and never come back. No one's going to hunt her down over eight thousand dollars," she said with a laugh.

Kam frowned at his mother-in-law. "Yeah, Anne. They do. She'd have to live her life on the run if she'd run away like you wanted her to. That's the kind of life you'd force on a woman you don't even know because I happened to fall in love with her?"

Anne licked her lips and studied the table before looking at him. Her eyes were full of anger. "Bailey would hate you," she said with a sneer. "You've completely betrayed her memory and the love she had for you."

Kam's lips thinned with anger and his eyes narrowed at the cruel words. "And how do you know that?"

Anne leaned forward, staring him down. "I'm her mother and I know my daughter. How could you choose to be with another woman after my daughter gave her heart to you? She gave her life to have your son, does that mean nothing?"

Kam frowned at Anne and tried to have compassion but couldn't find any. "Bailey loved her son from the moment she knew she was pregnant. And she'd be so happy to know that Natano will have a mother who loves him. You don't know Bailey at all if you can believe those things. And what about you, Anne? Your husband died and yet here you are remarried. Doesn't that make you a hypocrite?"

Anne lifted her chin in the air and pointed a finger at him. "It's only been three and a half years since Bailey died. *You* have no shame."

Kam rubbed his forehead before he answered. "No, Anne. You have no shame and you have no heart. I hope you stay in here for a very long time, because Sefe doesn't deserve to have a wife like you. And just so we're clear, you are no longer welcome in my life or my son's. Goodbye, Anne," he said and stood up, walking away as he heard pounding on the glass behind him.

He walked out, too upset to even talk to Tate or Pule. He headed over to Tai's diner, knowing he needed to cool down before he went back to work.

He walked in and was grateful that the diner was mostly empty. He picked a booth at the back and hunched over, leaning his head in his hands. He felt a tap on his shoulder and looked up to see a waitress looking at him expectantly.

"What can I get you?" she asked with a smile.

"Hi, June," he said, recognizing her. June was a middle aged, single mom who worked at the diner during the day so she could be home with her kids at night. He always tipped her generously, knowing the financial struggles she had.

"Just a water and maybe a pastrami and beef sandwich."

June wrote it down and looked up. "Horseradish? Fries or onion rings?"

Kam nodded. "Yes to the horseradish and I'd love some fries. Thanks, June."

She walked off and Tai magically appeared in her place. He sat down without an invitation, frowning at him.

"You look like you just lost your best friend and since I'm right here and I'm not lost, you're going to have to tell me what put that sad look on your face."

Kam groaned and massaged his temples as the headache from talking to Anne was still very much there, pounding away.

"I was just at the jail, talking to Anne. I swear, Tai, she'd do it again. Do you know what she said to me? She said that if I'd just listened to her, none of this would have happened. She told me that her stealing the money and framing Grace was all my fault."

Tai's eyes widened and he shook his head in sympathy. "So what did you say to that?"

Kam waited while June put a water glass and silverware in front of him and walked away before he answered. "I told her that she was no longer welcome in my life or Natano's life. I told her I couldn't trust her."

Tai whistled and shook his head. "Oh, Man, that's rough. I'm so sorry. Who knew Anne was so crazy?"

Kam laughed bitterly. "Oh, we all did. Trust me, we knew she had potential."

Tai smiled and waited as June brought out Kam's sandwich and fries.

"Thanks, June," Kam said and took a big bite.

"Won't that be hard on Natano, not having his grandmother in his life anymore?" Tai asked softly.

Kam wiped his mouth on his napkin and shook his head. "He's got my mom and all of his aunts and he'll have Grace now. How can I trust my son with her, Tai? She might get mad at me for being with Grace again and kidnap my son to punish me."

Tai winced but nodded. "You do have a point, but man, I kind of hate this. I feel like this town is coming apart at the seams. Anne is in jail and Sefe is torn up. Meredith and Asher aren't speaking to each other and who knows what's going to happen there. And everyone's taking sides. It makes me sad," Tai admitted, looking out the window.

Kam frowned and looked at his plate. "And all because I decided to love Grace."

Tai whipped his head up and grabbed his cousin's hand. "No, Dude. *No.* This is not your fault. If Anne and Meredith want to act crazy because they're not ready for you to move on with your life, then that's on them. No one can blame any of this on you, and I would never stand by and allow anyone to try."

Kam smiled sadly and picked up his sandwich again. "Maybe Grace and I should move away? Maybe this town is better off without us. Life could go back to normal if I wasn't here causing drama with my love life."

Tai ran his hands through his short, cropped hair. "Now you're the one talking crazy. Kam, you're the heart of this town. Everyone here loves you and needs you. Things will settle down in time."

Kam smiled and remembered why he loved Tai so much. "Thanks, Tai. I appreciate that. But you're right. This town isn't the same now. I want people to go back to loving each other and being kind and thoughtful. Who would have ever thought that Anne would be in jail for trying to ruin my girlfriend's life? Or that Asher and Meredith would be on the brink…"

"Brink of what?"

Kam and Tai looked up to see Asher standing next to their table, frowning at them.

Tai scooted over and patted the seat. "Sit down and help me eat Kam's fries, Ash."

Asher frowned but sat down, looking at Kam with sad eyes.

Kam nodded his head and reached across the table. "We good?"

Asher shook his hand and nodded. "Yeah, we're good."

Tai sighed loudly and picked up one of Kam's fries. June

walked by to refill Kam's water and took Asher's order for a hamburger and a chocolate milkshake.

Kam wasn't sure what to say to Asher and decided to let someone else start the conversation.

"So my brother made an appointment for me with a divorce lawyer today," Asher said in a low voice.

Kam and Tai looked at each other in shock before staring at Asher. Asher stared at his hands. "I know my brother wants me to leave Meredith, but I love her. She begged me yesterday to give her one more chance. She says she's going to prove her love for me. So I agreed to hold off on the divorce lawyer."

Kam sighed in relief and shook his head. "Dude, I know Meredith loves you. Don't listen to Garrett. He's always been too overprotective of you. This is your life and *your* marriage and your decision. Only you can say if your marriage is over."

Asher looked at him with haunted eyes. "If I could truly believe that Meredith was over you… but I just don't know."

Kam put his sandwich down and pulled his plate away from Tai who was eating all of his fries. "Bro, you own the place. Get your own fries," he said and then turned to Asher.

"Ash, Man, you can take my word for it. Her heart is yours. All yours."

Asher shrugged and stole one of his fries. Kam narrowed his eyes at Asher and was surprised when Asher grinned at him.

"You owe me," he said and dipped it in his fry sauce.

Kam laughed and decided not to kill him. "So you're going to give it another try?"

Asher nodded. "I love her. There's no one else I'd want to be the mother of my children. I want to grow old with her. I want everything with her. But Garrett will disown me if I take her back."

Tai snorted. "Lame. I'll have a talk with Garrett if you want me to. Seriously, he's pulling an Anne and overstepping himself."

Kam nodded in total agreement. "No one's disowning you. Not on my watch."

Asher grinned and sat back as June put his plate in front of him. "Thanks, June. How're the kids?"

June took a moment to chat and brag about her son being on the football team before she walked over to greet a new customer.

"You guys better tip good," Tai said.

Kam glared at his cousin. "You know I'm always good to June."

Asher held up his hands. "I'm her favorite customer, Tai. Thirty percent, every time."

Kam snorted. "I always tip at least forty."

Tai sighed. "Those football cleats are so expensive."

Kam laughed. "We get it, we get it. Stop being pushy."

Tai grinned and began stealing Asher's fries. They sat and talked about rugby and the Fine Dining experience on Saturday and when Kam and Asher walked out of the diner together, Kam felt like maybe something had been put right. He hugged Asher like a brother and made him promise to be nice to Meredith before he headed back to work.

He smiled, because even though things hadn't gone well with Anne, there was hope for Meredith and Asher. And that right there, was something to be very happy about.

CHAPTER 37

Friends and Enemies

GRACE WALKED OUT of the store with her dress over her arm and closed her eyes in relief. She'd been so embarrassed to go back and see if it was still there, but she was glad she had checked her pride and gone in. The clerk had been kind and even showed her some earrings that had gone on clearance that week that would be perfect with the dress.

She looked up at the blue sky and smiled to herself. It was amazing what a few days could do. She'd gone from despair and thinking her life was ruined to now thinking her life was simply incredible.

"It's kind of rude to stand there, looking so pleased with yourself, you know."

Grace looked around and shielded her eyes from the sun to see Meredith Murphy standing a few feet away. *Great.*

"And to think I was having such a good day," she said and looked down at her phone. "Catch you never," she said and began walking toward her truck.

"*Uh, uh.* I don't think so."

Grace grimaced and turned around, grateful that there

weren't too many people walking by. "Was there something I could do for you?"

Meredith walked over to her, wearing jeans and a gray t-shirt. Not her usual look. Every time Grace had seen her, she'd been dressed perfectly with perfect makeup and hair, razor sharp in it's gleaming blond perfection. Grace ran a hand through her own, windblown, blond streaked, and no where near perfect hair and felt good that Meredith looked just like everyone else did today. Normal and stressed.

"Well, I think it's only fair that you do. From what I hear from Jane, you and Kam are practically engaged and I'm on the edge of divorce. There's a lot you could do for me."

Grace frowned and motioned towards her truck. "Look, I only have forty-five minutes left on my break and I don't want to stand here in the middle of the sidewalk. If you want to talk to me, we can go to Belinda's. I need some calories."

Meredith pursed her lips but nodded. "Fine. But if those witches try to do anything weird with my food, I'm suing."

Grace laughed and opened her truck door, slipping her dress over the seat. "Jane would never do anything like that."

Meredith snorted and jumped in the other side. Grace had been hoping that Meredith would just follow her in her own car, but nope.

"But Kit would and I bet you Layla would too. Super judgey and mean."

Grace frowned at Meredith and pulled out into traffic. "Judgey and mean? They're angels."

Meredith laughed bitterly and turned the air vent toward herself. "That's because they *like* you. Watch your back when they don't."

Grace rolled her eyes and turned the corner. It was just one more block to Belinda's. Too bad her beautiful day was being ruined by Meredith's toxic company.

"Look, Meredith, they were just sticking up for me against you and Anne. From where I'm sitting, that was pretty awesome of them. I'm sorry you're on the edge of divorce, but that's not their fault, and it's not my fault either."

Meredith raised an eyebrow at that and crossed her legs. "We'll have to agree to disagree on that."

Grace tightened her hands around the steering wheel as she tried to remain calm. "If you're having problems with your marriage, I'm not the cause. All of this stuff that happened? You being mean to me because you were mad I was interested in Kam? That's all a symptom of a bigger issue. But it's not the cause."

Meredith frowned at her and then looked out the window. "You might have a point there," she said softly.

Grace blinked in surprise that Meredith was able to think rationally. She pulled into the parking lot and they walked up the steps to the bakery.

"I'm not buying you lunch, by the way," Grace said and stopped to smell the wonderful smells as she opened the door.

Meredith sighed. "I wasn't expecting you too. But I should probably buy you lunch. I guess I was a brat to you, especially at the gas station. That was kind of rude of me."

Grace grimaced, not stating the obvious and walked up to the counter, happy to see Kit there.

Kit's eyes were wide as she stared at Meredith behind her. "You two? You two are here *together*?" she asked.

Grace shook her head. "Not by choice. She says there's something she wants me to do to help her out."

Kit laughed at that. "Seriously? That's a lot of gall, even for you, Mer. If I were Grace and you were on fire, I wouldn't spit on you."

Meredith narrowed her eyes at Kit and pointed to the menu. "Just for that, I'm going to spit on your car on my way out. And I'll have the BLT on ciabatta bread with chips and a chocolate chip cookie."

Kit rolled her eyes and looked back at her. "The usual?"

Grace smiled, already imagining her delicious sandwich. "Yes, please. I'm addicted. Sorry."

Kit smiled back at her, completely ignoring Meredith. "I won't tell anyone. Have a seat and I'll bring it over."

The two women walked over to the last table by the windows and sat down. Grace tried to look everywhere but at Meredith but finally gave up and looked at her. And what she saw made her reconsider all of her resentment. What she saw, was a woman who looked painfully sad and a little desperate. She felt her heart go out to her and sighed.

"So what do you need help with?" she asked, as Meredith stared out the window.

Meredith swallowed hard and looked at her. "I don't even know you, but everyone seems to like you. They say you're kind and fun and beautiful, although, you seriously need a facial, a manicure and a day at the mall. But you seem like the type of person that might know how to help me. You see, I have a husband who has an older brother who made an appointment for him with a divorce lawyer. I begged him not to go and so he gave me a chance to win his heart back."

Grace put a hand over her heart, saddened that a marriage could crumble so easily and cause so much pain. "So what are you going to do to?"

Meredith shrugged helplessly. "I have no idea. That's where you come in."

Grace bit her lip. "I don't exactly have any experience in this department. My last boyfriend stole all of my money and I didn't exactly want to win his heart back."

Meredith laughed. "That's hilarious."

Grace frowned at her. "You know you're a little cracked, right?"

Meredith shrugged. "None of us are perfect, but yeah, I think that's funny. So help a girl out. If you had to win a man's heart, what would you do?"

Grace leaned back in her chair. "I'd cook for him, of course. I'd make him the most delicious food he's ever had until he was putty in my hands."

Meredith rolled her eyes. "Yeah, well, not everyone has your talents. What can a woman with, let's say, *no* talents do to win a man's heart?"

Grace smiled at her, almost liking her. "Well, let's be blunt. You already have your husband's heart. What you really have to do, is convince him that he has *your* heart."

Meredith's face fell. "Again, you might have a point."

Kit walked over with two trays and set the food in front of them. "Anything else, ladies?"

Grace nodded and pointed to the empty seat next to Meredith. "Yes, actually. We have to convince Asher that Meredith loves him with all of her heart. How does she do that?"

Meredith glared at her. "Why are you asking *her*? She probably poisoned my food."

Kit laughed. "I was sorely tempted. But no, eat up. You're safe today," she said and took a seat, looking at Meredith with a critical look on her face.

"I say you make a fool of yourself. You certainly made a fool out of him. The only way this will work is if you embarrass the snot out of yourself."

Meredith took a bite of her sandwich. "And you're suggesting this because you actually believe it will help, and not for your own personal enjoyment?"

Kit grinned. "Can't it be both?"

Grace laughed and took a bite of her sandwich. "Oh my word, Kit, this is divine."

Kit bowed her head, accepting the compliment as if she were a queen. "Of course it is. What do you think, Grace? Humiliation?"

Grace picked up a siracha potato chip and nodded. "I think it's brilliant actually. It would get his attention, it would make him feel a whole lot better and it would make him laugh. All of those things are good. People who laugh, relax. And you two are way too uptight right now."

Meredith sighed and took a sip of water. "I'll do anything. Seriously, I have no pride here. But how do I embarrass myself and show him I love him at the same time?"

Grace and Kit looked at each other frowning. Grace took a bite of her cookie and shook her head. "I say we go the whole ten yards. How about we put up a billboard with a picture of you guys on your wedding day and then something, super sappy that would embarrass you to pieces?"

Kit clapped her hands. "That would be perfect. And then we can get the whole town to wear t-shirts that have the same image. Asher won't be able to go anywhere without seeing your face."

Meredith laughed and wiped her mouth with her napkin. "Dang, this is going to take me deep. A billboard *and* t-shirts?"

Kit raised an eyebrow at her. "Trust me, it's a lot cheaper than a divorce."

Meredith groaned and nodded her head. "Fine. What else. Keep going."

Grace tapped her fingers on the table. "Hmmm, we could deliver something he loves to his office? His favorite meal or dessert?"

Kit nodded. "I know exactly what he loves. And I'll even

cover this one myself just to show you that Belinda's Bakery is behind you and Asher staying together."

Meredith smiled and looked away. "That's actually really sweet. Thanks, Kit. I take back all the times I called you a witch."

Kit shrugged. "If the name fits."

Grace laughed. "This is fun. But can we get it all done before Saturday night's Fine Dining? It would be so cool if you guys were back together so you could have a nice dinner together with romantic music and dancing."

Kit frowned. "I'll get Hunter to help you out. That man can get anything done, anytime, anywhere."

Meredith breathed in deeply and let it out slowly. "Okay, this might actually work. *Thank you.* I mean it. When I saw you standing on the street corner looking all happy and perfect, I just wanted to kick you, but then here you are actually helping me. I'm... I'm grateful and I'm truly sorry for being so mean to you," she said sounding sincere for the first time.

Grace smiled and shrugged. "It's all good. I'm glad to help. I love *love*, you know. If you and Asher can reconnect and be happy, then that makes all of us happy."

Kit put an arm around Meredith's shoulders and gave her a hug. "This will work. We'll throw all of this love stuff at him for the next few days and then Saturday night, you'll show up looking gorgeous and dance the night away with him. It'll work."

Meredith smiled. "I've been praying for help. Who would have thought that you two girls would be the ones to help me?"

Kit stood up, taking one of Meredith's chips. "In this town, we build each other up, we don't tear each other down," she said, looking deeply into Meredith's eyes before walking away.

Meredith looked back at her and smiled lopsidedly. "*Ouch.* That one hit home. And she's right. I'm really sorry that I acted like such a jerk to you. From now on, you and I are friends. Anything you need, you come to me."

Grace nodded her head in acceptance. "Sounds good. And if I can do anything to help you, just call me or come by the restaurant."

Meredith stood up and picked up her tray. "Lunch is on me and pick out any dessert you want, too," she said and walked away.

Grace smiled, feeling warm inside as she finished her lunch. She wasn't surprised when Kit walked back over and sat down.

"Well, you're a good person, Grace Jackson. If I had any doubts about the goodness of your heart, they're gone. Helping Meredith out after everything she's said and done, is pretty amazing."

Grace chewed on her last bite of chocolate chip cookie and smiled in happiness at eating something so perfect.

"Why hate her? Why spend all that energy hating someone and being mean when I can be her friend instead and turn something dark and mean into something light and good? Plus, she really needs help. I think she does love her husband."

Kit winced. "Well, she had a bad way of showing it, that's for sure, but I think she's learned her lesson. I think from here on out, she's going to appreciate her marriage and her husband and she'll never take him for granted again."

Grace stood up and stretched before picking up her tray. "I don't think any of us should take the people we love for granted. When that happens, hearts get broken."

Kit nodded. "Which reminds me, I need to pamper my hubby tonight. Especially since he's going to help me get a billboard for Meredith."

Grace grinned. "Lovely. Oh, and Meredith said I could pick out a dessert to take with me. What do you suggest?"

Kit walked behind the counter and pointed to what looked like a croissant. Grace frowned. "Really?"

Kit nodded and picked one up, sliding it into a bakery bag. "Would I ever steer you wrong? And besides, this is no ordinary croissant."

Grace looked at her suspiciously but took the bag. "Fine, I'll trust you. And thanks for being nice to Meredith. I think we both shocked her today."

Kit grinned and walked with her to the door. "I like keeping Meredith on her toes. She never knows what to expect from me."

Grace hugged Kit and waved goodbye. "Text me later and let me know what Hunter comes up with," she yelled over her shoulder.

Kit nodded and waved good-bye to her. Grace made it back to work and pointed at her bag and then at Kam's office as soon as he looked her way. Kam grinned and followed her back.

"Please tell me that's a Matafeo cupcake in there," he said, rubbing his hand together gleefully.

Grace shook her head and took the croissant out of the bag and laughed when Kam's face fell.

"Hey, I'm telling Kit that you're disappointed. She swears this is no ordinary croissant."

Kam took the croissant and broke it in half. Grace's eyes went wide with wonder as she saw custard and berries begin to ooze out. She grabbed a napkin and took her half and brought it to her nose, breathing in the scent.

"I do believe Kit was right," Grace said with a grin and took a bite.

Kam still looked disappointed but took a bite too. She groaned in pleasure as the flavors of the vanilla custard, the fresh berries and the flaky, buttery croissant melded together in her mouth.

"Oh. My. Word," she whispered.

Kam licked his lips and popped the rest in his mouth. "Still not as good as a Matafeo cupcake, but thank you for sharing with me," he said and pulled her into his arms.

He kissed her smoothly as if he'd been kissing her forever. She smiled as he kissed her and held her tight, savoring the moment.

He pulled away and pulled lightly on her hair. "No more tempting me with kisses and desserts, young lady. Time to get to work."

Grace fanned her face and walked toward the door, hoping she wouldn't look like she'd just been kissed. "You got it, Boss," she said and walked out into the kitchen.

The rest of the day, passed by quickly, filled with flirting, music, dancing and good food.

CHAPTER 38

Good Intentions

ANNE MATAFEO NODDED to Pule and Tate as Sefe held her hand and they walked out of the Police Station. Anne blinked up at the sun and rubbed her arms.

"It feels like I was in there forever," she said, feeling very sorry for herself.

Sefe nodded his head and held the door to his SUV open for her. "Watch your step," he said softly and then shut the door.

Anne frowned. Sefe was acting strange. He was very polite and kind, but he wasn't his usual smiling, flirting self. She buckled her seatbelt and sighed in relief as Sefe got in and started the car.

"It feels so good to be out and free. I knew Rob wouldn't press charges. Tate told me all the money was returned yesterday, so it's like none of this even happened," she said, with a smile as she looked out the window.

Sefe sighed, but didn't say anything. Anne frowned and looked at her husband. "What's wrong, Sefe? You're so quiet."

Sefe looked over at her and Anne saw what looked like sadness in his eyes.

"This is your first day of freedom. We don't need to talk

about it today. Why don't I take you to The Iron Skillet for lunch? You probably didn't get very good food in jail."

Anne frowned and reached over to grab Sefe's hand. "If something is wrong, just tell me. Sefe, *why are you sad?*"

Sefe shook his head and pulled into The Iron Skillet's parking lot. "Let's eat first," he said and turned the car off.

Anne followed him into the restaurant, confused and worried. Everything was fine now. There was nothing to worry about.

They were seated immediately and Anne had to admit, she was craving some decent food. She was going to complain to the City Council about the conditions in jail as soon as she recuperated from her experience.

"I don't know about you, but I need some of Grace's gnocchi and a big hunk of fish," Sefe said with a forced smile.

Anne frowned at Sefe, irritated that he would praise Grace's gnocchi. "Well, I'm sure *Kam's* gnocchi tastes just as good. What a thing to say," she said and continued to scan the options.

"And what can I get for you two?"

Anne looked up to see Taryn standing by their table and smiled. "What are you doing taking our order?" Anne said with a laugh. "You're the manager not a waitress."

Taryn nodded and put her hand on her waist. "Sorry, but I'm the only one here willing to wait on you. Everyone seems to know what you did to Grace. They're a loyal bunch here and we all like Grace."

Anne's mouth fell open in affront as she glared at all the waiters and waitresses talking to other patrons.

"That's so rude," she sputtered. "I'm the mother of the owner. That should count for something," she said, sitting up tall and straightening her napkin.

Taryn shrugged and took out a pad of paper and a pen. "Yeah, yeah. So what would you like?"

Sefe cleared his throat. "I'd love the blackened salmon and

the gnocchi with a Caesar salad, please. And thanks, Taryn. I appreciate it."

Taryn leaned over and hugged Sefe. "My pleasure. But it's mostly for you, Sefe. Rob and I think Mom have a lot of nerve showing up here after what she did to Kam and Grace. But you're always welcome of course."

Anne blinked in surprise. "Hold on a minute. Just hold on a minute, young lady. Who do you think you are, telling me I'm not welcome in my own son's restaurant. Kam works for Rob. Not the other way around," she said, feeling her temper start to rise.

Sefe sighed and looked down at his hands as if he was miserable. Taryn looked over her shoulder and made a tsking sound.

"Now you've done it. Someone's obviously complained about your loudness and now the owner is coming over."

Anne rolled her eyes. Rob would never kick her out. The thought was ridiculous.

"What seems to be the matter here?" Rob asked, looking unhappy to see her.

Anne smiled brightly at her son. "Rob, Taryn is being such a brat. She's telling me that no one will wait on me except for her and that you'd rather I didn't eat here anymore. That can't be true," she stated, folding her arms over her chest.

Rob looked up at the ceiling as if he was praying for heavenly help.

"Taryn happens to be right. I mean, how can I expect Kam or Grace to cook for you, Mom? It would be too much for me. If I were Kam and you'd hurt Wren like you hurt Grace, I wouldn't want you here."

Anne closed her eyes and shook her head as if she couldn't understand what Rob was saying. "I get it, I get it, you're punishing me. But it's over now. The money is back, and it's like it never happened. Everyone can just go on with their lives. Why are you making such a big deal about this?"

Rob's eyes widened and he turned and looked at Taryn who looked shocked too. Rob then turned to look at Sefe who held up his hands in defense.

Rob swallowed and licked his lips, nodding his head before looking her in the face. "I'm sorry, Mom but this is the last time you are allowed to eat here. Sefe, you of course are welcome to come in anytime. Enjoy your meals," he said and walked away, his shoulders stiff.

Anne frowned and stared after her son. "He better call me later and apologize for that nonsense. What has gotten into that boy?"

Taryn blew out a breath and tapped her notepad. "So, would you like the salmon too? Or a steak? How about those crab cakes you love? I need to get back to work, so can we hurry this up?"

Anne shrugged and pushed her menu toward Taryn. "I'll have a steak, medium rare with a garden salad and a bowl of clam chowder."

As soon as Taryn was out of earshot, Anne leaned across the table, and grabbed Sefe's hand. "Can you believe that? What is wrong with Rob, treating me like that?"

Sefe used his free hand to pinch the bridge of his nose. "So this might be a good time to bring up the fact that I think it's a good idea for us to move."

Anne's mouth dropped open. "*What?* Why? You moved here to be close to your family. You love your weekly dinners on Sunday. You love hanging out with your brothers and all of your nieces and nephews. Why in the world would you want to move?"

Sefe looked at her with his big brown eyes filled with misery. "We're no longer welcome at my brother's home for dinners on

Sunday. Kam doesn't want you there and his parents back him up. They think you're unbalanced and unkind."

Anne bit her lip and looked down at her hands feeling horrible that Sefe's family would turn their backs on him just like that.

"Well, that's a rotten thing to do," she said quietly and pulled her hand back.

Sefe shook his head. "No, it was the right thing to do. Anne, I love you with all of my heart, but sometimes I don't understand you. I don't understand how you can do the things you do sometimes. You've hurt so many people, Anne and you don't even care. You don't have any remorse. And now, I've lost my family and you're losing yours too. You've pushed Kam and Grace and Natano out of your life, and Rob and Taryn are close to walking away too. Anne, don't you get it? *You hurt people.* You need to start caring about that."

Anne frowned at her husband, shocked that he didn't have her back. "What about me? *Huh?* What about me, Sefe? Who in this town cares that they've hurt me?"

Sefe shook his head sadly at her. "And that's where you keep making the same mistake over and over. This isn't about you. This life isn't about you, Anne. It's about loving the people God has given us to love as best we can. Start thinking about Kam and Natano and our family for once."

Anne's head whipped back as if she'd been slapped. "That's a cruel thing to say, Sefe," she whispered.

Sefe sighed, sounding exhausted. "No, Anne. It's the truth. It was *your* cruelty that had you stealing from your son to frame Kam's girlfriend so you could ruin her life. *That's* cruel. Pointing out the facts to you and the consequences of your actions is not. It's being kind. Because you don't seem to get it. You blame everyone else for this misery, but Anne, it's you. All of this is on you."

Anne closed her eyes, and felt like crying. Nothing had turned out the way she hadn't wanted it to. Her intentions should be judged, not her actions.

"But I meant well," she said, her voice quivering.

Sefe shook his head. "That's not true, Anne. You can't lie to yourself anymore. You did everything you could to hurt Grace."

Anne looked away from her husband's intense eyes and bit her lip to keep from crying. They sat like that, in silence, until Taryn brought their food.

"Well, I can't believe it's not burnt and inedible, but it looks like they had pity on you and actually made you something delicious. Bon appetit and remember to tip fifteen percent although I'd prefer twenty."

Taryn walked away without another look and Anne knew she wouldn't be back by to refill their water glasses. She sighed and began to eat, but found she wasn't hungry anymore. She waited while Sefe ate his food and then followed him out after he put a few bills on the table.

They drove home in silence and when she walked in the door, she headed to the back porch. She sat in her rocking chair and stared at the cloudy sky and did some thinking. She thought about what Rob and Taryn and Sefe had said to her. She even thought about the things that Kam and Pule and Tate had said to her. And a couple hours later, she bowed her head in shame.

She had messed up and there was no way around it.

Now what?

CHAPTER 39

Forgiveness

GRACE AND KAM worked extra hard, alongside Candice, James and Manuel as they prepped for Saturday night's Fine Dining experience. They could hear the band that had been hired for the night practicing and Grace couldn't help herself from twirling around the kitchen, imagining herself dancing in Kam's arms later that night. Much later.

She used her arm to wipe her forehead and grinned at Kam who winked at her. Tonight was going to be magical, she could feel it. Everyone could. Kam was whistling to the music and teasing everyone. He'd kissed her at least five times in the past two hours and once in his office. There was something very special happening. She could feel it in the energy of the restaurant. Rob and Taryn had been back three times each, to check on how things were going.

They were going to be serving roasted artichoke hearts with prosciutto crisps and oven roasted tomatoes with a creamed garlic sauce to start with. Then they were going to bring out a quinoa salad with roasted peppers, grilled onion and egg-plant puree. She'd had it before in Seattle and it was divine.

For the entrée they were going to have two choices. The first choice was a braised oxtail ravioli with wild mushrooms with a perigourdine sauce and a shaved endive salad on the side. The second entrée was braised veal shank, with roasted peppers and gruyere cheese polenta with heirloom cauliflower on the side.

She'd worked so hard on the menu and had volunteered to make every single thing on the menu for Kam, Rob and Taryn to approve. They'd loved everything of course. She was excited to stretch not only herself but The Iron Skillet as well. This town was going to look at their restaurant a little differently after tonight. The Iron Skillet wasn't just going to be a family restaurant, it was going to be the place you wanted to take your date when you wanted to impress her. It was going to be the place where men dropped to their knees *and proposed...*

Grace blushed at the turn of her thoughts and glanced at Kam, who was smiling at her as he held a ladle.

"Interesting thoughts? You looked so pleased with yourself but then you turned bright red and you looked at me. I'm going to out on a limb here and say you were thinking about me," Kam said with a grin and a raised eyebrow.

Grace laughed nervously and went back to her cauliflower. "Your imagination is running away with you, Kam Matafeo. That or your ego is getting a little large," she said, trying to turn the tables on him.

Kam put his ladle down and pulled her into his arms, as he looked deep into her eyes, making her blush even brighter.

"*I knew it.* I knew you were thinking about me," he whispered in her ears. "So tell me. Were you thinking about kissing me? Were you thinking about later tonight, dancing in my arms?"

Grace nodded her head quickly. "*Yes.* That's it, that's exactly it," she said in relief.

Kam laughed and kissed her on the neck, before releasing

her. "I'll get it out of you tonight. I promise you," he said darkly, making a shiver go down her spine.

She laughed nervously and went back to work. She'd have to watch herself around Kam. That man could see right through her. They worked straight through the day, only taking short fifteen minute breaks. When their guests began to arrive promptly at seven all the wait staff was ready. They'd gone through the menu with everyone and allowed everyone to taste all the dishes so they knew how to describe them.

Rob and Taryn were walking around like worried parents at their child's first birthday party and Grace thought it was cute. Rob and Kam had been a little stiff with each other throughout the week, but they were relaxing with one another today and joking around again, which she was relieved to see.

Rob walked in as they began to send their first plates out and walked up to her and Kam at the stove.

"The place is packed!" he said, his voice high with excitement. "Wren and her dad and stepmom are out sitting with Pule and Posey. They want me to tell you that the artichoke hearts are divine. Wren's bitterly jealous right now. She's insisting on being able to cook with you guys for the next Fine Dining experience."

Grace laughed and nodded her head. "She's welcome to join us."

Kam smiled. "Wren misses the fun. Tell her she's welcome to come back right now if she wants."

Rob snorted. "In her new dress? No way. I know how much she spent. But seriously, this has been a homerun for The Iron Skillet. Our reservations have doubled and people are already asking to sign up for the next one. Once a quarter?"

Kam and Grace looked at each other and grinned before looking at Rob.

"We're in. But you have to hire more help for us though.

If we're going to be packed like this on a constant basis, we're going to have to have enough people. We can't work like this every day. Grace hasn't even had a lunch break and neither have I."

Rob winced. "Sorry, guys. I'll make it up to you. I promise. More help *and* bigger raises."

Kam winked at her. "Then it's a deal, Boss. Better get out there. People need to see what a charming owner we have."

Rob laughed and slapped Kam on the back. "Love you, Man. And don't forget, in an hour, you two come out. We're saving a table for you."

Grace smiled, thinking of her new dress upstairs, just waiting for her. "I can't wait."

Kam leaned over and kissed her on the cheek. "You have a very kind and forgiving heart. I'm glad you stayed here with me instead of quitting and going back to Seattle," Kam said, his eyes serious.

Grace shrugged and bumped her hip with Kam's. "I don't like walking around with heavy, bitter feelings. It's much better to just let things go when you can and move on."

Kam tilted his head as he looked at her. "When you can?"

Grace sighed and looked down at her veal. "There are times when I can't let go so easily. Like my mother. There's no way I can ever trust her again. That one's going to take me a *long* time."

Kam sighed and put his arm around her shoulders, giving her a squeeze. "You don't seem like you're very bitter or angry though. You just seem sad."

Grace blew out a breath. "I just don't know if I'd be sad if I didn't see her again. That thought makes me feel kind of hollow inside."

Kam sighed and kissed her forehead. "It will get better, I promise."

Grace tried to smile. "I know. Now come on, enough about me. Let's blow everyone's minds with how amazing we are."

Kam laughed and went back to his sauce pan. "You got it, Boss."

Grace grinned. "Hey! I like it."

An hour and a half later when Grace and Kam walked into the dining area. Grace loved the way her dress swished around her body and felt very sophisticated. Kam's eyes had gone big when she walked into the kitchen and he'd put his hand over his heart and just smiled at her. It made her stomach jump, just thinking of the look in his eyes.

Jenny, one of her favorite waitresses, appeared as soon as they sat down.

"I'll bring your first course out shortly," she said, as she filled their water glasses.

Kam was wearing a suit and his hair was pulled back neatly.

"If I haven't mentioned it, you look very handsome," Grace said primly and put her napkin in her lap.

Kam grinned and reached across the table for her hand. "If I haven't mentioned it at least five times since I saw you walk into the room, you're the most beautiful woman I know."

Grace smiled, feeling warmth fill her heart every time Kam looked at her with those big brown eyes of his.

"I don't know if that's actually true, but I have to say, I love hearing it," she said softly.

"Your dress is gorgeous."

Kam and Grace turned to see Meredith standing next to their table. Kam's smile faded but Grace stood up and gave Meredith a big hug. "I saw the billboard over by the library. So cute. Any response?"

Meredith shook her head with a worried frown. "Total silence."

Kam frowned, looking back and forth between the two women as if he was confused.

Grace sighed and took Meredith's hand. "What about all the t-shirts everyone's been wearing for the past two days?"

Meredith shrugged helplessly. "Jane and Kit have been passing them out to everyone. I walked in the diner and I swear, everyone was wearing a Meredith plus Asher t-shirt. I *know* he's seen them."

Grace frowned and looked at Kam who was staring at her with wide eyes. "Kam, what would you do if you were Meredith and you needed to embarrass yourself to win your man back?"

Kam blinked slowly a few times and then smiled at her, his eyes lighting up before he looked up at Meredith. "Well, I've heard you sing. That would have to be the most embarrassing thing you could do. I say you grab that mic over there and sing his favorite love song. You'll never be able to live it down and he'll smile every time he thinks about it."

Meredith groaned and looked over her shoulder. "He's sitting over there with his brother and Rayne. Every time I walk by, Garrett glares at me and Asher pretends he doesn't see me."

Grace took a sip of water. "I say do it. Probably before the dancing begins. Just slip the band a twenty and take a few minutes. Rob won't care."

Kam nodded. "Now's the perfect time."

Meredith closed her eyes and groaned again. "Okay, but nobody better film this or I'm suing."

Grace and Kam watched with twin grins as Meredith walked up to the band and talked to a man for a moment before he nodded his head. She walked over and picked up the mic, tapping it with her finger. Everyone turned to look at her.

"This one's going out to Asher Murphy, the best husband and friend a woman could ever have," Meredith said in a husky voice.

Kam grabbed her hand again. "You're going to have to fill me in on how you and Meredith became friends."

Grace shrugged as Kam looked at her with confusion in his eyes. "I'm actually a pretty likable person, you know."

Kam laughed as his eyes warmed. "Don't I know it."

Grace winked at him before looking back at Meredith. She looked back at the band and then nodded her head with a microphone in her hand. Holy cow, she was going for it. Grace was surprised when the band began playing the music to *Ordinary People* by John Legend. "Wow, she's going all out," Grace whispered as Kam smiled.

They listened as Meredith sang in a voice so off key it was laughable, yet sweet too. She stared right at Asher the entire time and even though she was singing as badly as anyone could, she didn't seem to care what anyone else thought. Grace turned in her seat to look at Asher. He was staring solemnly at his wife, his eyes glued to her. It looked like he was breathing fast as his chest went up and down. His hands were fisted in on his knees as if he was trying to control some great emotion. She glanced at Garrett and frowned. The man's expression said it all. He despised Meredith. She sighed sadly, hoping against hope that Meredith would be able to break through the wall that surrounded Asher so that they could reconnect. Because from where she was sitting, Meredith loved Asher. A lot.

She listened to the lyrics and hoped Asher was too. *I know I misbehaved, and you've made your mistakes, and we both still got room left to grow. And though love sometimes hurts, I still put you first, and we'll make this thing work...*

"*Wow.*" She heard Kam whisper and looked at him across the table. "I know," she whispered back. "This has to work."

When Meredith finally ended, there was a smattering of applause along with a few chuckles as Meredith walked slowly off the stage. Grace held her breath as she watched her walk slowly toward Asher. When she reached the table, Asher stood up and put his hands on his hips as the whole restaurant became quiet. He slowly reached out for his wife and pulled her into his arms, holding her tightly as he rested his chin on the top of her head.

Grace could see Meredith's shoulders begin to shake and Asher reach up and wipe his eyes as they stood there holding each other.

"Oh my word, that's the sweetest thing I've ever seen," she said, reaching for her napkin to wipe her own eyes.

Kam sighed. "Forgiveness is a beautiful thing. It's wonderful to be forgiven and it's beautiful to forgive. Especially someone you love."

Grace nodded and looked up in surprise as Jenny and another server brought their food. She'd completely forgotten about eating. They thanked their server and each took a bite of their veal.

Grace and Kam looked at each other as they focused on the flavors, grinning at each other at the same time.

"We're geniuses," she said, giving Kam a high five across the table. "Seriously, we're the best."

Kam laughed. "We do make a good team. Speaking of which…"

"*Did you guys see that?*"

Grace frowned, really wanting to know what Kam was going to say next. She looked up to see Jane, Kit and Layla standing next to her table and grinned, forgetting about Kam's unfinished words.

"I did! It was Kam's idea to humiliate herself by singing. Did you see Asher? He cried and then he hugged her," she squealed.

Jane grabbed her arm. "They're standing over in the corner talking now, but Asher's hand is on her waist and her hand is on his arm. This is actually working," she said, sounding surprised.

Kit nodded. "I still say the t-shirts and the billboard softened him up."

Layla laughed. "He's stubborn but he loves her. Look at his eyes. He's eating this up."

They all turned and looked at Asher and Meredith and she was right. Asher's eyes were lit up with love and happiness and Meredith was glowing.

Grace sighed happily and took another bite. "We're pretty good at this stuff. Anyone else need help?"

Layla and Kit shared a look and then turned and looked at a table in the far corner by the bathroom. Literally the worst table in the whole restaurant. Grace strained her eyes to see who it was and then frowned. *Anne Matafeo*, the woman who went to jail for stealing money in order to frame her.

"Oh, you guys are on your own for that one. She scares me," Grace said with a shiver.

Kam shook his head. "Sorry, Ladies, but our meddling in other people's lives is now at an end. We're happy for Asher and Meredith, but Anne is a wild card."

Jane shook her head. "She looks so sad though. And poor, Sefe. He's usually the life of the party and there he is just sitting there silently. No one's even talking to them. *Ugh*, I hate this. I'm going to go force Tate to talk to them," she said and walked away.

Kit winced. "Anne and I have had our differences, but I can't help feeling sorry for them," she said and walked back to her own table.

Layla tilted her head and looked at Anne one more time before looking back at them with a smile. "It will work out, but in the mean time, I just wanted to tell you guys that dinner was amazing. The best food I've ever had and I can't wait to see what's for dessert," she said with a smile and then walked away.

They had more and more people walk over and talk to them for the next half an hour as they ate their meal and Grace enjoyed every second of it. She'd never been in a position to actually sit and eat the food she'd imagined and created with other people enjoying her food. It was an exhilarating experience and one she hoped to enjoy again and again.

When their waitress brought their dessert, a seven-layer poppy-seed cake with passion fruit curd, she could feel her toes curl with joy. Listening to Kam's groans of pleasure made her laugh and giggle as they ate and talked. But as she and Kam finished their last bite, she could feel someone looking at her. She smiled and looked up, *and immediately felt her smile die.*

Anne and Sefe Matafeo stood next to their table.

Kam immediately stood up and shook his head. "I know Rob made an exception for tonight since you'd already bought your tickets, Anne, but I know for a fact that Rob told you to stay away from Grace."

Sefe held up his hand to Kam. "Kam, please calm down. Anne just wants to say something."

Kam's eyes were fierce as he crossed his arms across his chest. "She always wants to say something. That's what I *don't* want to happen."

Sefe's eyes looked miserable as he put a hand on his nephew's arm. "Kam, please."

Grace looked at Anne who was clasping her hands and looking at her feet. She looked beaten and sad. "Kam, it's okay. Let her say what she wants to say so we can get back to our dessert," she said softly.

Kam closed his eyes and sighed but nodded his head. "Okay, what would you like to say?" he asked tersely.

Anne cleared her throat, finally raising her eyes. "I just,... I just wanted to say…" she paused as if she didn't know what she was going to say.

She felt a rush of wind and then Rob and Taryn were standing right next to them.

"Mom! I told you to stay at your table and not talk to anyone," Rob said in a low, angry voice.

Taryn, who was dressed in a white evening gown, *and looking fabulous*, looked upset as well. "Grace, Kam, we're sorry. Mom is leaving *right now*," she said and put a hand on her mom's arm to pull her away.

Anne looked up, tears glistening in her eyes as she shook her head. "Please, just let me say one thing and then I'll go back to my table."

Rob looked horrified and glanced at Kam apologetically. "Absolutely not," he said and put his hand on Anne's arm too.

Sefe held both hands up as if he were trying to placate hungry dinosaurs. "Kam said it was okay. Just give her a moment, Rob. Please."

Rob and Taryn looked at Kam in surprise. "*Really?* You think this is a good idea?" Rob asked.

Kam shrugged and pointed to Grace. "Grace says okay. If it were me, absolutely not," he said, looking steadily at Anne.

Anne swallowed hard and then made a point to look everyone in the eyes before turning to Grace.

"I'm sorry," she said in a low voice. "I didn't realize before how much my actions had hurt everyone. I've even hurt my husband. But I know I hurt you the most, Grace. I'm sorry that I made a choice to not like you based on pain that I still have over Bailey's passing. I know now that Bailey would be happy for you and Kam and that she'd want Natano to have a mother."

Kam sighed and let his hands fall to his hips. Grace bit her lip and looked at him, wondering what to say to that.

Kam shook his head. "I have to be honest, I don't know if your words are sincere, or they're just the easiest way to get back to the way things were."

Grace winced at Kam's words, glad he was sticking up for her, but feeling sorry for Anne at the same time. She looked defeated and sad and very unlike the ball of energy that she always seemed to be.

Sefe put his hand on Anne's shoulder. "Well, at least you tried, Anne. Thank you for listening."

Anne nodded and looked up at her husband. "I was sincere, Sefe. I promise."

Sefe didn't say anything, but nodded. Rob and Taryn were looking at their mother suspiciously. Didn't look like they bought the apology either. She thought of everything Anne had done to her and for a moment, she felt pleased that Anne was finally getting what was coming to her. But then she saw the sadness in Sefe's face and the mortification on Rob and Taryn's. She looked at Kam and underneath his anger, she saw the sadness.

It was up to her whether or not she accepted Anne's apology. And maybe it was up to her whether or not to help the family heal.

"Anne, I accept your apology. I hope in the future when you come over to see Nate, that you'll remember that he loves me too, though."

Anne nodded her head quickly, reaching out to touch her arm. "I want us to be a family," she said, sounding desperate. "I truly do, Grace. And thank you. Thank you for being kinder than I was," she said, a few tears slipping down her cheeks before turning and walking away.

Sefe stayed where he was, looking stiff and awkward. "It would mean a lot to me if you could forgive my wife, Kamilo. Family means everything to me. I love my wife, but losing my family… it's devastating," he said and then nodded to Rob and Taryn and walked after his wife.

Grace felt sick to her stomach at the pain she'd seen in Sefe's face. She'd heard from Kam that they weren't welcome at family dinners on the weekends anymore.

Rob and Taryn gave Kam a hug and then touched her on the shoulder before walking to another table where their family was seated.

Grace shook her head and looked across the table at Kam with wide eyes. "Well, tonight has been interesting."

Kam took a sip of water and shook his head. "You know, I'm a lot like Sefe. Family is the most important thing to me in the world. But what he doesn't understand yet, is that you're part of my family now. You're part of my heart. And I can't let anyone, even his wife hurt you. If I feel that Anne is sincere in her apology, I'll consider allowing them back, but until then…"

Grace winced and looked away. "Kam, I feel so guilty, like I'm the cause of ripping your family apart. And the fact is, I'm not your family. I'm just… I'm just someone you're dating," she said, feeling the words come out of her mouth like sawdust. "When Anne talked about me being Nate's mom, it was wonderful and sad too. Because I'm not. But to be honest, I wish I was," she said shyly, looking at Kam.

Kam looked at her across the table and smiled slowly at her. "Not *yet*."

Grace smiled and looked away. "Really?"

Kam nodded. "You know I love you, Grace."

Grace licked her lips and shook her head. "Well, yes, I know you love me. But love doesn't make us a family either," she said softly as she stared at her lap.

She looked up as the band began playing and Rob stood up, walking over to take the microphone.

"Ladies and gentlemen, thank you for coming to our first

Fine Dining experience, we hope that you've enjoyed your dinner. And if you have, make sure you let our Head Chefs, Kam Matafeo and Grace Jackson know. But right now, enjoy dancing and just know that the band takes requests."

After the clapping ended, Kam stood up and held his hand out to her.

"Will you do me the pleasure?" he said.

Grace stood up and took Kam's hand as they walked out onto the dance floor. They saw Layla and Michael Bender, dancing in the corner, their arms wrapped around each other. Jane and Tate were standing next to Pule and Posey as the couples laughed and tried to do intricate dance moves. Cleo and Tai along with Garrett and Rayne and Becket and Ivy were dancing close to one another, laughing and talking too. Everyone was having a fabulous time.

Kam twirled her around and then pulled her into his arms. They swayed together, forgetting everyone else as they stared into each others eyes.

"Grace?" he asked, looking at her, his eyes serious.

She nodded and smiled at him.

"Do you want to be part of my family?" he asked in a warm, smooth voice.

Grace stumbled a little and stared at him with a little frown. "What are you talking about?"

Kam closed his eyes and shook his head. "I'm not doing this very well, am I? Grace, you said love doesn't make us a family. Well, I know what does. So do you? Do you want to be a part of my family?"

Grace closed her eyes, wondering if he was asking her what she thought he was asking. He couldn't be. *No way.*

"Kam, I love you. I think you might be the only man I've ever really loved now that I think about it. But being part of your family, *that means...*" she said, her words drying up as he smiled calmly.

Kam kissed her knuckles lightly and then looked into her eyes. "I want you in my life and in my son's life. We both love you and we both need you. I understand if you need more time. But Grace, I want to marry you."

Grace's mouth slowly dropped open as her eyes widened. He'd said the "M" word. *Holy Hannah.*

They stopped dancing and Grace could feel all of the other couples swirling around them as time stopped and Kam dropped to his knees. She gasped and covered her mouth with both hands as Kam pulled a small golden band out of his pocket and reached for her hand, slipping the ring on her finger.

"This is just a temporary until you can pick out what you want. But I want my ring on your finger. I want the whole world to know that I love you and that you're mine. Will you marry me, Grace Jackson? Will you be my family?"

Grace wiped the tears off her cheeks and nodded, unable to speak. Kam jumped up and pulled her into his arms as people began to surround them, clapping and yelling. Way too soon, she was pulled out of Kam's arms and into everyone else's. She'd never been kissed and hugged and congratulated so much in her life. She felt dizzy and weak and her face was hurting from smiling so much.

Kam picked her up and carried her out of the room and outside into the cool air. She was so grateful, she wrapped her arms around his neck and kissed him on the cheek. "You read my mind," she said and rested her cheek against his.

He drove her down to the water and they sat on his blanket and stared at the stars shimmering over the water and planned their lives together. When Kam dropped her off at her apartment, she practically floated up the stairs. Kam unlocked her door for her and made sure she locked up before he left.

Grace stared at the ring on her finger as the sound of Kam's car drove away. She walked into her room and collapsed on her bed as a wave of such intense happiness swept over her, she began to laugh and cry all at once.

"Crazy," she whispered softly before turning on her side. How crazy was it that she, *Grace Jackson*, was now engaged to an amazing man who loved her?

She went to sleep that night, smiling and remembering what it felt like to dance in Kam's arms.

CHAPTER 40

Bridal Shower

Five Months Later

GRACE LAUGHED AS Jane decorated her head with yet another bright bow, this one taken from Cleo's present.

"Guys, my head can't handle anymore," she protested as Layla handed her another gift to open.

"Yeah, right. Your head is huge and you know it," Meredith said, knocking a gold balloon away from her head. "I saw your review in the paper. That food critic raved about your food."

Grace blushed and pushed a ribbon off her nose. "Stan was very kind, true. But that doesn't mean I'm going to get a big head."

Wren laughed. "I would have a huge head if I was you. Trust me, you've earned it. Now, who is this present from?"

Grace frowned and looked for the card. "Um, I'm not seeing it. Does anyone recognize this present?" she said, holding the beautifully wrapped gift up in the air.

No one claimed it. Grace looked at Jane but she just shrugged.

"Open it, Grace. Maybe you have a secret admirer."

Grace bit her lip but tore the paper open. She lifted the lid off the box and frowned as it looked empty. She pushed the tissue paper aside and lifted out a card. She looked up at everyone and smiled as she opened the flap.

"Interesting," she said and pulled out a small square of heavy cream paper.

She read it out loud. "For you and Kam," she said with a frown and then looked at the empty box again. "Okay, I think someone is playing a joke," she said with a laugh and then looked at Meredith. "Is this you, Mer? You messing with me again?"

Meredith held up both hands as everyone turned and stared at her. "Hey, I spent a lot of money on a blender. That is not from me," she said, turning red.

Jane took the box from her and pushed through the paper some more. "Ah, here it is," she said and handed her another piece of paper.

Grace laughed and took the paper. "A seven-day cruise to the Bahamas!" she said with a gasp.

The whole room erupted in chatter as everyone stood up to see the paper. But it was legit. Someone had paid for her and Kam to go to the Bahamas. She tore the box apart trying to find some clue as to who it was from.

"Do you think Kam did this?" she asked Kit as she shook her head in awe.

Kit shrugged. "Well, everyone you know is here. If it's not from Kam, then who?"

Wren put her hand over her mouth. "Oh my heck, you guys. I bet you a million dollars this is from Anne. This is her big gesture to make everything up to you."

Grace slowly sat down and blew out her breath. "Okay then. I'm not sure what to think about that."

Meredith walked over and picked up the paper. "Wow, she sends you on a cruise and all I got you was a blender."

Kit snorted. "That's because Anne feels guilty."

Meredith rolled her eyes. "I'm a big believer in forgiving myself. Guilt is a huge waste of time," she added before turning and walking away.

Kit glared at Meredith's back, but Grace put her hand up. "She just said that to get a reaction out of you."

Kit closed her eyes and smiled. "Classic Meredith. Okay, on to the next present."

Grace spent the next half an hour opening presents and then they relaxed and ate all the delicious food supplied by Wren and the Belinda girls.

Grace took a sip of her punch and grinned at all of the women surrounding her, wearing their Love Witch t-shirts.

"I still can't believe I got all of these gifts and not one of them was a Love Witch t-shirt. I'm practically the only woman in town who doesn't have one. That's so unfair," she said to Taryn who had pushed Jane out of the way to sit next to her.

Taryn laughed and looked down at hers. "Hey, we deserve these shirts. Getting you and Kam together with all of the crazy surrounding you, took a village."

Layla leaned over from her other side. "I'll get you one for your birthday. Not that you're actually a love witch though..."

Grace stuck her tongue out and turned to Taryn. "Fircrest is so cliquey. Like, you have to be an actual witch or you don't fit in."

Taryn laughed. "Yeah I know what you mean. Look at all of these women here, spoiling you. I can tell you don't fit in."

Grace grinned and surveyed all of her new friends and shook her head. But the one person she'd always imagined being there, was her mom. Who didn't invite their own mother to their bridal shower? But after everything that had happened, it was a relief that she wasn't invited. Tate had informed her a few weeks ago that the Sacramento P.D. had caught up with Jocelyn and Billy. They were looking at serving five to ten years for robbing an empty house. Her heart broke for her mom, but knew that some people needed to learn the hard way.

Grace pushed away all the sad thoughts and focused on being present. "You're right. I am spoiled. Coming to Fircrest was the best decision of my life. If I hadn't, I would have never met Kam or any of you guys and I can't imagine my life without you all now," she said and surprised herself by tearing up.

Taryn put her arm around her shoulders. "Well, if it makes you feel any better, we can't imagine Fircrest without you either."

Meredith leaned around Taryn and smiled at her. "*I can*, but you're okay. Listen, this shower was all right, but for my baby shower next month, I want more balloons and less games."

Grace sighed, rethinking her decision to host Meredith's baby shower. She rolled her eyes at Meredith as she laughed at her and she couldn't help liking the prickly woman who had the bad habit of keeping Fircrest on it's toes.

"You've already emailed me everything you want for the shower. Are you sure you don't want to just throw it for yourself? That way you could be sure that it's done perfectly," she said with a big, toothy smile.

Layla and Taryn laughed at Meredith's shocked expression.

"Fine, I'll back off. Back to your celebration," she said with a queenly wave of her hand.

Taryn rolled her eyes. "Thanks."

The rest of the night, the women talked, laughed and ate everything in sight. It was absolutely the best party she'd ever been to.

CHAPTER 41

Happily Ever After

Two Days Later

G RACE STOOD IN the sand in her bare feet,
surrounded by all of her new friends as Kam stood
opposite of her and said his vows in a strong, solemn
voice that sent shivers up her spine. She felt the breeze off the
sound, flow over her as she held Kam's hands. The officiator's
strong, soothing voice filled her heart with peace and she felt
completely calm at the idea of spending the rest of her life with
this man, in this town and with these people.

She said her vows to Kam, echoing her commitment to
honor and love him and his son before nodding her head and
saying yes. Before she was even done saying the word, Kam was
picking her up and spinning her around as the man announced
them husband and wife.

The crowd exploded in cheers and Kam slowly put her
down. And then he was kissing her. She knew they weren't supposed to be kissing as long or as passionately as Kam was kissing her, but she refused to push him away. This was a day she

wanted to remember forever and if he wanted to kiss her all day, then by all means, kiss away.

When Kam finally stopped kissing her, laughter surrounded them. And happiness. And kindness. And love. So much love. She leaned down and picked up Nate, who had been very patiently waiting. She kissed Nate on the cheek as Kam's arms surrounded them both.

"Can I call you Mommy, now?" Nate asked so sweetly and shyly that her heart burst for the millionth time that day.

She looked at Kam first, biting her lip, not sure how he would react to his son's question. They hadn't discussed it yet.

Kam leaned down, ruffling Nate's hair and kissed him on his forehead.

"Of course you can, Natano. We've waited long enough."

Nate threw his arms around Grace's neck, squeezing her as hard as his little arms could.

"I love you, Mommy," he said in her ear as she squeezed him back.

Grace bowed her head for a moment, thinking of Bailey and her sacrifice and what an honor it was to be called mother by this special little boy. She would never take him or Kam for granted. Ever.

"Let's get this party over with, fellas, we have a plane to catch tonight. Disney World awaits us," she said, lifting her head to smile at Kam.

Nate began shouting in excitement as they walked into the crowd of people to accept everyone's congratulations.

*

Kam accepted the plate of food from Rob as he watched Grace dance with his son.

"I'm so happy for you, Bro. You deserve all the happiness you can handle," he said and Kam knew he meant it.

Kam gave him a one-armed hug. "Thanks, Rob. And I am happy. There were so many times I never thought I'd be happy again. Or be *me* again, you know? But Grace showed up one day out of the blue and my whole life changed. I could finally breathe again. She's amazing."

Rob looked at Grace and sent a silent prayer of thanks up to heaven.

"You've got a live wire there, you know. You prepared to be on your toes the rest of your life?" Rob asked as he laughed at her dance moves she was trying to teach Nate.

Kam smiled at his wife and son. "She does keep me busy. Laughing and living. And I love it," he said, handing the plate back to Rob and walking over to join his family. Life was meant to be lived, not endured. Grace had taught him that.

He leaned down and kissed Grace softly on the lips as he began to dance with her. She took his hand in hers and twirled herself around and he smiled, knowing that love could do miracles. It could even bring a hardened, bitter man like him back to life.

And he couldn't be more grateful.

ACKNOWLEDGEMENTS

Writing Free Fallin' was hard, my friends. *So hard.* I don't know why certain things happen, but they do. In books and in real life. And like I always say, I'm a big believer in happy endings, so I couldn't leave Kam sad and lonely. I love Kam! And I know it took me forever to write his book, and I apologize for that, but I had to wait for the story to come to me. So when Grace appeared, I knew she could bring Kam back to life. I hope you enjoyed his story as much as I did. And if you're like me, where hard things have happened to you, just know that it's not the end. Happy endings sometimes come later, *but they do come.*

Special thanks to Christina Tarbet and for my family's support. Also – thanks to all of my readers and friends who have forgiven me for taking some much needed time off. My bucket was empty but now it is full and although I won't be able to write as many books a year as I used to, I will be writing again. I love hearing from you all, so let me know what you think.

Hugs,
Shannon

BIOGRAPHY

I live in the Rocky Mountains with my husband and children and love my home when it's not snowing. I'm the author of 36 books so far. I also write YA Paranormal Romance under my pen name, Katie Lee O'Guinn. I enjoy the outdoors, reading and being with my family. I'm a huge believer in happy endings. Scarlett really should have been happy with Rhett and it's a darn shame Leo and Kate didn't float safely into New York on the Titanic. Don't even get me started on Romeo and Juliet. To find out the latest on my books, check out my blog at www.shannonguymon.blogspot.com or www.katieleeoguinn.blogspot.com. You can purchase all of my books at Amazon.com. I'm also a supporter of Operation Underground Railroad. Check out their website at ourrescue.org to learn more.

Books by Shannon Guymon

Fircrest Series:

The Love and Dessert Trilogy

You Belong with Me (Book 1) – Layla and Michael
I Belong with You (Book 2) – Kit and Hunter
My Sweetheart (Book 3) – Jane and Tate

The Love and Trust Trilogy

Come to Me (Book 1)
Wren and Rob
Be Mine (Book 2) – Kam and Bailey
Tough Love (Book 3) – Taryn and Brogan

The Love and Flowers Trilogy

Falling for Rayne (Book 1) – Rayne and Garrett
Dreaming of Ivy (Book 2) – Ivy and Becket
A Passion for Cleo (Book 3) – Cleo and Tai

The Love and Weddings Trilogy

My One and Only (Book 1) – Meredith and Asher
Free Fallin' (Book 2) – Pule and Posey
At Last (Book 3) – Maya and Tristan

Accidentally in Love

(Kam's Story) Final book in the Fircrest Series (Kam and Grace)

Books by Katie Lee O'Guinn (My pen name) YA Paranormal Books

The Lost Witch Trilogy

Freak of Nature (Book 1)
Blood Rush (Book 2)
Fate Changer (Book 3)

Taming the Wolf Series

Werewolf Dreams (Book 1)
Werewolf Rage (Book 2)
Werewolf Revenge (Book 3)
Werewolf Betrayal (Book 4)

Chasing the Wolf Series

Hunted (Book 1)
Taken (Book 2)
Lost (Book 3)

All of my books can be found at Amazon.com

Made in the USA
Middletown, DE
30 October 2018